P9-DHK-937

THE TOUCH

Also by F. Paul Wilson

HEALER

WHEELS WITHIN WHEELS

THE TERY

AN ENEMY OF THE STATE

THE KEEP

THE TOMB

THE
TOUCH

F. Paul Wilson

G. P. PUTNAM'S SONS
New York

G. P. Putnam's Sons
Publishers Since 1838
200 Madison Avenue
New York, NY 10016

Copyright © 1986 by F. Paul Wilson
All rights reserved. This book, or parts thereof,
may not be reproduced in any form without permission.
Published simultaneously in Canada by
General Publishing Co. Limited, Toronto

Library of Congress Cataloging-in-Publication Data

Wilson, F. Paul (Francis Paul)
The touch.

I. Title.
PS3573.I45695T6   1986   813'.54   86-1494
ISBN 0-399-13144-2

Printed in the United States of America
1 2 3 4 5 6 7 8 9 10

03040 0574

COPY1   7-9-86
DEERFIELD PUBLIC LIBRARY

Acknowledgments

The following individuals, all with doctorates in various fields, helped with the writing of this book in ways great and small in matters related and unrelated to their fields of expertise.

John DePalma, D.O.
Anthony Lombardino, M.D.
Martin Seidenstein, M.D.
Nancy Spruill, Ph.D.
Steven Spruill, Ph.D
Albert Zuckerman, D.F.A.

THE TOUCH

APRIL

1.

Dr. Alan Bulmer

"Can you feel this?"

Alan gently pricked the skin of her right leg with a needle.

Fear glittered in the woman's moist eyes as she shook her head.

"*Ohmygod,* she can't feel it!"

Alan turned to the daughter, whose face was the same shade of off-white as the curtains surrounding and isolating them from the rest of the emergency room.

"Would you wait outside for just a minute, please." He made sure his tone would indicate that he was not making a request.

The daughter found the slit in the curtains and disappeared.

Alan turned back to the mother and studied her as she lay on the gurney in the fluorescent-lit limbo, letting his mind page through what he remembered of Helen Jonas. Not much. Borderline diabetes and mild essential hypertension. She hadn't been to the office for two years, and on that occasion had been dragged in by her daughter. Half an hour ago, Alan had been sitting at home watching a rerun of *The Honeymooners* when the call had come from the emergency room that one of his patients had arrived, unable to walk or talk.

He had already made his diagnosis but followed through with the rest of the examination. He moved the needle to the back of Helen's right hand.

"How about this?"

Again she shook her head.

He leaned over and touched the point to her left hand and she jerked it away. He then ran his thumbnail up from her bare right heel along the sole of her foot. The toes flared upward. He raised her right hand and told her to squeeze. The fingers didn't move. He let go and the arm dropped back to the mattress like dead meat.

"Smile," he said, showing her a toothy grin.

The lady tried to imitate him, but only the left half of her face responded. Her right cheek and the right side of her mouth remained immobile.

"How about the eyebrows?" He oscillated his own, Groucho Marx style.

Both of the woman's eyebrows moved accordingly.

He listened to her heart and to her carotid arteries—normal rhythm, no murmur, no bruits.

Alan straightened up.

"It's a stroke, Helen. An artery—"

He heard the daughter say, "Oh, no!" behind the curtain, but he continued speaking. He would deal with her later. The main thing now was to reassure Helen.

"An artery on the left side of your brain has blocked off and you've lost the power on the right side of your body."

The voice came through the curtain again: *"Ohmygod,* I knew it! She's *paralyzed!"*

Why didn't she shut up? He knew the daughter was frightened, and he could appreciate that, but the daughter was not his primary concern at the moment, and she was only making a bad situation worse for her mother.

"How long it will last, Helen, I don't know. You'll probably get some strength back; maybe all of it, and maybe none. Exactly how much and exactly how soon are impossible to say right now."

He put her good hand in his. She squeezed. "We're going to get you upstairs right now and start running some tests in the morning. We'll start some physical therapy, too. We'll take good care of you and check out the rest of you while you're here. The stroke is over and done with. So don't waste time worrying about it. It's history. From now on you work on getting back use of that arm and leg."

She smiled lopsidedly and nodded. Finally he pulled his hand away and said, "Excuse me," as he turned and stepped through the curtains to where the daughter was talking to the air.

"Whatamygonnadoo? I gotta call Charlie! I gotta call Rae! Whatamygonnadoo?"

Alan put his hand on her shoulder and gave her trapezius a gentle squeeze. She flinched and stopped her yammering.

"You're gonna clam up, okay?" he said in a low voice. "All you're doing is upsetting her."

"But whatamygonnadoo? I've got so much to do! I gotta—"

He squeezed again, a little harder. "The most important thing for you to do right now is go stand by her and tell her how she's going to come stay with you for a while after she gets out of the hospital and how you're going to have everybody over for Easter."

She stared at him. "But I'm not . . ."

"Sure you are."

"You mean she's going to be coming home?"

Alan smiled and nodded. "Yeah. In a week, maybe. She thinks she's going to die here. She's not. But she needs someone holding her hand now and talking about the near future, how life's going to go on and how she's going to be part of it." He steered her toward the curtains. "Get in there."

McClain, head nurse for the ER, pushing sixty and built like the Berlin wall, saw him from the desk and held up an LP tray with a questioning look. Alan shook his head. He'd checked out Helen's eyegrounds and had seen no evidence of increased intracranial pressure. No use putting the old lady through a spinal tap if there was no need for it.

Alan signed the orders, wrote the admitting note, then dictated the history and physical.

After giving final reassurances and saying good night to Helen

Jonas and her daughter, Alan finally got out of the hospital, into his Eagle, and on his way back home. He drove slowly, taking the short route through downtown Monroe, where all the buildings clustered around the tiny harbor like anxious bathers waiting for a signal from the lifeguard. He liked the solitude of a late night drive through the shopping district. During the day the streets would be stop-and-go all the way. But at this hour, especially now that all the construction was done and he didn't have to dodge excavations or follow detour signs, he could cruise, adjusting his speed so he could hit the lights just right. A smooth ride, now that the trolley tracks had been covered with asphalt. He pushed a cassette into the player and The Crows came on, singing "Oh, Gee."

He watched the clapboarded shop fronts slip by. He hadn't been in favor of the downtown restoration at first when the Village Council—why did Long Island towns insist on calling themselves villages?—had decided to redo the harborfront in a Nineteenth Century whaling motif. Never mind that any whaling in this vicinity of the North Shore had been centered to the east in places like Oyster Bay and Cold Spring Harbor, the village wanted a make-over. Passing the newly faced seafood restaurants, clothing stores, and antique shops, Alan had to admit that it looked good. The former lackluster hodgepodge of storefronts had taken on a new, invigorated personality, fitting perfectly with the white-steepled First Presbyterian Church and the brick-fronted town hall. Monroe was now something more than just another of the larger towns along Long Island's "Preferred North Shore."

The illusion almost worked. He could almost imagine Ishmael, harpoon on shoulder, walking down to the harbor toward the *Pequod* . . . passing the new Video Shack.

Well, nothing was perfect.

A red light finally caught him and he pulled to a stop. As he waited, he watched Clubfoot Annie—the closest thing Monroe had to a shopping bag lady—hobble across the street in front of him. Alan had no idea of her real name; neither, so far as he knew, did anybody else. She was known to everyone simply as Clubfoot Annie.

He was struck now, as he was whenever he saw her, by how a

misshapen foot that no one had bothered to correct on a child could shape the life of the adult. People like Annie always managed to get to Alan, making him want to go back in time and see to it that someone did the right thing. So simple . . . some serial casting on her infant equinovarus deformity would have straightened it out to normal. Who would Annie be today if she'd grown up with a normal foot? Maybe she—

Something slammed against the right front door, jolting Alan, making him jump in his seat. A ravaged caricature of a human face pressed against the passenger door window.

"You!" the face said as it rolled back and forth against the glass. "You're the one! Lemme in! Gotta talk t'ya!"

His hair and beard were long and knotted and as filthy as his clothes. The eyes shone but gave no evidence of intelligence. Whatever mind he had must have been pickled a long time ago. The man straightened up and pulled on the door handle, but it was locked. He moved along the side of the car toward the hood. He looked like a Bowery derelict. Alan could not remember ever seeing the likes of him in Monroe.

He crossed in front of the car, pointing at Alan over the hood, all the while babbling unintelligibly. Tense but secure, Alan waited until the bum was clear of the front of the car, then he gently accelerated. The bum pounded his fist once on the trunk as the car left him behind.

In the rearview mirror, Alan saw the man start running behind the car, then stop and stand in the middle of the street, staring after him, a picture of dejection and frustration as he waved his arms in the air and then let them flop down to his sides.

The episode left Alan shaken. He glanced at the passenger window and was startled to see a large oily smudge in the shape of the derelict's face. As it picked up the light of a passing streetlamp, it seemed to look at him, reminding him uncomfortably of the face from the Shroud of Turin.

He was pulling up to another red light when his beeper howled, startling him into jamming on his brakes. A female voice spoke through the static:

"Two-one-seven—please call Mrs. Nash about her son. Complains of abdominal pain and vomiting." It gave the phone number, then repeated the message.

Alan straightened in his seat. Sylvia Nash—he knew her well; a concerned parent but not an alarmist. If she was calling, it meant something was definitely wrong with Jeffy. That concerned him. Jeffy Nash had come to occupy a special place in his heart and his practice.

He drummed his fingers on the steering wheel. What to do? His usual procedure in a case like this was to meet the patient at either his office or the emergency room. His office was on the far side of town, and he didn't want to go back to the emergency room tonight unless absolutely necessary. Then it struck him: The Nash house was a short way off the road between the hospital and his own house. He could stop in on the way home.

He smiled as he accelerated through the green light. He found the thought of seeing Sylvia invigorating. And a house call—that ought to flap the unflappable Widow Nash.

He followed Main Street around to where it passed the entrance to the Monroe Yacht and Racquet Club on the west side of the harbor, then turned inland and passed through the various economic strata that made up "The Incorporated Village of Monroe." The low-rent district with its garden apartments and rooming houses clung to the downtown area, eventually giving way to the postwar tract homes surrounding the high school. From there it was up into the wooded hills where the newer custom-built homes of the better-off had sprung up in the past decade. Alan lived there, and would have continued on Hill Drive if he had been going home. But he bore right at the fork and followed Shore Drive down to Monroe's most exclusive section.

Alan shook his head at the memory of his first day in town, when he had promised Ginny that someday they would own one of the homes along the waterfront at Monroe's western end. How naive he had been then. These weren't homes—these were *estates,* rivaling the finest homes in Glen Cove and Lattingtown. He couldn't afford the utilities, taxes, and upkeep on one of these old monstrosities, let alone the mortgage payments.

Stone walls and tall stands of trees shielded the waterfront estates from passersby. Alan wound along the road until his headlights swept the two tall brick gateposts that flanked the entrance, illuminating the brass plaque on the left that read:

TOAD
HALL

He turned in, followed a short, laurel-lined road, and came upon the Nash house—formerly the Borg mansion—standing dark among its surrounding willows under the clear, starlit spring sky as he pulled into the driveway.

There was only one window lit, the one in the upper left corner of the many-gabled structure, glowing a subdued yellow, making the place look like it belonged on the cover of a gothic novel. The front-porch light was on, almost as if he were expected.

He had driven by in the past, but had never been inside. Although, after seeing the spread *The New York Times Magazine* had run on it a week ago—one in a continuing series on old North Shore mansions—he felt as if he knew the place.

Alan could smell the brine and hear the gentle lap of the Long Island Sound as, black bag in hand, he stepped up to the front door and reached for the bell.

He hesitated. Maybe this wasn't such a good idea, what with Sylvia's reputation as the Merry Widow and all, and especially with the way she was always coming on to him. He knew it was mostly in fun because she liked to rattle him, yet he sensed there might be something real under the surface. That scared him most of all because he knew he responded to her. He couldn't help it. There was something about her—beyond her good looks—that appealed to him, attracted him. Like now. Was he out here to see Jeffy or see her?

This was a mistake. But too late to turn back now. He reached again for the bell . . .

"The Missus is expecting you?"

At the sound of the voice directly behind him, Alan jumped and spun with a sharp bark of fright, clutching at his heart, which he was sure had just gone into a brief burst of ventricular tachycardia.

"Ba!" he said, recognizing Sylvia's Vietnamese driver and handyman. "You damn near scared me to death!"

"Very sorry, Doctor. I did not recognize you from behind." In the glare of the porch light, the tall Asian's skin looked sallower, and his eyes and cheeks more sunken than usual.

The front door opened then and Alan turned to see the startled expression on Sylvia Nash's pretty, finely chiseled face through the glass of the storm door. She was dressed in a very comfortable-looking plaid flannel robe with a high cowled neck that covered her from jaw to toes. But her breasts still managed to raise an attractive swell under the soft fabric.

"Alan! I only wanted to talk to you. I didn't expect you to—"

"The house call is not entirely dead," he said. "I make them all the time. It happened that I was nearby in the car when I got the beep so I thought I'd save time and stop by and see Jeffy. But don't worry. I'll be sure to call ahead next time. Maybe then Ba won't . . ."

His voice trailed off as he turned. Ba was gone. Didn't that man make any sound when he moved? Then Sylvia was waving him inside.

"Come in, come in!"

He stepped into a broad, marble-floored foyer decorated in pastels, brightly lit by a huge crystal chandelier suspended from the high ceiling. Directly across from where he stood, a wide staircase wound up and away to the right.

"What was that about Ba?"

"He almost scared the life out of me. What's he doing skulking around in the bushes like that?"

Sylvia smiled. "Oh, I imagine he's worried about that *Times* article attracting every cat burglar in the five boroughs."

"Maybe he's got a point." Alan remembered the published photos of the elegant living room, the ornate silver sets in the dining room, the bonsai greenhouse. Everything in the article had spelled M-O-N-E-Y. "If the place is half as beautiful in real life as it was on paper, I imagine it would be pretty tempting."

"Thanks," she said with a rueful smile. "I needed to hear that."

"Sorry. But you have an alarm system, don't you?"

She shook her head. "Only a one-eyed dog who barks but doesn't bite. And Ba, of course."

"Is he enough?"

"So far, yes."

Maybe Ba *was* enough. Alan shuddered at the thought of running into him in the dark. He looked like a walking cadaver.

"They certainly made enough of a fuss over you in the article—famous sculptress and all that. How come no mention of Jeffy? I'm surprised they didn't play up the human interest angle there."

"They didn't mention Jeffy because they don't know about him. Jeffy is not for display."

At that moment, Sylvia Nash rose another notch in Alan's estimation. He watched her, waiting for her to start with the provocative comments. None came. She was too concerned about Jeffy.

"Come take a look at him," she continued. "He's upstairs. He quieted down after I called. I hated to disturb you, but he was in so much pain, and then he vomited. And, you know . . . I get worried."

Alan knew, and understood. He followed her across the foyer and up the curved staircase, watching her hips swaying gracefully before his eyes. Down a hall, a left turn, and then they were stepping over a knee-high safety gate into a child's room, gently illuminated by a Donald Duck night-light in a wall outlet.

Alan knew Jeffy well, and felt a special kinship with him that he shared with none of his other pediatric patients. A beautiful child with a cherubic face, blond hair, deep blue eyes, and a terrible problem. He had examined Jeffy so many times that his little eight-year-old body was nearly as familiar as his own. But Jeffy's mind . . . his mind remained locked away from everybody.

He looked at the bed and saw Jeffy sleeping peacefully.

"Doesn't look very sick to me."

Sylvia stepped quickly to the bedside and stared down at the boy. "He was in agony before—doubled over, grabbing his stomach. You know I'd never call you on a lark. Is something wrong with him? Is he okay?"

Alan glanced at her concerned face and felt her love for this child like a warm wave through the air.

"Let's take a look at him and find out."

"Off, Mess," Sylvia said. The black and orange cat that had been coiled in the crook of Jeffy's knees threw Alan an annoyed look as she hopped off the bed.

Alan sat beside Jeffy's sprawled form and rolled him over onto his back. He lifted his pajama shirt and pushed down his diaper to expose his lower abdomen. Placing his left hand on the belly, he pressed the fingertips of his right down onto those of his left. The abdomen was soft. He tapped around the quadrants, eliciting a hollow sound—gas. He paid particular attention to the lower right quadrant over the appendix. There was slight guarding of the abdominal wall there and maybe some tenderness—he thought he saw Jeffy wince in his sleep when he pressed there. He drew his stethoscope from his black bag and listened to the abdomen. The bowel sounds were slightly hyperactive, indicating intestinal irritability. He checked the lungs, heart, the glands in the neck, as a matter of routine.

"How'd he eat tonight?"

"As usual—like a little horse."

Sylvia was standing close beside him. Alan put away his stethoscope and looked up at her.

"And what?"

"His favorites: a hamburger, macaroni and cheese, celery stalks, milk, ice cream."

Relieved that he now had eliminated anything serious, Alan began rearranging Jeffy's pajamas. "Nothing to worry about that I can see. Either he's in the early stages of a virus or it's something he ate. Or *how* he ate. If he's swallowing air with his food, he'll develop some wicked bellyaches."

"It's not his appendix?"

"Not as far as I can tell. It's always a possibility, but I seriously doubt it. Usually, the first thing to go in appendicitis is the appetite."

"Well, his appetite's alive and kickin', I assure you." She put her hand on his shoulder. "Thanks, Alan."

Alan felt a warmth begin to spread from her long fingers through the fabric layers of his windbreaker and shirt. God, that felt good . . .

But sitting here in the almost-dark with her touching him could lead nowhere he felt he should go, so he stood up and her hand fell away.

"If there's any change during the night, yell, otherwise bring him by the office in the morning. I want another look at him."

"On *Wednesday?*"

"Right. I'll be out of town on Thursday so I'm having hours tomorrow. But bring him in early. I'm scheduled to be on a south-bound plane by late afternoon."

"Vacation?"

"Heading for D.C. I'm supposed to testify before Senator McCready's subcommitee on the Medical Guidelines bill."

"Sounds exciting. But a long way to go to talk to some politicians. Is it that important to you?"

"I'm tempted to say something about the last in public confidence wanting to regulate the first in public confidence, but I don't see a soapbox nearby so I'll refrain."

"Go ahead. Orate away."

"No . . . it's just that my professional life—my whole style of medicine—is on the line down there."

"I haven't heard about the bill."

"Most people haven't, but it's an idiotic piece of legislation that will affect every single person in the country by forcing doctors to practice cookbook medicine. And if that happens, I'll quit. I'd rather paint boat bottoms than practice that way."

"Going to take your ball and go home?"

Alan stared at her, stung. "You don't mince words, do you?"

"Not usually. But that's not an answer."

"It's not so much running off and sulking. It's . . ." He hesitated, unsure of what to say, but anxious to clarify himself to her. "It's more like shrugging and walking away from an impossible situation. My style of practice can't coexist with the paper-shufflers. It won't codify, and if they can't stick me into their computers, they'll want to either change me or get me out of the picture."

"Because you tend to fly by the seat of your pants?"

Alan couldn't help but smile. "I like to think of it as using intuition based on experience, but I guess you could call it that. I'm flying by that pants seat tonight with Jeffy."

Concern lit in her eyes. "What do you mean?"

"Well, according to the rules laid out in the Medical Guidelines bill, I'd be required to send you and Jeffy along to the ER tonight for a stat blood count and abdominal X rays to rule out appendicitis because the history and the physical exam suggest that as a possible differential diagnosis."

"Then why aren't you?"

"Because my gut tells me he doesn't have appendicitis."

"And you trust your gut?"

"My malpractice carriers would have a heart attack if they knew, but, yeah—I've learned to trust it."

"Okay," Sylvia said with a smile. "Then I'll trust it, too."

She was staring at him appraisingly, a half smile playing about her lips. Her stare had a way of stripping away all artificiality and pretense.

Alan stared back. He had never seen her like this. She was always dressed to kill, even when she brought Jeffy to the office. It was part of her image as the rich and wild Widow Nash. Yet here she was with no makeup, her dark, almost black hair simply tied back, her slim figure swathed in a shapeless robe, and he found her as attractive as ever. What did she have that drew him so? She was a woman he could not help being *aware* of—as if she were emanating something like a pheromone. He wanted to reach out and—

This was what he had been afraid of.

Her voice suddenly changed to an exaggerated seductive simper that broke the spell. "Besides, I kind of like the seat of your pants."

Here we go, he thought: *her Mae West routine.* Now that he had told her Jeffy was safe, she was back to the old, taunting Sylvia.

"As a matter of fact, if I'd known it was this easy to get you out to the house, I'd have made a night call years ago."

"Time to go," Alan said.

He led the way downstairs to the foyer. Something classical was playing softly through the speakers.

"What's that music?"

"*The Four Seasons.* Vivaldi."

"Not Vivaldi," Alan said, repressing a smile. "*Valli.* Frankie Valli sang with the Four Seasons. And that ain't them."

She laughed, and he liked the sound.

Then she spoke in a little voice. "Gee, Doc, I can't pay you tonight. I'm a little short. Will you take something else in place of money?"

Alan had been expecting this. "Sure. Gold will do. Jewelry."

She snapped her fingers in disappointment. "How about a drink then?"

"No, thanks."

"Coffee? Tea?"

"No, really I—"

"Me?"

"Coffee! Coffee'll do fine."

Her blue eyes flashed as she laughed. "Five points for you!"

"You asked for it, lady."

He wondered if she had always been like this, or if it was a trait she had developed after her husband had been killed. And he wondered too what she would do if he ever took her up on one of her offers. How much of her was for real and how much for show? He wasn't sure. Most of the time he was convinced she was putting him on, but then there was her wild reputation, and a sense that she really did want him.

"Oh, by the way," she said quickly as he put his hand on the doorknob. "I'm having a get-together here Saturday night. Why don't you and your wife—Virginia, isn't it?"

"Ginny."

"Why don't the two of you come over? It's nothing fancy. Just some friends—some of them are mutual, I'm sure—and a few politicos. Nobody really important."

"Politicos?"

She smiled that mischievous smile. "I've been known to make a contribution or two to the right candidate. So what do you say?"

Alan racked his brain for a quick excuse but came up empty. So he hedged. "I don't know, Sylvia. It's short notice and I don't know what Ginny's got planned for the weekend. But I'll let you know tomorrow."

Alan pulled the door open.

"You really have to go?" she said, suddenly serious.

"Yeah. I do." *And fast.*

She shrugged. "Okay. See you in the morning, I guess."

"Right."

And then he was out the door and into the cool air and on his way to the car. He didn't look back, didn't even breathe until he was headed down the driveway and passing through the gate.

Not a moment too soon, he thought, exhaling as he made his body relax into the seat. What that woman did to him . . .

As the drum opening from Little Richard's "Keep a-Knockin' " blasted from the car speakers, he gunned his car and headed for home.

*   *   *

"You'll never guess where I've been tonight," Alan said as he came into the bedroom.

On the way home he had figured out a solution to the Party Problem: He'd simply tell Ginny they were invited, Ginny would say *no,* and that would be it. She wouldn't go to a party at Sylvia's. After all, Sylvia had an unsavory reputation, and none of Ginny's crowd would be there and she'd have no one to talk to. Alan could then leave it up to Ginny to get them out of it. Easy.

Ginny was propped up in bed, eyes closed, a book on her lap. She opened her eyes and looked up. She was wearing her aqua-tinted contacts. She'd had them for six weeks now and Alan still wasn't used to them. She was a pretty, blue-eyed blonde without the contacts; a tall, attractive woman with curly hair close to her head. Definitely worth a second look. But with those contacts in place she was absolutely striking. Her eyes became a startling green that grabbed attention and held it.

She turned those eyes on him now. Would he ever get used to that color? Her long legs, lean and muscular from tennis year-round and golf whenever the weather permitted, slipped free of her robe as she stretched and yawned. She looked vaguely interested.

"The ER, you said."

"Yeah, there. But I made a house call on the way home."

"You should have been a dermatologist . . . no ER or house calls."

Alan made no comment. They'd been over this ground too many times before.

"Okay," she said after a while. "On whom did you make this house call?" Ginny had become very precise in her grammar over the years.

"Sylvia Nash."

Her eyebrows lifted. "What's she got? Herpes?"

"Pull in the claws, dear. I was there to see her little boy, who—"

Ginny bolted upright. "Wait a second! You were in that house? The one in the article? What was it like? Was it like the pictures? Did she give you a tour?"

"No. I was about to tell you that her little boy had abdominal pain and—"

"But didn't you get to see the *house?*"

"Well, the foyer and the boy's bedroom. After all—"

Ginny grimaced with annoyance. "Ohhh, I'd give anything to see that place!"

"Really?" Alan said with a sinking sensation. This wasn't going the way he had expected. In fact, it was going the worst possible way. He decided to cover all exits. "That's too bad. If I'd known you felt that way I'd have accepted her invitation to the party at her place on Saturday night. But I told her we couldn't make it."

She rose to her knees on the bed, hands on hips. "You *what?*"

"I told her we were busy."

"How *could* you without asking me?"

"I just figured that since you called her—what was it? A tramp?— the last time her name came up, that you wouldn't want to have anything to do with her."

"I don't! I just want to see that house! You call her back first thing tomorrow and tell her we're coming. With *bells* on!"

"I don't know if I can, Ginny." She had that gleam in her eye and he knew there would be no turning her around.

"Of course you can! And if you won't, *I* will!"

"That's okay!" he said quickly. "I'll handle it." God knew what Sylvia might say to Ginny on the phone. "Just didn't think you'd want to go to a party thrown by someone you consider a tramp."

"But don't *you* want to go?" she said with arched eyebrows. "As I remember, you came to her defense pretty quick when I made the remark."

"That's because I don't believe everything I hear."

"Everybody knows about her. And look at the way she dresses, the way she vamps around—"

"Vamps?"

"—and those wild parties where there's always a fight or something. And she's *got* to be into cocaine."

"I wouldn't know about that." Alan couldn't be sure, but he didn't think Sylvia was into anything stronger than champagne. He hoped not.

"You like her, don't you?" It sounded like a question but it wasn't. "Sure you don't have something going with her?"

"I can't hide it any longer, Ginny!" Alan shouted. "We've been lovers since the day Lou introduced us!"

Ginny yawned. "Figured as much."

Alan looked away. It was nice to know Ginny had that kind of faith in him. Did he deserve it?

Yes, he decided. Definitely. In all their years of marriage he had never cheated on her. Never even come close despite a good number of opportunities. But Sylvia . . . God, he was attracted to her! She was beautiful, but it was more than that. Beneath all her glittery posing there was a person he feared he could love if he let his feelings have their way.

Yet although he had shared no more than a handshake with the woman, he couldn't help but look on his feelings toward Sylvia as a kind of betrayal of Ginny. It was unfounded, but it plagued him. *You can't help the way you feel,* he always told himself; *you're only responsible for what you do with those feelings.*

"I still don't see why you always insist on defending her, though," Ginny was saying.

"Jeffy makes up for a multitude of sins, whatever they are."

"That strange little boy she took in?"

"Yeah. Only she didn't just take him in—she adopted him. That's a lifelong commitment. She gets a big drawing account of goodwill with me for that."

"Well, whatever," Ginny said, skittering away from the subject of adoption and suddenly becoming bubbly. "At least it will be an experience to see that house."

He tried to think of some way out of the party but saw it was useless. Ginny was off and running at the mouth.

"Wait'll I tell Josie and Terri! They'll *die!* They'll be green! Positively *green!*" She threw her arms around his neck. "This is perfect! Absolutely *per*fect!"

She kissed him. He kissed her back. And soon he was pulling her robe open and she was unbuttoning his shirt, and then they were together on the bed and into the positions and rhythms they had found comfortable and pleasurable over the years of their marriage.

When it was over, Alan lay beside Ginny, content and sated but a little disturbed by the knowledge that a couple of times during their lovemaking he had found his mind wandering to Sylvia Nash. That had never happened before and he didn't like it. It was like cheating. He knew all about fantasies during sex, but that was for other people, not him.

"Nice."

"That it was," Ginny said as she rolled away from him. "Mind if I turn on the tv? I want to see who's on *Letterman* tonight."

"Go ahead."

He went downstairs and got a Foster's from the refrigerator. The cold beer felt good going down. He finished it off as he wandered through the first floor, shutting off lights and locking windows. A lot of wasted space. The two-story brick colonial was really too big for just the two of them, but Ginny had refused to settle for anything smaller.

Finally he got back to the bed where a stack of journals waited on his night table. It was getting almost impossible to stay current with the new developments in all the fields his practice touched on every day. But he kept plugging, reading a little every night, no matter how tired he was. Still, he knew the cutting edge of medicine was slipping a little farther away each year. He felt like an overboard sailor, swimming for his life, and yet seeing the lights of his ship steadily fading farther and farther away into the night.

Ginny had fallen asleep with the tv on. Alan turned it off with the remote button and retrieved the latest issue of *Chest* from the night table. But he let it lie unopened on his lap. His mind was not on medicine but on how it used to be between Ginny and him. He could still see her as she had looked back in his residency days when they had met, her tan skin made darker by the white of her nurse's uniform, and how his throat had almost closed when she first spoke to him. That memory segued into others of the early years of their marriage and how they would snuggle together and whisper after making love. Those days were gone, it seemed. Was this the way marriage went after ten years?

He pushed it from his mind and picked up the journal. Maybe it was just as well tonight. He had a lot of reading to catch up on.

He twisted left and right, trying to find a comfortable position.

___ 2. ___
Ba Thuy Nguyen

Ba was used to Phemus' barking. The old dog had been skittish of late, baying at the slightest thing, waking the Missus and the Boy at all hours of the night. So Ba had taken him to his quarters over the garage where the howls would not disturb the household.

And where Ba could judge their import.

He had ignored the intermittent noise for the past hour as he concentrated on the pile of Immigration and Naturalization forms before him. He had met the residency requirement, and had decided he wanted to become an American citizen. Eventually he would have to take a test on the history and government of his new country, but first there were forms to fill out. Many forms. Tonight he was concentrating on form N400, the most important. The Missus had written out some of the entries for him on a separate sheet of paper and he was laboriously copying the English characters into the blanks. Later he would practice signing his name in English, another requirement for naturalization.

Phemus' barking suddenly changed. It was louder and carried a different note. A note much like it had carried when Dr. Bulmer had stopped by earlier.

Ba slipped from his chair and padded to where the dog stood with both front paws on the windowsill and howled again at the night.

Ba had learned over the years that Phemus was not to be underestimated. True, he was a pest at times, raising alarms at each passing rabbit or vagrant cat, but Ba had come to appreciate the old dog's keen ears and nose, and his remaining eye seemed to have compensated for its brother's loss by becoming twice as sharp. Ba had attuned himself to Phemus' alarms, and this particular pitch and tone, especially with the dog's fur on end at his nape and his low back, usually meant a human trespasser.

He crouched at the window with the dog and scanned the yard. He saw nothing. Phemus licked his face and barked again.

As Ba stood and pulled on his overalls, he wondered if it might be the same fellow he had chased away three nights ago. That had been easy: He had merely spoken from behind a bush and then stepped into view. That had been enough. The would-be thief had been so startled that he had tripped over his own feet in his haste to get away. Ba imagined that most of these sneak thieves were anxious to avoid any confrontation. They wanted to break in silently, take anything of value they could carry in their sack, then slink off unseen into the night.

But Ba also knew that he could not count on that. Among the jackals there might hide a few wolves with ready fangs. They were not hard to handle as long as one was prepared for them.

He knelt before his dresser and pulled open the bottom drawer. Beneath the neatly folded pairs of work pants lay a fully loaded U.S. Army .45 automatic pistol and a standard issue bayonet. Touching them loosed a flood of memories of home, and of how both had stood him well in the long sail from his village across the South China Sea. Fighting the winds and currents had been hard enough, but there had been the added danger of the pirates who preyed on the boats, boarding them repeatedly, robbing the refugees, raping the women, killing any who resisted. Ba remembered his gut-wrenching fear the first time they swarmed aboard his tiny boat: fear that there were too many of them, that they would overpower him and he would fail Nhung Thi and his friends. But he had met their attack with his own, fighting with a ferocity he had never dreamed he possessed, using every combat skill he knew and inventing new ones. The Americans had taught him well how to fight, and many unsuspecting pirates became food for the sharks that took to following Ba's boat.

And just as he had protected his family, friends, and fellow villagers then, Ba was determined to protect the Missus and the Boy now. They were all he had in the world. Nhung Thi was dead, his village was long gone, his friends either dead or scattered all over America. He owed the Missus a huge debt. She had aided him and his ailing Nhung Thi when life had looked the blackest: an unknown woman, appearing out of nowhere in Manila, saying she was the Sergeant's wife and offering help. Ba would never forget that. She still thought she was taking care of Ba, but he knew it was the other way around. For years now he had watched over her. Nothing would harm her or the Boy as long as he drew breath.

Ba picked up the bayonet and withdrew it from its scabbard. The blade was dark and dull except for the gentle curve of bright steel where he kept it honed to a fine edge. This old and silent friend would do, just in case. Not the gun. After all, the purpose of going out into the yard was to keep the Missus and the Boy from being disturbed.

He pulled on a dark sweater, slipped the naked blade through a loop in his overalls, and reached for the doorknob. Phemus was there in a flash, his nose to the door crack, growling.

Ba knelt down beside the animal.

"You'd die for her, too, wouldn't you, dog?" he said in his village dialect.

He remembered the day the Missus had found Phemus as if it were yesterday. He had been driving her back from the city and had taken a local route to avoid a tie-up on the Long Island Expressway. Suddenly the Missus had called to him to stop. As he pulled into the curb he saw why: A group of four boys in their early teens was chasing a limping, emaciated dog down the sidewalk, pelting it with rocks as it fled before them. Suddenly it stumbled and they were upon it, shouting as they surrounded it and kicked it repeatedly.

Before Ba knew it, the Missus was out of the car and running toward the group. She reached them just as one of the boys raised a heavy stone high over his head, ready to smash it down on the weak, exhausted creature. The Missus charged in and hurled him aside with a violent shove. The boy lost his balance and fell, but immediately leaped up at her, his fists raised, rage in his face. But Ba was approaching then. He looked at the boy and wished him death for even so much as considering the idea of striking the Missus. The boy must have read something of that wish in Ba's face, for he spun and ran. His friends quickly followed on his heels.

The Missus hovered over the panting dog and gently stroked the ridges of his heaving ribs. She picked him up and turned toward the car. Ba offered to take the dog for her but she told him to drive directly to the vet's.

In his mind's eye he could still see her in the rearview mirror, sitting in the back seat with the dog on her lap, unmindful of the blood that oozed onto her expensive dress and the velvet upholstery. The dog had the strength to lick her hand once and she had smiled.

On the way to the veterinary clinic, she had told him of people who moved away and simply abandoned their pets, leaving a faithful animal sitting at the back door of an empty house, waiting for days to be let in. Finally, when hunger and thirst got to be too much, the creature would take to the streets, ill-equipped to fend for itself after a lifetime as a house pet.

At the vet's they learned that the dog had a broken rear leg, three broken ribs, and a left eye that had been punctured by a stick.

Better to kill a dog and eat it rather than treat it so, Ba had thought.

The dog's bones healed, but the eye was permanently damaged. The Missus named him Polyphemus—a name Ba did not understand—and he had been a member of the household for five years.

"Not tonight," Ba told the dog as it tried to follow him out the door. "You've too gentle a heart. It might betray you."

He closed the door on Phemus' whines and barks and made his way down to the garage and out the side door to the grounds.

A half-moon was rising over the water. Ba kept to the shadows of the ground-brushing willows along the rim of the property until he could duck across a small area of lawn to the foundation plantings around the house. Quickly and quietly, he made his way through the shrubbery.

He found them on the west side. They already had one of the casement windows pried open and one of the pair was supporting the other as he climbed in.

Ba spoke from behind a rhododendron.

"The Missus does not want you here. Leave!"

The one up at the window dropped down and faced the spot where Ba was hiding. Ba recognized him then as the one he had frightened away the other night.

"It's the gook again!" the shorter one said. Two knives suddenly gleamed in the moonlight.

"Get him!"

___ 3. ___
Sylvia Nash

"Ba?"

Where is he? Sylvia wondered as she scanned the backyard from her work area off the hothouse that served as her arboretum. He almost invariably started off each day watering the trees in the hothouse. But the trays under the pots were dry and he was nowhere in sight.

Strains from Vivaldi, left on the stereo since last night, filled the air. Sylvia put down the chopsticks she had been using to loosen the soil around the ezo spruce bonsai before her and brushed her hands. The *ishi-zuki* was ready for transplanting and she needed someone to help her. The tree's new *Fukuroshiki* pot was layered with stone and soil and waiting for the tree. All that was missing was Ba.

Normally she would de-pot and transplant a tree by herself, laying it on its side, pruning the longer, heavier roots, then replacing it in its pot after freshening the soil. But the *ishi-zuki* was special. She had spent too many years working, watching, and waiting while she trained the roots of this little tree to grow over and around the rock upon which it sat to jeopardize it by trying to transplant it without assistance. If the stone fell free of the roots, she'd never forgive herself.

"Gladys?" she called. "Have you seen Ba?"

"Not this morning, ma'am," the maid answered from the kitchen.

"Come on, Mess," she said to the cat curled up in the sun by the door. "Let's go find Ba."

The cat raised its head and looked at her for a moment through slit eyes, then went back to dozing. Mess didn't like to move much. She had grown fat and lazy since the day Sylvia found her as a kitten and brought her home. Someone had bundled her and her four siblings into a trash can bag and dumped them in the middle of the road in front of Toad Hall. Mess, the only survivor after the bag had been run over by a number of cars, had truly been a mess when Sylvia had freed her—shaking, terrified, splattered with the blood of her brothers and sisters. To this day she would not go near the road.

Sylvia picked up her cup of coffee and walked out into the back. The forsythia were in full bloom, splashing buttercup yellow here and there around the awakening yard. Beyond the greening lawn was a narrow strip of sand; beyond that was the Long Island Sound, lapping high at the dock. Far on the other side lay Connecticut's south shore. A breeze blew the briny smell of the water across the yard and sighed through the willows that ringed the property. That sound—the wind in the willows—and the sight of this old, three-storied house looking like it had been transplanted whole from a Georgia riverbank had left her no choice but to buy the place and name it Toad Hall.

As she neared Jeffy's fenced-in play area, she saw two mallards standing before him, quacking softly. He used to feed the ducks, laughing like a little madman as they chased the bits of stale bread he threw to them. This pair probably thought he was the same old Jeffy. But he wasn't. He ignored them.

The ducks flew off at her approach. She thought she saw Jeffy's lips moving and she rushed over to him. But she heard nothing. He was still squatting in the grass, still rocking back and forth endlessly, totally absorbed in the bright yellow of the dandelion he had found in the grass.

"How's it going, Jeffy?"

The child continued to stare into the flower as if he had found the secrets of the universe there.

Sylvia pulled a box of Nerds from her smock pocket and squatted beside him. She had found Nerds the most suitable for her purposes because they released their flavor instantaneously and were not filling. She pinched one of the tiny candies at the tip of her thumb and forefinger and held it ready.

"Jeffy!" she said, pronouncing his name in a crisp, sharp tone. *"Jeffy!"*

His head turned a degree or two in her direction. At the first increment of motion, her hand darted out with an accuracy born of years of experience and pressed the Nerd between his lips. As he bit into it, she called his name again in an attempt to get him to turn a few more degrees her way.

"Jeffy! Jeffy!"

But he turned away again, back to the dandelion. Another half-dozen repetitions of his name elicited no response.

"Maybe you don't like Nerds anymore, huh?" she said. But she knew it wasn't the candy. Jeffy was slipping away. After doing so well for years with the operant techniques, he had become resistant to the therapy since sometime around the first of the year. Worse than that, he was regressing, slipping deeper and deeper into his autism. She didn't know what was wrong. She provided a structured environment and continued working with him every day. . . .

Sylvia swallowed hard past the constriction in her throat. She felt so *helpless!* If only . . .

She resisted the urge to hurl the candy out into the Sound and scream out her frustration. Instead, she tucked the Nerds back into her pocket. She would try a full-length operant therapy session with him this afternoon. She straightened up and gently ruffled the golden hair of the child she loved so much.

She had a flash of an old dream—Jeffy running across this same lawn toward her, a big smile on that round little face, his arms open wide for her as she lifted him up, laughing, swung him around, and heard him say, "Do it again, Mommy!"

It faded as suddenly as it had come. It was an old dream, anyway, browned and crumbling at the edges. Better to leave it undisturbed.

She studied Jeffy for a moment. Physically, he seemed fine this morning. No fever, no sign of a problem in the world since he had awakened. In fact, he had immediately gone to the refrigerator upon arising. But Sylvia had guided him out here to make him wait a bit before breakfast, just to see how he was acting. She had called the school and told them he wasn't going to be in today.

She turned and glanced toward the garage. The big double door was open but there was no sign of life. Then she heard Phemus' familiar bark from the west side of the house and went to investigate.

As Sylvia rounded the near corner, Ba came around the far corner, carrying the new tree. The sight startled her. When the twenty-foot peach tree had been delivered from the nursery two days ago, it had taken three men to off-load it from the truck. Ba now had his arms wrapped around the burlap-wrapped rootball and was carrying it by himself.

"Ba! You'll hurt yourself!"

"No, Missus," he said as he put it down. "Many fishing nets were heavier when I was a boy."

"Maybe so." She guessed hauling in fish-filled nets every day since boyhood probably would leave you pretty strong. "But be careful."

She noted that Ba had dug up a rather large section of the lawn. "What time were you up this morning to get so far already?"

"Very early."

She looked again. No doubt about it. The plot was large—considerably larger than necessary for the planting of a single tree.

"Flowers around the tree, don't you think, Missus?" Ba seemed to be reading her mind.

"A flower bed. Yes, I think that would be nice."

She glanced at the older peach tree thirty feet away to the south. That too would need a flower bed to even things out. Maybe this year, with two trees to cross-pollinate, they would get some peaches.

She watched him dig. For a man who had grown up on the sea,

Ba had a wonderful way with growing things, and an innate aesthetic sense. He had known nothing about yard work when he had first come here, but had learned quickly and well. He had also become a proficient assistant in her bonsai arboretum, wiring branches and pruning roots with the best of them. And since taking over as her driver, he had become a crack auto mechanic. There didn't seem to be anything he couldn't master.

She helped him slide the burlap-wrapped rootball into the hole in the center of the plot. As he began to back-fill, she saw the crude bandage on his arm.

"How did you cut yourself?"

He glanced at his forearm. "It is nothing. I was careless."

"But how—"

"Please do not worry, Missus. It will not happen again."

"Good." She watched him tamp down the soil around the newly planted tree with the flat of his shovel. "You seem to have an awful lot of dirt left over."

"That is because I have added peat moss and a special root food."

"You shouldn't fertilize a newly planted tree, Ba."

"This is a special food that will not burn the roots. I learned of it back home."

"What is it?"

"That is a secret, Missus."

"Fine. Meet me in the arboretum as soon as you're finished."

Smiling and shaking her head, Sylvia turned and headed for the backyard. *Secret root food* . . . but she let him have his way with the yard. He did an excellent job and she didn't believe in tampering with success.

She pulled Jeffy away from his dandelion and set him up with breakfast. Gladys had made him a bowl of Maypo and he attacked it. There didn't seem to be anything wrong with his stomach this morning.

As usual, Alan had been right.

Wandering back into her work area, Sylvia stood and considered the *ishi-zuki* from a distance. The gallery was really anxious for this one. Someone called at least twice a week asking when they could expect delivery.

Who'd have ever thought her hobby would make her the latest Big Thing with the New York art crowd and celebrity set? You weren't *anybody,* dear, unless you had a tree sculpture by Sylvia Nash somewhere in the house.

She smiled at how innocently it had all started.

The art of bonsai had fascinated Sylvia since her teenage years. She had come across a book on the miniature trees and had been touched by their delicacy, the sense of age about them. She decided to try her hand. She found she had a knack for the art, and after many years of working at it, became quite adept.

But after Greg's death, she neglected them and one of her prized trees died. She had pruned and wired that particular little five-needle pine for years, transforming it from an ordinary collection of needles and branches into a graceful living work of art. Its loss seemed all the more tragic after losing Greg. It sat in its pot with its needles turning brown, its roots rotting, beyond salvage. When the needles dropped off, only a naked trunk would remain.

Then Sylvia remembered seeing a demonstration of a laser technique used to sculpt heads and busts. She investigated, found a place that did it, and had her dead tree, pot and all, laser-sculpted from a laminated block of oak. She was delighted with the result: The outer needles were sharp, the intricacies of the bark and even the moss at the tree's base were all preserved forever. She painted it, and set it back in its former spot among her other bonsai. It needed no watering, no pruning, no wiring. It was perfect. Forever.

And that would have been that had not Christmas a few years later found her without the slightest idea of what to give half the people on her list. Her gaze had come to rest on the laser-sculpted bonsai and the idea struck her: Why not take one of her favorite bonsai to the laser studio and have a dozen or so replicas run off? Why not indeed? A unique personal gift.

And so it became an annual routine to favor certain special people in her life with a laser-sculpted bonsai. Probably it would have gone no further if she hadn't decided to use one of her experimental trees as a model.

That particular tree had been a lark, really—a mixture of bonsai and topiary techniques. She had allowed a rather tall boxwood to grow wild while letting it acclimate to its pot. For some reason, its cylindrical form had reminded her of a skyscraper, so on a whim she began pruning and shaping it into the form of the Empire State Building. She had ten laser-scuptures made from it and gave them away for Christmas. By the end of January there was a Manhattan art gallery owner knocking on her door, begging to speak to her. He went on and on about the Empire bonsai, literally cooing about its "subtle melding of the man-made and the natural," her "stunning brilliance in using the latest in modern technology to preserve an ancient art form," and so on. He *ooh*ed and *ahhh*ed as she toured him through her collection and actually *eek*ed when he saw her *sokan* tree with the double trunk on bottom growing into the New York skyline on top.

Since then, once a year, she issued a strictly limited edition of one hundred sculptures of one of her bonsai. She signed and numbered them and made the gallery charge an astronomical amount for each. She didn't need the money, but the high price tag and the limited supply made them all the more sought after. She had had numerous offers—extremely generous offers—for the original living trees from which the copies had been cut. She turned them down and refused to hear any counteroffers. No one other than Sylvia herself would ever own or care for her trees. Bonsai culture was a delicate, time-consuming task that took skill, practice, and devotion—*not* for amateurs.

Take the *ishi-zuki,* for instance. How could she allow some clown with a fat wallet, who thought all they needed was a little watering like a house plant, entrust them to his maid for care? *Especially* this one. The leafy area had been pruned into the shape of a neat little Cape Cod house, which was supported by a gently curved trunk whose roots were clasped tightly around a supporting rock. This tree spoke to her. Selling it would be unthinkable.

But she would gladly sell replicas, and people were waiting in line to buy them.

Which made her Someone to Know.

Sylvia knew she really didn't fit in with the celebrities who bought her sculptures and wanted to meet her and invite her to their parties.

Sometimes it seemed to her that she didn't fit anywhere. But she accepted the invitations and maintained tenuous contact with the rich and famous, staying on the fringes, riding along, waiting for something interesting to happen. She used them for some of her nights. The nights could be a hellish burden at times. Jeffy and her trees and her investments filled the days, but the nights went on forever.

Last night had been an exception, however. It had proved far too short. Alan's presence had injected a special kind of life into the old house, warming it, brightening it. She could so easily get used to having him come home to her every night, kissing him hello, touching him—

She shook off the thought with a touch of irritation. No sense getting lost in that little fantasy. She had had that kind of life once, in a tiny garden apartment downtown.

She caught herself. She hadn't thought of the old apartment in years. Those memories were supposed to be locked safely away for good. That kind of life was gone for good, as were the Sylvia Nash and the man who had lived it together. The man was dead, and the Sylvia Nash of today no longer wanted or needed that life. She had built a new one from scratch. The old Sylvia was gone. And no one was going to bring her back.

Besides, Alan Bulmer was taken.

Still, it was a nice, respectable little fantasy, as long as that was all it remained.

After all, she thought with a wry smile, she had her reputation to consider.

She went back into the kitchen. Jeffy was still at the table, scraping the bottom of his bowl. She pulled it away and gave him his glass of milk.

"Okay, guy," she said, lightly running her fingers through his curly hair as he drank his milk in huge gulps. "We're going to clean you up and get you over to Dr. Bulmer's before his office gets too crowded."

Jeffy didn't look at her. He had finished his milk and was busy staring into the bottom of the glass.

"Someday you're going to talk to me, Jeffy. You may not know it yet, but someday you're going to call me 'Mommy.' " She kissed him on the forehead. How could she feel so intensely about someone who did not acknowledge her existence? "You are, damn it. You are!"

*   *   *

The modern, brightly lit waiting room was crowded with people of all ages, shapes, and sizes. The receptionist said that Dr. Bulmer had penciled in Jeffy's name and they would get to him in a minute. Two of the children had started screaming at the sight of Ba, so he left to wait in the car. Sylvia seated herself next to a polyester princess who eyed her Albert Nipon suit with barely concealed hostility.

Wouldn't fit you anyway, honey, she thought as she snuggled Jeffy in against her on a seat and waited.

A little girl, no more than four or five years old, with blue eyes and straight blond hair, came up and stood before Jeffy. After looking at him for a while she said, "I'm here with my mommy." She pointed to a woman across the room engrossed in a magazine. "That's my mommy over there."

Jeffy stared over her left shoulder and said nothing.

"My mommy's sick," she said in a louder voice. "Is your mommy sick?"

She might have been a piece of furniture for all the notice Jeffy took of her, but her voice was attracting the attention of the other waiting patients. The room grew perceptively quieter as they waited for the reply that would never come from Jeffy.

Tense and watchful, Sylvia bit her lip, trying to think of a way to defuse the situation. The little girl, however, did it for her.

"My mommy's got diarrhea, that's why she's here to see the doctor. All the time she keeps going to the bathroom."

As the waiting room rippled with restrained laughter, the woman with the magazine, her face now red with embarrassment, came over and led the little girl back to her seat.

Jeffy neither laughed nor smiled.

It wasn't long before they were called back to an examining room. She sat Jeffy on the paper-covered table and undressed him down to his training pants. He was still dry. Jeffy would use the bathroom if it was convenient, but if he was absorbed in something or away from home, he simply went in his pants. The nurse took a rectal temperature, said it was normal, then left them to wait. Alan entered about ten minutes later. He smiled at her, then turned to Jeffy.

"So you made it through the night, Jeff? No more bellyaches? How about lying back and letting me check the old tummy."

As he went through the examination, he kept up the chatter, as if Jeffy were just like any other eight-year-old. That was what had immediately attracted Sylvia to Alan as a physician—the way he treated Jeffy. Most doctors in her experience had examined him thoroughly and gently, but never spoke to him. They would talk to her but never to Jeffy. True, he wasn't listening and wouldn't respond, so why talk to him? She had never noticed it until that day she brought him to see Alan after he had fallen and his elbow had swollen up. Sylvia had been sure it was broken and had been about to rush him over to her Uncle Lou's office when she remembered that he was out of town that day. But his former associate, Dr. Bulmer, had been available. They had been introduced briefly in a hallway of her uncle's office when the two had been partners and she didn't know anything about him except that her uncle had said at the time that he was "pretty sharp." *Anyplace but an emergency room*, she had thought, and had consented to letting the new guy examine Jeffy.

That one brief visit had been a revelation. Jeffy's autism didn't faze Alan at all. He had treated Jeffy like a real human being, not like some sort of deaf, dumb, blind block of wood. There was respect in his attitude, almost reverence—this was another human being he was treating. It wasn't an act, either. She had sensed that it came naturally to this man. And for just a second, as Alan had lifted him off the table, Jeffy had hugged him.

That had been it. From then on there had been no other doctor for Jeffy. Only Alan Bulmer would do.

Her Uncle Lou had been a little miffed when he learned about

Alan examining Jeffy, but that had been nothing compared to the explosion that had occurred when she transferred Jeffy's records to Alan's new office.

And now she watched Alan as he pushed and tapped on Jeffy's abdomen again. He kept getting better-looking as he got older. The little touches of gray flecking the dark brown hair of his temples didn't make him look older, just more distinguished. He was built the way she liked a man, tall and lean, with those long legs and piercing dark brown eyes. . . .

"You're fine, Jeff," Alan said as he sat him up. "But you're getting pudgy." He sat on the table, put his arm around Jeffy's shoulder in a casual gesture of affection, and turned to Sylvia. "He's got a lot of air in his intestines. He eats fast?"

"Like a vacuum."

"See if you can slow him down."

"Easier said than done."

"And either cut back on the amount he's eating or increase his activity."

"Maybe I should enroll him in Little League," she said with the slightest edge to her voice.

Alan winced at her sarcasm and sighed. "Yeah, I know. 'Easier said than done.' "

That was another thing she liked about Alan—they could communicate. After years of caring for Jeffy together, they had become attuned to each other regarding the rare ups and many downs of life with an autistic child.

"I'll try," she said. "Maybe I can take him for walks."

"Will he come?"

"Sure. As long as I take him by the hand and Ba's not there."

"Ba?"

"Ba spoils him terribly. Carries him all the time. Jeffy's legs don't work when Ba is around."

Alan laughed. "Well, whatever you can get him to do will help."

Sylvia pulled Jeffy's clothes back on while Alan scribbled in the chart.

"I want to thank you for coming over last night," she said, remembering the thrill she had felt upon opening the door and seeing him there. "I'm sorry it was for nothing."

"It wasn't for nothing. We both slept better."

"Speaking of house calls: Do you make them on lonely widows?" She loved to watch him blush. He didn't disappoint her.

"As a matter of fact, yes. There's a little old lady not far from here who's bedfast after a couple of strokes. I see her once a month."

"What about younger ladies?"

"Depends on the problem. The home is a lousy place to practice medicine."

She stifled a smile. Poor guy. Trying so hard to remain cool and professional.

"What if she's got an itch only you can scratch."

He smiled with the slightest trace of malice. "I'd tell her to take a bath. Or maybe a cold shower."

She laughed. She was so glad that for all his old-fashioned propriety and almost stuffy integrity, he still had a sense of humor.

"By the way," he said into her laugh, "is that invitation to your party this weekend still open?"

"You can make it?" A buoyant sensation came over her.

"Yes, we can. I thought we were busy but we're not."

"Wonderful! Nine o'clock. Semi-dressy."

"We'll be there."

"Great. Then I can sneak you upstairs and show you some of my erotic Japanese etchings."

He looked squarely at her, his expression tinged with annoyance. "You know, one of these days I just might call your bluff."

Don't you dare! The phrase leaped to her lips but she bit it back. "Who's bluffing?" she said as she opened the examining room door and ushered Jeffy out. "Good luck in Washington. See you Saturday night."

As she walked up the hall, she wondered at the stab of panic she had felt when Alan had mentioned calling her bluff. She didn't want that. She was aware that much of the attraction was based on his inaccessibility. It made him unique among so many of the men she knew—such as some of Greg's friends and the husbands of her female friends who had come around to "comfort" her after Greg's death. Their idea of comforting, however, seemed to require a bed. That had been an eye-opening time in her life. She'd had her share of flings since then, but not with any of them.

Alan had turned a deaf ear to her frequent offers. And she knew he was attracted to her, which made the little game all the more charming—and Alan all the more honorable.

But why did she do it?

She never could answer that question. Alan was the only man she teased so, yet she respected him more than any man she knew. So why make him squirm? Why tempt him? Was it because she knew he was safe? Or did she want to bring him down somehow, prove that the shining knight had feet of clay?

No. She did *not* want to prove that!

Then why did she so enjoy teasing him?

The questions went 'round and 'round, with never an answer.

She wondered if there might be something wrong with her—a wire crossed somewhere in her psyche—but brushed that uncomfortable thought away.

It was all in fun, she thought determinedly. All in fun.

4.
Alan

"Sure you don't want to come?"

Ginny looked at him through her green contacts and smiled. "You know I'd love to, Alan, but I can't let Josie down. We're—"

He knew: the Tennis Tournament at the club. Ginny and Josie were in the quarter-finals for women's doubles.

"How many times am I going to testify before a senate subcommittee? I could use you there for some moral support."

"I know, honey," Ginny said as she put her arms around him. "And I never would have entered the tournament if I'd thought we had the slightest chance of getting this far. But Josie's depending on me, Alan. I can't let her down."

A caustic remark rose to Alan's lips but he held it back. He didn't want to leave on a tense note.

"But I'll drive you down to JFK," Ginny said.

"Better if you didn't. I don't know when I'll be back tomorrow, so I'd rather have the car sitting in the lot there."

He gave her a kiss and a hug, and then he was on his way out the door with his overnight bag in his hand.

"Good luck!" she said with a wave as he got into the car. He smiled and hoped it looked genuine. He hurt more than he wanted to admit, even to himself.

*   *   *

Mike Switzer had told him that all doctors who gave pro-guidelines testimony had all their expenses paid for by the committee, including limousines to meet them at the airport. Those testifying against the guidelines had to shift for themselves.

So Alan shifted himself from National Airport and checked into Crystal City in Arlington, where he got a room with a view of the Potomac. The night was cool and clear, and from his window he could see the lighted images of the monuments on the far side of the river reflecting brightly in the rippling water.

He hated to travel. He felt strangely disconnected when he was away from his practice and his home, as if someone had pulled the plug on him and he'd ceased to exist. He shook himself. He didn't like the feeling.

He opened his suitcase, pulled out a bottle of scotch, and settled back on the double bed with a couple of fingers' worth and watched the tv without seeing it.

No sense in kidding himself: He was nervous about tomorrow. He had never testified before a committee of any sort, let alone one being run by the ferocious Senator James McCready. Why on earth had he agreed to do it? Why would anyone set himself up for a grilling by a bunch of politicians? Crazy!

It was all Mike—pardon: *Congressman*—Switzer's fault. If he hadn't sweet-talked Alan into this, he'd be home safe and sound in his own bed before his own tv set.

No, that wasn't true. Alan knew he really had no one to blame but himself for being here. He had wanted a chance to say something against the Medical Guidelines bill, and Mike had given it to him.

But would it matter?

He had begun to wonder if maybe he wasn't a vanishing breed . . . a dinosaur . . . a solo physician practicing a personal brand of medicine, developing one-to-one relationships with his patients, gaining their trust, dealing with them person-to-person, becoming someone they came to with their problems, someone they called when their children were sick, someone they placed high on their Christmas card list.

The coming thing seemed to be the patient-as-number served by the doctor-as-employee who worked for a government or corporate clinic, seeing X number of patients per hour for Y hours per day, then signing off and going home like everybody else.

Alan was not totally immune to the allure of the 9-to-5 setup: normal hours, guaranteed income and benefits, no calls in the middle of the night or on Sunday afternoons in the middle of the Jets game. Enticing . . .

Great for robots, maybe, but not for dinosaurs.

Switzer was styling himself as the champion of the American doctor, but how much was real and how much was a role, Alan couldn't say. He had known Mike in their undergraduate days at N.Y.U. and they had been fairly good friends until their post-graduate paths parted: Mike to law school and Alan on to medicine. Mike had always struck Alan as a decent sort, but the fact remained that he now held—and intended to continue to hold—an elected office; and that meant he had to keep an eye on which way the wind was blowing.

Switzer certainly seemed to know how to keep his name in the paper, what with his feud with the City MTA on the home front and his butting heads with Senator McCready on the national level. But how much of his opposition to McCready's Medical Guide-lines bill was real commitment and how much was because McCready and the MTA's Cunningham were members of the other party?

Not knowing for sure made Alan slightly queasy. For the moment, however, he would have to trust Switzer. He had no choice.

And tomorrow I put my head on the block.

The hearings started at the unheard-of hour at 7:00 a.m., so he turned off the tv, undressed, made himself another scotch, and lay there in the dark. He tried to find an oldies channel on the radio, but the reception was poor, so he resigned himself to waiting for sleep in silence. He knew he'd have to be patient, because he could tell already it was going to be one of those nights.

Here we go, he thought as he lay there.

It never failed. Whenever he left town, he spent the first night running through his own peculiar variation on *A Christmas Carol.*

He wrestled with the covers on the unfamiliar mattress, plagued by the ghosts of Patients Present: the sick ones he had left behind. They were in good hands, but he was out of town and they were out of reach. He wondered if he'd made any diagnostic blunders or therapeutic errors that wouldn't be found in time. The same worries nagged him every night, but never with the same intensity as when he was out of town.

He wondered if other doctors lay awake nights worrying about patients. He never mentioned it to anyone because it sounded phony, like cheap PR, like dime store Marcus Welbyism.

The worries about current patients flowed naturally into the ghosts of Patients Yet to Be, products of Alan's chronic anxiety over keeping up to date in all the fields his practice touched on. A virtually impossible task, he knew, but he fretted about not knowing of a new diagnostic tool or a new therapy that could change the course of a patient's disease.

And last—his subconscious always saved the worst for last—the ghosts of Patients Past. He feared them the most. Like a silent crowd around an accident, all the failures of his medical career ringed the bed, crouched on the covers, and hovered overhead as he slipped toward sleep. The failures . . . the ones who had slipped through his fingers, the lacerated lives that got away.

Caroline Wendell was first tonight, appearing at the foot of the bed, baring her shoulders and legs to show him all those utterly gross bruises that kept popping out and threatening to like simply ruin her prom because her gown was, you know, off the shoulders. She hadn't known then that her bone marrow had gone wild, destroying her along with itself. Alan hadn't known immediately, either; but now he relived the weak, sick feeling that came over him when he spun down a hematocrit and saw the much-too-thick buffy coat of white cells in the capillary tube. Eventually she faded away, just as she had in real life from the acute lymphocytic leukemia that had kept her from seeing the end of her senior year.

Little Bobby Greavy crawled up on the bed to demonstrate that what a wild bone marrow did to a young girl's body was nothing compared to what people did to each other. Bobby was a visitor from Alan's training years, and now he gracefully turned to show off the red, blistered second-degree burn in the skin of his back— a perfect triangular imprint of his mother's steam iron.

Bobby almost always brought along Tabatha, the little seven-month-old who had been clouted on the head so many times she was blind. Despite Alan's pleas and demands and strident protests, both had been returned to their respective parents by the court and he never saw them again.

Bobby and Tabatha dissolved into Maria Cardoza. She was a frequent visitor. Slim, beautiful, nineteen-year-old Maria. As usual, she floated in on her ICU bed, naked, bleeding from her nose, her mouth, her abdominal incisions, her rectum and her vagina. That was how he had last seen her, and the image was branded on his subconscious. Four years ago he had been passing through the ER when the first aid brought her in from a two-car head-on accident on 107. He had seen her only once before in his office for a minor respiratory infection. Since there was no one else available, he had assisted the surgeon on call in removing her ruptured spleen and sewing up her lacerated liver. The procedure had been effective, but all the clotting factors in her blood had been chewed up and she simply would not stop bleeding. Alan dragged a hematologist out of bed but nothing he did would make Maria's blood clot. Once again, fresh as that very night, he felt the grim, almost hysterical frustration of his impotence, of the futility of every effort to save her as he stayed by her bed until dawn, watching liter after liter of the various solutions and plasma fractions that poured into her veins run out the drains in her abdominal cavity. She went into renal shutdown, then congestive heart failure, then she went away.

But not for good.

Maria and her touring company lived on, visiting Alan on a regular basis.

*   *   *

It was almost time.

Mike Switzer, all eyes behind his horn-rimmed glasses, wavy brown hair falling over his angular face, had hovered at Alan's side all morning.

"Just stay cool, Alan," he kept saying. "Don't let them rattle you."

Alan kept nodding. "Sure. Don't worry. I'm fine."

But he wasn't fine. He felt as if he were about to be fed to the lions. His stomach kept twitching and his bladder urged him to the men's room again despite the three trips he had already made there.

He'd heard about McCready and how he could cut you up and eat you alive before you even knew he was talking to you.

The hearing room was just like the ones he had seen now and then on cable tv: oak paneled, with the politicos and their aides sitting up behind their desks on the raised platform like Caesars in the Coliseum, and the testifiers below like Christians waiting for their turn in the ring. Bored-looking reporters strolled in and out of the room or slouched about in chairs at the rear until The Man Himself limped in and sat behind the nameplate that said: SEN. JAMES A. MCCREADY (D-NY). Then they were all attention.

Alan studied McCready from his vantage point among the plebeians. With his stooped frame and sagging jowls, he looked older than his reputed fifty-six years. The impenetrable dark glasses that had become his trademark over the past few years were in place, shutting him off from everyone around him, masking whatever hints his eyes might let slip about what was going on in his mind. Whatever was said, Senator McCready remained expressionless and insectoid behind those dark glasses.

Some confusing chatter went back and forth among those on the podium, followed by someone finishing testimony that had begun yesterday, then it was Alan's turn to sit before the microphones.

__ 5. __
The Senator

James McCready let his mind wander as the latest doctor—what was his name? Bulmer?—began to speak. He had heard all he wanted to hear on this subject long ago.

Besides, he didn't want to be here. He felt tired and weak. He felt *old*.

Fifty-six and he felt like a hundred. Thank God he could sit now and regain the strength he had spent just walking here from his office . . . and sitting down. If they only knew what it cost him to seat himself slowly when every muscle in his body screamed to allow him to flop into his chair.

And mornings were his *best* times! That was why he scheduled these hearing for the crack of dawn. By the afternoon he could barely fake it. Good thing he'd been wounded in Korea. That old, nearly forgotten injury had finally served some useful purpose.

Keeping his head still and moving only his eyes behind his dark glasses, McCready scanned the committee room. He had started wearing the heavily tinted lenses when his upper lids had begun to droop. He had feared at first that people would think he was trying to look like a movie star. Instead, they said it made him look like General Douglas MacArthur. Well, if he had to look like somebody, he could certainly do worse than MacArthur.

His gaze came to rest on Congressman Switzer.

There's a man to watch out for. He smells the weakness in me and he's readying himself for the kill. The first time I stumble, he'll be on me. Look at him there, the little weasel bastard! Hanging on his pet doctor's shoulder, egging him on. Probably coached him for weeks. These doctors can't think on their own unless it's about medicine, and even then they screw up plenty!

McCready, above all else, knew about medical screw-ups. But he chided himself for begrudging Switzer a pet doctor. After all, he had plenty of his own.

He focused in on the doctor. What was his name again? He looked at the list. Oh, yes—Bulmer. He couldn't resist a smile. *Poor Dr. Bulmer . . . probably thinks he has a real ally in Switzer. Wonder if he realizes that his buddy will drop him at the first hint that it would be advantageous to do so?*

He heard the doctor say the magic words, "In closing . . ." and decided he'd better tune in. It had been a brief address and he was ending it while he still had everyone's attention. Maybe this doc wasn't so dumb.

". . . that these so-called guidelines are cookbook medicine of the lowest sort. It allows a doctor no leeway in tailoring therapy to a particular patient under particular conditions. It reduces doctors to robot mechanics and reduces their patients to assembly-line cars. It is the most dehumanizing piece of legislation I have ever had the misfortune to read. It will drive out the kind of doctor who shapes his therapeutic approach to the individual patient, and will encourage the rise of the physician-bureaucrat who does everything unswervingly by The Book. Medicine will become as personal as welfare, as efficient as the Post Office, and as successful as the war against the Viet Cong.

"Only one party will suffer in the long run: the patient."

From somewhere in the room there came the sound of one pair of hands clapping, then two, and then many.

Obviously ringers, McCready told himself. But then more and more hands joined in until the whole room—some committee members included!—was clapping. What had this Bulmer character said? He'd brought no graphs or charts, and he couldn't have gone over too many facts and figures because McCready would have noticed lots of glazed eyes. Which meant that he'd probably done a "Dr. Sincerity" number on the room. He clenched a fist. He should have listened.

Well, no matter. He'd have a little fun with him, then cut him down to size. He cleared his throat and the room silenced.

"So tell me, Dr. Bulmer," he said, noting the persistent rasp in his voice, "if American medicine doesn't need guidelines, how do you explain the health care crisis in this country?"

Bulmer nodded toward him. He seemed ready for the question.

"Besides you, Senator, who says there's a crisis? A recent nationwide study showed that only ten percent of the people polled were dissatisfied with their personal health care, yet fully eighty percent were under the impression that there was a health care crisis in America. So I have to ask myself: If ninety percent of the people are satisfied with their own health care, and have not personally experienced a 'health care crisis' of any sort, where do they get the idea that there's a crisis? The answer is obvious: They have been *told* so often about a health care crisis in America that they believe it exists, despite the fact that ninety percent of them have no beef with their personal health care. As inheritor of a chain of newspapers, Senator, I figure you're in a better position than I to explain how this *perceived* crisis in health care might have been manufactured."

The bastard! McCready thought as a smattering of applause died out before it really got started. The doctor was trying to put him on the defensive. He debated mentioning that the McCready newspaper chain was being held in trust and run by a board of directors while he was in office, but decided against it. Better to ignore the remark—not even dignify it with an answer. He waited until the silence bordered on the uncomfortable. When he finally spoke he treated Bulmer's last remark as if it had never been uttered.

"So everything's just hunky-dory with American medicine, eh?"

The doctor shook his head. "No, Senator. Everything's far from 'hunky-dory' in American medicine. Doctors in general aren't doing their job as well as they should or could. I'm not talking about competence—anyone graduated from a U.S. school can be assumed to be competent. I'm talking about the void growing between doctors and their patients. The technology that allows us to diagnose and treat illness as never before is building a wall between patient and physician."

McCready wasn't too sure he liked the way this was going. He had expected some bromides about how doctors were only human and were doing the best they could. He didn't know what Bulmer was leading up to.

The doctor paused, then continued. "I really hate to bring it up before a committee such as this, but here goes: As doctors, we must—we need to—keep *touching* people, and by that I mean an actual laying on of hands, even when it's not necessary. It's letting that person know that there's another human being among all this hardware.

"A simple example: A doctor can listen to a heart by standing to the patient's right, grasping the head of the stethoscope with the fingers of his right hand, reaching over, and pressing it against the patient's chest wall—only the diaphragm of the stethoscope touches the patient. Or he can lean close and steady the patient by placing his left hand on the patient's bare back. He's not hearing any better, but he's in *contact*. It's a very simple but very personal thing. And there are diagnostic bonuses that come with touching. You can often pick up little cues from the feel of the skin and tissues beneath. It's not something you can get from a textbook, it's something you can learn only by doing. It's hands-on medicine, and too few doctors are doing it today."

The committee room was silent. Even the reporters had stopped their chatter.

They like him. The senator decided he'd do better being gentle with Bulmer rather than trying to cut him up.

"That was very well put, Dr. Bulmer," McCready said. "But why did you say you hesitated to bring it up before this committee?"

"Well . . ." Bulmer said slowly, obviously measuring his words. "The operating premise of this committee seems to be that you can actually lay out guidelines for good medical care. So I wouldn't be surprised if my comments inspired a new federal guideline requiring every doctor to touch each patient for a predetermined number of minutes during each examination."

There were a few titters, then a couple of guffaws, then the room erupted into laughter. Even a few of the committee members broke into sheepish grins.

McCready was furious. He didn't know if he had been set up or if Bulmer's remark had been genuinely off the cuff. Either way, this pipsqueak doctor was ridiculing him and the committee. His words had been carefully padded with humor, but the sting was still there. McCready glanced at the other committee members. The looks on their faces sounded an alarm in him.

Until this moment he had harbored not the slightest doubt about his bill's inclusion in the latest Medicare appropriations. These hearings had been mere formality. Now he experienced his first twinge of uncertainty. Bulmer had struck a nerve and the committee members were twitching.

Damn him!

This bill had to pass! The country needed it! *He* needed it! He had to put an end to the kind of medical oversights that had left him undiagnosed for so long. And if the medical establishment couldn't or wouldn't do it, then he'd goddamn well do it for them!

But right now he had to act. Top priority was to get this doctor away from the microphone and off the floor immediately.

He leaned close to his own mike. "Thank you for your time and valuable input, Dr. Bulmer."

And then the room was applauding and Congressman Switzer was clapping his pet doctor on the shoulder. McCready watched the pair from behind his dark lenses. He would have to do something about Switzer. And soon. And Dr. Bulmer . . . Dr. Alan Bulmer . . .

He would remember that name.

__ 6. __
Alan

It turned out to be an only partially wasted Thursday. Alan managed to duck a lunch with an ebullient Congressman Switzer, grab a shuttle home, and get over to the Monroe Yacht and Racquet Club in time to see Ginny and Josie win their doubles match and progress to the semifinals. He couldn't help but get caught up in Ginny's excitement over the match. Maybe it was just as well she had stayed home—he would have felt rotten depriving her of the victory.

He made quick afternoon rounds at the hospital, then met Ginny back at the club for dinner. He was all set to spend a nice, quiet evening at home when the answering service patched through a call from Joe Barton, a longtime patient. He was coughing up blood. Alan told him to get right over to the emergency room and he'd meet him there.

Joe turned out to have a heavily consolidated lobar pneumonia. But because he was a smoker and there was the chance that something sinister might be lurking in the infiltrated area of lung, and because Alan knew Joe as the type for whom bed rest was impossible, he admitted him for treatment.

As he approached the ER nursing desk, a voice called out from the corner gurney.

"You! Hey, you! You're the one!"

The overhead light in the corner was out. Alan squinted into the dimness. A disheveled old man in shapeless clothes lay there, gesturing to him. Alan didn't recognize him, but threw him a friendly wave in passing.

"Who's in the corner cot?" he said to McClain when he reached the desk. "Anybody I know?"

"For your sake, I hope not," she said. "He's drunk as a skunk and doesn't smell much better. Doesn't even know his name."

"What's wrong with him?"

"Says he came here to die."

"That's encouraging."

McLain snorted. "Not on my shift, it ain't. Anyway, we've got lab and a chest X ray cooking, and EKG is on the way."

"Who's on service?"

"Your old buddy, Alberts."

McClain was one of the few nurses still around who would remember that Alan and Lou Alberts had been partners—how many years ago? Could it be seven years already since they'd split?

"I'm sure they'll get along fine together," he said with an evil grin.

McClain barked a laugh. "I'm sure!"

On his way back to say good night to Joe, the man in the corner cot called to him again.

"Hey, you! C'mere! S'time!"

Alan waved but kept walking. The man was in no distress, just drunk.

"Hey! S'time! C'mere. *Please!*"

There was a note of such desperation in that last word that Alan stopped and turned toward the corner. The man was motioning him over.

"C'mere."

Alan walked over to the side of the gurney, then backed up a step. It was the same bum who had banged on his car Tuesday night. And McClain hadn't been kidding. He was filthy and absolutely foul-smelling. Yet even the stench from his pavement-colored clothes and shoeless feet couldn't quite cover the reek of cheap wine on the breath wheezing from his toothless mouth.

"What can I do for you?" Alan said.

"Take my hand." He held out a filthy paw with cracked skin and blackened, ragged fingernails.

"Gee, I don't know," Alan said, trying to keep the mood light. "We haven't even been introduced."

"Please take it."

Alan took a breath. Why hadn't he just walked on by like everybody else? He shrugged and reached out his right hand. The poor guy did look like he was dying, and this seemed important to him. Besides, he'd had his hands in worse places.

As soon as his fingers neared the derelict's, the filthy hand leaped up and grabbed him in an iron grip. There was pain, but from more than pressure. Light blazed around him as a jolt like high-voltage electricity coursed up his arm, convulsing his muscles, causing him to thrash uncontrollably like a fish on a hook. Dark spots flared in his vision, coalescing, blotting out the derelict, the emergency room, everything.

And then the grip was broken and he was reeling backward, off balance, his hands reaching for something, anything to keep him from falling. He felt fabric against his left hand, grabbed it, realizing it was a privacy curtain as he heard its fasteners snap free of the ceiling track under his weight. But at least it slowed his fall, lessening the blow to the back of his head as it struck the nearby utility table.

His vision blurred, then cleared to reveal McClain's shocked expression as she leaned over him.

"What happened? You okay?"

Alan rubbed his right hand with his left. The electric shock sensation was gone, but the flesh still tingled all the way down to the bone. "I think so. What the hell did he do to me?"

McClain glanced at the corner gurney. "Him?" She straightened up and gave the derelict a closer look. "Oh, shit!" She darted out toward the desk and came back pushing the crash cart.

From the overhead speaker the operator's voice blared, *"Code*

Blue—ER! Code Blue—ER!" Nurses and orderlies appeared from every direction. Dr. Lo, the ER physician for the night, ran in from the doctors' lounge and took charge of the resuscitation, giving Alan a puzzled look as he darted by.

Alan tried to stand, intending to help with the CPR, but found his knees wobbly and his right arm numb. By the time he felt steady enough the help, Lo had called the resuscitation to a halt. Despite all their efforts, the heart had refused to start up again. The monitor showed only a wavering line when McClain finally turned it off.

"Great!" she said. "Just great! Don't even know his name! A coroner's case for sure! I'll be filling out forms for days!"

Lo came over to Alan, a half smile on his Oriental face.

"For a second there, when I saw you on the floor, I thought we'd be working on you. What happened? He hit you?"

Alan didn't know how to explain what had happened when he had touched the man's hand, so he just nodded. "Yeah. Must have been some sort of Stokes-Adams attack or something as he arrested."

Alan went over to the corner cot, stepped inside the drawn curtains, and pulled down the covering sheet. The old man's head was half turned toward Alan, his mouth slack, his eyes half open and glazed. Alan gently pushed the lids closed. With his features relaxed in death, he didn't look so old. In fact, Alan was willing to bet that given a good shave, a shower, and a decent set of teeth, he would look no older than forty, Alan's age.

Alan cradled his right arm in his left. It still felt strange.

What the hell did you do to me?

He could think of no explanation for the shock that had run up his arm. It had come from the derelict, of that he was sure. But where had *he* got it? He had no answer, and the derelict wasn't going to tell him, so he pulled the sheet back over the face and walked away.

7.
Sylvia

"No hurry, Ba," Sylvia said from her seat in the rear of the Graham. "Take your time."

She was not particularly anxious to hear what Sara Chase had to say today. She had resigned herself to the fact that it was not going to be good.

Fighting the melancholia that clung to her like a shroud, she ran her hand over the polished mahogany that framed the tinted side windows, sliding it down to the plush upholstery. Usually she took such pleasure in the interior refurbishing job she had commissioned on this old 1938 sedan, transforming it from a rusting derelict into a warm, safe place, a bright red home away from home. A passenger had once remarked that it reminded him of a luxury stateroom on the *QE2*. Today it left her cold.

She hadn't gone into this with her eyes closed. She had known from the beginning that it wasn't going to be easy raising a child like Jeffy. She had expected and had been prepared for trouble, aggravation, and frustration. She hadn't counted on heartbreak.

But the heartbreak was there. For months now, Jeffy had receded from her a little bit each day, and each tiny increment of withdrawal was a stab of pain.

She wondered: If she had known from the start that things would turn out this way—slow progress over more than four years, teasing her into a false hope, only to see those hopes dashed in the space of a few months—would she have adopted Jeffy?

A difficult question, but she knew only one answer: yes.

She clearly remembered how she had lost her heart to that little boy from the moment she opened the Monroe *Express* five years ago and saw his picture. The three-year-old had been left on the steps of the Stanton School for Special Education, secured to the front door by a leash fastened to the dog collar around his neck. A note saying *"Please take care of Jeffy I cant do it no more"* was found pinned to his shirt. The picture had been published in an attempt to identify him and locate his parents.

It had accomplished neither. But it did capture Sylvia. Jeffy reached through that grainy black and white photo and touched a spot in Sylvia's heart that refused to let her rest until she brought him home.

They had warned her. Right from the start, the people at the Stanton School—Dr. Chase the most vocal among them—had told her that he was profoundly autistic and would be a tremendous financial, psychological, and emotional burden. The entire range of Jeffy's behavior consisted of rocking back and forth, humming tunelessly, eating, sleeping, urinating, and defecating. He never even *looked* at another person, directing his gaze always just to the right or left of anyone facing him, as if they were an inanimate object obstructing his view. The most rudimentary rewards of motherhood, such as the simple return of love and affection showered on a child, would be denied her.

But Sylvia hadn't listened. She had *known* she could reach Jeffy. And she had.

While waiting for all the legal machinery to process Jeffy and clear him for adoption, Sylvia had taken him into her home as a foster child. She immersed herself in his care, spending her nights reading every available reference on autism, her days structuring his environment and using the theories she was studying. Operant behavior-modification techniques worked best with Jeffy.

The operant sessions had been grueling at first. Endless repetitions, positively reinforcing each tiny fragment of a desired response, building a repertoire of behavior, increment by increment, from nothing—it was a seemingly impossible task. But Sylvia's efforts paid off. She smiled now, reliving a hint of the joy she had felt as, bit by bit, Jeffy began to come around, began to respond. Dr. Chase and the staff at the Stanton School had been amazed. Sylvia and Jeffy became celebrities of sorts there.

The dream of the little boy with open arms running toward her across the lawn had looked like it would eventually come true. Until last winter.

She felt her lips tighten as her smile withered.

Jeffy had never come near to being a "normal child"—whatever that was—but he had begun responding to people to the extent that he would look up when someone came into the room—something he had not been doing when found. He responded to animals and inanimate objects much more readily, going so far as to play with Mess and Phemus, and even say a few words to the air. He never spoke a word to another human being, but at least he proved he had the capacity for speech. Sylvia had felt they were on the verge of a breakthrough when Jeffy suddenly began to regress.

It had been so subtle at first, Sylvia had refused to even acknowledge that it was happening. Finally, reluctantly, she was forced to admit that Jeffy was losing ground. She had fervently hoped that she was wrong, but Dr. Chase had begun to notice it, too. She was doing a behavioral evaluation of Jeffy this week and the results were due today.

"I'm afraid the results aren't good," Sara Chase said without preamble as Sylvia seated herself in the chair beside the desk.

Sara was a pleasant-looking woman of about fifty, with ruddy cheeks and wispy brown hair. She never wore makeup and was perhaps twenty pounds overweight. She had long ago told Sylvia to stop calling her "Doctor."

Sylvia sank deeper into the chair. She bit her lip to keep it from quivering. She wanted to cry. "I've done everything. Everything."

"I know you have. The progress he made with you is incredible. But . . ."

"But I didn't do enough, right?"

"Wrong!" Sara said sternly as she leaned forward on her desk. "I won't have you blaming yourself. Autism isn't simply an emotional disorder; it's a neurological disease as well. I shouldn't have to tell you this. You know almost as much about it as I do."

Sylvia sighed. She knew she had done all that could be done for Jeffy, but it *hadn't* been enough.

"And Jeffy's disease is progressing, is that it?"

She nodded.

Sylvia pounded her fist against the arm of the chair. "There's a beautiful little boy in there and he can't get out! It's not fair!"

"Oh," Sara said in a placating tone, "I don't know if any of us knows what Jeffy's really like . . ."

"*I* do! I can feel him in there, trapped. He's been locked away so long he doesn't even know he's a prisoner. But he's in there. I know it! Last summer I saw him pick a Monarch butterfly out of a puddle, dry off its wings with his shirt, and let it fly away. He's kind, he's gentle, he's—"

There was sympathy in Sara's eyes as she sat and watched Sylvia in silence.

Sylvia knew what the psychologist was thinking—that she was romanticizing Jeffy's condition.

"No new medication?" she asked.

Sara shook her head. "We've tried them all and he's refractory. We could arrange another trial—"

"No." She sighed as depression settled on her like a mantle. "They only made him jittery or put him to sleep."

"Keep working with him, then. Keep using the operant techniques. Maybe you can slow his slide. Maybe it will turn around by itself. Who can say?"

Sylvia walked out into the crystalline daylight. *The sun shouldn't be shining,* she thought. Dark and rainy were more in tune with her mood.

8.
Alan

It began late Friday morning.

The only incident of note before that was the call from Fred Larkin.

Connie buzzed back with the word that Dr. Larkin was calling.

"Dr. Larkin himself, or his secretary?"

Alan already knew the answer. Fred Larkin was the local glamor-boy orthopedist who took in something like $750,000 a year, owned three homes, a forty-two-foot cabin cruiser, and traveled the 35-mile-an-hour roads from his home to the hospital in a 200-mile-an-hour, $90,000 Maserati with license plates that read FRED MD. Alan never referred patients to him, but one of his regulars had somehow landed under Larkin's care in January. He had been expecting this call.

"His secretary, of course."

"Of course." Fred Larkin was not the type to deign to dial a phone number himself. "Put her on hold and hurry back here for a second."

As Connie bustled her short, plump frame into his office, Alan hit the button on his phone and said, "Hello?" When a female voice on the other end said, "Just a minute, Dr. Bulmer," and put him on hold, Alan handed the phone to Connie. She smiled and held it to her ear. After a short pause, she said, "Hold on, Dr. Larkin," and hit the hold button. Giggling, she handed the phone to Alan and hurried out of the office.

Alan waited for a slow count of five and then opened the line.

"Fred! How are you?"

"Fine, Alan," he said in his officious voice. "Listen, I don't want to take up much of your time, but I thought you should know what one of your patients is saying about you."

"Really? Who?" Alan knew who, what, and why, but decided to play dumb.

"Mrs. Marshall."

"Elizabeth? I didn't even know she was mad at me!"

"I don't know about that. But as you know, I arthroscoped her right knee in January and she's refusing to pay the last two-thirds of her bill."

"Probably because she doesn't have the money."

"Well, be that as it may, she says"—he gave a forced laugh here—"that *you* told her not to pay it. Can you believe that?"

"Sure. In a sense, it's true."

There was a long silence on the other end of the line, then: "You admit it?"

"Uh-huh," Alan said, and waited for the explosion.

"You son of a bitch! I half figured you put her up to it. Where the hell do you get off telling one of my patients not to pay my bill?" He was shouting into the phone.

"To say you charge too much is an understatement, Fred. You *gouge.* You never gave that old lady a clue that your fee for a look into her joint plus a little trimming of her cartilage would cost her two grand. You did it in twenty minutes in the outpatient surgery department—which meant your overhead was *zero,* Fred—and you charged her two thousand bucks! Then—and this is the kicker—*then* she had to come to me for an explanation of exactly what it was you did for her. You charge at a rate of six thousand bucks an hour and *I* have to do the explaining! Which I couldn't do because as usual you never bothered to send me a copy of the procedure summary."

"I explained *everything* to her."

"Not so she could understand it, and you probably had four more procedures lined up. Answering a few questions would take too much time. And when she told your office that Medicare and her other insurance only covered six hundred of the bill, she was informed that that was *her* problem. And you know what she said to me?"

Alan had now arrived at the point that infuriated him the most. He could feel himself coming to a boil. He tried to control it, but knew he could slip into a shouting rage at any minute.

"She said, 'You doctors!' She lumped *me* with *you!* And that pissed me off. Ill will from guys like you who treat patients like slabs of meat spills over onto me, and I don't take kindly to that at all."

"Don't give me any of your holier-than-thou crap, Bulmer. Nothing gives you the right to tell a patient not to pay!"

"I didn't tell her that, exactly." Alan's temper was stretched to the breaking point, but he managed to keep his voice low. "I told her to send your bill back to you in the shape of a rectal suppository. Because you're an asshole, Fred."

After a second or two of shocked silence, Larkin said, "I can buy and sell you, Bulmer."

"A rich asshole is still an asshole."

"I'm taking this to the hospital board and to the medical society. You haven't heard the last of this!"

"Yes, I have," Alan said, and hung up.

He was annoyed with himself for sinking to name-calling, but could not deny that he had enjoyed it.

He glanced at his watch. Nine-thirty already. He would be playing catch-up the rest of the morning.

*   *   *

Alan's mood lightened immediately when he saw Sonja Andersen waiting for him in the examining room. He smiled at the pretty little ten-year-old he had been following for the past three years and mentally flipped through her medical history. Sonja had been a normal child until age four when she contracted chicken pox from her older sister. It was not the usual uncomplicated case, however. A varicella meningitis developed, leaving her with a seizure disorder and total hearing loss in her right ear. She was a brave little soul and had been doing well lately. No seizures for the past year, and no visible ill effects from the Dilantin she took twice a day to control them.

She held up a Walkman tape player with lightweight headphones.

"Look what I got, Dr. Bulmer!" Her face was bright and open, her smile unstudied sincerity. She seemed genuinely glad to see him.

Alan was just as happy to see her. He loved pediatrics more than any other facet of his practice. He found something in caring for a child, whether sick or well, that gave him a special satisfaction. Perhaps this communicated itself to the children and their parents, explaining why an unusually large segment of his practice, nearly 40 percent, was devoted to pediatrics.

"Who gave you that?"

"My uncle. For my birthday."

"That's right—you're ten now, aren't you? What kind of music do you like?"

"Rock."

He watched as she put on the headphones and began bouncing to whatever she was hearing. He lifted the left earpiece away from her head and said,

"What's playing?"

"The new song by Polio."

He forced a smile, acutely aware of the generation gap. He'd heard Polio's music—a mindless blend of punk and heavy metal. They made Ozzie Ozbourne sound refined and were one of the reasons he kept the stack of oldies tapes in his car. "What say we turn it off for the moment and let me give you the once-over."

He checked her heart, lungs, blood pressure, checked her gums for the telltale signs of long-term Dilantin therapy. All negative. Good. He turned on the otoscope, fitted it with a speculum, and moved to her ears.

The left looked fine—the canal was clear, the drum normal in color and configuration with no sign of fluid in the middle ear. He came around to the other side. As usual, her right ear looked as normal as the left. Her deafness there was not caused by a structural defect; the auditory nerve simply didn't carry the messages from the middle ear to the brain. He realized with a pang that she would never hear her tapes in stereo—

And that was when it happened.

First the sensation in his left hand where he gripped the auricle of her ear, a tingling, needling pleasure, surging from there through his whole body, making him tremble and break out in a sweat. Sonja whimpered and clutched at her ear with both hands as she lurched away, toppling off the examining table and into her mother's arms.

"What?" was all the startled woman could say as she hugged her child against her.

"My ear! He hurt my ear!"

Weak and more than a little frightened, Alan sagged against the examining table.

The mother came to his defense. "He barely touched you, Sonja!"

"He gave me a shock!"

"It must have been from the rug. Isn't that right, Dr. Bulmer?"

For a second Alan wasn't exactly sure where he was. "Right," he said. He straightened up and hoped he didn't look as pale and shaky as he felt. "That's the only explanation."

What he had felt just now reminded him of the shock he had received from the derelict in the emergency room last night. Only this afternoon he'd felt more pleasure than pain. An instant of searing ecstasy and then . . . what? Afterglow?

He managed to coax Sonja back up onto the table and complete the examination. He checked the right ear again. No problem this time. No sign of injury, either. Sonja left a few minutes later, still complaining of pain in her ear.

Alan went into his consultation room to sit at his desk for a moment. What the hell had happened in there? He couldn't explain it. He had used the same technique with the same otoscope and speculum in her ear for years without incident. What had gone wrong today? And that feeling . . . !

Alan didn't like things he couldn't explain. But he forced his mind to file it away for later and rose to his feet. He had a full schedule and had to keep moving.

The next half hour went smoothly. Then Henrietta Westin showed up.

"I just want a checkup."

Alan was immediately alert. He knew Henrietta Westin was not the checkup type. She was a Born-Again Christian who herded her three kids and husband in at the first sign of a cold or fever, but trusted in the Lord for herself. Which meant she usually waited until she was well into bronchitis and on the way to pneumonia or 10 percent dehydrated from an intestinal virus before she dragged herself into the office.

"Anything wrong?" Alan asked.

She shrugged and smiled. "Of course not. A little tired maybe, but what do you expect when you're pushing forty-five next month? I suppose I should praise the Lord I've had my health this long, at least."

That had an ominous ring to it.

Alan checked her over. He found nothing remarkable other than a slight elevation in her blood pressure and pulse rate, the former no doubt secondary to the latter. She had a gynecologist whom she saw regularly "for any female problems" she might have; her last gyn exam had been four months ago and everything had been normal.

Alan leaned back against the counter and looked at her. He had touched her palms and found them slick with perspiration. Those hands were now clutched tightly in her lap, the knuckles white. This woman was about to explode with tension. He decided to arrange some thyroid studies but he doubted that was the problem since her weight hadn't changed in the last two years.

He closed her chart and pointed to his consultation room door. "Get dressed and meet me in there and we'll talk."

She nodded. "All right." As he stepped toward the door she said, "Oh, by the way . . ."

Here it comes, he thought. *The real reason for the visit.*

". . . I found a lump in my breast."

He flipped her chart back onto the counter and moved to her side.

"Didn't Dr. Anson examine you?" Alan knew her gynecologist to be a painstakingly thorough physician.

"Yes, but it wasn't there then."

"When did you first notice it?"

"Last month."

"You check your breasts monthly?"

She averted her eyes. "No."

So it could have been there three months!

"Why didn't you come in sooner?"

"I . . . I thought it might go away. But it didn't." A single sob broke through. "It got *bigger!*"

Alan gently put a hand on her shoulder. "Hang on now. It might be a cyst—which is nothing but a fluid-filled sack—or something equally benign. Let's check."

She unsnapped her bra and pulled it off under the paper cape. Alan lifted the cape and looked at her breasts. He immediately noticed a little dimpling of the skin two inches from the left nipple at two o'clock.

"Which breast?"

"The left."

This was looking worse all the time. "Lie back."

In an effort to stave off the inevitable, Alan examined the right breast first, starting at the outer margin and working toward, around, and finally under the nipple. Normal. He did the same on the other side, but started under her arm. There, beneath the slippery mixture of perspiration, deodorant, and shaven stubble, he felt three distinctly enlarged lymph nodes. *Oh, hell!* He moved over to the breast itself, where he found a firm, fixed, irregular mass under the dimpled area. His stomach tightened. Malignant as all hell!

—and then it happened again.

The tingling, the ecstasy, the small cry from his patient, the instant of disorientation.

"What was *that?*" she said, cupping her hands over her left breast.

"I don't . . . I'm not sure," Alan said, alarmed now. This was the second time in less than an hour. What was—?

"It's gone!" Mrs. Westin cried, frantically running her fingers over her breast. "The lump—praise God!—it's not there anymore!"

"Of course it is," Alan said. "Tu—" He almost said *tumors.* "Lumps don't just disappear like that." Alan knew the power of denial as a psychological mechanism; the worst thing that could happen now was for her to fool herself into believing that she had no mass in her breast. "Here. I'll show you."

But he couldn't show her.

It was gone.

The mass, the dimpling, the enlarged nodes—*gone!*

"How did you do it, Doctor?"

"Do it? I didn't do anything."

"Yes, you did. You touched it and it disappeared." Her eyes glowed as she looked at him. "You healed it."

"No-no." He hunted for an explanation. "It must have been a cyst that broke. That's it." He didn't believe that—breast cysts did not rupture and disappear during examination—and from the look on her face, Henrietta Westin didn't believe it either.

"Praise the Lord, He has healed me through you."

"Now just hold on there!" This was getting out of hand. Almost frantic now, Alan rechecked the breast again.

This can't be! It's got to be here!

But it wasn't there. There wasn't a trace of the mass.

"Bless you!"

"Now wait a minute, Henrietta. I want you to have a mammogram at the hospital."

As she straightened up and refastened her bra, her eyes still held that glow. "If you wish, Doctor."

Don't look at me like that!

"Today. I'll call the hospital now."

"Anything you say."

Alan fled the examining room for his desk. He picked up the phone to call the radiology department at Monroe Community Hospital. And stopped. For a few seconds he couldn't think of the hospital's main number, one he called at least a dozen times a day. Then it came back to him. This thing must have shaken him up more than he had realized.

Jack Fisher, the chief radiologist, was not crazy about the idea of squeezing another xeromammography into his schedule, but Alan convinced him of the urgency of this particular request and Jack reluctantly agreed to find a slot for Mrs. Westin.

Alan managed to do a competent job on the rest of the morning's patients, even though he knew he gave a couple of them the bum's rush. He couldn't help it. It was an effort to concentrate on their problems when his mind throbbed with the question of what had happened to the tumor in Henrietta Westin's breast. It had been there! He had felt it! And there was no way it could have been anything less than a malignancy with those nodes in the axilla.

And then it had been gone.

This was crazy!

His state of distraction had one unexpected benefit: He hardly heard Mr. Bradford as he went through his usual catalog of the color, caliber, and frequency of each of his stools since his last visit.

Finally, lunchtime came and he'd made his call-backs and sent Connie and Denise out to eat. He wished Ginny were still working here. She'd started off as his receptionist when he first moved into the building but soon decided it wasn't for her. Maybe she was right. After all, none of the other doctors' wives she hung around with worked for their husbands.

He heard the phone ring up front at Connie's desk, saw a light start blinking on the phone beside him. It was the private line he reserved for the hospital, pharmacists, and other doctors. He stabbed at it.

"Hello."

"Nothing there, Alan." It was Jack Fisher, the radiologist. "A little fibrocystic disease, but no mass, no calcifications, no vascular changes."

"And you checked the axilla like I asked you?"

"Clean. Both sides. Clean."

Alan didn't speak. *Couldn't* speak.

"Okay, Alan?"

"Yeah. Yeah, sure, Jack. And thanks a lot for squeezing her in. I really appreciate it."

"Anytime. Sometimes the only way to handle these kooks is to humor them."

"Kook?"

"Yeah. The Westin lady. She was going on and on to anyone who'd listen about how you had 'the healing touch.' How she'd had a tumor there for the past month and with a single touch you made it disappear." He laughed. "Every time I think I've heard it all, somebody comes up with a new one."

Alan managed to get off the phone with a modicum of grace, then slumped into his chair and sat staring at the grain in the oak paneling on the opposite wall.

Henrietta Westin now had a left breast that felt normal and showed clean on xeromammography. But that hadn't been the case two hours ago.

He sighed and stood up. No use worrying about it. She wasn't going to lose her breast or her life, that was the important thing. When he had more time he'd try to figure it out. Right now it was time for a bite to eat and then into the afternoon session.

The phone rang again. It was a patient line this time. He hadn't signed out to the answering service yet so he picked it up.

It was Mrs. Andersen and she was sobbing. Something about Sonja. About her ear.

Oh, Christ! Just what he needed now.

"What's wrong?" he asked. "Is she still in pain?"

"No!" the woman wailed. "She can hear out of her right ear again! She can *hear!*"

*   *   *

"How do I look?"

Alan snapped back to the here and now. He had made it through the afternoon hours without committing any medical negligence, but now that he was home, his mind was constantly tugged toward Sonja Andersen and Henrietta Westin.

He looked up. Ginny was standing at the far side of the kitchen table, modeling slacks and a blouse of different shades of green. "You look great." It was the truth. Clothes fit her perfectly right off the rack. The greens of the fabric caught the green of her contacts. "Really great."

"Then how come I always have to ask?"

"Because you always look great. You should know that."

"A girl likes to be told sometimes."

For perhaps the hundredth time this year—the first time was New Year's Eve—Alan promised to be more attentive to Ginny and less absorbed in his practice. They didn't have much of a life together anymore. To an outsider they probably looked like the perfect couple—all they needed was two and a half children and they'd be the ideal American family. They had talked about getting their lives on the same track again countless times, but all their good intentions seemed to remain intentions. The practice kept demanding more and more of Alan's time, and Ginny seemed to be getting increasingly involved with the club, along with her civic and hospital-related groups. Their paths crossed at breakfast, dinner, and, occasionally, at bedtime.

He *would* be more attentive and he *would* be less self-absorbed. Soon. But tonight was certainly a special case, especially after what had happened today.

Ginny set a plate of shrimp salad on a bed of lettuce, plus a loaf of sourdough bread before him.

"You're not eating?" he asked as she continued to buzz around the kitchen.

She shook her head. "No time. Why do you think I'm dressed up? Tonight's the Guild meeting and I've got to give a progress report on the fashion show."

"I thought the Guild met on Thursday nights."

"Tonight's a special meeting because of the fashion show on Sunday. I told you about it."

"Right. You did. Sorry. Just wanted to talk."

Ginny smiled. "Great. Talk."

"Sit," he said, pointing to the chair opposite him.

"Oh, I can't, honey. Josie and Terri are going to be here any minute to pick me up. Can't you tell me quick?"

"I don't think so."

"Give it a try." She sat down across from him.

"Okay. Something weird happened in the office today."

"Mrs. Ellsworth paid her bill?"

Alan almost laughed. "No. Weirder."

Ginny's eyebrows rose. "This ought to be good."

"I don't know if it is or not." He took a deep breath. This wasn't going to be easy. "Somehow, some way, I . . . I cured two people of incurable illnesses today."

After a short pause, Ginny shook her head slowly, a puzzled expression constricting her features. "I don't get it."

"Neither do I. You see—"

There was a honk from outside in the driveway. Ginny leaped up.

"That's Josie. I've got to go." She came around the table and gave Alan a quick kiss. "We'll talk about it later tonight, okay?"

Alan managed to smile. "Sure."

And then her coat was on and she was out the door.

He jabbed his fork into the shrimp salad and began to eat. Maybe it was just as well. Both he and Ginny knew doctors who had developed God complexes. All he had to do was start talking about healing with a touch and she'd have him ready for the funny farm.

And maybe she'd be right.

He swallowed a mouthful of shrimp, put the fork down, and leaned back. He wasn't hungry; he was just eating so he wouldn't get hungry later.

What right did he have to think he had anything to do with Sonja regaining her hearing or with the disappearance of the lump in Henrietta Westin's breast? Thinking yourself some sort of magical healer was the road to *big* trouble.

Yet certain facts persisted and he couldn't wish them away: Sonja Andersen's deafness had been verified time and again by audiometry, and now she could hear; Mrs. Westin had found the breast mass herself and he had confirmed its presence, yet it was gone now.

Something was up.

And in each case the turning point seemed to be his touch.

There was no sane explanation here.

With a growl of frustration, disgust, and bafflement, Alan threw down his napkin and headed out to make late rounds at the hospital.

*   *   *

Alan turned toward his office on the way back from the hospital. Tony DeMarco had left a message with the answering service that he wanted to see him—a fortunate coincidence, because Alan wanted to talk to Tony. He had a job for him.

On the way, he found he was hungry and looked for a place to eat. He almost pulled into a downtown sandwich shop but turned away when he remembered that he had treated the owner a number of times for various venereal diseases . . . and the owner made the sandwiches. He decided instead on Memison's, where he ordered a fish dinner.

As he pulled into his parking lot of the free-standing building he half-owned, he saw that the lights were still on in the law office. Tony answered Alan's knock.

"Ay! Alan! C'mon in."

Alan smiled at the man who was perhaps his closest friend, his partner in the office building they shared, and whom he hardly ever saw. Shorter than Alan, with close-cropped dark hair and a mustache, Tony was still whipcord lean as only an unmarried chain-smoker could be at his age.

"Just finished up some dictation and was about to call it a day. Drink?"

"Yeah. I could use one."

Tony handed Alan a glass with two fingers of Dewar's, neat. "Brooklyn," he said, lifting his glass.

"And a new Ebbets Field," Alan said, lifting his.

"And the return of da Bums."

They both drank and Alan let it burn down the back of his throat. Oh, that was good. He looked around the lavishly appointed office. He and Tony had both come a long way from their roots in Brooklyn— only a few miles on the map, but income and prestigewise they had traveled light-years.

They small-talked, and then Alan asked Tony, "You wanted to see me?"

"Yeah," Tony said, indicating a chair and lighting a cigarette as he seated himself behind his desk. "Two things. First—know what today is?"

Alan didn't have the foggiest.

"It's our eighth anniversary, you dumb shit!"

Alan smiled at the ease with which Tony reverted to his Brooklyn accent and the street patois of their youth. Alan had quickly learned in medical school in New England that with his Brooklyn accent he could discuss baseball or hot dogs or streetlife with authority, but shouldn't say anything about internal medicine, because nobody who talked like that could know anything about internal medicine. So he developed a neutral, regionless brand of English that was now as much an integral part of him as the way he walked.

Tony used his "lawyer English," as he called it, only when he was being a lawyer. When he was relaxing with friends, he was the old Tony DeMarco, street fighter and toughest kid on the block.

"Really? That long?"

Alan found it hard to believe eight years had gone by since he had picked out Tony's name under the *Lawyers* listing in the phone book—his office had been the most convenient for a lunchtime appointment then—and had learned to his delight that they had grown up only a few blocks apart in Brooklyn.

He had asked Tony about getting out of his practice agreement with Lou Alberts. Personally, he got along fine with Lou, but their styles of practice didn't mesh. Alan had found it utterly impossible to keep Lou's pace, which was eight patients an hour on an average day, and ten or more per hour when things got busy. Lou's technique was to hit the patient's most immediate problem with an injection or a prescription, then shoo him out to make room for the next. He was a doctor with his hand forever on the doorknob. Trying to emulate him had made Alan feel like a pieceworker on an assembly line. Not at all the brand of medicine he wanted to practice.

But Alan didn't want to break his contract unless Lou hadn't been holding up his end of it. Unfortunately, Tony's analysis revealed that Lou had been living up to the letter of the contract. But that was no problem—Tony could get him out of it and slide him past any of the restrictive covenants described therein.

"Yeah. Eight years ago you changed my life when you said you were going to finish out your second contract year with Lou Alberts."

"Get out!"

"I'm serious, man! I offered you half a dozen finagles out of your contract and you sat there with your white-bread mouth and said, 'No. I signed my name and so that's it.' Do you know how you made me feel? Like a scumbag! Never had a client say that to me. *Never!* You didn't care if you had a legal escape hatch—you'd given your word and you were gonna stick by it. I felt like slipping down under the table and crawling out the door."

"You hid it well," Alan said, amazed at the revelation. He had never imagined—

"So from that day on I changed my style. No more weasel shit like that. I've lost clients because of it, but I can sit in the same room with you now."

Something was suddenly made clear to Alan in that moment. He had never known why Tony had called him only a month or so after that first meeting and asked him if he wanted to go into partnership on a small office building on the other end of town, exactly one tenth of a mile outside that radius of the restrictive covenant in Alan's contract with Lou Alberts. They could both share the first floor and maybe even find a tenant for the second.

He and Tony had been close friends and partners ever since. He wished they could spend more time together. He felt more kinship with this feisty lawyer than with any of his fellow physicians.

"Tony . . . I never realized—"

"Forget it!" he said with a wave of his hand. "But on to the second thing: I overheard some real weird shit today."

"Like what?"

"I was having a drink with this lawyer friend while he was waiting for a client. When the client came in they took the booth right behind where we had been sitting, so while I'm finishing my drink I hear this dapper dude, who happens to be a doctor, tell my friend that he wants to sue another doctor—a guy by the name of Alan Bulmer. I later call my friend and in my casual roundabout way find out that this doctor's name is Larkin." He stared at Alan a moment. "So how come you don't look too damn surprised?"

Alan told him about his conversation with Fred Larkin that morning.

Tony shook his head. "You can be a real jerk at times, Alan. I did a quick check on this Larkin guy. He's a bigshot, has lot of influence with the hospital Board of Trustees. Never know when you're gonna need a friend or two in high places."

"What for?" Alan said. "I've no intention of ever running for chief of staff, even if I had the time for it. Hospital politics bore me to tears."

"Still, never hurts to have a friendly contact."

"That's the politician in you talking."

"Ay! Don't call me no fucking politician!"

"Scratch any lawyer and you'll find a nascent politician," Alan said with a laugh.

"Don't act so high and mighty about friends in high places. How do you think you got into that high-class club."

Alan shrugged. Lou had been his partner then and Lou had been serving on the club membership committee. "Wasn't my idea. Ginny wanted it . . . I just went along."

"Yeah, but it was *connections* that got you in—that and not having your name end in a vowel or a '-berg.' "

Alan shrugged again. His practice left him little time for tennis or yachting, so he was almost a stranger at the club. "Anyway, you're a friend, aren't you, Tony?"

"Yeah. But I ain't in what you might call a High Place."

Alan had an urge to tell Tony what had happened today. He tried to think of a way to phrase it so he wouldn't sound delusional, but couldn't fine one. *Damn,* this was frustrating! He needed to talk to someone about this, yet he couldn't bring himself to spill it for fear of what people would think. He knew what *he* would think.

So he turned the conversation away from himself.

"How's business?"

"Great! Too great. Had to pass up a big party this weekend to fly up to Syracuse for a meeting with a client. Hate to miss one of Sylvia Nash's parties."

Alan was startled. "You know Sylvia Nash?"

"Sure. Did a few closings for her around here. That lady either really knows what she's doing with real estate or she's just plain lucky. Everything she touches turns to gold."

"Them that has, gets."

"Well, from what I can gather, she didn't always have. Greg Nash came back from Nam, joined his father's insurance agency, married Sylvia, insured himself to the eyeballs with term, then got blown away in that Seven-Eleven. With double indemnity and all, Sylvia became a millionairess overnight. She's tripled and quadrupled that since then. Good *business*woman. Unfortunately, she doesn't quite live up to her reputation as a *loose* woman."

"Oh?" Alan said, trying to sound casual.

Tony's eyebrows rose. "Got your interest now, ay?"

"Not really."

"Yeah? You should've seen your eyes bug when I mentioned her name."

"Just wondering how you got to know her."

"*Riiiight.* You got something goin' with her?"

"You know me better than that. I just treat her little boy, that's all."

"Yeah. I do remember her talking about you—like you could walk on water."

"She's very perceptive. But how do you know she doesn't live up to her reputation?"

"We dated a few times."

The thought of Sylvia in Tony's arms pained him. "And?"

"Never got to first base with her."

That was a relief. "Maybe it's your technique."

"Maybe. But I don't think so. There's a lot of anger in that woman, Alan. A *lot* of anger."

They both lapsed into silence, Alan thinking about Sylvia and how he had never thought of her as angry. He had only seen her with Jeffy, however, and then there was only love for the child. But Tony was a perceptive guy. Alan couldn't easily brush off his impressions.

Finally, he broached the subject he had wanted to see Tony about.

"Tony . . . could you look into something for me?"

"Sure. What?"

"It's about a patient who died in the ER last night."

"Malpractice potential?"

"I doubt it." Tonight at the hospital, Alan had taken a look at the pathology report on the derelict. He had been suffering from early lung cancer and end-stage alcoholic cirrhosis. A walking dead man. "His name was Walter Erskine—no identification on him, but his prints were traced through the V.A. He was born in 1946, grew up in Chillicothe, Missouri, and served in Nam in the late sixties. He was treated once for a mental condition at Northport V.A. Hospital in 1970. That's all that's known about him."

"Isn't that enough?"

"No. I want to know more. I want to know what he was like growing up, what happened to him in Nam, and what happened to him since Nam."

"Why?"

Alan shrugged, wishing he could tell Tony. But not yet. He couldn't tell anybody yet.

"It's a personal thing, Tony. Can you help?"

"I think so. I'll have to hire an eye, which is no problem—I use them on occasion."

"Great. I'll pay all expenses."

"You bet your ass you will."

They had a little laugh over that and Alan felt himself relaxing for the first time all night. At least now he felt he was doing something about whatever it was that had happened. In his gut he sensed that this Walter Erskine was the key. He had done something to Alan last night. And somehow, some way, Alan was going to find out just what.

— 9. —
At the Party

Sylvia was standing at her bedroom window on the second floor when Charles Axford strolled into the room. His tuxedo jacket was open and his hands were thrust into his pants pockets. She liked the way clothes fitted on his solid, just-under-six-foot frame; he looked his forty-four years, with his rugged face, his salt-and-pepper hair thinning a bit on top, and the wrinkles at the corners of his eyes, but she liked the look.

"Where've you been?" Sylvia asked him.

"Down the hall discussing the national debt with Jeffy," he said blandly.

Sylvia smiled and shook her head. Charles was testing the limits of bad taste again. She framed a nasty remark about his daughter, Julie, but didn't have the heart to say it. Besides, it would only spur Charles to elaborate on his opening comment. And where Jeffy was concerned, he was on very thin ice.

"What did he say?" she asked with equal blandness.

"Not much. He's getting a bit of kip, actually." He sat on her bed and leaned back on his elbows. "Anybody special coming tonight?"

"The usual crowd, plus a special treat: Congressman Switzer and Andrew Cunningham of the MTA."

Charles' eyebrows lifted. "Together? In the same bloody house?"

She nodded, her smile mirroring his. "Only they don't know it yet." She was definitely looking forward to seeing what happened when those two enemies ran into each other tonight.

"Oh, this is going to be jolly!" he said with a laugh as he got up from the bed and kissed her on the lips. "That's why I love you, Sylvia."

Sylvia said nothing. She knew he didn't really love her. He was simply responding to her sense of mischief.

She had met Charles Axford, M.D., at the McCready Foundation when she had taken Jeffy there for a comprehensive evaluation. Charles had been and still was chief of neurological research at the Foundation. Although he had taken no particular interest in Jeffy, he had taken a very definite interest in her. They had had an on-again, off-again relationship for three years now.

Sylvia wasn't sure what attracted her to Charles—or "Chuckie" as she liked to call him when she wanted to get under his skin. It certainly wasn't love. And it certainly wasn't because he was irresistibly handsome.

Simply put: He fascinated her.

She had never met anyone like him. Charles Axford could find something to dislike or distrust in anyone. *Anyone!* That along with the fact that he did not give a damn about what anyone thought of him resulted in one of the most sarcastic, cynical, verbally offensive human beings on earth. His acid wit coupled with his British accent made him a devastating gadfly. No treasured belief, no sacred cow, no religious, moral, or political dogma was safe from him. Charles believed in nothing, cared for nothing except his work, and was not above putting even that down if the mood struck him. In a rare, self-revelatory moment after too much to drink one night, he had told Sylvia that a man with no illusions can never become disillusioned.

Perhaps that was the key, she thought as she disengaged herself from his embrace. Perhaps that was why at the slightest provocation he gored anyone who came within range. No one was safe. Not

Jeffy, not even her. He was like a rare jungle frog she had seen on a television special—harmless-looking enough until it spit venom in your eyes. Sylvia found that the sense of imminent danger when he was around added a little zest to life.

"I hope it won't crush you to learn that you won't be the only doctor here tonight."

"Hardly. Doctors are the bloodiest boring people on earth—except for me, of course."

"Of course. The other two are both G.P.s, by the way. And they used to be partners."

"Really?" A gleam sparkled in his eyes and his thin lips curved into an impish grin. "I'm glad I came tonight."

"I told you it would be interesting."

She glanced out the window at the sound of a car on the drive. The first guests had arrived. She checked herself in the full-length mirror set on the closet door. The black dress looked just right—a bit too low in the front, a bit too low in the back, a bit too tight across the hips. In perfect keeping with her image.

She linked her arm through Charles'.

"Shall we go?"

*   *   *

"Isn't that a *Rolls,* Alan?" Ginny said as they pulled into Sylvia Nash's driveway.

Alan squinted through the windshield at the silver-gray car parked near the front door. "Sure looks like one. And there's a Bentley right next to it."

Ginny made a small, feminine grunt. "And here we are in an Oldsmobile."

"A Toronado isn't exactly a pickup, Ginny." Alan cringed at the knowledge of where this conversation was headed. The two of them had been down this road before, many times, and he knew every turn. "It gets you to Gristede's and the tennis courts in style and comfort."

"Oh, I don't mean for me. I mean for you. Instead of that awful Beagle—"

"It's an Eagle, Ginny. An *Eagle.*"

"Whatever. It's a dull car, Alan. No pizzaz."

"Back in January you thought it was great when we popped it into four-wheel drive and cruised through the blizzard and wound up being the only people to show up for Josie's fortieth birthday party."

"I'm not saying it doesn't have its uses. And I know it allows you to feel you can get to the office or hospital no matter what the weather—God forbid someone else should have to take care of one of your patients!—but so would a tractor. That doesn't mean you have to drive around town in one. You should get one of those cute little sports cars like Fred Larkin just got."

"Let's not talk about Fred Larkin. And I wouldn't own a ninety-thousand-dollar car even if I could afford one."

"You can write it off."

"No, I *can't* write it off! You know we don't have that kind of money lying around!"

"You're shouting, Alan!"

So he was. He clamped his lips shut.

"You usually don't get so hyper about money. What's the matter with you?"

Good question.

"Sorry. Just don't feel like going to a party tonight, I guess. I told you I didn't want to come."

"Just loosen up and try to enjoy yourself. Vic is covering for you, so why don't you have a few drinks and relax."

Alan smiled and sighed. "Okay." He would have a few drinks but he doubted he would relax or enjoy himself. There was too much on his mind tonight. Especially after the phone call he had received this afternoon.

Murray Raskin, the hospital neurologist, had been catching up on reading the hospital EEGs today and had come across little Sonja Andersen's. He had immediately called Alan at home, stuttering with excitement. Sonja's routine EEG last year had been grossly abnormal with a typical epileptic pattern in the left parietal lobe—the same as it had been for the past half-dozen years. The one Alan had ordered yesterday was completely normal.

All traces of her epilepsy were gone.

Alan had been stewing ever since. He knew now there would be no peace for him until he had unraveled the Andersen and Westin incidents and made sense out of them.

But that wasn't all that was eating at him tonight. He didn't want to be here. He didn't want to be in a social situation with Sylvia Nash where he couldn't play "Dr. Bulmer." He'd have to drop the professional mask and be "Alan." And he was afraid then that Sylvia and anyone else within half a dozen blocks would know exactly how he felt about her.

"Isn't that the Nash lady's car?" Ginny said, pointing to the bright red car under the lights of the front door.

"Sure is."

He parked the Toronado and they walked past Sylvia's car on their way to the front door.

"With all her money, you'd think she'd get something nice and new instead of this ugly old thing."

"Are you kidding?" Alan said, lightly running his fingers over the glossy red finish of the long hood to where it ended at the chromed, forward-leaning grille. He loved that huge grille with its vertical chromed rods gleaming like teeth. "This is a 1938 shark-nosed Graham, fully restored." He peered through the tinted windows. "*More* than restored. It was considered an economy car in its day. Look inside—she's even put in a bar."

"But why this awful red color? It would look better on a fire engine."

"Red was Mr. Toad's favorite color."

"I don't get it, Alan."

"*The Wind in the Willows*—this is Toad Hall, and you remember Mr. Toad, always stealing motorcars, don't you? Well, red was his favorite color. And the author's name was Kenneth *Grahame* . . . get it?"

Ginny stared at him, a frown forming. "Since when have you had such an interest in children's books?"

He reined in his enthusiasm. "Always been one of my favorite stories, Ginny. Let's go in."

He didn't mention that he had bought a copy of *The Wind in the*

Willows only after learning that Sylvia's place was called Toad Hall.

No, Alan thought as they approached the front door, he could not see how it was going to be a pleasant evening.

*   *   *

"Ah! Here comes a special guest!" Sylvie said.

Charles Axford glanced at her, then into the foyer, then back at Sylvie's face. She had suddenly become animated. That annoyed him.

A chap with average good looks with a slim, athletic-looking blonde on his arm—Charles guessed them both to be slightly younger than he—was approaching. The woman was beaming, the man looked ill.

"Which one's so bloody special?"

"Him. He's one of the doctors I told you about."

"I'm a doctor, too, you know."

"He's Jeffy's doctor."

"I was Jeffy's doctor for a while."

The corner of Sylvie's mouth pulled to the right. "You only did some tests on him. Alan's a *real* doctor."

"Two points for that one, Love."

Sylvie smiled. "That was worth five and you know it."

"Three, tops—because I'm precisely the kind of doctor I want to be. But let's go meet this 'special guest.' It's been so long since I've spoken to a *real* doctor."

"Come along, then, but try to limit the 'bloodys' to ten per minute."

Sylvie introduced them. Alan Bulmer was the fellow's name. Decent-looking chap. The woman was a pert, beaming blonde with the most captivating green eyes; she gushed over Sylvia and burbled on about the house and grounds.

Charles studied the doctor while he and the wife made nice-nice with their hostess. He looked acutely uncomfortable, like he was going to crawl out of his skin. His eyes kept moving to Sylvie and then richocheting off in all directions like misspent bullets.

What's the bloody matter with him?

Just then some other overdressed bird toddled over and tapped

Bulmer's wife on the shoulder. They squealed and hugged and did everything but call each other "Dahling!"

Charles turned away. *Bloody doctor's wife.* How well he knew the type. He had been married to one for eight very long years, and free of her for half again as long. This one reminded him of his ex: Probably a decent girl once, but now she was a Doctor's Wife and on the status trip.

Ba came by, resplendent in a white jacket and shirt, with a black bow tie and pants, carrying a tray full of tall, slim glasses of champagne. Some guests seemed afraid to take anything from him. Charles signaled to him.

While passing out the glasses to all those around him, he appreciated the awed expressions on Bulmer's wife and her friend as they looked up at Ba. Most hostesses would keep someone like Ba out of sight for a party. Not Sylvie. Good old Sylvie liked the stir he caused in the uninitiated.

Charles decided to start some friendly—for the moment—chatter with Bulmer and maybe find out what this *real* doctor was made of. He nudged him and nodded toward Ba's retreating form.

"Big fellow, what?"

Bulmer nodded. "Reminds me of Lurch from *The Addams Family.*"

"Lurch? Oh, you mean that show on the telly . . . the butler. Yes, does remind one of him a bit, although I do believe Lurch's face was more expressive."

"Possibly," Bulmer said with a smile. "I imagine Ba's height gave him some rough times as a kid. I mean, the average Vietnamese male is five-three, and Ba's got to be at least a foot over that."

"Pituitary giant, wouldn't you say?"

Bulmer's reply was immediate. "Uh-huh. Arrested in his mid-teens, I'd guess. Certainly doesn't show any acromegalic stigmata."

Five points to you, Doc, Charles thought with a rueful mental grin. The bloke already had a diagnosis filed away and waiting. Sharp for a G.P.

"Is that English you two are speaking?" Sylvie was saying.

"Doctor talk, Love," Charles said. "We use it to befuddle the masses."

"But it was about Ba. What were you saying?" She seemed genuinely concerned.

"We were saying that he probably had an overactive pituitary as a kid, maybe even a pituitary tumor. Made him a good foot taller than the average Vietnamese."

Bulmer chimed in. "But his pituitary must have slowed down to normal when he reached adulthood because he doesn't have any of the facial and hand deformities you see with adult hyperpituitism."

"Lucky for him it stopped on its own. It's eventually fatal if untreated."

"But doesn't he ever smile?" Bulmer asked. "I've known him all these years but never once seen him smile."

Sylvie was silent a moment. "I have a picture of him smiling."

"I've seen that picture," Charles said. "It answers the old Pepsodent question about where the yellow went."

Sylvie was studiously ignoring him. Her eyes were on Bulmer, and they glowed in a way he had never seen.

"Want to see the picture?"

Bulmer shrugged. "Sure."

"Good," Sylvie said with a smile and a lascivious wink. "It's upstairs in my bedroom . . . with my erotic Japanese etchings."

Charles bit his lip to keep from laughing as he watched Bulmer almost drop his glass and begin to stutter. "I . . . well . . . I don't really know—"

Sylvie turned to Charles and looked him squarely in the eyes. Her gaze was intense. "Charles, why don't you show Virginia and Adelle around the ground floor. You know it almost as well as I do."

Charles resented the twinge of jealousy that stabbed through him. "Sure, Love," he said as nonchalantly as he could. "Be glad to."

As he guided the two women away, he noticed Bulmer's wife looking over her shoulder with a puzzled expression as Sylvie linked an arm through her husband's and led him up the wide, winding stairway.

Charles watched, too.

There was something going on between those two, but bloody-damned if he could figure it out just yet.

Does she fancy him, I wonder?

*   *   *

Alan felt like a lamb led to slaughter. If she had been sly and sneaky about getting him up here he would have backed straight out, no problem. But she had been so open about it, dragging him away right in front of Ginny. What could he do?

She led him down the hall as she had Tuesday night, but this time they passed Jeffy's room and traveled farther on, farther away from the party downstairs. And tonight she wasn't swathed chin to toe in flannel. She wore a filmy black something that exposed the nearly flawless skin of her back and shoulders just inches away from him.

A turn of a corner and they were in her bedroom. Thank God it wasn't dark—there was a light on in the corner. A nice bedroom, stylishly furnished with a king-size bed flanked by sleek, low night tables, long satiny curtains framing the windows. Feminine without being too frilly. And no Japanese erotica on the walls. Just mirrors. Lots of mirrors. At one point in the room, the mirrors reflected each other back and forth, and he saw an infinite number of Alans standing next to an endless line of Sylvias in an infinity of bedrooms.

She went over to a dresser and picked up a Lucite-framed eight-by-ten color photo. She said nothing as she handed it to him.

There was Ba—a much younger Ba—in a jungle setting, standing next to a shorter, redheaded American soldier. Both were in fatigues, each with an arm around the other's shoulder, and grinning from ear to ear. Obviously somebody had said, "Smile!" and they were complying with a vengeance. Ba's teeth were indeed yellow. And very crooked. Small wonder he didn't smile.

"Who's the soldier?"

"The late Gregory Nash. That was taken in 1969, somewhere outside Saigon."

"Sorry. Never knew him."

"Don't apologize." She took the picture from his hands, gave it a lingering look, then replaced it on the dresser.

Alan wondered if she thought of him often.

"And I didn't realize they had known each other. I mean, Ba—"

"Right. Ba didn't arrive until four years after Greg died. It turned out to be pure chance. I happened to be watching the evening news one night years back when they were doing all those stories on the continuous flow of Boat People from Nam. They showed some film from the Philippines about this fellow who had just piloted a fishing boat full of his friends and neighbors across the South China Sea. I recognized him at once. It was Ba."

"You brought them back here?"

"Sure," she said offhandedly. "They said his wife was ill. I flew out there and got them. I figured what good was Greg's blood money if I couldn't use it to help out one of his friends? You know the rest . . . about Nhung Thi and all that."

Alan knew about Ba's wife. She had been sicker than anyone had guessed. He wanted to move the conversation to a lighter level. He glanced out the window into the floodlit yard and saw two trees in full blossom.

"Are those new?"

Sylvia moved up close behind him. "Only one—the one on the right."

Alan was surprised. "I would have guessed this one here—that other one has so many more blossoms."

"Some secret root food Ba is trying. Whatever it is, the new tree is really responding to it."

She was so close. Too close. Her perfume was making him giddy. Without saying anything more, Alan eased out into the hall and waited for Sylvia there. She caught up and they strolled back toward the party. She was more subdued than he could ever remember.

At Jeffy's door he stopped and waited in the hall while she tiptoed in to check on him.

"All's well?" he said as she returned.

She nodded and smiled. "Sleeping like a baby."

They walked on and stopped at the banister overlooking the front foyer. A glittering crowd swirled in conflicting, intermingling currents below, eddying into side pools of conversation in its ceaseless flow from one room to another. He recognized the bulky form of one of the Jets' better-known defensive backs as he passed through. The familiar face of a longtime New York TV weatherman was there, and Alan swore he recognized the voice of his favorite morning disk jockey but couldn't find the face.

That friend of Sylvia's, Charles Axford, passed through below. He wondered what Axford was to Sylvia. Her current lover, no doubt. She probably had a lot of lovers.

Then he saw a face he recognized from the newspapers.

"Isn't that Andrew Cunningham?"

"Right. I told you there'd be a few politicos here. Congressman Switzer is somewhere around, too."

"You know Mike?"

"I contributed to his campaign last year. I hope he won't be too disappointed when he doesn't get any money from me this time around."

Alan smiled. "Was he a bad boy in Washington?"

"I wouldn't know. But I have a rule: I never support incumbents." Her eyes narrowed. "Once they get comfortable, they get dangerous. I like to keep them off balance."

Alan sensed that he was seeing a hint of the anger Tony had mentioned last night.

"Why?"

Her features were taut as she spoke. "Comfortable incumbents sent Greg off to Vietnam, and he came back thinking he could handle anything. It got him killed."

Alan recalled the story. It had happened before he came to Monroe, but people were still talking about Gregory Nash's murder back then. Apparently the Vietnam vet had been waiting on line in the local 7-11 when someone pulled a gun on the clerk and told her to empty the cash register. According to witnesses, Nash stepped in and neatly disarmed the robber. But he hadn't known about the man's accomplice, who shot him in the back of the head. He was DOA at the hospital.

He looked down again at Cunningham, and thought of Mike Switzer, and suddenly remembered their feud.

"God, Sylvia! When Switzer and Cunningham run into each other tonight, all hell could break loose!"

Sylvia's hand darted to her mouth. "Oh, my! I never thought of that!"

*   *   *

Sylvia wanted to get away from the subject of politicians and onto the subject of Alan. She had known him all these years and had never had a chance to ask him about himself. Now that she had him all to herself, she wanted to make the most of the opportunity.

She put her hand on his arm and felt him flinch. Did she make him that nervous? Her heart stumbled over a beat. Could he possibly feel . . . ? No, that would be too much to ask.

"You know, I've always wanted to ask you how come you aren't a pediatrician? You have a way with kids."

"For the same reason I didn't specialize in any other area: I need variety. In my practice I can see a five-day-old infant with colic and a hundred-and-two-year-old man with prostate trouble back to back. Keeps me on my toes. But as for pediatrics, I had a more specific reason for not going into that. I rotated through the peds ward in my senior year of medical school and that cured me of a career in that field." A look of pain passed over his face. "Too many terminally ill kids. A few years of that and I knew I'd be an emotional basket case. And anyway, with the type of training I had, it was hard to go into anything *but* family practice."

Sylvia leaned forward with her elbows on the banister. She loved listening to him, hearing about a side of him that was otherwise hidden from her. "How's that?"

"Well, my school had this philosophy of teaching you all about every organ in the body but never letting you forget that it was part of a person. They always stressed the old cliché of the whole being greater than the sum of its parts. We were never supposed to treat John Doe's heart disease—we were always to treat John Doe who happened to have heart disease."

"Sounds like semantics."

"Yeah. I thought it was a word game, too. But there's a world of difference when you put the two approaches into practice. But getting back to pediatrics, I've come to see that I can practice better office pediatrics as a family doctor than as a pediatrician."

Sylvia laughed. She knew a few pediatricians who might take issue with that.

"I'm serious. Best example I can think of is a nine-year-old girl in a few months ago with stomach pains, weight loss, and sinking grades in school. If I were a pediatrician I'd start ordering a battery of blood tests, and when they came out negative, maybe even some barium X-ray studies. But I didn't."

"Flying by the seat of your pants again?" she said, remembering Tuesday night and Jeffy's bellyache.

"Not at all. Because over the past year I'd seen the mother three times for sprains, bruises, and contusions. Each time she'd say she had fallen, but I know what it looks like when someone gets punched in the nose. I confronted her; she admitted that her husband had been getting physically abusive over the past year; I sent them for family counseling, and when I last saw the girl her stomachaches were gone, she had regained her lost weight, and was performing back up to par in school."

"And you don't think a pediatrican could do that?"

"Of course. I'm not saying I'm a better pediatrician per se. I'm saying that because I treat whole families, I have a more direct line into what's going on in the home, which allows me a perspective no specialist has."

Sylvia saw Virginia Bulmer and Charles stroll into view below, and noted with a flash of satisfaction the relieved expressions on both their faces when they looked up and saw Alan and her standing in plain sight.

Lou Alberts, her uncle and Alan's old partner, came out to make it a threesome.

Alan apparently saw them, too.

"I guess I'd better get you back to your guests," he said.

Was that a note of reluctance in his voice?

"If you must," she said, looking him in the eyes.

Alan offered her his arm.

She sighed and allowed him to lead her down. It really was time to get back to the party—Switzer and Cunningham would be bumping into each other soon and she didn't want to miss *that*.

*   *   *

Mike Switzer came up and grabbed Alan's arm as he reached the bottom of the stairs.

"Alan!" he said, all smiles. "You did it!"

"What? Did what?" Alan said. Sylvia smiled, gave his arm a squeeze, and drifted away.

"The Guidelines bill! It's gone back to committee!"

"Is that good?"

"Hell, yes! It means it won't get tacked onto the Medicare appropriations, which puts it in limbo for a while."

Alan's rising spirits dipped. "So it's still alive."

"Yes, but it's wounded. And nowadays that's the best we can hope for." He slapped Alan on the back. "And *you* helped wound it, buddy!"

"The pleasure was all mine."

"Great! Just don't run against me in my district."

"Never fear," Alan said with heartfelt sincerity. "If I never see one of those committee rooms again it will be too soon."

"That's what I like to hear!" Switzer suddenly sobered. "But be alert for any of the senator's aides who may come around and say they want to 'get you on the team' where they can have 'easy access to your valuable insight.' They'll offer positions on things like study groups and the like. Ignore them."

"Why? Not that I have time for that kind of thing—but why ignore them?"

"It's an old trick," Mike said in an exaggerated conspiratorial whisper from the corner of his mouth. "You get your most articulate critics off guard by appearing open to their ideas, then you lose them in your study groups, sub-sub-committees, brain trusts, etcetera. You muffle them by burying them under tons of paper and red tape."

"Nice town you work in."

Mike shrugged. "If you know the rules, you can play the game."

"When it starts worming its way into my examining rooms," Alan said, "it's not a game anymore."

As Congressman Switzer drifted off to press flesh with other guests, Axford strolled by and stopped at Alan's side.

"So what field are you in?" Alan asked in an apparent attempt at making small talk with Axford; actually, he was curious as to what sort of man interested Sylvia.

"Research. Neurology."

"One of the schools? Pharmaceutical company?"

Axford shook his head. "Private. The McCready Foundation."

"Oh, God!"

Axford smiled. "Now don't get your knickers in a twist."

Alan couldn't help the sour look on his face. "But McCready . . . Christ! Wasn't it his kind that drove most of the good doctors out of England?"

Axford shrugged. "The famous 'Brain Drain'? I don't know and I don't bloody much care. National Health was already on the scene when I entered medical school. I just go where the research dollars are."

Alan felt an almost instinctive hostility rise in him. "So you come from a tradition of doctors as government employees. Must make it easy for you to work for McCready. Ever meet him?"

"Of course."

"What do you think of him?"

"His Circle of Willis is clogged with fecaliths."

Alan burst out laughing. Axford was anything but charming, but his candor was endearing. So was his wit. Alan had never heard anyone called a shithead in such an oblique manner.

"Do I detect a note of hostility toward academic medicine?" Axford said.

"No more than the average clinician."

"And I suppose you think you can get along just ducky without the research physician and the academician?"

"They have their places, but when a guy who hasn't laid a finger on a living patient since 1960 condescends to tell me how to practice clinical medicine—"

"You mean you actually *touch* people?" Axford said with an exaggerated grimace of distaste.

Lou Albert was passing by then and Axford caught him by the elbow.

"I say, why don't we three doctor-types stand around and talk shop, what? I understand you two were partners once upon a time. Is that so?"

Lou looked decidedly unhappy, but he stopped and nodded. He was shorter than either Alan or Axford, and at least a decade older, but he stood tall as always with his military-straight spine and gray, crew-cut hair. "You know damn well that's so. You asked me about it an hour ago."

"That's right, that's right. I did, didn't I?" Alan saw a gleam begin to glow in Axford's eyes. His smile became vulpine. "Years ago, wasn't it? And didn't you tell me that Alan here stole a lot of patients from you?"

Lou's face reddened. "I said no such thing!"

"Oh, do come along, old fellow. I asked you how many patients he stole from you and you said . . . ?" Axford's voice curved up at the end like the barb on a hook.

"I said 'a few,' that's all."

Alan couldn't fathom what Axford was after, but he knew he was up to no good. Still, he found himself unable to keep silent.

" 'Stole,' Lou?" Alan heard himself saying. "Since when do patients *belong* to anybody? I haven't seen any yet that came with your Social Security number stenciled on them."

"They wouldn't be going to you now if you hadn't had your secretary call them all up and tell them where your new office was!"

I don't believe I'm getting sucked into this! Alan thought as he glared at the contentedly smiling Axford.

"Look, Lou," he said. "Why don't we drop it for now. I'll just say that the only reason I had my secretary call all those patients was because the few who found me on their own said your office told them I'd left town."

"Gentlemen! Gentlemen!" Axford said in a mock-conciliatory tone. "It wounds me to see two primary-care physicians, two foot soldiers on the bloody frontlines of medicine, bickering so! I—"

"I've had just about enough of this!" Lou said. "My niece's taste in friends is equal to her taste in doctors!" He stormed off.

"Really, old boy," Axford said, turning to Alan. "What *did* break you two up?"

Alan was about to suggest a dark place where Axford could store his curiosity when Ginny and Sylvia walked up. Alan thought the presence of the women might blunt Axford's goading, but it only seemed to spur him on.

"I mean, was one of you using too much B-12? Not shooting enough penicillin? Tell me: Doesn't general practice get bloody boring, what with all those endless sore throats?"

"At times," Alan said, keeping cool and pretending to take Axford very seriously. "Beats abusing white rats for a living, though."

Axford's eyebrows rose halfway to his hairline. "Does it now? And how many colds have you treated this week? How many stomach viruses? How many hangnails? How many boils and carbuncles?"

"Careful, Charlie," Sylvia said somewhere to the right of Alan's shoulder. Alan couldn't see her. His face was no more than a foot from Axford's and their eyes were locked. "You're getting yourself too exercised."

"None," was all Alan said.

Axford's face parodied shock. *"None?* Pray tell, then, old sock, what *do* you treat?"

"People."

Alan heard Ginny clap and laugh and Sylvia say, *"Touché,* Chucko! A ten-pointer!"

Axford's third-degree interrogator's expression wavered, then broke into a rueful smile. "How did I let myself get maneuvered into *that* old saw?" He looked at Sylvia. "But ten points is a bit much, though, wouldn't you say? After all, I gave him all those openings, unintentional though they might have been."

Sylvia wouldn't budge. "Ten."

What's going on here? Alan felt like a species of game fish that had spit a hook. He was about to say something when angry shouting arose in the living room. They hurried in as a group to find the cause.

Had to happen, Alan said to himself from his vantage point behind a couch as he saw florid, overweight Andrew Cunningham of the MTA squared off against dapper Congressman Switzer in the center of the room. Cunningham had evidently had too much to drink, as evidenced by his unsteady stance. Alan and the rest of the New York Metropolitan area had been watching the two swap accusations and insults via the TV and the newspapers for the past three or four months. The situation had escalated from the political to the personal, with Switzer painting Cunningham as the ringleader of the most graft-ridden, featherbedded transportation system in the country, and Cunningham calling the congressman a headline-grabbing traitor to the district that elected him. As far as Alan could tell, neither was completely wrong.

As Alan and most of the other guests watched, Cunningham roared something unintelligible and threw his drink in Switzer's face. The congressman went livid, grabbed the MTA chief by the lapels, and swung him around. They pushed and shoved this way and that across the room like a couple of barroom brawlers while the rest of the guests either called for them to stop or shouted encouragement to one or the other.

Alan saw Ba standing off to the side in a corner of the room. But he was not watching the fight; instead, his eyes were fixed somewhere to Alan's left. Alan looked and there stood Sylvia. He had expected to see a look of dismay on her face, but he was wrong. She stood on tiptoes, her eyes bright, a tight smile on her face as she pulled short, quick breaths between her slightly parted lips.

She's enjoying this!

What was it with her? And what with *him?* He should have been repulsed by the pleasure she took from these two grown men, two public figures, making fools of themselves. Instead, it drew him more strongly to her. He thought he knew himself, but where this woman was concerned . . . everything was new and strange.

Alan turned back to the struggle in time to see Cunningham lose his grip and stumble backward toward the fireplace. His heel caught the lip of the outer hearth and he lost his balance. As his arms flailed helplessly in the air, the back of his head struck the corner of the marble mantelpiece. He went down in a heap.

Alan leaped over the couch, but was not the first to reach the fallen man. Ba was already there, crouched over the bulky, unconscious form.

"He's bleeding!" Alan said as he saw the characteristic red spray of an arterial pumper along the white marble of the mantelpiece. Probably a scalp artery. A small puddle had pooled around the back of Cunningham's head and was spreading rapidly.

The room, filled a moment ago with shouting and catcalls, had gone deathly still.

Without being told, Ba lifted the head and rolled the man onto his side so Alan could inspect the wound. Alan immediately spotted the jagged two-inch gash in the lower right occipital area. Wishing he carried a handkerchief, he pressed his bare hand over the wound, applying pressure. Warm blood filled his palm as he tried to press the slick, ragged edges closed with his fingers.

It happened then: The tingling ecstasy and euphoria started where his hand covered the wound, darting up his arm, then spreading throughout his body. He shuddered. Cunningham shuddered with him as his eyes fluttered open.

Alan took his hand away and looked. Terror, wonder, and disbelief mingled furiously within him when he saw the scalp. The wound had closed; only a shallow, irregular scratch remained.

Ba leaned over and looked at the wound. Abruptly, he released Cunningham and rose to his feet. For a moment, as Ba towered over him, the giant seemed to sway, as if he were dizzy. Alan saw shock and amazement in his wide dark eyes . . . and something else: Alan couldn't be sure, but he thought he saw recognition there. Then Ba turned to the people crowding forward.

"Please, back! Please, back!"

Sylvia came forward and crouched beside him. The tight smile was gone, replaced by a mask of genuine concern. Axford was behind her but remained standing, aloof but watchful.

"Is he all right?" she asked Alan.

Alan couldn't answer. He knew he must look silly, kneeling here with his mouth hanging open and a puddle of another man's blood clotting in his palm, but he couldn't speak just yet. All he could do was stare at the back of Cunningham's head.

"Of course I'm all right!" Cunningham said and sat up. He didn't appear the slightest bit groggy. All signs of inebriation were gone.

"But the blood!" She looked at Alan's hand.

"Scalp wounds bleed like crazy—even little ones," Alan managed to say, then he looked pointedly at Axford. "Right?"

He watched Axford's eyes travel over the spray of blood along the mantelpiece and wall, to the puddle on the floor. He hesitated, then shrugged. "Right. *Bloody* right."

*   *   *

The party was in its final spasms and Ba was glad. He did not like so many strangers in the house. For the Missus it had no doubt been just another party, but for Ba it had been a revelation.

Dat-tay-vao.

As he stood at the front door and watched the Doctor's car cruise toward the street, the phrase reverberated through his mind, echoing endlessly.

Dat-tay-vao.

Dr. Bulmer possessed it.

But how? It wasn't possible!

Yet he could not deny what he had seen tonight: the gout of blood, the open wound—stopped and closed at the Doctor's touch. He had felt his knees go weak and rubbery at the sight.

How long had the *Dat-tay-vao* been with him?

Surely not long, for Ba had seen the surprise on the Doctor's face when the wound had healed under his hand. If only . . .

Ba's mind leaped back over the years to the time when his dear Nhung Thi was wasting away from the cancer that had started in her lungs and spread throughout her body. He remembered how Dr. Bulmer had returned again and again to her side during the endless torment, the year-long days, the epochal months as she was devoured from within. There had been many doctors treating Nhung

Thi in those days, but for Ba and his wife, Dr. Bulmer had come to be *The* Doctor.

If only he had possessed the *Dat-tay-vao* then!

But of course he hadn't. He had been an ordinary physician then. But now . . .

Ba felt a pang in his heart for the Doctor, because all the tales about the *Dat-tay-vao* hinted that there was a balance to be struck. Always a balance . . .

And a price to be paid.

*   *   *

I can do it! Alan thought as he drove home.

There was no longer any doubt that he had come to possess some sort of healing power. Tonight's episode proved it. Cunningham's scalp had been hanging open, bleeding like crazy, and he'd put his hand over it and changed it to a scratch.

Eleven p.m. He had made a mental note of the time it happened.

Sonja Andersen and Henrietta Westin weren't freak coincidences! He could *do* it! But how to control it? How to use it when he wanted to?

Ginny's voice broke through.

"Josie and Terri won't believe tonight when I tell them about it!"

"Won't believe what?" Alan said, suddenly alert to what she was saying. Had she seen? If she had, they could talk about it without him sounding crazy. He desperately needed to share this with someone who *believed.*

"The party! All those celebrities! And the fight between Cunningham and Switzer! *Everything!*"

"Oh, that." He was disappointed. Obviously she hadn't seen anything.

He thought Ba might have seen what had happened, but perhaps he hadn't quite believed his eyes. That would be the normal reaction—disbelief. Which was why Alan had to keep this to himself. If *he* couldn't quite believe what was happening, how could he expect anyone else to accept it?

"You know," Ginny was saying, "I can't figure that Sylvia. She seems hard as nails, yet she took in that little retarded boy and cares for him by herself. I just don't—"

"Jeffy's not retarded. He's autistic."

"Just about the same thing, right?"

"Not really. Most autistic kids test out retarded, but there's a lot of debate as to whether they all are. I don't think Jeffy is." He gave her a quick summary of the latest theories, then said, "Sylvia once showed me a photo of a house he had built out of blocks. So I know there's intelligence in that boy: It's just locked away."

Ginny was staring at him. "That's the most you've said in days!"

"Is it? I hadn't realized. Sorry."

"That's okay. You've been only a little bit more preoccupied than usual. I'm used to it by now."

"Again, sorry."

"But back to our hostess: How did she come to adopt that little boy? I asked her but she never got around to answering me. As a matter of fact, I got the distinct impression she avoided answering me."

Alan shrugged. "I don't know, either. I figure it's something she doesn't feel is anybody else's business."

"But isn't there something that can be done for him?"

"Every known therapy has been tried."

"With all her money, I'm surprised she doesn't take him to see some bigwig pediatrician in the City—" She stopped abruptly.

Alan finished for her. "Instead of making do with a local family doc?" he said with a sour smile.

Ginny looked uncomfortable. "I didn't mean that at all."

"It's okay." Alan was not angry, nor was he hurt. He had developed a thick skin on this topic. He knew Ginny wished that he had specialized in some field, *any* field, of medicine. She said she wanted it for *him* so he wouldn't have to work such long hours, but he knew the real reason. All her friends were the wives of specialists, and she had come to think of a family doctor as the bottom of the medical pecking order.

"I didn't," she said quickly. "I simply— *Alan!* That's our street!"

Alan braked and pulled in toward the curb.

"Are you all right?" Ginny asked, genuine concern on her face. "Were you drinking much?"

"I'm fine," Alan said in a meticulously steady voice. "Just fine."

Ginny said nothing as he backed the car along the deserted road and turned into their street. Alan didn't understand how he could have missed the street. He had been paying attention to the road. He had even seen the street sign. He simply hadn't recognized it. And he hadn't the vaguest notion why.

10.
Alan

Alan spent all day Sunday aching to get to the office to see if he could make the power work again. Finally, morning came and he was chafing to get started.

It was 8:00 a.m. He was going to be scientific about this—get all the data down as it happened: dates, times, names, places, diagnoses. He had fresh batteries in his microcassette recorder. He was ready for his first patient and his first miracle of the day.

No such luck.

His first three patients consisted of an elderly couple, each with stable hypertension, and a woman with mild, diet-controlled, type II diabetes. There was no ready means of confirming a cure with these diagnoses. He wouldn't feel right telling the first two to stop their medications, nor could he tell the third to throw away her 1500-calorie diet and rush down to Carvel's for a hot fudge sundae.

He needed an acute illness or injury. It came with the fourth patient.

Six-year-old Chris Bolland was home from school because of a sore throat and a fever of 101.6 degrees. Alan looked in the child's throat and saw a white exudate coating both tonsils: tonsilitis.

"Again?" said Mrs. Bolland. "Why don't we take them out?"

Alan glanced back through the chart. "This is only his third episode in the past year. Not enough to warrant that. But let's try something."

He swung around behind Chris and placed his fingertips lightly over the swollen glands below the angles of the jaw. He concentrated—on what, exactly, he did not know; but he tried thinking of a nice, pink, healthy throat with normal-sized tonsils; tried willing that ideal throat into little Chris.

There was no outcry from Chris, no tingle in Alan's fingers and arms. Nothing.

Out of the corner of his eye he noticed the mother looking at him strangely. He cleared his throat, adjusted the earpieces of his stethoscope, and began listening to Chris' lungs, hiding the frustration that welled up in him.

Failure! Why was this power, if it really existed, so damn capricious? What made it work?

He didn't know, but he dutifully dictated a brief, whispered account of the failure into his hand-held recorder.

His next patient was an unscheduled emergency. Marla Springer—a new patient, twenty-three years old, brought in by a neighbor who had been coming to Alan for a long time—had cut her right hand earlier this morning. After half an hour of applying ice and direct pressure, the wound was still bleeding. Denise placed her in an empty examining room immediately.

Alan examined Marla's hand and found a crescent-shaped laceration, an inch from end to end, on the fleshy edge of the palm below the fifth finger. Blood was oozing slowly but steadily from under the flap of cut skin. He noticed the hand was cold. He looked at the woman and saw the pallor of her face, her tight features, her lower lip trapped between her teeth.

"Hurt much, Marla?"

She shook her head. "No. But it won't stop bleeding!"

"Sure it will—as soon as I get through with it." He could feel some of the tension go out of her as she realized she wasn't about to bleed to death. Now to use a little razzle-dazzle to get her confidence. "And maybe you can use this as an excuse to talk your husband into getting you a dishwasher. Or if not that, at least a sponge with a handle."

"What do you mean?"

"I mean, this is what you get for trying to get the bottom of the glass spotless."

Her eyes widened. "How did you know?"

Alan winked at her. "Karnak knows all, sees all."

What he didn't say was that he had seen dozens of similar wounds over the years, all from the same cause: a bit too much vigor in washing out the inside of a waterglass, causing it to shatter and cut either the index finger or the edge of the palm.

As he had her lie back and relax, Alan realized that he had been presented with a perfect opportunity to test the power. It had worked on a much larger laceration Saturday night; there should be no problem with a little cut like this. He glanced at his watch: 9:36 a.m. He wanted to document everything as accurately as possible.

He pressed the flap of skin tightly closed and wished-hoped-prayed for the wound to heal. He held it there for a good twenty seconds, but felt no shock, no rush of ecstasy. He released the pressure and examined the wound.

The edges of the cut were closed together in a thin crimson line with no sign of further bleeding. Alan felt exultation swell toward bursting within him—

—and then the wound edges gapped and fresh blood began to flow again.

He'd done nothing.

"Are you going to use a needle to numb it up?" Marla Springer asked.

"Getting ready to do just that," Alan said, swallowing the bitter disappointment as he reached for the Xylocaine bottle next to the suturing set.

Another failure.

But he wasn't giving up. As soon as he finished here, he would go into his consultation room, dictate the failure, and move on to the next patient.

*   *   *

(Transcribed from microcassette)

Monday, April 12.
10:18 a.m.
MARIE EMMETT: 58-yr-old white female hypertensive on In-
deride 40/25 BID. Bp = 136/84. Says "I think I've got shingles."
She's right. Typical vesiculating rash on left flank along T-10
dermatome. Placed hand over the rash and wished it gone. Tried
x 3. No change. Rash still present. No decrease in pain.

10:47 a.m.
AMY BRISCO: 11-year-old asthmatic. Mother states child short
of breath all night. Auscultation reveals tight expiratory wheezing
throughout lungs. Placed right hand on front of chest, left hand
over back, and squeezed, willing lungs to loosen up and clear.
No change other than odd expression on her mother's face—
probably thinks I've gone a little strange. Bronchospasm sounded
as tight as before. Started usual therapy—0.2 cc of aqueous ep-
inephrine subcutaneously, etc.

11:02 a.m.
CHANDLER DEKKS: 66-yr-old white male with bilateral lower
limb deep and superficial varicosities; severe associated stasis
dermatitis. Presents with 2 x 2 cm. ulceration on posterior aspect
of left lower leg of approximately 1 week's duration. Examined
carefully, all the time wishing and willing it to heal/fill in/dis-
appear. No change. Prescribed usual treatment.

11:15 a.m.
JOY LEIBOV: 16-year-old white female. Unscheduled appoint-
ment. Helped in by father and brother after injury to right ankle
during high school intramural soccer game. Typical inversion
injury with swelling, tenderness, and ecchymosis in area of lateral
malleolus. Cupped my hands around the ankle—gently—and
willed the damn thing to heal. No change. Nothing!

This is idiotic.

(end of transcription)

*   *   *

Alan pushed all thoughts of mystical healing powers from his mind
as he struggled to keep up with the patient load for the rest of the

morning. He didn't do too badly. He stepped into the room with his last patient, scheduled for noon, at 12:30.

He saw Stuart Thompson sitting on the edge of the examining table looking worried. Alan immediately knew something was wrong. Stu was a forty-two-year-old construction worker with tattoos on both arms and moderate essential hypertension. He was the macho sort who never let his feelings show, never admitted a frailty. If not for his wife virtually putting the Tenormin tablet in his mouth every morning and badgering him to get checkups, his blood pressure would have remained untreated all these years.

If Stuart Thompson looked the slightest bit frightened on the outside, it meant he was absolutely terrified on the inside.

"I ain't no pussy, Doc, but somebody said this thing on my back looks like cancer and it's got me spooked. Take a look at it and tell me it's okay."

"Sure thing. Lie on your stomach and we'll see."

Alan bit his lip when he saw what Stu was talking about. It looked bad: a blue-black lesion on the left scapula, measuring about two centimeters across, with an irregular border and an uneven surface.

Alan's thoughts were ranging in all directions as he leaned closer over Stu's back. This thing had to be removed, probably with a wide excision, and as soon as possible, too. He was trying to think of a way to phrase his suspicions without shooting Stu's blood pressure through the ceiling when he lightly touched a fingertip to the dark area.

The now-familiar feeling raced up his arm as Stu arched his back. "*Shit*, Doc!"

"Sorry," Alan said quickly. "Just seeing how sensitive it is."

Alan stared at the man's back. The lesion was gone! There was no trace of pigment left in the area.

He looked at his hand. So many unanswered questions, but they sank in the exultation of knowing that he still had the power.

"Well, now that you know," Stu said, "what are you going to do—amputate my back?" The tone was sarcastic but Alan sensed the fear beneath.

"No," Alan said, thinking fast. "I'm just going to burn off that ugly little wart you've got there, and then you can try out for Mr. Universe."

"A wart? Is that all?" There was profound relief in his voice.

"It's nothing," Alan said, realizing he was literally telling the truth. "I'll get the hyfrecator and we'll have this done in a minute."

Alan stepped outside the room and took a deep breath. All he had to do was anesthetize the area, make a little burn where the lesion had been, and send the unsuspecting Stuart Thompson home cured of a malignant melanoma. That way he could avoid any difficult questions.

Then he heard Stu's voice from the other side of the door.

"Hey! It's gone! Hey, Doc! It's *gone!*"

Alan stuck his head back into the room and saw Stu examining his back in the mirror.

"What are you? Some kinda miracle worker?"

"Naw," Alan said, swallowing and trying to smile. "It must have fallen off. That's the way it is with warts sometimes . . . they just . . . fall off."

Alan brushed off the ensuing questions, all the while minimizing what had happened, and ushered the puzzled but happy man from the examining room.

He ran to the next examining room—empty! The ceiling light was off and the room was clean and ready for the afternoon patients.

But the afternoon would be too late! He needed somebody *now*, not later! He was *hot!* The power was on and he wanted to use it before it left him again! Denise and Connie were getting ready to go for lunch. Both were in excellent health. There was nothing he could do for them.

He turned in a slow circle, wanting to laugh, wanting to shout his frustration. He felt like a millionaire who had decided to give his fortune to the needy but could find only other millionaires.

For want of anything better to do, he rushed into his office and picked up the microcassette recorder. He had to get all the details down while they were fresh. He thumbed the *record* button, opened his mouth . . . and stopped.

Funny . . . he couldn't think of the patient's name. He could picture his face perfectly, but his name was lost. He glanced down at the appointment sheet. There it was in the last slot: Stuart Thompson. Of course. Amazing how a little excitement could jumble the mind.

He began dictating—time, age and condition of the patient, his own feelings at the time. Everything.

He was going to cage this power, learn everything there was to know about it, train it, bend it to his will, and make damn good use of it.

In the back of his head he heard Tony Williams of The Platters singing, "You-oo-oo've got the maaaaagic touch!"

MAY

__11.__
Charles Axford

McCready had invited him to the upper office for another of what the senator liked to call "informal chats." Charles called them pumping sessions. Which was just what they were. As namesake of the Foundation, McCready seemed to feel it was his prerogative to sit down with his director of neurological research and quiz him on the latest developments in the field. Perhaps it was. But Charles knew the Foundation was the furthest thing from the senator's mind when he asked about neurological diseases. The interest was strictly personal.

As he waited for the senator, he wandered to the huge windows that formed the outer walls of the corner office. If he leaned his head against the panes of the left wall, he could see Park Avenue and its flowering islands twenty stories below.

The door opened and McCready hobbled in. He fell into the big padded chair behind his desk. He wasn't looking good at all these days. His features sagged more than usual, and he had to tilt his head back in order to see past his drooping upper eyelids. Charles made a quick mental calculation: _Six months and he'll be in a wheelchair._

He had known the man all these years; he owed his present economic security and prestigious position to him; yet he found he could not dredge up a bloody ounce of pity for James A. McCready. He wondered why. Perhaps it was because he knew what drove the man who had been born with more money than he could spend in two lifetimes. He had been present during some of the senator's most unguarded moments, and had seen the naked power lust shine through. Here was a man who could be President merely by choosing to run. Yet he could not run, and Charles was one of the few people in the world who knew the reason.

Maybe it was all for the best. Men like McCready had brought Great Britain to the edge of economic ruin; perhaps Charles' adoptive country was lucky that this particular senator had an incurable disease.

He seated himself and listened to the questions: Always the same: Any new developments? Any promising lines of research we can encourage?

Charles gave his usual answer: No. He used the Foundation computers to keep tabs on all the medical literature worldwide. As soon as anything of the slightest potential interest to the senator showed up in the most obscure medical journal in the remotest backwater, it was flagged and brought to his attention. The senator could access the information as readily—perhaps more readily; after all, they were his computers—but preferred "a personal touch" from Charles.

In other words, he wanted Charles to predigest it and spoon-feed it to him.

Well and good. Charles kept up on the field anyway. Small price to pay for the latitude he was given in his research at the Foundation.

The conversation followed its usual course to its customary dead end, and Charles was getting ready to make his exit when the senator shifted to a new topic.

"What did you think of Dr. Alan Bulmer when you met him?" His voice was getting weaker and raspier as the afternoon wore on.

"Who?" Charles drew a complete blank on the name for a second.

McCready prompted him: "You met him at that Nash woman's party last month."

"Oh, the G.P.! I don't—" And then it occurred to Charles: "How did you know I met him?"

"There's been some talk about him."

"What kind of talk? This wouldn't have anything to do with his testimony before the committee, would it?" Charles knew that it was not good to get on the bad side of Senator James McCready.

"Not at all, not at all. That's over and done with, gone and forgotten. This talk has to do with healings. Cures. That sort of thing."

Charles groaned mentally. *Here we go again: another try for a bloody miracle cure.*

McCready smiled. The expression seemed to take a lot of effort. "Now, now, my esteemed Dr. Axford—don't get that cynical look on your face. You know I like to investigate every one of these faith healers. One of these days—"

"Bulmer's no faith healer. He's a bloody ordinary family practitioner. And I stress the word *ordinary*. You're going to drive us both dotty if you keep looking for a miracle!"

McCready laughed. "I could listen to you talk all day, Charles. I wish I had a British accent."

It never failed to impress Charles how easily Americans were impressed with a British accent. It always sounded "classy" to them. But he knew that back in London his accent would have been recognized immediately as Paddington and his class identified as working.

"Still," the senator said, hanging on to the subject, "there's talk."

"What do you mean by 'talk'?"

"You know how things get around. Comments dropped here and there in laundromats and supermarket checkout lines eventually get around to a stringer or a reporter who works for one of my papers. Then it gets to me."

"Fine. But talk about what?"

"About people with long-term illnesses, chronic conditions, progressive disorders, acute illnesses—all sorts of things—cured after he touches them in a certain way."

"That's bloody foolishness!"

McCready smiled again. " 'Bloody.' How apropos. I was just going to ask you about a very bloody wound sustained by a certain Mr. Cunningham last month."

"Jesus bloody Christ—!"

"There's that word again."

"—Did you have a spy at that party?"

"Of course not. But it would be rather silly of me to own a string of newspapers and have all those editors and reporters at my command and not avail myself of their talents when the need arose, don't you think?"

Charles nodded silently. He didn't like the idea of anyone snooping into his off-hours, but he didn't see any point in protesting. McCready seemed to read his mind.

"Don't worry, Charles. You weren't the object of investigation. I was just having someone look into the incident between my esteemed colleague, Congressman Switzer, and the MTA chief of this fair city. I've found one can deal more effectively with one's colleagues if one is up to date on their improprieties and indiscretions."

Charles nodded again. *Looking for dirt on Switzer,* he thought. But he said: "Works that way in research foundations, too."

"Right. Unfortunately, the only impropriety on the congressman's part was not turning the other cheek, but rather giving as good—or perhaps better—than he got from Cunningham in the physical abuse department. And to many of his constituents, that would seem a virtue rather than a fault. So the inquiry was dropped."

He paused for a moment. The extended monologue was obviously tiring him.

"But something interesting was turned up serendipitously. One of the guests who saw the struggle mentioned during her interview that she thought Cunningham had received a terrible gash to the back of the head. She spoke of blood spouting like . . . 'like a geyser,' I believe she said. Yet after this unknown man—later identified as Dr. Alan Bulmer—put his hand over the wound, it stopped bleeding and closed itself up."

Charles laughed. "She was probably drunker than Cunningham!"

"Possibly. That's what this reporter thought. But not long ago, he heard some idle talk about 'miracle cures' at a Long Island doctor's office. The name Bulmer clicked and he told his editor, who told me." His eyes bored into Charles from under their half-closed lids. "You were there. What did *you* see?"

Charles thought for a moment. There *had* been an awful lot of blood. He could see it now, spurting against the mantel and the wall. But when he had seen the wound, it had only been a scratch. Could it—?

"I saw a lot of blood, but that means nothing. Scalp wounds bleed far out of proportion to their length and depth. I've seen heads literally *covered* with blood from a two-centimeter laceration barely a centimeter deep. Don't waste your time looking for a miracle cure from Alan Bulmer."

"I never waste my time, Charles," the senator said. "Never."

12.

The Senator

Ah, Charles, McCready thought after Axford had gone. *Doubting Charles.*

He leaned far back in his chair and, as he often did, thought about his chief pet doctor. And why not? Their lives were tightly entwined, and would remain so as long as he remained ill.

Despite the fact that Charles was a doctor and an arrogant bastard to boot, McCready privately admitted to a soft spot in his head for his chief of research. Perhaps that was because there was no pretense about Charles. He made no bones about being a devout atheist and confirmed materialist who was constitutionally unable to accept anything that did not yield to the scientific method. If he couldn't observe it, qualify and quantify it, it didn't exist. Refreshingly free of bullshit, his Charles. Humans were nothing more than a conglomeration of cells and biochemical reactions to him. He had once told McCready that his dream was to reduce the human mind to its basic neurochemical reactions.

All fine and well when you had your health. But when you didn't, and when modern medicine failed you . . . then you looked for something more. You prayed, even when you didn't believe in prayer. You investigated faith healers even when you had no faith. The sneers and the derogatory remarks no longer came so easily. You looked under every rock and followed every trail to its inevitable phony end. And then sniffed out another one to follow.

Hopelessness was a bitch.

He had given up hope on current research into neuromuscular diseases—he couldn't trust it to go in the direction he needed. Thus the Foundation was born, with Charles Axford as its core. He had made Axford chief because he felt he owed him something.

Because the day he met Axford was the most traumatic day of his life. It had altered the course of his life, altered his perception of life, the world, the future. Because Charles Axford had been the first to know what was wrong with him.

All the other doctors before Charles had been wrong. To a man they had blamed his episodic fatigue on "overwork" and "stress." That was the new catchword in medicine: If you can't figure it out, it's stress.

McCready had bought that for a while. He had been working hard—he'd always worked hard—but he'd never felt so tired. He would get up in the morning a ball of fire and by midafternoon he was useless. He had stopped eating steak because it was too much work to chew it. His arm tired while shaving. *Overwork and stress.* He'd gone along with the diagnosis because time and again his physical examination, reflexes, blood tests, X rays, and cardiograms had come out completely normal. "You're the picture of health!" a respected internist had told him.

His first episode of double vision had sent him in a panic to the nearest neurologist who would give him the earliest appointment. That had been Charles Axford. He later learned that Axford had not squeezed him into that day's schedule out of doctorly concern for a patient in distress, but because his afternoon appointment book had been virtually bare.

McCready had found himself seated before a cool, aloof, thickly accented Britisher in a white coat who chain-smoked cigarettes in his chair on the far side of an old desk as he listened to McCready's symptoms. He asked a few questions, then said:

"You've got myasthenia gravis, a rapidly progressive case, and your life is going to be hell."

McCready still remembered the slow wave of shock that had passed through him by inches, front to back, like a storm front. All he could see was Aristotle Onassis fading away month after month, year after year. He managed to say, "Aren't you even going to examine me?"

"You mean tap your knees and shine lights in your eyes and all that rubbish? Not if I can bloody help it!"

"I insist! I'm paying for an examination and I demand one!"

Axford had sighed. "Very well." He came around and sat on the front edge of the desk. Holding out both his hands to McCready, he said, "Squeeze. Hard." After McCready had gripped them and squeezed, Axford said, "Again!" And then, "Again!"

And with each successive squeeze, McCready felt his grip grow weaker and weaker.

"Now rest up a bit," Axford had said. After smoking half another cigarette and further fouling the office air, he stuck out his hands again. "Once more now."

McCready squeezed with all he had, and, with no little satisfaction, saw Axford wince. After a brief rest his strength had returned.

"See," Axford said, wiping his hands on his lab coat. "Myasthenia gravis. But just to be absolutely sure, we'll do an EMG."

"What's that?"

"Nerve conduction study. Which in your case will show the classic decremental pattern."

"Where do I get this done?" He was suddenly desperate to have the diagnosis confirmed or denied.

"Lots of places. But my rig here in this office affords the most nutritional value."

McCready was baffled by this Brit. "I don't understand."

"The fee I'll charge you," Axford said with the barest hint of a smile, "will help keep food on my table."

McCready fled Axford's office, fully convinced that the man was a lunatic. But second and third opinions, along with exhaustive testing, proved the Brit right. Senator James McCready had a particularly virulent case of myasthenia gravis, which he learned was an incurable neuromuscular disease caused by a deficiency of acetylcholine, the substance that transmits messages from nerve cells to muscle cells at their junction.

Out of a sense of loyalty, he returned to Axford for therapy. And, as he had long ago learned about such supposedly noble impulses, it was a wrong move. Axford's bedside manner embodied all the concern and personal warmth of the average cinder block. Axford didn't seem to care how the medications were affecting his patient— the muscle cramps, the twitching, the anxiety, and insomnia. He cared only about how they improved the responses on his damned EMG machine.

And McCready went the route—the *whole* route. He had his thymus removed, he was juiced up with drugs like neostigmine and Mestinon, then bloated up with cortisone. He went through plasmapheresis. All to no avail. His case progressed slowly but relentlessly no matter what Axford or anyone else did.

But he had never fully accepted his illness, not even to this day. He had fought it from the beginning and would keep on fighting it. He had plans for his life and his career that went beyond the Senate. Myasthenia gravis threatened to stop him. It wouldn't. He would find a way—over it, around it, or through it.

And toward that end, he began investigating Charles Axford years ago. He learned he'd been born into a working class family in London, and that he saw his parents and his home destroyed during the Blitz when the Paddington section had been heavily bombed. He proved brilliant in his studies, graduating from medical school in England at the top of his class; he was considered equally brilliant by anyone who knew him during his neurology residency here in Manhattan—admired by all but considered far too abrasive for anyone's comfort. After countless bids for research grants and fellowships had been turned down, he had reluctantly opened up a private practice, where he was quietly starving. Brilliant though he was in the science of medicine, he was virtually an idiot in the art of dealing with people.

To add to his problems, his wife had run off to "find" herself, leaving him with a chronically ill daughter.

Charles, of course, had never mentioned a word of his personal problems to the senator. McCready had ferreted them out through the contacts he still maintained with his publishing empire.

It became evident to McCready that the two men were made for each other: Axford was a whiz in neurology and McCready had a neuromuscular disease that was considered incurable at medicine's present state of knowledge; Axford was looking for a research post and McCready had more money than he could spend in many lifetimes—at last count his personal fortune had totaled somewhere in the neighborhood of 200 million dollars.

Two ideas were born then. The first was the seed of the Medical Guidelines bill. Doctors had explained to him over and over that myasthenia gravis was subtle and difficult to diagnose in the early stages. He didn't care. It should have been discovered years before he went to Axford. These doctors needed a lesson or two in humility. If they wouldn't do their jobs right, he'd show them how.

The second idea became reality sooner than the legislation: The McCready Foundation for Medical Research was begun, with Charles Axford, M.D., as its director. The setup was tax-advantaged and allowed McCready to direct the course of all research done. Axford seemed delighted—he was well paid and could follow his interests without having to deal too much with patients.

McCready had his first pet doctor. He too found the situation delightful.

With an influx of grants and donations, the Foundation grew until it presently provided inpatient as well as outpatient services and occupied its own building on Park Avenue in Manhattan, a former office building raised in the thirties that looked like a smaller version of Rockefeller Center. He had started off with one pet doctor; now he owned a whole stable of them. That was the only way to keep doctors in line: Own them. Make them dependent on you for their daily bread and they soon lost their maverick ways. They learned to toe the line like anybody else.

Axford still showed a lot of maverick tendencies, but McCready laid that off to the fact that he gave his research chief plenty of room. Someday he would yank on a few strings and see how the Brit danced. But not yet. Not while he needed Axford's research know-how.

That might not be much longer, though. Not if one *tenth* of what he had heard about this Bulmer character were true. After years of false leads, it was almost too much to hope for. But those stories . . .

His mouth went dry. If those stories were even half true . . .

And to think that Bulmer had been in his committee room only last month. He hadn't come across as a nut case then—anything but. But was it possible he had been sitting a few yards away from a cure and not known it?

He had to find out. He had to *know!* He didn't have much time!

__ 13. __
Charles

"C'mon, Daddy," Julie said, her voice a shade away from a whine. "Tonight's a dialysis night." She stood there in her cut-off jeans and long-sleeved Opus the Penguin T-shirt, holding the glass out to him. "Let me have some more. I'm thirsty."

"How many ounces have you had already?" Charles asked.

"Six."

"Only two more."

"Four! *Please!*" She hung her tongue out of her mouth and made a choking sound.

"All right! All right!"

He filled her eight-ounce tumbler halfway to the top, but restrained her arm as she lifted the glass.

"Use it to wash down your last three Amphojels."

She made a face but popped them in her mouth and began chewing. Of the twenty-eight pills Julie had to take a day—the calcium, the activated vitamin D, the iron, the water-soluble vitamins—she hated her aluminum hydroxide tablets the most.

When she had finished gulping down the juice, he pointed toward the back end of the apartment.

Julie slumped her shoulders and pouted. "Can't it wait?"

"Toddle on, and no more lolly-gagging. It's after six already."

He followed her into the back room where she plopped herself into the recliner, rolled up her sleeve, and placed her bared forearm on the arm of the chair.

Charles had the dialyzer all warmed up and ready to go. He seated himself next to his daughter and inspected her forearm. The fistula was still in excellent shape after five years. The thickened, ropy veins about as big around as his little finger bulged up under her skin. A few years ago one of the kids at school had seen her fistula and given her the name "wormy arms." She had worn long sleeves ever since—even in the summer.

After cleaning the area with Betadine and alcohol, he made the skin punctures and cannulated the arterial and venous ends. He hooked her up to the dialyzer and watched the blood begin to flow toward the machine.

"You want the telly?"

She shook her head. "Maybe later. I want to read this first." She held up the latest *Bloom County* collection. The comic strip was her current favorite and Opus the Penguin her latest fave.

Charles placed the remote control for the tv next to her on the seat, then stood over the dialyzer—which came up to his chest—and watched it do its thing, drawing the red blood and the clear dialysate past each other on different sides of the membrane, then sending the freshened blood, relieved of most of its toxins, back to Julie's vein while it stored away the tainted dialysate. Charles was happy with this particular hollow-fiber dialyzer. There was seldom trouble with the transmembrane pressures, and Julie had got shocky only twice so far this year—a pretty good record.

He sank into the couch across the room from her.

How does she do it? he wondered for the thousandth time as he watched her smile and occasionally giggle as she paged through the book. *How does she keep from going crazy?*

How much longer did this have to go on? Something had to break soon. He couldn't see how she could put up with this for the rest of her life. It was living hell . . .

. . . three hours on the machine three times a week. He always timed it as the last event of the day because it exhausted her. All those pills . . . the ones that didn't nauseate her made her constipated. She had to measure every bloody ounce of fluid that passed her lips so as not to overload her vascular system. And the diet—rigidly restricted sodium, protein, and phosphorus, which meant no pizza, no milk shakes, no ice cream, no pickles, no cold cuts, or anything else that kids like. She was constantly anemic and tired, so she couldn't get into any school activities that required exertion.

That was no life for a kid.

But that wasn't the worst of it. Typical of a kid on long-term hemodialysis, she wasn't growing or developing at a normal rate. As they became teenagers, they didn't . . . become teenagers. They stayed small; they didn't develop much in the way of secondary sexual characteristics, and that took a terrible emotional toll after a while. Julie wasn't to that stage as yet, but she would be before too long. And she was already small for her age.

Charles studied Julie, with her big brown eyes and raven hair. So beautiful. Just like her mother. Lucky for her that was the only thing she had inherited from the bloody bitch. He felt his teeth grinding and banished his ex-wife from his mind. Every time he thought of her, or someone even mentioned her name, he felt himself edged toward violence.

She didn't have to leave. It was hard living with a child in chronic renal failure, but lots of parents lived with lots worse. And Jesus, look at Sylvie—she'd gone out and adopted a bloody autistic boy! If only his ex had been like Sylvie—what a life they could have had!

But no use gnawing on that subject. He'd chewed it to death over the years. There were more important concerns to be dealt with in the here and now.

Like the call from Julie's nephrologist just an hour ago. Her circulating levels of cytotoxic antibodies were still high, years after her body had rejected the kidney he'd donated to her. She hadn't been a good transplant candidate in the first place, and until those antibody levels came down, she was no candidate at all.

So she went on day by day, producing her ounce or so of urine per week, feeling tired most of the time, and getting her thrice-weekly hemodialysis treatments here in this room. An unimaginable existence for Charles, but the only life Julie had ever known.

He watched television for a while, and when he glanced her way at 8:30, she was asleep. He waited until her dialysis was done, then he disconnected her from the machine, bandaged up her arm, and carried her into her bedroom, where he changed her into her pajamas and slipped her under the sheet.

As he sat there for a moment stroking her hair and looking at that innocent little face, she stirred and raised her head.

"I forgot to say my prayers."

"That's okay, Love," he said soothingly and she went back to sleep immediately.

There's nobody listening anyway.

It never ceased to amaze him how people could believe in a provident God when so many children in this world suffered from the day they were born.

There was no God for him. There was only Julie and this world and today—and, hopefully, tomorrow.

He kissed her on the forehead and turned out the light.

14.
Alan

The patient was lying.

A new patient. His file said he was Joe Metzger, age thirty-two, and he was complaining of chronic low back pain. He said he wanted a cure for his backache.

The cure bit threw him. Alan had thought he'd had him pretty well pegged as a drug abuser looking for some Dilaudid or Percodan. He ran into his share of them—always a chronic painful condition, always "allergic" to the non-narcotic analgesics, always with a story about how "Nothing works except one kind of pill—I'm not sure what it's called, but it's yellow and has something like 'Endo' on it."

Yeah. Right.

Perhaps Alan would have been less suspicious if he hadn't happened to glance out the window just as Joe Metzger of the terrible back pain limberly hopped out of his little Fiat two-seater in the parking lot.

"Just what do you mean by 'cure'?" He had recounted an extensive work-up—myelograms, CT scans, and all—and consultations with bigshot orthopedists. "What do you expect from me that you haven't been offered elsewhere?"

Joe Metzger smiled. It was a mechanical expression, like something Alan would expect to see on Jerry Mahoney or Charlie McCarthy. His thin body was bared to the waist, with the belt to his jeans loosened. His bushy hair stuck out on all sides and a thick mustache drooped around each side of his mouth; wire-rimmed granny glasses completed the picture, making him look like a refugee from the sixties.

"A healing. Like you did for Lucy Burns' sciatica a couple of weeks ago."

Oh, shit! Alan thought. *Now it starts.* He couldn't quite place the name Lucy Burns, but he'd known something like this would happen sooner or later. He couldn't expect to go on working his little miracles without talk getting around.

He hadn't exactly caused the blind to see as yet—although old Miss Binghamton's cataracts had cleared after he'd examined her—but he had caused the deaf to hear and performed many other . . . he could think of no better word than *miracles*.

He was still unable to control the power and doubted he ever would. But he had learned a lot about it in the preceding weeks. He had the power twice a day for approximately one hour. Those hours were approximately twelve hours apart, but not exactly. Therefore he possessed the power at a different time each day, anywhere from forty to seventy minutes later than he had the day before. Day by day, the "Hour of Power," as he now called it, slowly edged its way around the clock. It occurred in conjunction with no biorhythm known to medical science. He had given up trying to explain it—he simply used it.

He had been judicious with the power, not only for reasons of discretion, but for safety as well. For instance, he could not try a cure on an insulin-dependent diabetic without informing the patient of the cure; otherwise the patient would take the usual insulin dose the next morning and wind up in hypoglycemic shock by noon. He had never promised results when he used the power, never even *hinted* that he possessed it. He did everything he could to make the cure appear purely coincidental, purely happenstance, brushing off any cause-effect relationship to him.

He didn't know what would happen if word got around about his little miracles, and he didn't want to find out.

But if this Joe Metzger sitting here before him had heard something, so had others. Which meant it was time to lie low, hold back from using the power until the rumors died out. It would be such a shame, though, to waste all the healing he could do in those hours. The power had come suddenly and without warning—it might leave the same way.

But for now, he'd do what he'd planned to do: stonewall it.

Today the Hour of Power was scheduled to begin around 5:00 p.m., which was three hours away.

Not that it mattered to Joe Metzger, if indeed that was his real name.

"Mr. Metzger, I'll do what I can for you, but I can't make any promises—certainly not of a 'cure' of any sort. Now let's check you out and see what's what."

Alan went through the routine of checking the range of motion in the spine, but then stopped. He was annoyed that this phony, for whatever reason, was taking up his time. He was also tired. And, to be frank with himself, he couldn't think of the next step in the routine low-back examination.

This was happening a lot lately. He wasn't sleeping well, and therefore he wasn't thinking well. This power, or whatever it was, had turned all his beliefs on their heads. It was blatantly impossible. It went against everything he had learned in life, in med school, and in a decade of practice. Yet it *worked*. There was no getting around the reality of that, so he had surrendered to it and accepted it.

"What would a cure cost me?" Metzger asked.

"If I could perform a 'cure,' it would be the same as an office visit: twenty-five dollars. But I can't: Your back's in better shape than mine."

Joe Metzger's eyes widened behind his granny glasses. "How can you say that? I have a—"

"What do you *really* want?" Alan said, deciding on a hardline approach. "I've got better things to do than waste my time with clowns looking for drugs for nonexistent problems." He jerked his thumb over his shoulder toward the door. "Take off."

As Alan reached for the doorknob, Joe Metzger reached into his pocket. "Dr. Bulmer—wait!" He pulled a card from his wallet and extended it toward Alan. "I'm a reporter."

Oh, God.

"I'm from *The Light*."

Alan looked at the card. A photo of Metzger's face looked back at him. His name really was Joe Metzger and he did indeed work for the infamous scandal sheet. "*The Light*? You mean you actually admit that?"

"It's not such a bad paper." He had retrieved his shirt from behind him and was putting it on.

"I've heard otherwise."

"Only from people with something to hide—dishonest politicians and celebrities who like the spotlight but don't like anyone to know what they did to get there. Have you ever read an issue, Doctor, or does your low opinion come secondhand?"

Alan shook his head. "Patients bring in copies all the time. They show me articles about DMSO, Laetril, curing psoriasis with B-12, preventing cancer with lettuce, or losing ten pounds a week eating chocolate cake."

"Looks like the tables are turned, Dr. Bulmer," Metzger said with his marionnette smile. "Lately your patients have been coming to *us* with stories about *you!*"

Alan had a sinking feeling inside. He had never imagined things getting this far out of hand so soon.

"And *what* stories!" Metzger continued. "Miracle cures! Instant healings! If you'll pardon the cliché: What's up, Doc?"

Alan kept his expression bland. "What's up? I haven't the faintest. Probably a few coincidences. Maybe some placebo effect."

"Then you deny that you've had anything to do with any of these cures your patients are talking about?"

"I think you've wasted enough of my time already today." Alan held the door open for the reporter. "If you can't remember the way out, I'll gladly show you."

Metzger's expression became grim as he hopped off the table and walked past Alan.

"You know, I came here figuring I'd find either a quack who'd jump at the chance for some publicity or a small-time charlatan ripping off gullible sick old ladies."

Alan put a hand on Metzger's back and gently propelled him toward the rear of the building.

"Instead, I find someone who denies any power and who was only going to charge me twenty-five bucks if he could cure me."

"Right," Alan said. "You found nothing."

Metzger turned at the back door and faced him. "Not quite. I found something I want to look into. If I can produce evidence of genuine cures, I may have found the real thing."

The sinking sensation deepened in Alan. "Aren't you worried about ruining that real thing if it exists?"

"If someone can do what I've heard, everyone should know about it. It should be spread around like a natural resource." He flashed that mechanical smile again. "Besides—it could be the story of the century."

Alan closed the door behind the reporter and sagged against it. This was bad.

He heard his phone ringing in his office and went to pick it up.

"Mr. DeMarco on ninety-two," Connie said.

He punched the button.

"Alan!" Tony said. "Still interested in Walter Erskine?"

"Who?"

"The bum in the ER you wanted me to check out."

"Oh, yeah. Right." Now he remembered. "Sure."

"Well, I know all about him. Want to hear?"

Alan glanced at his schedule. He wanted to run next door right now, but he had three more patients to see.

"Be over at five-thirty," he said.

At last!

__ 15. __
Ba

"What on earth did you feed that new peach tree, Ba?" the Missus said as she looked out the library window. "It's growing like crazy!"

The Missus had been quizzing him on the material for his Naturalization test. He had filed the forms. After they were reviewed, he would hear from an examiner if he qualified for citizenship. They were taking a break now.

The Missus was disturbed. Ba could tell. She was hiding her troubles with small talk.

Over the years Ba had come to recognize the signs—the way she held her shoulders high, the stiffness of her back, and her pacing. On those rare occasions when the Missus gave the slightest hint of a disturbed inner face, she always paced. And smoked. It was the only time she smoked. The afternoon sun was slanting through the high windows of the two-story library, illuminating the haze in the air from her cigarette, silhouetting her as she passed back and forth through the light, puffing on the cigarette while she slapped a folded newspaper against her thigh.

"Is there something Ba can do, Missus?"

"No . . . yes." She threw the newspaper onto the coffee table. "You can tell me why people spend money on garbage like this!"

Ba picked up the newspaper. *The Light.* He had seen it often at the supermarket checkout aisle. This issue was folded open to an article on a Long Island doctor named Alan Bulmer whose patients were claiming miracle cures at his hands.

Ba had seen the MIRACLE CURES ON LONG ISLAND banner on the front page yesterday and had bought the issue. He knew the Missus would eventually learn of it and would be disturbed. He had wanted to be ready to help her, so he had gone to the New York Public Library and found Arthur Keitzer's book, *The Sea Is in Us.* He had remembered the author passing through his village during the war, asking many questions. He remembered that the author had written down the song of the *Dat-tay-vao.* To Ba's immense relief, he found that Keitzer had included a translation in his book. Ba would not have trusted his own translation. He had photocopied the page and returned to Monroe.

"Do you know what's going to happen now?" the Missus was saying, still puffing and pacing. "Every kook from here to Kalamazoo will be knocking on his door, looking for a miracle! I can't *believe* someone's printing a story like this about him! I mean, if there was ever a more conservative, cautious, touch-all-bases kind of doctor, it's Alan. I don't get it! Where do they dig up this nonsense?"

"Perhaps it is true, Missus," Ba said.

The Missus whirled and stared up at him.

"Why on earth do you say that?"

"I saw."

"When? Where?"

"At the party."

"You must have been sampling too much of the champagne."

Ba did not flinch, although the words cut like a knife. But if the Missus wished to speak to him so, he would allow her. But only her.

The Missus stepped closer and touched his arm. "Sorry, Ba. That was as cruel as it was untrue. It's just that . . ." She tapped a finger against the paper he still held in his hand. "This infuriates me."

Ba said nothing more.

Finally the Missus sat on the sofa and indicated the chair across from her. "Sit and tell me what you saw."

Ba remained standing, speaking slowly as he reran the scene in his head.

"The man, Mr. Cunningham, was bleeding terrible. I saw when I turned him over for the Doctor." He spread his thumb and index finger two inches. "The wound was that long"—then reduced the span to half an inch—"and that wide. The Doctor put his hand over the wound and suddenly the bleeding stopped and the man woke up. When I looked again the wound was closed."

The Missus crushed out her cigarette and looked away for a long moment.

"You know I trust your word, Ba," she said without looking at him. "But I can't believe that. You must be mistaken."

"I have seen it before."

Her head snapped around. "What?"

"At home. When I was a boy, a man came to our village and stayed for a while. He could do what Dr. Bulmer can do. He could lay his hand on a sick baby or on a person with a growth or an old sore that wouldn't heal or an infected tooth and make them well. He had what we call *Dat-tay-vao* . . . the Touch." He handed her the photocopied sheet from the Keitzer book. "Here are the words to a song about the *Dat-tay-vao*."

The Missus took it and read out loud:

> *"It seeks but will not be sought.*
> *It finds but will not be found.*
> *It holds the one who would touch,*
> *Who would cut away pain and ill.*
> *But its blade cuts two ways*
> *And will not be turned.*
> *If you value your well-being,*
> *Impede not its way.*
> *Treat the Toucher doubly well,*

> *For he bears the weight*
> *Of the balance that must be struck."*

"It sounds much better in my village tongue," Ba told her.

"It sounds like a folktale, Ba."

"I had always thought so, too. Until I saw. And I saw it again at the party."

"I'm sorry, Ba. I just can't believe that something like that can happen."

"The article lists many of his patients who say it has."

"Yes, but . . ." A look of alarm crossed her face. "If it's true—God, they'll eat him alive!"

"I think there might be another danger, Missus." Ba was silent a moment as he pictured the face of the man with the *Dat-tay-vao* as he remembered it from some thirty years ago: the vacant eyes, the confusion, the haunted look about him. "I once spoke to a Buddhist priest about the man with the Touch. He told me that it is hard to tell whether a man possesses the *Dat-tay-vao,* or the *Dat-tay-vao* possesses the man."

The Missus stood up. Ba could tell by her expression that she still did not believe. But she was deeply concerned. "Would you be willing to tell Dr. Bulmer what you told me?"

"If you wish it, of course."

"Good."

She stepped over to the phone and punched in a number. "Yes. Is the doctor in? No, never mind. I'll call him tomorrow. Thank you."

She turned to Ba again. "He's left the office and I don't want to disturb him at home. We'll catch him tomorrow. He should know about this." She shook her head slowly. "I can't believe I'm buying this. I just don't see how it can be true."

Lost in thought, she walked slowly from the room.

It is true, Missus, Ba thought as he watched her leave. He knew beyond all doubt. For he had been touched by the *Dat-tay-vao* in his youth, and the awful growth that had stretched him so far above his fellow villagers was finally halted.

___ 16. ___
Alan

Ginny met him at the door as he returned from the office.

"Alan, what's going on?"

Her lips were slightly parted as they tended to be when she was annoyed, and she had taken her contacts out, leaving her eyes their natural blue. Tonight they were a very worried shade of blue.

"I don't know." It had been a long day and he was tired. A game of Twenty Questions didn't appeal to him. "You tell me."

She held up a newspaper. "Josie dropped this off."

Alan grabbed the paper and groaned when he saw the logo: *The Light.* Then he saw the banner across the top of the front page: MIRACLE CURES ON LONG ISLAND! (SEE PG. 3).

It was all there: five of his patients—Henrietta Westin, Lucy Burns, and others—all documenting their former chronic or incurable illnesses, now cured after a trip to Dr. Alan Bulmer. There was no malice in them. Quite the contrary. They sang Alan's praises. Anyone reading their comments would come away convinced he walked on water as well.

He looked up and found Ginny's gaze fixed on him.

"How did something like this get started?"

Alan shrugged, barely able to hear her. He was too shaken to think straight. "I don't know. People talk—"

"But they're talking about *miracles* here! Faith-healing stuff!"

Alan scanned through the article again. It was worse the second time through.

"That reporter says he spoke to you. He even quotes you. How can that be?"

"He came by the office, posing as a patient. I threw him out."

"How come you didn't tell me about it?"

"It didn't seem worth it," Alan said. Actually, he had forgotten to tell Ginny. Perhaps he had simply blotted it out of his mind. "I thought that would be the end of it."

"Did he quote you right?" She pulled the paper away and read from the article. " 'Probably a few coincidences. Maybe some placebo effect'?"

Alan nodded. "Yeah. I believe that's about what I said."

"That's all?" Her face was getting red. "How about something like 'Bullshit!'? Or 'You're nuts!' "

"Come on, Ginny. You know he'd never print that. It would ruin the story."

"Maybe so," she said. "But I can tell you one thing he *is* going to print, and that's a retraction!"

Alan felt a twinge of despair. "That would only magnify the problem and give the story more publicity, which is just what *The Light* would love. If we simply refuse to dignify the story with a reply, interest will slowly die out."

"And what are we supposed to do in the meantime? Nothing?"

"Easy, easy," Alan said, rising and moving toward her. She was working herself up into one of her rages. He went to put his arms around her but she pushed him away.

"No! I don't want to be known as the wife of the local witch doctor! I want this junk straightened out and fast! You just tell me why—!"

Her voice was reaching a screechy pitch that frazzled Alan's nerves.

"Ginny . . ."

"You just tell me why you can't call Tony and have him sue this rag for defamation of character or libel or whatever it's called and print a retraction!"

"Ginny . . ." Alan felt his own patience wearing thin.

"You just tell me!"

"Because it's true, goddamnit!"

Alan regretted the explosion immediately. He hadn't wanted to say that.

Ginny stepped back as if she had been slapped in the face. Her voice was tiny when she spoke.

"What?"

"It's true," Alan said. "I tried to tell you last month but I knew you wouldn't believe me."

Ginny reached a shaking hand behind her, found a chair, and sat down.

"Alan, you've got to be kidding!"

Alan sat on the sofa across from her. "At times, Ginny, I almost wish I were. But it's true. Those people aren't lying and they aren't crazy. They've really been cured. And I did it."

He saw her mouth form a question that found no voice. He asked it for her:

"How? I don't know." He didn't mention the incident with the derelict. This was all hard enough to believe without adding *that* and what Tony had recently told him about the man. "All I know is that at certain times of the day I can cure people of whatever ails them."

Ginny said nothing. Neither did Alan. Ginny watched her hands; Alan watched her.

Finally she spoke, falteringly.

"If it's true—and I really can't believe I'm sitting here talking about this—but if it's true, then you've got to stop."

Alan sat in stunned silence. He couldn't stop. Not permanently. He could cut back or hold off for a while, but he couldn't stop.

"It's *healing*, Ginny," he said, trying to catch her eyes. She wouldn't look at him. "I don't know how long I'll have this power. But while I have it, I've got to use it. It's what I'm about. How can I stop?"

Ginny finally looked up. There were tears in her eyes. "It will destroy everything we've worked for. Doesn't that mean anything to you?"

"Ginny, you've got to understand—"

She shot to her feet and turned away. "I see it doesn't."

Alan gently turned her around and pulled her to him. She clung to him as if she were about to fall. They stood there in silence, arms wrapped around each other.

"What's happened to us?" he finally asked.

"I don't know," Ginny said. "But I don't like the way things are going."

"Neither do I."

As they held the embrace, Alan thought, *This is the way it used to be. This used to be the simple answer to everything. I'd hold Ginny and she'd hold me, and it would be enough. Everything would be all right.*

"Let's not talk about this any more tonight," she said finally, and pulled away. "Let me sleep on it."

"We should talk this out, Ginny. It's important."

"I know it's important. But I can't handle it right now. It's too much. You're talking like someone who belongs in a mental hospital, and I'm tired and I want to go to bed."

As Alan watched her go up the stairs, he remembered that tomorrow was the twenty-seventh. His receptionist had reminded him that his office hours started late in the morning because of that. He always started late on May 27. Now was hardly the best time to ask, but maybe this year Ginny would come.

"Ginny? Would you come with me?"

She turned at the top of the stairs and looked at him questioningly.

"It's the twenty-seventh."

Her face suddenly went blank, devoid of any feeling. She shook her head silently and turned away.

He wandered around the first floor aimlessly for a while. He felt lost and very much alone. If only he could talk to someone about this! The pressure was building to explosive proportions inside him. If he didn't let it out soon, he'd *really* be crazy.

He went to the kitchen, made a cup of instant coffee, and brought it back to the living room. He stopped and stared in surprise when he saw another cup of coffee already there.

When had he made that?

Shaking his head, he dumped both in the kitchen sink. He returned to the living room and lay back in the recliner, thinking about the power.

How could something that seemed like such a miraculous boon become such a curse?

He closed his eyes and tried to sleep.

17.
Sylvia

"There he is now," Sylvia said as she spotted Alan's Eagle. She leaned forward and pointed past Ba's shoulder.

Ba nodded from the driver's seat. "I see him, Missus."

"We'll follow him to his office and catch him before he goes in."

Jeffy had been dropped off at the Stanton School and Sylvia was on her way to Alan's office, determined to speak to him before he saw his first patient.

She leaned back in the rear seat, wondering how she would broach the subject to Alan. Last night she almost had been able to accept what Ba had said about this healing touch, this *Dat-tay-vao,* as he called it. Now, with the sun flickering and slanting through the oaks along the road on a beautiful spring morning, it seemed preposterous. But she had decided to follow through with her decision to speak to Alan about it, and pass on Ba's warning. She owed him at least that much.

They were approaching the office now. But Alan didn't turn into the parking lot. She saw his car slow momentarily as it passed, then pick up speed again. There were two cars and a van in the parking lot, and one man sitting on the front steps.

"Do I follow him, Missus?" Ba said as he slowed the car.

Sylvia hesitated. He wasn't headed toward the hospital—that was in the other direction. "Yes. Let's see where he's going. Maybe we'll still get a chance to speak to him."

They didn't have far to go. He turned into Tall Oaks Cemetery. Ba stopped the car at the gate and waited.

Sylvia sat tense and quiet while invisible fingers of ice encircled her stomach and squeezed.

"Go on," she said at last.

Ba turned the Graham through the gate and followed the winding asphalt strip through the trees. They found Alan's car pulled to the side about a third of the way along the drive. Sylvia spotted him a few hundred feet off to the left, kneeling in the grass on a gentle rise.

She watched him a moment, puzzled. She didn't know much about his past, but she knew he was not from around here and had no family in the area. On impulse she got out of the car and walked toward him.

She knew Tall Oaks well. Too well. It was one of those modern cemeteries that didn't allow standing markers. All headstones had to be flat little slabs laid in the ground in neat rows to facilitate groundskeeping. Gone was the old-fashioned creepy cemetery with its mausoleums and cracked, tilted headstones. In its place was this open, grassy field ringed by trees.

As she came up behind Alan she saw that the ground around him was littered with colorful cardboard and clear plastic packaging, all torn to pieces. When she saw what he was doing, she stopped in shock.

He was lining up little *Star Wars* action figures along the edges of a headstone plaque. The three human leads were there, plus a variety of bizarre aliens, of which Jabba the Hutt was the only one she knew by name.

She moved closer to get a look at the inscription of the headstone:

THOMAS WARREN BULMER
Tommy, we hardly knew ye.

Her throat tightened. She took another step to see the dates at the bottom of the brass plaque. The date of birth was eight years ago today. She caught her breath involuntarily when she saw that the date of death was only three months later.

Oh, God! I didn't know!

Filled with guilt and embarrassment for intruding on him at a moment like this, she spun and began to hurry back down the rise.

"Don't go," he said.

Sylvia stopped, turned. He was still squatting, but he was looking up at her. His eyes were dry and he was smiling.

"Come say happy birthday to Tommy."

She went and stood at his side while he gathered up the toy packaging.

"I didn't know."

"No reason you should." He stood up and surveyed the toys he had displayed on the headstone. "How's it look?"

"Great." She didn't know what else to say.

"Well, it won't last long. One of the groundskeepers will rip them off for his kids. But that's okay. Better than having them ground up by the lawnmowers. At least somebody will be getting something out of them. Tommy would have loved *Star Wars,* you know. Especially Jabba the Hutt. Mean as he was, big fat Jabba would have made Tommy laugh."

"How did he—?" She caught herself. The question had filled her mind since the instant she had read the plaque, but she hadn't meant to ask.

Alan didn't seem to mind. "Tommy had a congenital heart defect: endocardial fibroelastosis. For the sake of simplicity, let's just say that his heart wasn't up to the job. We took him to the city. We had every specialist in Manhattan look at him. They tried everything they knew. But nobody could save him." His voice cracked. "And so he died. He was just learning to smile when he up and died on us."

He raised his free hand to his eyes as a sob racked him. Then another. He dropped the wrappings and covered his face with both hands.

Sylvia didn't know what to do. She had never seen a man cry before, and Alan's grief was so deep that she wanted to cry herself. She put an arm around his hunched shoulders. Touching him and feeling the tremors within him made his pain a physical thing. She wanted to say something comforting . . . but what could she say?

Alan suddenly regained control and wiped his face dry on his sleeves.

"Sorry," he said, looking away, obviously embarrassed. "I'm not a crybaby. I come here every May twenty-seventh, and I haven't cried for the last five or six times." He sniffed. "Don't know what's the matter with me today."

A thought struck Sylvia with the force of an explosion. "Is it because you think that maybe if he had been born this year, you could have saved him?"

Alan's eyes were wide as he turned toward her.

"Ba told me," she said.

"Ba?" It almost seemed as if he didn't recognize the name.

"You know—the big Vietnamese guy. He says he saw you do something at the party."

"The party," Alan said in a flat, vacant tone. "It seems so long ago." And then his eyes lit. "The party! That MTA guy's head! Yeah . . . Ba could have seen."

There was silence for a moment, then Alan took a deep, shuddering breath. "It's true, you know. I can . . . do things I would have laughed off as utterly impossible two months ago. I . . . I can cure just about anything when the time is right. *Anything*. But it doesn't do Tommy any good, does it? I mean, what goddamn good is it if I can't use it on Tommy, who was the most important little sick person in my life!"

Biting his lip, he turned and walked a few steps away, then returned.

"You know something?" he said, slightly more composed. "Before you came I was sitting there actually thinking of digging up the grave and seeing if I could bring him back."

With a quake of fear, Sylvia remembered the old story of *The Monkey's Paw*.

"Sometimes I think I'm going crazy," he said, shaking his head sharply.

Sylvia smiled and tried to lighten the mood. "Why should you be any different from the rest of us?"

Alan managed to return the smile. "Did you come here to see someone?"

Sylvia thought of Greg, whose marker was on the other side of the field. She had buried him close to home rather than in Arlington, but she had never returned to the site.

"Only you." He gave her a puzzled look. "Ba has some things to tell you."

He shrugged. "Let's go."

18.
Alan

"And you say this man simply touched you?"

Ba nodded in response to the question.

Alan sat with Sylvia in the back of the Graham; it was the first time he had been in the car, and he marveled at its plush interior. Ba sat up front, half-turned toward them. The car was still parked in the cemetery.

Ba had told them of his freakish growth as a teenager and how his mother feared he would grow too tall to live among others. When the man who had what Ba called the *Dat-tay-vao* came to his village, his mother had brought him forward for healing.

"What did you feel?" Alan asked. He could barely suppress his excitement. The folky-mythical aspects of Ba's tale were hokey, but they didn't matter. Here was proof! Eyewitness corroboration that such a power existed!

"I felt a pain deep in my head and almost fell to the ground. But after that I grew no taller."

"That backs up the Vietnam connection. It all fits!"

"What's the Vietnam connection?" Sylvia asked.

Alan decided it was best to start at the beginning, so he told her about the derelict, Walter Erskine, and the incident in the emergency room.

"The healings started shortly after that. I've always been sure that bum passed on the power to me—how and why, I don't know, but I had my lawyer, Tony DeMarco, look into Erskine's past. Tony found out he was a medic in Vietnam. Came home crazy. Thought he could heal people. Diagnosed as a paranoid schizophrenic by the V.A. Joined a faith-healing tent show in the South but got kicked off the tour because he wasn't healing anybody and was never sober."

"Alcohol puts the *Dat-tay-vao* to sleep," Ba said.

Alan wondered if that could be why Erskine became a drunk— to stifle the power. "Evidently he lived on the Bowery for years when for some reason he came out here to Monroe and found me, gave me some sort of electric shock, and died. Is that how the *Dat-tay-vao* is passed on?"

Ba said, "I'm sorry, Doctor, but I do not know. It is said that the Buddha himself brought the *Dat-tay-vao* to our land."

"But why *me,* Ba?" Alan desperately wanted to know the answer to that question.

"I cannot say, Doctor. But as the Song tells: 'It seeks the one who would touch, / Who would cut away pain and ill.' "

" 'Seeks'?" Alan was uneasy about the idea of being sought out by this power. He remembered the derelict's words: *You! You're the one!* "Why seek me?"

Ba spoke simply and with conviction. "You are a healer, Doctor. The *Dat-tay-vao* knows all healers."

Alan saw Sylvia shudder. "Do you still have that poem, Ba?" The driver handed her a folded sheet of paper and Sylvia passed it to Alan. "Here."

Alan read the poem. It was confusing and sounded more like a riddle than a song. He found one line particularly disturbing. He said, "I'm not too keen on this part about the balance. What's that mean?"

"I'm sorry, Doctor," Ba said. "I do not know. But I fear it might mean that there is a price to be paid."

"I don't like the sound of that!" Sylvia said.

"Neither do I," Alan said, his uneasiness growing. "But so far I've kept my health. And I haven't got any rotting portrait in the attic. So I think I'll just keep on doing what I've been doing—only a little more discreetly."

"A *lot* more discreetly, I hope," Sylvia said. "But just what *have* you been doing?"

Alan glanced at his watch. He still had a good hour and a half until his first patient showed up. And there was something very important he wanted to discuss with Sylvia.

"I'll tell you over breakfast."

Sylvia smiled. "Deal."

__ 19. __
Sylvia

Alan sat across from her, sipping his fourth cup of coffee, silent at last. They had left Ba so he could run some errands and Alan had driven her to this Glen Cove diner where he swore they made the best hashbrowns on the North Shore.

While polishing off scrambled eggs, bacon, a double helping of the famous hashbrowns, and a torrent of coffee in a rear booth, Alan had talked nonstop about what he had accomplished since the *Dat-tay-vao* had found him.

Sylvia listened in wonder and awe. If all this were really true . . . she thought about Jeffy for an instant, and then blocked the thought. If she let herself hope for a single minute. . . .

Besides, as much as she respected and admired Alan, she simply couldn't believe all the cures he described had really happened. This was the real world. *Her* world. Miracles didn't happen in her world.

"God, it's good to be able to talk to someone about this," he said as he hunched over his cup.

"Doesn't your wife . . . ?"

He shook his head. There was pain in his eyes. "She doesn't want to hear about it. She's frightened about the publicity."

"She should be. You both should be."

"I can handle it."

"And you should be concerned about what Ba told you about who is the master with the Touch."

"I can handle that, too. I'm going to cut back on when and how I use it. Don't worry. I can control it." He laughed. "I sound like a drunk, don't I?" He suddenly switched to an authentic Brooklyn accent. " 'Don't worry, Doc. I may put away a fifth now an' den, but I ain't no alcoholic, y'know? I can han'le it.' "

Sylvia laughed. "That's good. Where'd you pick that up?"

"From life. I grew up in Brooklyn. Mine was the token Wasp family between Jewish and Italian neighborhoods. We lived on . . ." His brow furrowed. "I don't know. The street name slips my mind. Doesn't matter. I think the only reason they tolerated us was because we were poorer than they were."

They sat in silence a moment, then he said:

"Ginny and I have had our problems since Tommy died. She changed. Maybe it would have been different if he'd been stillborn or had died in the first couple of days. But he held on." She saw a wavering smile pull up the corners of Alan's mouth. "God, what a little fighter he was! He wouldn't give up. He shouldn't have lasted as long as he did. And that was the real problem, I guess. A priest told us it was better to have had him for a little while and lose him, than not to have had him at all. I don't know about that. You can't ache like this for what you've never known." His hands gathered into fists. "If only Tommy hadn't become a real person to us, a little guy who could grab your finger and smile, and even giggle if you tickled him in the right spot. But to have him and love him and hope for him for those three months—eighty-eight days, to be exact— and then to lose him, to see the life drain from his face and the light in his eyes go out. That was cruel. Ginny didn't deserve that. Something inside her died right along with Tommy, and nothing has been the same since. She . . ."

Alan let the word dangle as he leaned back in the booth. Sylvia hung on, waiting for him to continue, dying to know what went on in his marriage.

"I shouldn't be talking about her," he finally said. "But the fact remains, I can't talk to Ginny about this . . . this *thing* I have. I can't talk to any other doctor about it, because I know they'll all want me to see a certain kind of specialist—stat."

"A shrink."

"Right. So excuse me for running off at the mouth, but this has been dammed up for too damn long."

"Glad to be of service."

His gaze burned into her. "Do you believe me?"

Sylvia hesitated, taken aback by the directness of the question. "I don't know. I believe in *you* as a person, but what you've told me is so . . . so . . . "

"Yeah, I know what you mean. Took me a while before I could accept it myself, even with the cures happening right before my eyes. But now that I have, and I've learned how to use it, it's just . . ." He spread his hands. "It's wonderful!"

Sylvia watched his face, feeling the glow of his enthusiasm.

"I can't tell you what it means to actually be able to *do* something! Most of medicine is just buying time, staving off the inevitable. But now I can make a real difference!"

"You always have," Sylvia told him. "You shouldn't sell yourself short."

"Why not? I was like a guy trying to swim the Channel with both arms tied behind his back. God! There was so much I could have done! So many lives . . ."

His eyes got a faraway look, as if he had wandered into a private world and couldn't find his way back right away. Which was fine with Sylvia. It made her angry to hear him put down his pre-Touch self.

"You *always* had something special!" she told him as his eyes focused again. "You had compassion and empathy. I still remember the second or third time I saw you with Jeffy and told you how you were the only doctor who made me feel I wasn't imposing by asking a few questions."

"Good. Then let me ask *you* a question."

"Okay." The intensity of his gaze made her uncomfortable. "What?"

"Jeffy."

Her stomach twisted. She sensed what was coming. "What about him?"

"I've been thinking about him ever since I found I really had this power, this Touch, or whatever it's called. But I didn't know how to approach you. And you haven't brought him in since he had that abdominal pain and, I mean, I couldn't exactly come knocking on your door." He seemed to be fumbling for words. He took a deep breath. "Look: I want to try the Touch on Jeffy."

"No!" Sylvia said automatically. "Absolutely not!"

Alan blinked. "Why not?"

She didn't know why, exactly. She had refused reflexively. The thought of placing Jeffy at the mercy of some power she couldn't quite believe in frightened her. It was too mystical, too scary. But it went deeper than mere fright. A nameless dread, baseless and formless, had risen within her as Alan was speaking. She didn't understand it, but knew she was helpless before it. Who knew what the *Dat-tay-vao* might do to Jeffy? Bad enough if she got her hopes up and it didn't work. But what if it backfired somehow and made him worse? She couldn't risk anything happening to Jeffy.

"I-I-I don't know." The words tumbled out. "Not yet. Not now. I mean, you said yourself you don't know how it works, or exactly when it will work. There's too many unknowns here. And besides, all the cures you've told me about have been for physical ills. Jeffy's problem isn't purely physical."

Alan was watching her closely, searching her face. Finally he nodded.

"Maybe you're right. Maybe we should wait. It's up to you. Just remember: I'm at Jeffy's service anytime you say."

"Thank you, Alan," she said, feeling the dread and near panic recede.

He glanced at his watch. "Getting late. I'll get Ba to drive you back."

Sylvia felt a nudge of concern. Alan seemed to be forgetting a lot. She had always been struck by the keenness of his memory in the past.

She shrugged it off and laughed as she reminded him that Ba was gone and that Alan was supposed to drive her back. With the strain he must be under—between grappling with this miraculous power and now with the press—it was a wonder he could concentrate on anything.

"And thank you for thinking of Jeffy."

"Oh, I think of him a lot. Tommy would be just Jeffy's age if he had lived."

__ 20. __
Alan

Alan drove toward his office in an almost lighthearted mood. He had finally found someone with whom to discuss the Hour of Power. It was like having a great weight eased from his shoulders; there was someone to share it with now.

Too bad it wasn't Ginny. He truly enjoyed talking to Sylvia. Enjoyed it too much, perhaps. He had revealed more of himself than he had wished today. Perhaps the fact that she had seen him crying had opened the door. He had always preferred to leave his feelings for Sylvia unexplored, but he could see the day approaching when he would have to confront them. An intimacy was growing between them, almost in direct proportion to the lengthening distance between Ginny and him. He wished it weren't so, but there was no use denying the obvious.

He knew when it had started. He had almost blurted it out to Sylvia today but had caught himself. It was a private thing, between husband and wife, and he wouldn't have felt right talking about Ginny behind her back like that.

Saying that something in Ginny had died with Tommy had been

true enough. But it was only part of the story. There was the guilt and the self-flagellation that had poisoned a part of her forever.

Ginny had smoked during the pregnancy. Only an occasional cigarette—she had been a pack-and-a-half-a-day smoker for years, but had ostensibly stopped when she had become pregnant. Ostensibly. When the house was empty she would sneak a smoke. Only one or two a day, and heavily filtered.

Tommy's cardiac defect had had nothing to do with her smoking. Nicotine had ill effects on the fetus, but this type of heart problem was completely unrelated to smoking. The pediatricians and cardiologists had assured her of that, her obstetrician had reinforced it, and Alan had repeated it like a litany.

It didn't matter to Ginny. She had decided that she was responsible and no one could convince her otherwise. Over the years, she had slowly poisoned herself with guilt and self-loathing. She locked a part of herself away forever and refused to even consider the thought of another pregnancy. She had decided that she wasn't fit to raise a child and that was that. She had walled off the memory of Tommy, too. She never mentioned him, never visited the grave site. It was as if he had never existed.

Alan sighed as he drove. He almost wished he could do the same. Maybe it would ease the pain of the wound that never seemed to heal; the wound that tore open every May 27.

*   *   *

The parking lot was jammed. So was the front entrance. Alan didn't recognize any of the faces. And the way all those strange people stared at him as he drove by on his way to the rear of the building made him glad he had given up his M.D. plates years ago. Having his car broken into and ransacked twice had been enough to convince him that the few prerogatives granted the M.D. plates were not worth the hassle of drug-hungry junkies popping the lock on his trunk.

His nurse, Denise, met him at the back door.

"Thank God you're here!" she said, red-faced and breathless. "The waiting room's filled with new patients! I don't know what to do! They all want to be seen today—now!"

"Didn't they see the sign? 'Patients Seen by Appointment Only'?"

"I don't see how they could miss it. But they've all seen that newspaper, *The Light*. Most of them have a copy with them, and they ask if you're the Dr. Bulmer in the article, and even when I say, 'I don't know,' they say they've got to see you—*got* to see you and they plead and beg with me to give them an appointment. I don't know what to tell them. Some of them are dirty and smelly and they're crowding out our regular patients."

Alan cursed *The Light* and he cursed Joe Metzger, but most of all he cursed himself for letting things get to this point. He should have known, should have foreseen . . .

But what to do now? This was an impossible situation, yet he shied from the unpleasant decision it called for.

He should say no to these people. They had come to him expecting to be healed, and anything less would disappoint them. To agree to see them and then withhold the power would be unconscionable.

The trouble was, they were looking for miracles. And if he supplied them, they would talk. God, how they would talk! And then the *National Enquirer* and the *Star* and all the rest would be knocking on his door. Followed soon by *Time* and *Newsweek*.

To protect himself and his ability to practice any sort of medicine, he would have to lie low for a while. With nothing new to fuel it, the controversy would die down and eventually be forgotten. Then he could start using the power again.

Until then he would be just another G.P. Good ol' Doc Bulmer.

He had no choice. He was backed into a corner and could see no way out.

"Tell them I'm not taking any new patients," he told Denise.

The nurse rolled her eyes skyward. "Thank God!"

"Why do you say that?"

"Well," she said, suddenly hesitant and uncomfortable, "you know how you are about turning people away."

"This is different. This is chaos. I won't be able to see *any*body with that mob outside. They've got to go."

"Good. I'll tell Connie and we'll shoo them out."

Alan headed for his office as Denise bustled toward the front. As he flipped through some of the morning mail, he heard Connie's voice rise to make the announcement. She was answered by a rising babble of voices, some angry, some dismayed. And then he heard Denise shouting.

"Sir! Sir! You can't go back there!"

A strange voice answered: "The hell I can't! My wife's sick and she needs him and I'm gonna get him!"

Alarmed at the commotion, Alan stepped out into the hall. He saw a thin, balding, weathered-looking man in an equally weathered-looking double-knit leisure suit striding down the hall toward him.

"Just where do you think you're going?" Alan said in a low voice, feeling anger boil up in him.

That anger must have shown in his face, for the man came to an abrupt halt.

"Are you Dr. Bulmer? The one in the paper?"

Alan jammed a finger into the man's chest. "I asked you where you're going?"

"To . . . to see the doctor."

"No, you're not! You're leaving! Now!"

"Now wait. My wife—"

"Out! All of you!"

"Hey!" someone yelled. "You can't kick us out!"

"Oh no? Just watch! Connie!" His receptionist's worried face appeared around the corner behind the crowd. "Call the police. Tell them we have trespassers in the building interfering with patient care."

"But *we* need care!" said a voice.

"And what's that mean? That you own me? That you can come in here and take over my office? No way! I decide whom I treat and when. And I don't choose to treat any of you. Now get out, all of you. *Out!*"

Alan turned his back on them and returned to his office. He threw himself into the chair behind the desk and sat there, watching his trembling hands. His adrenaline was flowing. His anger was genuine and had been effective in confronting the crowd.

His heart finally slowed from its racing tempo; his hands were steady again. He stood up and went to the window.

The strangers were leaving. In singles and pairs—walking, limping, in wheelchairs—they were returning to their cars. Some were scowling and muttering angrily, but for the most part their faces were withdrawn, vainly trying to hide the crushing disappointment of one more lost hope.

Alan turned away so he would not have to see. They had no right to take over his office, and he had every right to send them packing. It was a matter of self-preservation.

Then why did he feel so rotten?

People shouldn't have to feel that way. There was always hope. Wasn't there?

Their forlorn expressions hammered at him as he sat there, assaulting him, battering his defenses until he felt them crumble. He flung open his office door and strode up the hall. He couldn't let them go away like that, not when he had the power to help them.

I'm going to regret this.

He hated stupidity. And he had decided to do something very stupid. He was going to go out into the parking lot and tell those people that if they went home and called up and said they had been here this morning, his receptionist would make appointments for them.

I can do it, he told himself.

If he was scrupulously careful to swear each of them to secrecy, maybe he could make it work without screwing himself.

It would be like walking a tightrope.

How good was his balance?

JUNE

21.
Alan

"I knew it would come to this!" Ginny said from behind the morning paper at the breakfast table.

"Come to what?" Alan said. He was pouring himself a second cup of coffee at the counter.

"As if things weren't bad enough already—now this!" She pushed the paper across the table onto his place mat.

It was the local weekly, the Monroe *Express*. She had it folded open to the editorial page. Alan's gaze was immediately drawn to the headline in the upper left corner:

THE SHAME OF SHAMANISM

"Cute," Alan said.

"You won't think so after you've read it." Ginny's voice had taken on the belligerent tone that had become too familiar during the past few weeks.

Alan glanced down the column. It took up half the editorial page. He spotted his name. Uneasy now, he began reading.

Most of the first half was a rehash of the notoriety that had surrounded him for the past few weeks; then it became more pointed. It spoke of the fund-raising drive for Monroe Community Hospital's new expansion program, of how extra beds were desperately needed in the area, of how the hospital had to keep a dozen or so patients on cots in the hallways at all times because of the chronic need for new beds.

The closing paragraphs chilled Alan:

> And so we wonder here at the *Express* what the Board of Trustees of Monroe Community Hospital will do. Will they wait until a single staff member's unsavory notoriety undermines the institution's credibility as a health care facility, thereby jeopardizing its certificate of need applications? Or will they take the reins of leadership in their teeth and confront Dr. Bulmer on this matter?
>
> Granted, Dr. Bulmer is not solely to blame for the brouhaha that surrounds him, but the fact remains that he has done nothing to stem the rising tide of speculation and hysteria. Under normal circumstances we would respect his right to decline comment on the wild stories about him. But when that silence acts only to feed the fire, a fire which threatens the expansion of a facility so vital to the health care of our community, then we must demand that he speak out and refute these sensational tales. And if he will not, then we see it as the duty of the Board of Trustees to reconsider his position on the staff of Monroe Community Hospital.

"They've got to be kidding!" Alan said, a knot of disquiet tightening in his stomach. "They're identifying me with the hospital. That's ridiculous! I could see it if I was a board member but I'm—"

"You're a doctor on the staff!" Ginny said. "If you look like a kook, then they look like kooks for keeping you on. Simple as that."

"Why can't they just leave it alone?" Alan said, more to himself than to Ginny.

"Why can't *you?* That's the question! Why can't you give an interview or something and say it's all a crock?"

"I can't do that." He didn't tell her that *People* Magazine had called three times last week for just that purpose and he had turned them down flat. Or had it been this week? Time seemed so jumbled lately.

"In God's name, why not?"

"Because I told you—it's *not* a crock!"

"I don't want to hear that, Alan. I don't want to hear that kind of talk from you."

Alan knew she had shut her mind to the possibility that it might be true.

"All right, then: Let me ask you a hypothetical question."

"I'm not interested in hypo—"

"Just hear me out. Let's just say for the sake of argument that I can heal people."

"I don't want to hear this, Alan!"

"Ginny—!"

"You need help, Alan!"

"Just play along with me. What should I do? Deny it?"

"Of course."

"Even if it's true?"

"Sure."

"And continue using it in secret?"

"No!" She rolled her eyes in exasperation. "You couldn't hide something like that! You'd just have to forget about any weird power and go back to regular medicine. Don't you see how you're becoming some kind of leper around here?"

"No."

"Of course you don't! You're walking around like you're on drugs lately. But *I* do! So put a stop to this once and for all. Tell everybody it's all bull. Please!"

Was she right? He had hoped it would all die down, but it hadn't. He realized now that as long as he used the *Dat-tay-vao* and cured more and more of the incurables, it would never die down. It would only get worse.

"Maybe you're right. Maybe I should put a stop to this once and for all."

Ginny smiled. The first genuine smile he had seen on her face in weeks. "Great! When?"

"Soon. Real soon."

*   *   *

"Dr. Bulmer!"

He heard Connie hurrying down the hall. She burst into his office and shoved a magazine under his nose.

"Look!"

It was the waiting-room copy of the latest issue of *People*. Connie had it opened to an article titled "The Miracles in Monroe." There were photos and case histories of a number of his patients. At the end of the article was a grainy, long-range shot of him exiting the private door to his office building.

The caption read: "The secretive Dr. Bulmer who has refused all comment."

"Wonderful!" he said, feeling sick. This capped it. Things couldn't possibly get any worse.

*   *   *

Connie brought him the registered letter two days later.

The return address was for Monroe Community Hospital. The letter said that he was "invited" before the Board of Trustees "to explain and clarify the rumors and sensational stories" concerning him that were coming to have "a deleterious effect on the hospital's reputation." They expected him on Friday—three days from now.

Here it comes, he thought. He had realized all along in some corner of his mind that sooner or later he was going to run afoul of the medical establishment. Not so much the individual practitioners themselves, but the administrative types who lived off disease and trauma without ever treating or coming near a patient.

"Start canceling all my appointments for the rest of the week. And see if Mr. DeMarco is in his office next door. Tell him I have to speak to him right away."

A moment later she called him back. "Mr. DeMarco is in court and will not be back until this afternoon. He'll call you then. And there's a Mrs. Toad on the phone. She said she must speak to you immediately."

22.
Sylvia

"I think you've got trouble."

"So what else is new?"

Alan smiled at her from across the table. It was a weak smile, but it seemed genuine. He looked more worn and haggard than the last time she had seen him, when they had sat at this same table after meeting in the cemetery. She had been shocked that the board would even think of calling Alan on the carpet, and had rushed to lend him whatever support she could.

"I just got word about this hearing of yours before the Board of Trustees."

"Bad news travels fast."

"Not as fast as you might think. I'm a big contributor to the building fund over there and I hear things sooner than most. So I made some calls and . . ." She didn't want to say this, but he had to be told. He had to be ready.

"And?"

"It doesn't look good."

He shrugged.

"Don't take this lightly, Alan. The four board members I spoke to are really upset with that editorial in the *Express* and are taking its implications very seriously. They're beginning to see you as a real threat to the hospital's expansion bid."

"Who'd you speak to?"

"My father-in-law, naturally. He sells the hospital all its insurance—an expanded hospital means expanded premiums for him. Two others made me promise not to mention their names to anyone, but I can tell you that one runs the bank where I keep my accounts and the other brokers some real estate for me now and then."

She waited for the light of recognition in Alan's eyes and a conspiratorial smile that would reflect her own. Neither came.

"I'm sorry . . ." he said with a baffled shake of his head. "I don't . . ."

How could he forget the board members? Was it possible to be on the staff of the hospital all these years and not know the names on the Board of Trustees?

"Never mind," she said quickly to cover his obvious embarrassment. "Their names aren't important. It's what they think that counts, and they think you're a liability."

"You're making my day," he said with a wry twist of his mouth. "Who was the fourth?"

"My uncle, naturally—your esteemed ex-partner."

"I'm sure he'll give a stirring speech in my defense."

"Right—when water flows uphill. So you can see why I'm worried. That's four out of ten. I don't know the others but I doubt they feel any different."

Alan leaned back and mused in silence. She watched his troubled face, sharing his anguish.

"You don't deserve this," she said. "You haven't hurt anybody. You've—"

"Maybe I should just resign from the staff," he said as if he hadn't heard her. "I hardly use the hospital nowadays anyway."

"I'm sure they'd love that. It would save them a lot of trouble if you made the decision for them."

"I'll tell you quite frankly, Sylvia: The thought of standing before that board scares the hell out of me. I don't want to have to explain myself to them or anyone else."

"But if you don't show, that will give them more ammunition against you."

"Well, I don't want to make it easy for them, and I don't want to put another bullet in their gun," Alan said, straightening up. "So that leaves me with showing up and toughing it out."

"I guess so." *But you're going to get hurt,* she thought with a tightening in her chest.

"They're not going to shut me off," he said with sudden determination.

He gave her a tight smile and she smiled back with her lips only. She knew he was putting on a show for her, but she saw through it. He was afraid.

And he should be.

23.
Alan

Alan swerved in toward the curb when he saw Tony standing there, waving.

"What are you doing here?" he asked as Tony got in. "We were supposed to meet at the office."

"You can't get into the goddamn parking lot," he said, lighting a cigarette as soon as he settled himself in the seat. "It's loaded with cripples."

"Handicapped," Alan said.

"You speak Newspeak, I'll speak Oldspeak. Whatever they are, they've taken over the whole fucking lot. I figured there'd be a mob scene if you showed up so I walked up a couple of blocks to head you off at the pass."

He dragged on his cigarette, rolled his window down two inches, and let the smoke flow through the opening.

"I spoke to some of them, you know. Most of them are here because of that article in *People*. Like they've been to Lourdes and the Vatican and Bethlehem already, looking to be cured of something. But others know somebody who's already seen you and been cured of something incurable."

They passed the office then. Alan was startled at the congestion of cars and vans and people that filled the lot and overflowed onto the street and lined the curbs. He hadn't been to the office in days. He hadn't realized . . .

Guilt filled him. He hadn't used the Touch in days. He had wasted hours of power.

"And so now they're all here—looking for you. It's taken me a couple of days, Al, but I got to tell you, I'm a believer. You've got *something.*"

Alan feigned a wounded expression. "You mean you doubted me?"

"Shit, yes! You threw me some real curves there. I thought that maybe you needed a checkup from the neck up, if you know what I mean."

Alan smiled. "So did I at first. But then I realized that if I was having delusions, an awful lot of formerly sick people were sharing them."

When he had called Tony for help, he had told him the truth about the *Dat-tay-vao*. He had felt it necessary to lay everything out for the man who would be advising him at the hearing. He had told him about the incident in the emergency room, about how his new power dovetailed with the life history of the derelict Tony had researched.

Tony had been skeptical, but not overtly so. Alan was glad that he seemed to be convinced now.

"No lie, Al: It's still pretty hard for me to swallow, even after talking to the pilgrims on your doorstep. But the one thing we can't do is tell the Board Bastards that you really have this power."

At the mention of the board, Alan's palms became slippery on the wheel and his stomach went into spasm. In fifteen minutes or so he'd be seated before the board like some juvenile miscreant. He hated the idea. It angered him, but it frightened him even more.

"Why not bring it out in the open once and for all?" Alan asked. "Get it over with."

"*No!*" Tony fumbled his cigarette, dropped it on the floor of the car, and hastily retrieved it. "Christ, don't even consider it! That'll open up a can of worms I don't even want to *think* about dealing with!"

"But sooner or later—"

"Al, old buddy, trust me with this. I've looked over the medical staff bylaws and there's nothing in there that threatens you. You don't even have to show up today—and I've advised you not to but you choose to ignore that advice. So be it. But the fact remains: They can't touch you. Let them play their little head games on you all they want. Just sit back and relax. If you haven't been convicted of a felony or found guilty of moral turpitude or gross negligence of your duties as an attending physician in the department of medicine, they can't lay a finger on you. They're just blowin' smoke, man. Let 'em blow."

"If you say so, Tony. I just—"

"Just nothing, Al. You don't take nothin' from these moneylenders, real estate shills, and used car salesmen. You just sit mum and look clean and neat while I do the dirty work."

Alan could see that Tony was working up a head of steam in preparation for the meeting. He let him roll.

"If those turkeys think they can hang you because of a little yellow journalism, they got another think comin'! Let 'em try. Just let 'em try!"

Alan felt his fear and uneasiness slip away in the wash of Tony's belligerent confidence.

*   *   *

"Now, gentlemen," Tony was saying, "I'm sure you're all aware of how embarrassing this is to Dr. Bulmer, to be called before the Board of Trustees like some errant schoolboy before the principal because of some graffiti written about him on the schoolyard wall."

Alan sat in wonder and watched Tony pacing back and forth before the board members. He was eloquent, respectful, and deferential, yet never obsequious. He made it seem as though Alan had granted them an audience out of the goodness of his heart.

There they sat, the twelve of them—ten trustees plus Alan and Tony—seated around the oblong table in this small rectangular meeting room on the hospital's first floor. A coffee urn was set up in the corner, its red light beckoning; maritime paintings by local artists depicting the North Shore broke the muted beige of the walls. All were at the same table, yet unquestionably separated into two groups: Alan and Tony were down at their end, the members of the board—two physicians and eight local businessmen who devoted their spare time to "community service"—clustered around theirs. He knew both physicians well—Lou, of course, was his former partner, and old Bud Reardon had practically run the surgery department single-handedly in the hospital's early days. Bud was showing his years, lately. Alan had noticed him limping as he came in.

Alan really didn't know the others as individuals. He didn't do business with them, didn't get involved in hospital politics, and although he belonged to the same club as most of them, he didn't spend enough time there to have more than a nodding acquaintance with them.

While none of them actually stared, they all looked at him and glanced away as if he were a stranger, as if they were trying to put some mental distance between themselves and the doctor they might have to discipline. But they didn't frighten him now. Tony was right. He had broken no laws, either civil or criminal, had done nothing that would put him outside the bylaws. They couldn't touch him. He was safe.

"What I would like to know, Mr. DeMarco," the car dealer said, interrupting Tony, "is why Dr. Bulmer thinks he needs a lawyer here today? This isn't a trial, you know."

"Precisely. I am aware of that, and so is Dr. Bulmer. And I am heartened to hear that *you* are aware of that, sir. In fact, I had to talk Dr. Bulmer into allowing me to speak for him today. He didn't want me here, but I insisted on coming to make sure that none of you tries to turn this little informal gathering *into* a trial."

The white-haired Dr. Reardon cleared his throat. "All we want is to discuss the rather peculiar publicity Dr. Bulmer's gotten lately and ask him how it started, why it keeps on going, and how come he's done nothing to discourage it."

"Dr. Bulmer is under no obligation to respond. The 'peculiar publicity' you mention is nothing of a criminal nature. He can't be expected to hold a press conference every time some—"

"I would prefer to hear Dr. Bulmer's reply from Dr. Bulmer himself," the banker said.

The other board members nodded and murmured in agreement. Tony turned to Alan.

He said, "It's up to you."

Alan felt his heart pick up its tempo as he let his eyes scan the faces of the board members. "What would you like to know?"

Lou spoke up immediately. His words were clipped, his tone frankly irritated.

"Why in God's name haven't you done or said anything to squelch the ridiculous stories about these miracle cures you supposedly perform?"

Alan opened his mouth and then closed it. He had been about to give his usual reply about not dignifying the stories by taking the trouble to deny them, then changed his mind. Why not get it out in the open? He was tired of the half-truths, the surreptitious cures, the constant tension. Why not put an end to all that and come clean? He pushed himself to speak quickly before he had a chance to change his mind.

"I haven't made any denials because the stories are true."

There—I've said it.

A dead hush fell over the room, broken only briefly by Tony's muttered, "Christ on a crutch!"

"Let me get this straight, Alan," Lou said with an incredulous, half-amused, tell-me-I'm-wrong smile on his face. "Do you mean to say that you can actually cure incurable illnesses with a touch?"

"I know it sounds nuts," Alan said with a nod, "but yes—it's been happening for . . ." How long had it been? He couldn't remember when it had begun. "For months."

The board members exchanged worried glances. As they began to bend their heads together to confer, Bud Reardon said:

"Alan, do you realize what you're saying?"

"Believe me, I do. And if I were in your shoes, I know I'd be looking at me just the way you are."

Alan's statement seemed to have a disarming effect on the board, but only for a moment. The consternation on their faces remained, and they all seemed to be urging an opinion from the two medical members. Alan looked over at Tony and found him glaring his way in frustration. The lawyer made a punching motion with his fist. He wasn't encouraging Alan—he was angry.

Finally there was silence. Lou spoke. "We simply can't accept what you've said, Alan. You've put us in a dreadful position with this. We thought maybe you were simply ignoring the wild stories in the hope they would go away; some of us even thought you might be letting the stories continue because of the tremendous boost the publicity gave your practice. But none of us ever even considered the possibility that you would stoop to propagate such nonsense—"

"Now just a minute!" Tony said, leaping to his feet. "Just a goddamn minute! Nobody's going to call this man a liar while I'm around. This isn't a court and I don't have to be constrained by court decorum. Anybody who calls him a liar will answer to me!"

"Now, now," said the car dealer. "There's no call for that sort of—"

"Bullshit, there ain't! When this man tells you something is so, it's *so!*"

Bud Reardon cleared his throat again. "I would tend to agree, Mr. DeMarco. I've know Dr. Bulmer since he first came to this community—interviewed him when he applied here to the staff, in fact. And having observed him over the years, I can say that his level of care and sense of medical ethics are beyond reproach. Which leaves us with a critical and most uncomfortable question: What if Dr. Bulmer is indeed telling the truth, *but only as he sees it?"*

There were puzzled expressions all around Dr. Reardon, but Alan knew exactly where he was going.

"He means," Alan said to the group, "that although I may be telling the truth, I might be having delusions which lead me to honestly believe that I can cure with a touch, even though I can't."

Reardon nodded. "Exactly. Which would classify you as a psychotic."

"I can show you documentation if you—"

"I was thinking of something a little more immediate and concrete," Reardon said. He pushed back his seat, pulled off his left loafer and sock, and placed his bare foot on the table. "This has been killing me since about three a.m."

Alan saw the angry, reddened, slightly swollen area at the base of his great toe. Gout. No doubt about it.

Bud Reardon looked him in the eye. "Let's see what you can do about this."

Alan froze. He hadn't expected this. Not now. He had been certain he would be called upon eventually to prove his fantastic claim, but he had never dreamed it would be here in the conference room.

The Hour of Power—when was it scheduled to begin today? He had been out of the office for a few days so he had lost track. Damn! If only he could remember! He made some rapid calculations. Monday it had been . . . when? Late afternoon, about 4:00. His mind raced through a series of calculations. He would have to depend solely on those calculations, because he felt nothing when the Hour of Power was upon him.

If his calculations were correct, he could count on about thirty minutes of the Touch right now.

But were his calculations correct? It all depended on Monday's Hour of Power occurring at 4:00 p.m. Had it? Had it really? His memory had been so haphazard lately, he didn't know if he could trust it on this. He strained to remember. Yes. On Monday he remembered using the Touch on his last patient. That had been late afternoon. Right. It had been 4:00 p.m., he was sure of it.

Tony's low voice stirred him back to the here-and-now.

"You don't have to do this, Al. You can tell them you don't put on exhibitions and you'd prefer—"

"It's all right, Tony," he told his worried-looking friend. "I can handle this."

Alan stood up and approached the board's end of the table. The silent members swiveled in their seats as he passed behind them, as if afraid to take their eyes off him for a fraction of a second. Lou Albert's jaw hung slack and open as he watched from the far side of the table. Bud Reardon's smile became hesitant as Alan approached. He was clearly astonished that Alan had accepted his challenge.

Alan paused before the spot where Reardon's foot rested on the table. He was taking a terrible risk here. If his calculations were off by a single hour, he would be branded a quack or worse by these men. But it was *going* to work, he was sure of it. And that would wipe the frank disbelief off these smug faces in the blink of an eye.

He reached forward and touched the toe, wanting to heal it, *praying* that it would be healed.

Nothing happened.

With his blood congealing in his veins, he held on, although he knew in his very core that he was going to fail. The Touch never delayed; if it was working, it worked right away or not at all. Still, he hung on and gripped the angry-looking joint with increasing pressure until Bud Reardon winced in pain and pulled his foot away.

"You're supposed to make it better, Alan, not make it hurt worse!"

Alan was speechless. He had been wrong! His calculations had been off! Damn his sieve of a memory! He could feel their eyes boring into him. He could hear their thoughts—*Charlatan! Phony! Liar! Madman!* He wanted to crawl under the table and not come out.

Dr. Reardon cleared his throat once more. "Assuming we were in your office and you tried what you just tried with similar results, what would be your next move?"

Alan opened his mouth to speak and then closed it. He had prescribed the medication thousands of times, yet its name crouched over the far edge of his memory, just beyond his reach. He felt like a castaway on a desert isle watching the smoke from the stacks of a passing ship that was just over the horizon.

Reardon mistook Alan's hesitation for uncertainty about what was being asked of him and tried to clarify.

"What I'm saying is, what tests would you order now? What medication?"

Alan's mind was completely blank. He stabbed at an answer. "An X ray and a blood test."

"Oh, I hardly think an X ray would be necessary," Reardon said in a jovial tone, but his smile quickly faded as he stared at Alan. " 'Blood test' is a little vague, don't you think? What, specifically, would you order?"

Alan racked his brain. God, if he could only *think!* He played for time.

"A profile. You know—a SMAC-20."

Alan saw the concern and suspicion growing in Reardon's face. It was reflected in the other faces around him.

"Not very specific, Alan. Look. I know this is very elementary, but for the record, tell me the etiology of gout."

Tony jumped in then. "First of all, there *is* no record. And secondly, Dr. Bulmer is not here to be examined on gout or whatever's wrong with Dr. Reardon's foot!"

"It was not intended as such," Reardon said, "but we seem to be faced with an incredible situation here. I've asked Dr. Bulmer a question any first-year medical student could answer, and I'm still waiting for a reply."

Alan felt the room constrict around him as he sank into a fog of humiliation. Why couldn't he think? What was wrong with him?

"Well, don't hold your breath!" Tony said as Alan felt himself grabbed by the arm and pulled toward the door. "Dr. Bulmer didn't have to come here and he sure as hell doesn't have to stay here!"

Alan allowed himself to be led to the door. He heard Reardon's voice behind him.

"It would be better if he stayed. From what I've seen this morning, Dr. Bulmer appears mentally impaired and the board will have to take appropriate action."

And then they were out in the hall and heading for the parking lot.

*   *   *

"Shit, Alan! Shit, shit, *shit!*"
That was all Tony had said since they had reached the car.

"And the worst part of this whole thing is that you didn't even have to *be* there! Christ! What happened in there!"

Alan shook his head as he drove. He felt absolutely miserable, and Tony wasn't helping matters with his rantings.

"I don't know. I couldn't come up with the answer. I've diagnosed and treated gout countless times, but it just wasn't there. It was as if part of my memory had been blocked off, like it was there but it was hiding, or hidden. It still is."

"If they decide you're impaired, they can suspend your privileges—I remember seeing that in the bylaws. They can put you on suspension until you've been evaluated by a shrink or a drug-rehabilitation guy—"

"Drugs! You think I'm on *drugs?*"

"No. I know you better than that. But, Al, you haven't been yourself lately. And you looked spaced this morning when he started quizzing you. I'm sure the board thinks you're either on something or you've cracked."

Alan couldn't argue with him. He'd seen their expressions. One face lingered in the front of his memory. As Tony had propelled him from the room, Alan had glanced back and seen Lou Alberts staring after him. It was as if all their years of ill-feeling and competition had been washed away; Lou's face was a study of shock, dismay, and—worst of all—pity.

"And there's worse coming, let me tell you. The hospital is required by law to notify the State Board of Medical Examiners if any staff member is suspended because of suspected impairment or any other form of incompetence."

Impairment . . . incompetence . . . the terms rankled in Alan's brain. After fighting constantly to stay on top of clinical medicine, to be judged incompetent while so many other doctors coasted along with outdated knowledge and practices.

He slowed to a stop at an intersection and sat there, staring at the road ahead as a crystalline ball of fear formed and grew in his chest.

"Maybe they're right," he said. "Maybe I do need help."

"What are you talking about?"

"I'm lost, Tony. I don't know which way to go."

"Don't worry, Al. I'm with you all the way. We'll sit down and—"

"No!" Alan said, hearing his voice rise in pitch as the fear spread down his arms and legs, encompassing him completely. "I mean now. Here. This road! I know I've been here thousands of times, but I'm lost!"

He turned and stared into Tony's shocked eyes.

"How do I get home from here?"

__ 24. __
Sylvia

"You didn't have to come along," Alan said as he got into the car and sat beside her.

"I wanted to," Sylvia said and forced a smile. He looked so haggard and tired; his eyes had a haunted look.

As Ba put the car in gear and began to drive, Alan said, "I'm glad you did, though. That was why I asked if I could borrow Ba instead of hiring a cab. I need a friend along, and you're it."

His words warmed her. She was glad he considered her someone he could turn to in time of need. "But what about . . . ?" She didn't finish the question.

"Ginny?" He sighed. "We're barely speaking. She wants me to see a psychiatrist. Even Tony wants me to see one."

"Is that who you're seeing at Downstate? A psychiatrist?" She wanted to tell him that he was the sanest man she knew, but thought better of it. Her opinion was purely personal.

"No. No psychiatrist—at least not yet. There's something I've got to rule out first."

"Going to tell me about it?" she asked after a lengthy pause during which he seemed to go into a trance. But when he spoke, the words froze her blood.

"Got to rule out a brain tumor."

"Oh, God! You can't—"

"I can't bury my head in the sand any longer, Sylvia. My memory has gone to hell. Why do you think I'm not driving myself? Because I could get lost! Or forget where I'm going! Hell, I got lost on the way back from the hospital the other day!"

"Couldn't that just be stress?" she asked, praying for a simple answer.

"It could, but that's a wastebasket diagnosis. It could be directly related to the *Dat-tay-vao,* for all I know. But I have to face the possibility that a tumor could be behind it all. I had a patient a few years back with exactly the same symptoms, but he was older so I laid it off to an organic brain syndrome—Alzheimer's or the like. But the progression of his symptoms was too rapid for my comfort— as rapid as mine—so I ordered a brain scan. Guess what? He had a big midline frontal meningioma. Benign. They shelled it out and his memory was back to normal in a couple of months. So before I do anything else"—he tapped his forehead with a finger—"I've got to make sure I haven't got something growing in here."

The thought of Alan with a brain tumor made her almost physically ill. "I can see why you wouldn't want it done in Monroe Community."

"Right. Too close to home. Too many nosy trustees."

"Those trustees!" she said. "I can't believe the rotten way they've treated you! Suspending your privileges and then releasing the news immediately to the *Express*!"

"Yeah," he said softly. She sensed his hurt and humiliation. "I didn't expect the public execution before a hearing. Anyway, I went to school with one of the radiologists at Downstate. He fitted me in for a CT scan this morning."

"Have you seen another doctor about any of this?"

Alan smiled. " 'The physician who treats himself has a fool for a patient.' Is that what you mean? I'm not treating myself, just doing a little diagnostic work."

"But if you had to see someone, who would you choose?"

"Oh, there's any number of men I'd trust. A bunch of us in the area have this unofficial network of cross-referrals and cross-coverage. After a while you learn to sense which consultants give a damn about patients as people and which don't. Considering that competence is pretty much equal, those are the ones who get my referrals. Vic O'Leary would probably be my first choice for a consultation. I trust him to cover my practice when I'm away, and I'd trust him with my own health. But at the moment I don't want to put him in the hot seat."

Sylvia sat in silence, stewing in the fear that Alan might have something seriously wrong with him, until she realized that if she was terrified, how must *he* feel?

She found his hand and squeezed it.

"Scared?"

"A little," he said with a shrug. Then he looked at her and smiled. "Okay—a lot."

"Then I'm glad I'm along. No one should have to face this alone."

Her hand rested in his for the rest of the trip.

* * *

As she waited on the top floor of the multilevel garage near University Hospital, Sylvia tried to read the newspaper, tried the *Times* crossword puzzle, tried a novel—nothing seemed to get her mind off Alan. Except thinking about Jeffy's continued regression. That was hardly a relief.

Please, God. You can't let there be anything wrong with Alan. He's one of the good guys. Let one of the bad guys have a brain tumor. Not Alan.

She leaned back in the seat and closed her eyes, as much to shut out the world as to rest them. Why? Why did death and disease and misfortune swallow up everyone she cared for? First Greg's senseless death, then Jeffy's regression, and now Alan. Was there some sort of black cloud hanging over her? Maybe everyone would be better off if she just threw an iron gate across the driveway entrance and never left Toad Hall.

Ninety minutes crawled by. Sylvia was getting a headache from the tension, and muscle aches in every part of her body from sitting in the back seat for so long. She was about to suggest to Ba that they get out and stretch their legs when it started to drizzle. Then she saw Alan threading his way through the parked cars in their direction. He opened the door on the other side and hopped in.

"Well?" she said, holding her breath.

"I've got one."

She gasped. "*A tumor?*"

"No. A brain—a perfect one. No problem."

Without thinking, she threw her arms around him and clutched him.

"Oh! I'm so glad!"

Alan returned the hug. "*You're* glad! Let's celebrate!" He pulled a cassette from a pocket and handed it forward to Ba. The interior of the car was soon filled with falsetto "Oooohs" and basso "Bowms."

"Good lord!" Sylvia laughed. "What is *that?*"

" 'I Laughed' by the Jesters. Great, huh?"

"It's awful! I can't believe you listen to Doo-wop!"

His face fell. "You don't like oldies? They're not all Doo-wop, you know." He leaned forward. "I'll tell Ba to turn it off."

"No," she said, laying a hand on his shoulder. She had such an urge to touch him. "I like some of the old stuff, but listening to it all the time seems like such a dead end."

"You could say the same about opera . . . or Vivaldi."

"*Touché.*"

"Wait'll you hear the next one!" he said. He was like a teenager.

"That's 'Maybellene' by What's-His-Name!" she said, recognizing it almost immediately.

"Chucker! The Berry!"

"Chuck Berry! Right. I didn't think anybody listened to him any-more."

"He's the best. The Beatles, The Rolling Stones, The Beach Boys—they all borrowed from him. And he's the man who got me into rock 'n' roll."

He leaned his head back as he settled into the seat.

"Let's see . . . it was back in the summer of fifty-five and I had two passions in the world: rocket ships and the Brooklyn Dodgers. On summer nights I liked to listen to the Bums in bed, but the noise of the radio would keep my younger brother awake. So my father bought me a little Japanese radio—shaped like a rocket, of course— that had a tiny earplug instead of a speaker; you tuned by pulling up or down on the aerial in the nose cone.

"And so it was on a hot, muggy August night as I was trying to tune in the Brooklyn Bums that I came upon this strange music with twanging bass and some guy singing about chasing a Cadillac and a girl named Maybellene. I'd heard of Elvis but had never actually heard his music. In those days a kid listened to what his parents listened to. And my folks listened to stations that played stuff like 'Mr. Sandman,' 'How Much Is That Doggie in the Window?', 'The Tennessee Waltz,' 'Shrimp Boats Is a-Comin',' and so forth. Get the picture? Those songs did nothing for me. But *this!* This went directly from the radio to my central nervous system. And then that manic guitar solo in the middle came on—here it is. Listen!"

Sylvia listened. Yes, it was certainly manic. So was Alan. She could almost see the tension pouring out of him.

"Anyway, I sat up in the dark, electrified by what was shooting out of that little earplug. It was my rock 'n' roll epiphany. And to top it off, the DJ—I later learned his name was Alan Freed—said something like, 'So nice, we'll play it twice,' and he *did!* He played the same damn song twice in a row!

"That was it—I was converted. Still liked the Dodgers, but I kept the radio tuned to WINS all night except during the commercials, when I checked out the score of the game. While my folks blithely assumed I was up in bed listening to the national sport, I was really listening to what some people called nigger music."

And I was worried about his memory! Sylvia thought with a mental shake of her head.

"You're really into this stuff, aren't you?" she said.

Alan shrugged. "It makes me feel good. And I need some good feelings these days. What else can I say?"

"Nothing more. That's what matters."

"Here comes 'Florence' by the Paragons," he said. He grinned at her as he sang along with the falsetto opening.

She winced at his sour notes. She felt so close to him at that moment, and realized with a bittersweet pang that she was very much in love with a man she could never have.

25.
Alan

"What are you doing?" Alan asked as he entered their bedroom. He had rushed upstairs to tell her about the CT scan.

Ginny's reply was terse and she didn't look up when she spoke. "I should think that would be pretty obvious."

It was. She was taking clothes from her closet and her drawers and placing them in any of the three suitcases lined up in descending order of size on the bed.

"Where are we going?" He knew with a sick feeling in the pit of his stomach that there was no "we" involved here, but he used the word anyway. The drum of the rain against the windows filled the room as he waited for an answer.

"Florida. And it's just me. I . . . need some time to myself, Alan. I need to get away and just think about things for a while."

"You mean about us."

She sighed and nodded. "Yeah. Us. What's left of us."

Alan stepped toward her but she held up a hand. "Don't. Please don't. I just want to get away by myself. I can't take it around here anymore."

"Everything's going to be all right, Ginny. I know it."

"Oh, *really?*" she said, throwing a pair of slacks into the big suitcase. "And who's going to make it all right? You? You made a fool out of yourself in front of the Board of Trustees! You've lost your hospital privileges! You can't even get into the office with all those kooks around it! And all you do is hang around the house and have conferences with Tony about how to keep from losing your medical license altogether!"

"Ginny—"

"Nobody wants to know us anymore!" Her voice rose steadily in pitch and volume. "It's like we're living in a vacuum. All our friends either have something else to do when I call or don't even bother to return my calls. They think I'm married to a nut! And I can't argue with them!"

"Thanks for the vote of confidence."

"It's not just me! Tony may be on your side, but I'm sure he thinks you're coming unwrapped, too!"

"Is that so?" Alan was suddenly angry—with Ginny and Tony for their lack of faith, and with himself for expecting them to accept something as bizarre as his power without seeing it for themselves.

He went to the phone at the bedside. "Okay. If I can prove that I'm not crazy, will you stay?"

"No games, Alan. And no deals."

"Will you give me a chance?"

"I've got a six o'clock flight out of JFK. If you can change my mind by then, fine. But I hope you won't mind if I finish packing."

Six o'clock! That gave him five hours. He didn't know if he could—

He dialed Tony's business number and told him to go next door into his office and take a file marked "Timetable" from his desk, then bring it here to the house. Tony agreed, although he sounded hesitant.

Alan paced the first floor of his home like an expectant father while Ginny labored upstairs with the suitcases. Then a rainsoaked Tony was at the door with the folder. Alan snatched it from him, told him to wait, and took it to his study.

He pored over the figures, dimly aware that Ginny had come downstairs and that she and Tony were exchanging worried glances behind his back. He saw at once his mistake on the day of the board hearing. Again, it was his memory that had failed him—he had been only forty minutes off with his calculation of the arrival of the Hour of Power. *Forty minutes! Forty rotten minutes!* If the meeting had started an hour later, he would have been golden. Instead . . .

But he couldn't dwell on that now. Here, with all the figures in black and white in front of him, he couldn't go wrong. He even double-checked on a hand calculator. No doubt:

Today's Hour of Power would start in approximately twenty minutes.

He strode into the living room and waved the car keys in the air.

"Let's go—both of you!"

"Wait a minute—" Ginny began.

"No waiting. I'm going to prove I'm not crazy. Call my bluff and give me an hour. If you're still not convinced, I'll drive you to the airport myself in plenty of time for your six o'clock flight."

Tony looked surprised at the remark about the flight but only said, "I want to see this."

"I don't know . . ." Ginny said.

Alan and Tony together managed to convince her to come along. Then they were in the car and heading through the rain toward the office. Alan had a fairly clear picture of the route he would take and was reasonably sure he wouldn't get lost. He planned to go to the office, let a few of the people in, and heal them before Ginny and Tony's eyes. Alan knew it would be risking a mob scene, but if he could demonstrate to them that he truly had this power, he would have two firm allies. Maybe if he could anchor himself to them, he wouldn't feel so alone and adrift.

As he slowed for the light at Central and Howe, Clubfoot Annie hobbled out of Leon's Superette. Her usual tattered dress was sheltered under an equally tattered umbrella; a plastic shopping bag hung from her free hand. Alan checked his watch, then slammed on the brakes and leaped out of the car, ignoring the startled noises from Ginny and Tony.

Why go to the office? he thought. Here was someone who really needed healing and wasn't clamoring for it. Someone who had been tearing at his heart for years.

"Miss!" he said as he hopped over a puddle onto the curb. "Can I speak to you a minute?"

She whirled, startled. Her eyes were wide and fearful. "What? I ain't got no money!"

"I know that," Alan said, approaching more cautiously. "I just want to help you."

"Get away. Don't want no help!"

She turned and started to hobble away.

"Miss! I just—"

She hobbled faster, her body jerking left and right like a trip-hammer.

Alan could feel the rain soaking through his shirt, plastering down his hair. But he couldn't let her go. He trotted after her.

"Wait!"

She glanced over her shoulder, her eyes full of fear. His heart broke for her. How many times throughout her life had people made fun of her, picked on her, teased her, tormented her, pushed her around, tripped her, just because of that foot?

"I'm not going to harm you!"

And then she tripped. She was looking at him and not at the sidewalk; her foot caught a raised section of walk and she went down in a muddy puddle.

She was crying when Alan reached her.

"Don't hurt me! I ain't got no money!"

"I don't want anything from you. I just want to do *this*." He grabbed her malformed left foot and ankle and twisted them toward the normal physiologic position. He felt the tingle, the rush, heard her cry out, and then it was over. He took both her hands.

"Stand up."

She looked at him with a puzzled, still-fearful expression, but accepted his help. Her eyes nearly bulged from their sockets when she regained her feet and felt her left sole lie flat against the ground for the first time in her life. She gasped, tested it, then walked in a slow circle, her mouth gaping, utterly speechless. Alan picked up her umbrella and shopping bag and put them back into her hands.

"Take these and get home and get out of those wet clothes."

"Who . . . who are you?"

"Just someone who wishes he could have been here for you forty or fifty years ago."

He walked back to the car in a cloud of jubilant euphoria. Oh, that had felt good!

Ginny and Tony were staring out the side windows of the car.

Tony's eyes kept darting between Alan and the woman, now walking back and forth on the sidewalk on her normal left foot. "Holy shit, Alan!" he kept saying. "Holy *shit!*"

Ginny said nothing. She simply stared at him, her face a tight, unreadable mask.

Alan opened the door on her side. "Would you mind driving home, honey? I'm a bit shaky after that."

Actually, he had suddenly realized that he didn't know the way home. But it didn't bother him. He felt too damn *good!*

Wordlessly, Ginny slid over and put the car in gear.

*   *   *

"Now you know," Alan said as they waved good-bye to Tony from their front steps.

Ginny turned and went into the house.

"I still can't believe it," she said. "I saw it, but . . ."

"So you can see why I can't come out and say that the stories aren't true."

Ginny dropped onto the couch and sat staring at the far corner of the room.

"God, Alan."

"You can see that, can't you?"

He desperately wanted to hear her agree. She had been so quiet and pensive since his little demonstration at Central and Howe. He hadn't a clue as to what was going on in her mind.

She shook her head. "No," she said. "I can't see that at all. Not only have you got to deny it—you've got to stop using it."

He was stunned. *"What?"*

"I mean it, Alan." She rose and began to circle the couch, head down, her arms folded in front of her. "It's ruining our life!"

"You mean forget I have it? Ignore it? Pretend it doesn't exist?"

Finally she looked at him, face to face, eyes blazing. "Yes!"

Alan stared at her. "You really mean it, don't you?"

"Of course I do! Look what it's done to you! You can't practice medicine anymore—the hospital won't let you admit patients and you can't get into your office without being mobbed by all the kooks hanging around outside it. Can you imagine what would happen if you publicly admitted that you *can* cure people? They'd tear you to pieces!"

Alan was numb. *Deny the power exists? Not use the Hour of Power when it comes?*

"So . . ." Ginny hesitated, took a deep breath, then began again. "So, I want a decision, Alan. I want a promise. I want you to hold some sort of news conference, or put out a press release, or whatever it is people do in a case like this, and tell the world that it's all a pack of lies. I want you to go back to being a regular doctor and me back to being your regular wife. I can't deal with what's been happening here!"

There were tears in her eyes.

"Oh, Ginny," he said, stepping toward her and taking her hands, "I know it's been tough on you." He didn't know what else to say.

"You haven't answered me, Alan."

He thought of a future full of sick and miserable people with no hope passing through his office, looking for help, and he saw himself letting them pass by as he stood mute and still with his hands in his pockets.

"Don't ask this of me, Ginny."

"Alan, I want things as they were!"

"Tell me: Could you stand on a dock and hide a life preserver behind your back while a drowning man cries for help ten feet away?"

"Never mind the hypothetical stuff! This is real life—*our* life! And we've lost control of it! I want our old life back!"

Regret and resignation suddenly flooded through him. This was it. This was the end.

"That life is gone, Ginny. Things will never be the same again. I can't stop."

She jerked away from him. "You mean, you *won't* stop!"

"I won't stop."

"I knew it!" she said, her features hardening into an angry mask. "I knew you wouldn't do this for me, for us, but I made myself ask. You didn't disappoint me! If nothing else, you're consistent! I've never come first with you—never! So why should I have expected any special consideration this time?" She whirled and headed for the stairs. "Excuse me. I've got a plane to catch."

Alan stood and watched her go, unable to refute her. Was she right? Had he really put her and their marriage second all along? He had never really thought about it before. He had taken it for granted that they were both leading the kind of lives each of them wanted. But maybe that was the problem: the taking for granted and the living of separate lives. The bonds that had united them early on had long since dissolved and they had formed no new ones.

And then the Touch had come along.

Alan shook his head and walked to the window to watch the rain. The Touch—it would test the strongest marriage. It was exploding his.

But I can't give it up! I can't!

He didn't know how long he stood there, brooding, mulling the past and the future, watching the rain sheet the screen, wondering how long Ginny would stay in Florida to "think things over." But he wasn't giving up yet. He would use the time they'd have together in the car during the trip down to JFK to try to convince her to change her mind. He'd—

A taxi pulled into the driveway and honked.

Ginny was suddenly on her way down the stairs, somehow managing all three suitcases at once.

"I'm driving you, Ginny," he said, angry that she thought he'd let her go off to the airport by herself.

She pulled on her raincoat. "No, you're not!"

"Don't be ridiculous. Of course I—"

"No, Alan! I'm leaving here to get off by myself. I don't want to be with you, Alan. Can I make it any clearer than that?"

That hurt. He hadn't realized things had got to this point. He shook his head and swallowed.

"I guess not."

He picked up the two biggest bags and carried them out into the downpour to the taxi. Ginny got in the back seat and closed the door while he and the cabbie loaded the trunk.

Ginny didn't wave, didn't roll down the window to say good-bye. She huddled in the back of the cab and let it drive her away, leaving Alan standing in the driveway, in the rain, feeling more alone than he'd ever felt in his life.

JULY

26.
Alan

The divorce papers arrived on Monday morning a week later. Alan fought a sinking sensation as he unfolded them, and shook his head sadly when he read that he was being charged with mental cruelty. Tony dropped by shortly after the mailman left. Alan showed him the papers.

"Things like this don't happen so fast," Tony said as he folded the sheets and slipped them into his inside jacket pocket. "I can almost guarantee you she had this in the works before she left."

"So she wasn't going to her folks' place 'to think things over.' She was going for good. Great."

Alan sighed. The marriage had been over for years; he simply hadn't realized it. He wanted to be angry, and he should have been hurt. All he could do was shrug. He wanted to feel *something*. He couldn't seem to feel much of anything anymore. He spent his days hanging around the house waiting to see what the State Board of Medical Examiners was going to do. Not knowing from one day to the next whether he was going to be able to keep his medical license was paralyzing him. He hadn't left the house once over the long

July Fourth weekend just past—one day had become pretty much like any other.

"Heard from the Board of Examiners yet?"

Tony smiled. "That's why I stopped over. The board's not going to do anything until after Labor Day. I talked to one of the members today and he said since there hasn't been a single complaint registered against you by a patient, or any malpractice suits started, no civil or criminal charges, and no intimation that you've harmed anyone, and since a couple of board members are out of state on vacation, he said there was no reason for an immediate hearing."

Alan felt as if an enormous weight had been lifted off him. "Really?"

"Really. That gives us two whole months to prepare for the hearing. And I think we'll really be able to put it to the hospital board by then. They're either going to have to shit or get off the pot. And after what I saw last week—I still can't quite believe I saw what I saw—I have a feeling they're going to go into acute anal retention, if you know what I mean. And then we can sue their asses off!"

"I just want my privileges reinstated."

"Don't be a jerk, Al! They released your suspension to the *Express* within an hour! That's pretty goddamn low!"

"They deny it."

"They lie. We're gonna nail these clowns to the wall!"

"Okay, Tony," Alan said, placing a hand on his friend's shoulder. "Okay. Just calm down."

"I'm fine. Just don't go playing Mr. Forgiveness with those bastards. Once you put on your little show like you did for me last week, we'll—"

"No show, Tony."

"What?" Tony's face went slack. "What do you mean, no show?"

Alan dropped into the recliner. "I've thought about it a lot since Ginny left. Let's face it—I haven't had much else to do. But I've come to the realization that if I admit to the public what I can do, and if I effectively demonstrate it to prove I'm not crazy, my personal life will be destroyed. Worse than that, I'll become some sort of natural resource, to be metered out. Cripes, I might even become the object of a religious cult. I'd be in the spotlight around the clock.

I'd have no freedom, nothing. I'd probably even become a favorite target for assassins." He shook his head slowly, back and forth. "No way."

Tony was silent for a moment, then: "Yeah. I see what you mean. Well, okay. I can get you clear without the magic show." He pointed his finger at Alan. "But just don't screw up like you did before the hospital board. You wouldn't be in this spot if you'd listened to me and kept quiet!"

Alan folded his hands as if in prayer and bowed his head. "Amen, brother."

Tony laughed. "That's the attitude!"

"How are things at the office?" Alan said as he rose and led him to the door. "Quieted down any since word got out about suspension of my hospital privileges?"

"Just the opposite. The crowd's bigger than ever. I mean, some of them have been there for *weeks* now, waiting for a chance to see you, and you haven't even shown. You'd think they'd give up by now."

"They're the type who can't give up," Alan said. "They've been everywhere else and tried everyone else. They haven't got anyplace else to go."

Alan stood at the door, looking down the driveway without seeing Tony drive off.

They haven't got anyplace else to go. God, what an awful feeling that must be. And then to wait and wait and have the miracle you've been praying for never show up.

He went to his charts on the Hour of Power. After making some quick calculations, he grabbed the phone and called his receptionist.

"Connie? Can you get down to the office right away? Great! We're going to work!"

_27._
Charles

Another "informal chat" with the senator.

Charles stifled a yawn. He had taken Julie out to Montauk for the long weekend—Friday, Saturday, and Sunday at the beach. The purely American holiday held a special significance for him, allowing him to celebrate his own personal independence from England. The sunburn he'd developed on the beach—and he deserved it for leaving his shirt off most of yesterday—had kept him awake half the night.

"By the way," the senator said as Charles got up to leave, "I heard a strange story over the weekend. Seems that sometime last month a woman in Monroe with a lifelong history of a clubbed left foot was accosted by a man who chased her, knocked her down, and straightened out her foot right there on the side of the road."

Charles rolled his eyes. The man never tired of the subject! He didn't want to waste more time here. He was to meet Sylvia shortly when she dropped Jeffy off for a few days of testing. He was looking forward to seeing her. "An apocryphal tale if I ever heard one. Which one of the saints was it? Anthony? Bartholomew?"

The senator smiled. "No. Actually, the description she gave matches Dr. Alan Bulmer quite closely."

Bulmer again! The senator seemed to be developing an obsession with the man. Between Sylvia and the senator, every conversation seemed to turn to Alan Bulmer lately. Charles had met him only once, but he was getting bloody sick of hearing about him.

"Just let me guess," Charles said before Senator McCready could go on. "Her supposedly deformed foot is now bloody perfect. Right?"

The senator nodded. "Right. Only 'supposed' isn't quite accurate. I understand the woman's deformity has been common knowledge for many years. There's no evidence of it now."

Charles smirked at the senator's gullibility. "Got any before-and-after X rays?"

"None that can be found. Apparently the woman suffered from an unfortunate combination of poverty and ignorance—she never sought help for it."

"How convenient," Charles said with a laugh.

"Would X rays convince you?"

"Not likely. Especially not old ones. They could be of someone else's foot."

It was the senator's turn to laugh, and there seemed to be genuine good humor in the sound.

"That's what I like about you, Charles! You accept nothing at face value. You trust no one! I take great comfort in knowing that if *you* believe in something, it's certainly safe for me to do the same."

"I've told you before, Senator—I don't believe in things. I either know something or I don't. Belief is a euphemism for ignorance combined with sloppy thinking."

"You've got to believe in something sometime."

"You are free to believe that if you wish, Senator. I bloody well don't."

Deliver us all from men who "believe," Charles thought as he walked out into the hall.

Marnie, his secretary, held up a yellow slip of paper as he walked into his office.

"Mrs. Nash is at the front desk."

Charles' spirits lifted. Sylvia had been so bloody preoccupied lately, she seemed to have no time left for him. He knew she was worried about Jeffy, but there seemed to be more to it than that.

Well, she was here now and that offered an opportunity to revive the relationship. Perhaps it wasn't going to be a Blue Monday after all.

__ 28. __
Alan

It threatened to become a mob scene at first. The people in the parking lot recognized him immediately and surrounded his car, pressing so tightly against it that he couldn't get the door open. Finally, after he had leaned on the horn for a full minute, they backed off enough to let him out.

And then it was a sea of hands and faces pressing close, touching him, grabbing his hands and placing them on their heads, or upon the heads of the sick ones they had brought with them. Alan fought the panic that surged through him—he could barely breathe in the crush.

This bunch was noticeably different from previous crowds. These were the diehards, the most determined of the pilgrims, the ones who had stayed on despite news of the suspension of Alan's hospital privileges and rumors that he either had lost his power or had been proven a fake after all. As a group they were scruffier, dirtier than any others Alan could remember. All the women seemed to have ratty hair, all the men seemed to have a two-day growth of beard. They appeared much worse for the wear, much poorer for their illnesses. But most striking was the look of utter desperation in their eyes.

Alan shouted for them to let him through, but no one seemed to hear. They kept reaching, touching, calling his name. . . .

He managed to crawl up on the roof of his car, where he cupped his hands around his mouth and shouted. Eventually they quieted down enough to hear him.

"You've got to back away and let me into the office," he told them. "I'll see you one at a time inside and do what I can for you. Those I don't see today, I'll see tomorrow, and so on. But all of you will be seen eventually. Don't fight, don't push and shove. I know you've all been waiting here a long time. Just be patient a little longer and I'll see you all. I promise."

They parted and let him through. Connie was already inside, having sneaked by while the crowd's attention was on him. She opened the door and quickly locked it behind him.

"I don't like this," she told him. "There's something ugly about this group."

"They've been waiting a long time. You'd be disheveled and short-fused too if you'd been living in a parking lot for two weeks."

She smiled uncertainly. "I guess so. Still . . ."

"If they make you nervous, here's what we'll do. We'll let them in two at a time. While I'm seeing one, you can be filling out a file on the next. That way we'll keep a good flow going."

Because I'm only going to have an hour or so to do what these people came for.

It began on a sour note, with a surge of pushing and shoving and scuffling to get in when Alan first opened the door. He had to shout and threaten to see no one unless there was order. They quieted. A middle-aged man and a mother with her child were admitted. Both man and child were limping.

Five minutes or so later, Connie brought the mother and child back to the examining room. As Alan stepped into the room, the mother—dressed in a stained housecoat, with dark blue socks piled around her ankles—tugged at the child's hair and it came off. A wig. She was completely bald. Alan noted her pallor and sunken cheeks. She looked to be no more than ten.

"Chemotherapy?"

The mother nodded. "She got leukemia. Least that's what the doctors tell us. Don't matter what they give her, Laurie keeps wastin' away."

The accent was definitely southern, but he couldn't place it. "Where are you from?"

"West Virginny."

"And you came all the way—?"

"Read aboutcha in *The Light*. Nothin' else's worked. Figure I got nothin' to lose."

Alan turned to the child. Her huge blue eyes shone brightly from deep in their sockets. "How are you feeling, Laurie?"

"Okay, I guess," she said in a small voice.

"She always says that!" the mother said. "But I hear her crying at night. She hurts every hour of the day, but she don't say nothin'. She's the bravest little thing you ever saw. Tell the man the truth, Laurie. Where does it hurt?"

Laurie shrugged. "Everywhere." She pressed her hands over her painfully thin thighs. " 'Specially in my bones. They hurt somethin' awful."

Bone pain, Alan thought. Typical of leukemia. He noticed the scars on her scalp where she had been given intrathecal chemotherapy. She'd been the route, that was for sure.

"Let's take a look at you, Laurie."

He placed a hand on either side of her head and willed all those rotten little malignant centers in her bone marrow to shrivel up and die.

Nothing happened. Alan felt nothing, and neither, apparently, did Laurie.

Alan experienced an instant of panic. Had he miscalculated again?

"Excuse me," he said to the mother, and stepped into his adjoining office. He checked his figures. All the calculations seemed right. The Hour of Power should have started at 4:00 p.m. and here it was 4:05 already. Where had he gone wrong? Or had he? He had never been able to chart the power to the exact minute. It had never failed to appear, but his calculations had been off by as much as fifteen minutes in the past. Hoping the failure a moment ago was due to the quirky margin of error in his charts, he returned to the examining room. Again he placed his hands on Laurie's head.

The charge of ecstasy came, and with it, Laurie's cry of surprise.

"What's the matter, Honeybunch?" the mother said, at her child's side in a flash, pulling her away from Alan.

"Nothin', Ma. Just felt a shock is all. And . . ." She ran her hands over her legs. "And my bones don't hurt no more!"

"Is that true?" The mother's eyes were wide. "Is that true? Praise the Lord! Praise the Lord!" She turned to Alan. "But is her leukemia cured? How can we tell?"

"Take her back to her hematologist and get a blood count. That will tell you for sure."

Laurie was looking at him with wonder in her eyes. "It doesn't hurt anymore!"

"But how—?" the mother began.

With a quick wave, Alan ducked out and crossed the hall to the next room. He felt exultant, strong, *good*. It was working! It was still there. The Hour of Power was not perfectly predictable—at least not by him—but he still had it, and he had no time to waste with explanations.

There was work to be done.

*   *   *

Time to quit.

Alan had just effected one of his most satisfying cures. A forty-five-year-old man with a long history of ankylosing spondylitis had come in with the typically rigid spine curved almost to a right angle at the upper back and neck so that his chin was pushed down against his chest.

Sobbing his thanks, the man walked out with his spine straight and his head high.

"That man!" Connie said as she came to the rear. "He was all bent over when he came in!"

Alan nodded. "I know."

"Then it's really true?" Her eyes widened steadily in her round face.

Alan nodded again.

Connie stood before him, gaping. It was making him uncomfortable.

"Is the next patient ready?" he said finally.

She shook herself. "No. You told me to stop bringing them in as of five. It's ten after now."

Five-ten. The Hour of Power was over.

"Then tell them that's it for today. We start again at five tomorrow."

"They're not going to like that," she said and bustled away toward the front.

Alan stretched. It had been a satisfying hour . . . but he wasn't really practicing medicine. It took no skill, no special knowledge, to lay his hands on someone. The *Dat-tay-vao* was doing the work; he was merely the carrier, the vessel, the instrument.

With a start he realized that he had become a tool.

The thought disturbed him. The whole situation was bittersweet—emotionally satisfying but intellectually stultifying. He didn't have to get to know the patient or build a relationship. All he had to do was touch them at a certain time of day and *wham!*—all better. Not his kind of medicine. There was the high of seeing the relief and joy and wonder in their faces, but he was not using any of his training.

Then again, none of his training had anything to do with what he had accomplished today. His fellow doctors would find ways to write off most of the results as "placebo effect" and "spontaneous remission." And why not? In their position he'd do the same. He'd been taught not to believe in miracles.

Miracles—how easily he'd come to accept them after witnessing a few. After *causing* them. If only he could find a way to get Sylvia to let him try the Touch on Jeffy. She seemed afraid of it and he couldn't understand why. Even if the Touch were useless against Jeffy's autism, he couldn't see how it would hurt to try.

If he could make little Jeffy normal, it would make all the trials he had been through because of the Touch worthwhile. If only Sylvia would give him—

He heard shouting from up front and went to investigate. A number of people from the parking lot had pushed their way into the waiting room. When they saw him they started shouting, pleading, begging for him to see them.

Alan raised a hand in the air and held it there, saying nothing until they finally quieted down.

"I'll say this once and once only. I know you're all sick and hurting. I promise I will see every one of you and do everything I can for you, but my power lasts only one hour a day, no more. I have no control over that. Just one hour a day. Understand? That hour is over and done for today. I'll be back tomorrow for another hour at five p.m."

There was some rumbling from the rear.

"That's all I have to say. I'll be back tomorrow, I promise."

"That's what you said two weeks ago and we never saw you again until today!" a voice called out. "Don't play games with us!"

"Maybe we'll just stay in here until you *do* come back!" said another.

"If you're going to threaten me, I won't be back at all."

There was sudden silence.

"I'll see you here tomorrow at five."

He watched as they reluctantly shuffled out. Connie leaned her plump frame against the door after she locked it and sighed with relief.

"I don't like this bunch, Doctor. I tell you, there's something mean and ugly about them. They frighten me."

"They're all right one on one."

"Maybe, but not all together. As each cured patient walked out, the rest got meaner and meaner, the bigger and stronger ones pushing the smaller and weaker ones out of the way."

"A lot of them have waited a long time, and they're sick of being sick. They're tired of hurting. When relief is in sight, another night can seem like a year."

Connie shook her head. "I guess you're right. Oh, Dr. Bulmer," she said as he turned to go, "my mother suffers something terrible from arthritis in her hips. I was wondering if . . ."

"Of course," he said. "Bring her with you tomorrow."

They closed up and Alan walked her out to her car and made sure she was on her way before he got into his own. The crowd had gathered at a decent distance and stood there staring at him like a starving horde watching the owner of a fully stocked supermarket.

But their hunger was of a different sort, and he knew he would have nothing in his cupboard for them until tomorrow.

He drove away feeling tense and uneasy. He wondered if they had believed him.

29.
Sylvia

She hated the idea of leaving Jeffy here for one night, let alone three, but Charles insisted it was the best and quickest way to have him evaluated.

"We'll scan him head to foot," he said from behind his desk. "We'll monitor and record him awake and asleep, collect twenty-four-hour urines, and you can have him back in seventy-two hours. By then we'll know everything there is to know about him. Otherwise it will take forever on a piecemeal basis."

"I know," she said, sitting with Jeffy on her lap, her arms tight around him. "It's just that it's been years since he's been away overnight. What if he needs me?"

"Sylvie, dear," Charles said, and she resented the touch of condescension in his voice, "if he calls for you in the night, I will personally send the Foundation helicopter to pick you up and bring you here. It will be an unprecedented breakthrough."

Sylvia said nothing. Charles was right. Jeffy interacted with no one now. Not even the pets; not even himself. She wondered if he would even know she was gone.

"What else is wrong?" Charles said. She looked up to see him watching her face. "I've never seen you so blue."

"Oh, it's a bunch of things. Little things, big things—from my favorite bonsai getting root rot to Alan having his hospital privileges suspended, and very possibly about to lose his license. Everything was going so well for so long; now everything seems to be going sour at once."

"Bulmer's problems aren't yours."

"I know." She hadn't seen much of Charles since the party, so he couldn't know how her feelings for Alan had intensified.

"It's not as if you're bloody married to him." Was there a trace of jealousy in Charles' voice? "And from what I've heard, most of his troubles are his own doing. Sounds to me as if he's come to believe what the yellow press has been saying about him."

"According to Alan, the stories are true. And Ba told me he saw something similar in Vietnam when he was a boy."

Charles snorted in contempt. "Then Bulmer's license *should* be revoked for practicing medicine without a mind!"

Sylvia resented that and instantly came to Alan's defense.

"He's a good, kind, decent man who's being crucified!" But her anger cooled quickly, for what Charles had said reflected the tiny doubts that had been clawing at the walls of her mind for weeks now. "You met him. Did he seem unbalanced to you?"

"Paranoids have a knack for appearing perfectly normal until you tread on their forbidden ground. Then they can be bloody dangerous."

"But Ba—"

"With all due respect to your houseman, Sylvia, he is an uneducated fisherman from a culture that worships its ancestors." He came out from behind the desk and leaned against it, looking down at her, his arms folded in front of him. "Tell me: Have you ever seen him perform one of these miraculous cures?"

"No."

"Have you ever personally known someone incurably ill who has returned in perfect health from seeing him?"

"No, but—"

"Then watch out for him! If something breaks all the known rules, and can't be seen or heard or touched, then it isn't there! It only exists in someone's head. And that someone has broken with reality and is potentially dangerous!"

She didn't want to hear this. She couldn't conceive of Alan being dangerous to anyone. Charles was simply lashing out at someone he was coming to see as a rival.

And yet what if he were right?

___ 30. ___
Alan

Alan poured himself a scotch as soon as he entered the house. It *was* scotch he liked, wasn't it? He sipped and decided he liked the taste. He flopped onto the couch and let his head fall back.

The ride had been an ordeal. If he hadn't had the presence of mind to write down the directions from his home to his office and back again before leaving here earlier, he'd still be driving around. His memory was shot. He couldn't *think!* Even in the office, when that fellow with the bamboo spine had come in, he'd had to go look it up in a textbook to find the name—Strümpell-Marie disease, also known as ankylosing spondylitis.

God, what was happening to him? Why couldn't he remember everyday things anymore? Was it related to the *Dat-tay-vao,* or was he getting senile? There was a name for the condition but he couldn't think of it at the moment. At least he didn't have a brain tumor— he had proof of that in black type on yellow paper from the radiology department at University Hospital.

He closed his eyes. He was tired.

When he opened them again, it was dark. He jerked upright. He

couldn't have dozed off that long. A glance at his watch revealed
that barely an hour and a half had passed. Then he heard a rumble
of thunder and understood: A summer storm was brewing.

The front doorbell rang. Was that what had awakened him? Alan
turned on the lights, then opened the door and found a man standing
there. He was short and thin, wearing a Miami Dolphins jacket; he
was nervously twisting a baseball cap in his hands as he looked up
at Alan.

"Dr. Bulmer, could I speak to you a minute?"

He had that look, that *hungry* look. Alan swallowed.

"Sure. What can I do for you?"

"It's my wife, Doc. She—"

Alan had a sudden queasy feeling. "Were you over at my office?"

"Yeah. But they wouldn't let me in to see you. You see, my—"

"How did you find out where I live?"

"I followed you from the office."

My God! He hadn't even thought of that!

Alan looked beyond the man to the street. The light was rapidly
being swallowed up by the storm, but the lightning flickers revealed
a caravan of cars and vans and Winnebagos pulling up to the curb.

"I see you didn't come alone."

The man looked around with obvious annoyance. "A couple of
other guys followed you, too. They must've told the rest. I was
gonna wait till you came out, but when I saw them coming, I figured
I better get to you first."

"I can't do anything for you now," Alan said. Is this what it was
going to be like? People ringing his doorbell, camped on his lawn?
"I told you: tomorrow at five."

"I know that. But y'see, we live in Stuart—that's a ways north
of Palm Beach in Flahda—and the wife's too sick to be moved, so
I was wondering if maybe you'd sorta like come down and see her."
He laughed nervously. "A long-distance house call, if you know
what I mean."

Despite the uneasiness that was growing by inches and yards
within him, Alan couldn't help being touched by this little man who
had come all the way up the coast on behalf of his sick wife.

"I don't think so," Alan said. He couldn't keep his eyes off the growing crowd outside. "At least not now."

"I'll drive you. Don't worry about that. It's just that"—his voice caught—"that she's dying and nobody seems to be able to do anything for her."

"I really can't leave here," Alan said as gently as he could. "I've got too many people here to care—"

"You're her only hope, man! I seen what you did today and if you can help those people, you can help her, I know it!"

There were people crossing the lawn toward them. Thunder rattled the windows. The sky was going to open up any minute. Alan started to close the door.

"I'm sorry, but—"

"Sorry, hell!" the man said, stepping forward and blocking the door's swing. "You're comin' with me!"

"But don't you see, I—"

"You've *got* to, man! I'll pay you anything you want!"

"Money has nothing to do with it." There were people on the walk, almost to the front steps. "I'm sorry," he said as he tried to push the door closed.

"No!" chorused from the man and the others directly behind him as they all leaped forward and slammed the door open, sending Alan reeling backward, off balance.

But they didn't stop at the door. In a blind, frantic rush, squeezing through the open doorway two and three at a time, eyes wild, faces desperate, hands outstretched and reaching, they came for him. Not to hurt him. He could see no malice in their eyes, but that didn't lessen his terror. There was no stopping them. They wanted to touch him, to grab him, to pull him toward their sick loved ones, or toward their cars and pickups to drive him where the needy ones waited, to use him, to own him for a minute, just a few seconds, just long enough for him to work his miracle and then he could have his freedom back and go about his business with their eternal thanks.

That was what frightened him the most—he had become a *thing* to them.

There were so many of them, and as they pushed and shoved at each other to get to him, he tripped and stumbled to the floor. And then some of the others around him tripped too and fell on him, driving him down, knocking the wind out of him with explosive force. More fell on top of them. Alan felt the thick fibers of the shag rug grind into his left cheek from below as someone's belly molded itself around his face from above. An elbow drove into his stomach. Frantic, he tried to cry out his pain, his fear, but he couldn't breathe.

If they didn't get off him and give him some air, he was going to suffocate!

Then everything went black.

31.
Ba

The Missus had been silent all the way in from the city. Lately she had spent much of their time in the car quizzing him for his Naturalization exam. He was glad for no questions today; he had been having second thoughts about citizenship. Not because he didn't love this new country—he truly did—but because naturalization seemed so *final,* like a deathblow to his homeland, a final slap in the face, saying *You are dead and gone and useless to me, so I've found another place and hereby renounce you forever.* Could he do that?

And yet, his village was gone, his friends were no longer in the country, and those ruling his homeland would probably execute him if he returned.

He wished there were an easy answer.

The Missus watched the threatening sky and flickering lightning in silence. As they passed Dr. Bulmer's office, she finally spoke.

"Well, look at that—the lot's empty."

Ba slowed and glanced to his left in the pre-storm dimness. The lot was not completely empty—there were still two cars there—but it was a far cry from the congestion that had been present around the clock for the past few weeks.

"I wonder what happened?"

"Perhaps they gave up and left, Missus."

"I doubt it. They waited this long . . . hard to believe they'd all lose patience at once."

"Perhaps the police drove them off."

"Maybe. Tony must have finally got fed up with the mob scene around his office and blown the whistle. But I'm sure he wouldn't have done it without checking with Alan, and I can't see Alan agreeing to that. Maybe . . ."

Her voice trailed off. Although the Missus thought she hid them from the world, Ba knew her deep feelings for Dr. Bulmer. The tales warned against loving the one with the *Dat-tay-vao*. But what could he say to her? How could one warn against feelings? Besides, the die was cast. The *Dat-tay-vao* sought those whose lives were already pointed along a certain path. Ba knew that the Doctor would follow that path at all costs. It was his karma.

Still, for some unaccountable reason, the nearly deserted parking lot struck an uneasy note within him.

He accelerated to cruising speed and was ready to bear right toward Toad Hall at the fork in the road when the Missus spoke.

"Swing by Dr. Bulmer's house before we go home."

"Yes, Missus," Ba said with a secretly approving smile. The Missus too sensed that something was wrong.

The lightning grew brighter, the sky darker, and the thunder was now audible through the car's soundproofing. As rain began to pour from the sky in a sudden torrent, Ba turned on the headlights and heard the Missus gasp as they revealed the street ahead lined on both sides with a motley assortment of vehicles. Either someone was throwing a very big party or—

"They've found his house!" Her voice was a hoarse whisper behind his right ear as she leaned forward and stared ahead.

He pulled to a stop in the middle of the road before the Doctor's house. Through the sheets of rain he could see a crowd of people pushing and squeezing their way through the front door.

"Oh, Ba! They're in there!"

The anguish in her voice was all he needed to hear. He slammed the Graham into neutral, set the emergency brake, took off his chauffeur's cap, and leaped out into the pelting rain. He did not run, but a quick stride with his long legs moved him along almost as quickly as another man at a run. He reached the crowd from its rear and began working his way through it. Those who would not or could not move aside he grabbed by the back of the shirt or blouse or nape of the neck and pulled from before him and deposited behind, one after the other in a rhythmic swimming motion.

He was soon in the house. Although he could not see the Doctor, he knew immediately where he was—in the flailing knot of humanity lumped in the middle of the living room. Were these people mad? Were they trying to crush the life out of the Doctor? How long had he been under them? He had to get to him!

Ba waded into the crowd, roughly pushing aside anyone who was in his way until he reached the knot.

The lights flickered, then went out. It didn't matter to Ba. He simply reached into the knot and yanked on anyone he contacted, using the sporadic flashes of lightning through the windows to adjust his course. He worked hard, knowing he didn't have much time. The people here were more determined—some fiercely so. They struck back at him, aiming fists at his face, kicks at his groin. Ba was rougher on these, literally hurling them aside. The room became filled with sound, shouts of pain and anger breaking through the nearly continuous roar of the thunder.

The lights suddenly went on again and he found himself standing over the form of Dr. Bulmer, white-faced, gasping, disheveled. He held his hand out to the man. As the Doctor grasped it and pulled himself to his feet, Ba heard the babble of voices around him die to the point where he could understand snatches of sentences here and there.

. . . "Who the hell is he?"—"Where'd *he* come from?"—"Gawd he's big!"—"Looks sicker than you, pal!" . . .

The people backed away, leaving Ba and the Doctor in a rough circle of clear floor. Ba knew that his appearance was forbidding as he stood there dripping water, his thin wet hair plastered to his skull and hanging over his forehead. Perhaps that alone would be enough to get them out to the car without further violence.

"The Missus awaits you in her car," he told Dr. Bulmer.

The Doctor nodded. "Thanks, but I'll be okay."

Ba knew that was a very slim possibility. "Perhaps, but would you please speak to her to assure her of your safety?"

"Sure." He started toward the door.

A man stepped in his way. "You ain't goin' nowhere till you've seen my sister, pal."

Ba stepped forward but the man was apparently waiting and ready for him: Without warning, he swung a vicious uppercut at Ba's jaw. Ba blocked the blow with his palm and wrapped his long fingers around the man's fist. He would have to make an example of this one. He held the man's hand trapped in his own so that all could see how powerless he was, and then he twisted it back sharply. There was a loud crack and the man screamed and went down on his knees.

"Jesus!" the Doctor said. "Don't hurt them!"

"The Missus awaits you."

"Okay," said the Doctor. He turned to the crowd. "I want you all out of here when I get back."

Amid angry murmuring, Ba followed him out through the rain to the car. As the Doctor opened the door to the Graham, and leaned in, people began to shout.

. . . "Sure! He's got plenty of time for the rich but none for us!"— "Is that what I've got to do to get to him, buy a classic car?" . . .

Over the roar of the thunder, Ba heard glass crash behind him as he reached the curb. He turned and saw a lamp land on the lawn after smashing through a front window. More shattering: Some of the people were pulling bricks from a garden border and hurling them through the windows. Others were turning Ba's way. Even before the bricks started flying toward him and the car, Ba was moving. He pushed Dr. Bulmer into the back seat and closed the door after him. Then he jumped into the driver's seat, threw the car into gear, and sped off.

"What in the name of—" the Doctor said from the back, and then a brick bounced off the trunk with a loud *thunk*.

"My car!" the Missus cried, turning to stare out the tiny rear window. "Why would they want to hurt my Graham?"

"They're angry, frustrated, and afraid," the Doctor said.

The Missus laughed. "Anybody else I'd call a sap for saying something like that. But you, Alan, you've really got the curse."

"What curse?"

"Empathy."

Peering through the rain as he drove toward Toad Hall, Ba realized that his own reply to the Doctor would have been, "The *Dattay-vao*."

__ 32. __
At Toad Hall

Sylvia stood at the library doors and watched Alan as he gazed out the tall windows at the lightning. She wished the drapes were drawn. Lightning had terrified her ever since five-year-old Sylvia Avery in Durham, Connecticut, had seen a bolt of lightning split a tree and set it ablaze not twenty feet from her bedroom window. She had never forgotten the terror of that moment. Even now, as an adult, she could not bear to watch a storm.

Alan must have sensed her presence, for he turned and smiled at her.

"Good fit," he said, tugging on the lapels of the blue bathrobe he was wearing. "Almost perfect. You must have known I was coming."

"Actually, it belongs to Charles," she said, and watched closely for his reaction.

His smile wavered. "He must be a pretty regular visitor."

"Not as regular as he used to be."

Was that relief in his eyes?

"Your clothes will be out of the dryer soon."

He turned back to the windows. "My memory keeps betraying me—I could swear you told me the new peach tree was on the right."

"I did. It's just that it's been growing like crazy. It's now bigger than the older one."

The phone rang and she picked it up on the first ring.

It was Lieutenant Sears of the Monroe Police Department, asking for Dr. Bulmer. "For you," she said, holding it out to him.

The first thing he had done upon arriving at Toad Hall was to call the police and report the disturbance at his home. He had said he didn't want to press charges, just wanted everybody out of his house and off his property. The lieutenant was probably calling to say mission accomplished.

She watched him speak a few words, then saw his face go slack. He said something like, "*What?* All of it? Completely?" He listened a bit longer, then hung up. His face was ashen when he turned to her.

"My house," he said in a small voice. "It's burned to the ground."

Sylvia's body tightened in shock. "Oh no!"

"Yeah." He nodded slowly. "Jesus, yeah. They don't know if it was the mob or lightning or what. But it's gone. Right down to the foundation."

Sylvia fought the urge to take him in her arms and say it would be all right, everything would be all right. She just stood there and watched him go back to the window and stare out at the storm. She let him have a few moments to gather himself together.

"You know what keeps going through my mind," he said at last with a hollow laugh. "It's crazy. Not that I lost my clothes or all that furniture, or even the house itself. My records! My moldy-goldy-oldy forty-fives are gone, reduced to little black globs of melted vinyl. They were my past, you know. I feel like someone's just erased a part of me." He shrugged and turned toward her. "Well, at least I've still got the cassettes I duped off the records. Got them in my office and my car. But it's not the same."

Something about his speech had been bothering her since he had leaned into the car during the storm. Now she identified it: A trace of Brooklyn accent was slipping through. He had used it jokingly before; now it seemed part of his speech. Probably due to the tremendous strain he was under.

"Maybe you'd better call your wife," Sylvia said. "She'll be worried if she calls and learns the phone's out of order."

Sylvia knew his wife was in Florida. She didn't know exactly why, but assumed that the lady found the storm around her husband easier to weather from a thousand or so miles away.

"Nah. Don't worry about that," Alan said as he walked around the room, inspecting the titles on the shelves. "Ginny hasn't much to say to me these days. Lets her lawyer do her talking for her. His latest message was a packet of divorce papers that arrived today."

Oh, you poor man! Sylvia thought as she watched him peruse the bookshelves with such studied nonchalance. He's lost everything. His wife has left him, his house has burned to the ground, he can't even get into his own office, and he stands a good chance of losing his license to practice medicine. His past, his present, his future— all gone! God! How can he stand there without screaming out to heaven to give him a break?

She didn't want to pity him. He obviously wasn't wallowing in any self-pity and she was sure he would resent any pity from her.

Yet it was certainly a safer emotion than the others she felt for him.

She wanted him so badly now. More than she could ever remember wanting any other man. And here he was, in her home, alone— Gladys had gone for the night after putting Alan's wet clothes in the dryer, and Ba had beat a hasty retreat to his quarters over the garage. Alan had nowhere else to go, and all the moral restraints that had separated them were now gone.

Why was she so frightened? It wasn't the storm.

Sylvia forced herself to go to the bar. "Brandy?" she said. "It'll warm you."

"Sure. Why not." He came closer.

She splashed an inch or so into each of two snifters and handed him one, then quickly retreated to the far corner of the leather sofa, tucking her legs under her and hiding them in the folds of her robe. Why in God's name had she undressed and put on this robe? Just to make him feel more comfortable in Charles'? What was the matter with her? What had she been thinking?

Obviously she hadn't been thinking at all. Her hands trembled as she tipped the glass to her lips and let the fiery liquid slide down her throat.

She didn't want this. She didn't want this at all. Because if she and Alan came together, it wouldn't be another casual affair. It would be for keeps. The Real Thing—again. And she couldn't bear another Real Thing, not after what had happened to Greg. She couldn't risk that kind of loss again.

And she *would* lose Alan. He had an aura of doom. He was one of those men who was going to do what he had to do, no matter what. Greg had been like that. And look what had happened to him!

No. She couldn't let it happen. Not again. No matter how she felt about Alan. She would keep her distance and help him out and treat him as a dear friend and that would be it. No entanglements.

So she put on her just-good-friends face and watched him stalk the room.

But as she watched him, she felt a flame inside glowing, trying to grow and warm her, trying to ignite her need to touch him and be touched by him. She smothered it.

She was not going to get burned again.

*   *   *

Alan watched Sylvia out of the corner of his eye as he pretended to scan the titles on the library shelves. He barely saw the books. Like the song: He only had eyes for her.

Jeez, she was beautiful sitting there in her burgundy robe with her hair down and falling about her face. He had always felt attracted to her, but now . . . fate seemed to have thrown them together. She was sitting on the sofa over there with her robe demurely tucked around her, but he had caught sight of a length of long white thigh before she had arranged herself, and it was as if one of those lightning bolts arcing across the sky outside had struck him in the groin.

This was crazy! His life had completely fallen apart—he didn't even have a home anymore, for Chrissake!—and all he could think about was the woman across the room from him.

Yet where was all her banter, where were her come-ons when he needed them? He didn't know how to handle this, what to do, what to say.

Hi! You live around here? Come here often? What's your sign?

He took a gulp of the brandy and felt the fumes sear his nasopharynx.

But at last he could admit to himself that he wanted Sylvia, had wanted her for a long time. And now they were here, alone, with all the walls broken down. But instead of playing Mae West, she was suddenly Mary Tyler Moore.

He couldn't let the moment pass. He wanted her too much, *needed* her too much, especially now. Especially tonight. He needed someone to stand up with him, and he wanted Sylvia to be that someone. She had the strength to do it. He could go it alone, but it would be so much better with her beside him.

He wandered along the wall, gazing at the spines of the books, not seeing their titles. Then he came around behind the couch where she was sitting and stood directly behind her. She didn't turn around to look at him. She said nothing. Merely sat there like an expectant statue. He reached out toward her hair and hesitated.

What if she turns me away? What if I've read her wrong all these years?

He forced his hand forward to touch her hair, laying his fingers and open palm gently against the silky strands and stroking downward from where they fell from the center part. The tickling sensation in his palm sent a pleasurable chill up his arm. He knew Sylvia felt it too, for he could see the gooseflesh rising on the skin of her forearm where it protruded from the sleeve of her robe.

"Sylvia—"

She suddenly jumped up and spun around. "Need a refill?" She took his glass. "Me too."

He followed her over to the bar and stood at her side, desperately searching for something to say as she poured more brandy into the snifters. Alan noticed her hand trembling. Suddenly there was a

deafening crash of thunder and the lights went out. He heard Sylvia
wail, heard the brandy bottle drop, and then she was in his arms,
clutching him in fear, trembling against him.

He put his arms around her. God, she was quaking! This wasn't
an act. Sylvia was genuinely frightened.

"Hey, it's all right," he said soothingly. "Just a near miss. The
lights will go on soon."

She said nothing, but soon the tremors stopped.

"I hate thunderstorms," she said.

"I love them!" he said and held her tighter. "Especially now.
Because I was racking my brain for a way to get my arms around
you."

She looked up at him. Although he could not see her expression
in the darkness, he felt a change come over her.

"Stop it!" she said. Her voice was strained.

"Stop what?" She was still against him, but it was as if she had
just pulled herself a step or two away.

"Just stop it!"

"Sylvia, I don't know what—"

"You know and don't pretend you don't!"

She slammed her right fist against his chest, then her left, then
she was pounding at him with both at once.

"You're not going to do this to me! It's not going to happen again!
I won't let it! I won't! I won't!"

Alan pulled her tightly against him, as much to comfort the pain
he sensed within her as to protect himself.

"Sylvia! What's wrong?"

She struggled fiercely for a moment, then slumped against him.
He heard and felt her sobs.

"Don't do this to me!" she cried.

"Do what?" He was baffled and shaken by her outburst.

"Don't make me need you and depend on you to be there. I can't
go through that again. I can't lose one more person, I just can't!"

And then he understood. He tightened his arms around her.

"I'm not going anywhere."

"That's what Greg thought."

"Nobody can guarantee against that kind of tragedy."

"Maybe not. But sometimes it seems like you're courting disaster."

"I think I learned a big lesson tonight."

"I hope so. You could have been killed."

"But I wasn't. I'm here. I want to be with you, Sylvia. And if you let me, I *will* be with you—tonight and every night. But especially tonight."

After a long pause he felt her arms wriggle out from between them and slip around his back. "Especially tonight?" she said in a small voice.

"Yeah. It's been a long time coming and I don't think I can turn back now."

He waited patiently through another long pause. Finally she lifted her face to him.

"Me neither."

He kissed her then and she responded, bringing her hands up to his face and then clasping her fingers behind his neck. Alan pressed her against him, nearly overwhelmed by the feelings growing within him, old feelings that had lain dormant so long he had almost forgotten they existed. He opened the front of her robe and she parted his, and then her skin was hot against the length of him. Soon the robes had fallen to the floor and he led her to the couch, where he explored every inch of her with his fingers and his lips as she explored him. Then they were together, straining against each other, strobe-lit by lightning, the thunder and pounding rain all but drowning out the sounds they made as they peaked with the storm.

*   *   *

"God! Is that what it's like?" she heard him say after they had caught their breaths and lay together on the couch.

"You mean it's been so long you've forgotten?" Sylvia asked with a laugh.

She could almost see him smile in the dark.

"Yeah. Seems like forever since it's been like this. I've been going through the motions so long I've forgotten what passion feels like. I mean real *passion*. It's great! It's like being cleansed. Like being run through a wringer and hung up to dry."

The lights remained out. Lightning still flickered, but not as brightly, and there were increasingly longer intervals between the flashes and the rumbles.

Alan pulled away and went to the window. He seemed to love the storm.

"Do you know that you're the second woman I've ever made love to?"

Sylvia was startled. "Ever?"

"Ever."

"You must have had plenty of opportunities."

"I guess so. Lots of offers, anyway. I don't know how many were serious." She saw the silhouette of his head turn her way. "Only one offerer ever attracted me."

"But you never took her up on them."

"Not because she didn't appeal to me."

"But because you were married."

"Yeah. The Faithful Husband. Who committed adultery every day."

That puzzled her. "I don't get you."

"My paramour was my practice," he said in a low voice, as if talking to himself. "She came first. Ginny had to be satisfied with what was left over. To have been the kind of husband she needed, I would have had to settle for being something less than the kind of doctor I wanted to be. I made my choice. It wasn't a conscious decision. And I never really saw it before. But now that Ginny's gone and the practice is gone, it's all very clear. Too often my mind was someplace else. I cheated on her every hour of every day."

Is he trying to scare me off?

"And now that they're both gone, I feel free to be with you, and that's the most important thing in the world right now."

Sylvia felt a glow upon hearing those words. "Come back over here," she said, but he didn't seem to hear. She decided to let him talk. She sensed it was good for him. Besides, she wanted to hear what he had to say.

"And I'm talking about how I *feel*. I can't tell you the last time I opened up to anybody. *Any*body. Trouble is, I feel lost. I mean, what am I going to do with myself? For the first time in my life I

don't know what I want to do. Ever since I was a kid I've wanted
to be a doctor. And do you know why? For the money and the
prestige."

"I don't believe that!"

"Actually, I wanted to be a rock star but found I had no musical
talent. So I settled on medicine." He laughed. "Seriously, though—
money and prestige. Those were what were important to the kid
from Brooklyn all the way through pre-med and most of med school."

"What changed you?"

"No big deal. I didn't renounce all things material and don sack-
cloth and ashes. I just changed. Gradually. It started during my
clinical training, when I got my first contact with patients and realized they were more than just case histories—they were flesh-and-
blood people. Anyway, I achieved both my goals. The prestige
automatically came with the degree, and the money came, too. Like
one of my professors had told us: 'Take good care of your patients
and you won't have to worry about balancing the books.' He was
right.

"So I came out determined to be the best goddamn doctor in the
whole world. And after I got into practice, it was an all-day job to
try to be that kind of doctor. But now I'm not *any* kind of doctor.
I'm a tool. I've become some sort of organic healing machine. Maybe
it's time to quit." He grunted a laugh. "You know, Tony and I used
to say that when the legal jungle got too thick and the politicians
made twenty minutes of paperwork necessary for each ten minutes
spent with a patient, we'd chuck it all and open a pizzeria."

He finally turned away from the window.

"Speaking of pizza, I'm starved. Got anything to eat, lady?"

Sylvia slipped into her Mae West voice. "Of course, honey. Don't
you remember? You were just—"

"*Food*, lady. Food!"

"Oh, *that* stuff. Come on."

They groped for their robes and put them on, then she took him
by the hand to the kitchen. She was fumbling in a drawer for a
flashlight when the lights came on.

"Whatcha got?" Alan said, hanging over her shoulder as she
peered into the refrigerator.

The shelves were almost bare. With taking Jeffy into the Foundation, she hadn't got around to shopping today.

"Nothing but hot dogs."

"Oh, my!" Alan said. "What would Dr. Freud say about that?"

"He'd tell you to eat them or go hungry."

"Any port in a storm. Pop them in the microwave and we'll have byproducts-in-a-blanket."

"That sounds awful!"

"Can't be worse than the meatloaf I had last night. Made it myself—all the flavor and consistency of a Duraflame log." He stuck his tongue out in a disgusted grimace. "Blech!"

Sylvia leaned against him and began to laugh. This was a side of Alan she had never known. A little-boy side that she hadn't even dreamed existed. Whoever would have guessed that the handsome and dedicated Dr. Bulmer could be charming and witty and fun? *Fun!*

She stretched up on tiptoe and kissed him. He returned the kiss. Without separating her lips from his, she tossed the package of hot dogs back into the refrigerator and closed the door. As she put her arms around his neck, he lifted her and carried her back to the library.

Later, as they lay exhausted on the couch, she said, "We've got to try this in a bed sometime."

He lifted his face from between her breasts. "How about now?"

"You've got to be kidding!"

"Maybe I am," he said with a smile. "Maybe I'm not. All I know is I feel like my life has just begun tonight. I feel giddy, high, like I can do anything. And it's because of you."

"Oh, now—"

"It's true! Look at what's happened to me in the past few weeks. None of it matters now that I'm with you. I can't believe it, but touching you, loving you, it shrinks all those troubles to nothing. For the first time in my life I don't know what I'm going to be doing tomorrow and *I . . . don't . . . care!*"

He got up and put Charles' robe on again. Seeing him in the light now, she noticed how thin he was. He couldn't have been eating well at all since his wife walked out on him.

"Maybe you should open that pizzeria on your own. Put some meat on your bones if nothing else."

"Maybe," he said, walking back to the window.

She put on her own robe and followed him.

"Maybe, like hell," she said, snaking her arms around him and snuggling against his back. The storm was completely gone now. Still he stared out at the sky. "You'll never quit medicine and you know it."

"Not voluntarily anyway. But it looks like medicine is quitting me."

"You still have the Touch, don't you?"

He nodded. "It's still there."

She still hadn't one-hundred-percent accepted the existence of the *Dat-tay-vao*. She believed Alan, and she believed Ba, but she hadn't as yet seen it *work,* and the idea was so far beyond anything in her experience that the jury was still out for a small part of her mind.

"Maybe you should lay low with it for a while."

She felt him stiffen. "You sound like Ginny. She wanted me to deny it existed and never use it again."

"I didn't say that!" She resented being compared to his wife. "I just think maybe you should back off a bit. Look what's happened to you since you began using it."

"You're probably right. I probably should let things cool down. But, Sylvia . . ."

She loved to hear him say her name.

". . . I don't know how to explain this, but I can *feel* them out there. All those sick and hurting people. It's as if each one of them is sending out a tiny distress signal, and somewhere in the center of my brain is a little receiver that's picking up every single one of them. They're out there. And they're waiting. I don't know if I could stop—even if I wanted to."

She hugged him tighter. She remembered the day in the diner after they had been to the cemetery when he had first told her about it. It had seemed like such a gift then. Now it seemed like a curse.

He suddenly turned to face her.

"Now that I'm here, don't you think it's about time I used the touch on Jeffy?"

"No, Alan, you can't!"

"Sure! Come on. I want to do this for you as well as him!" he began pulling her toward the stairs. "Let's go take a look at him."

"Alan," she said, her voice quavering with alarm, "he's not here. I told you before—he's at the McCready Foundation until Thursday."

"Oh, yeah," he said quickly. Perhaps too quickly. "Slipped my mind."

He gathered her into his arms.

"Can I stay the night? If I may be permitted to quote Clarence Frogman Henry"—his voice changed to a deep croak—" 'I Ain't Got No Home.' "

"You'd better!" she laughed. But the laugh sounded hollow to her. How could Alan have forgotten about Jeffy being away? She didn't know what it was, but something was wrong with him.

33.
Charles

Charles looked up and was shocked to see Sylvie wending her way toward him through the tables of the staff cafeteria. In the bright red and white print dress that hugged her waist and bared her shoulders, she was a breathtaking mirage floating across a wasteland of white lab coats. Her smile was bright, but it didn't seem to be for him alone—it was for the world at large.

"You're early," he said, rising as she reached his table. She hadn't been due for another two hours.

"I know." She pulled out the chair across from him and sat down. Her words came rapid-fire. "But it's been three days and I've missed Jeffy and couldn't wait any longer. Your secretary told me you were here, told me how to get here when I asked her not to page you. What's that you're drinking?"

"Tea. Want one?"

She nodded and made a face in the direction of his cup. "But not hot and milky like that. Iced, if you don't mind. And clear."

He went and got it for her, and a refill of hot for himself, conscious of all the eyes on them, wondering no doubt where Charles Axford had been hiding the lovely bird.

She sipped it appreciatively. "Good." She looked around, a mischievous smile playing about her lips. "Never thought of you as the type for the staff caf."

"Every once in a while," he said with his best deadpan expression, "when I feel the approach of a hint of self-doubt, I find it therapeutic to move among the lesser of my fellow creatures. It restores my faith in myself."

Sylvie favored him with a smile. "How's Jeffy?"

She had asked him that question every day since she'd left him here on Monday and he had managed to put her off. Now it was Thursday and he had to answer. He would lay it out straight for her.

"Not good. He's definitely withdrawing. The clinical evaluations confirm it across the board when compared to his last work-up. We did the works on him—CT, PET, and BEAM scans, MRI, waking and sleeping EEGs, and computer generated spectral analysis of those EEGs. All normal. There's nothing structurally or electrically wrong with his brain."

"Which means there's nothing you can do for him."

"Probably not."

Anyone else watching Sylvie's face would have thought it calm, impassive. Charles saw the fleeting twist to her lips, the single prolonged blink, and knew how deeply disappointed she was.

"There's a new medication we can try."

"None of the others worked, not even that last one, whatever it was."

"PPA—phenylpropanolamine. It works in some autistics. Not Jeffy, unfortunately."

"And this one?"

He shrugged. It was a structural analog of PPA—probably useless where Jeffy was concerned. But he wanted to give her hope. "It may help, it may not. At least it won't hurt him."

"How can I refuse?" Sylvie said with a sigh.

"You can't. I'll ring you up later on and come by. I'll drop some off then."

Sylvie glanced away. "Maybe you should know . . . I have a houseguest."

"Who?" He couldn't imagine what she was getting at.

"Alan."

"Bulmer?" Jesus bloody Christ! Everywhere he went—Bulmer, Bulmer, Bulmer! "What happened? Wife kick him out or something?"

"No. She left him."

Charles held his breath. "Because of you?"

Sylvie looked puzzled, then: "Oh, no. It was because of all this healing business."

"So he came knocking on your door with an empty sugar bowl in his hand, right?"

"Why, Charles!" she said with a humorless smile. "I believe you're jealous! What happened to all that talk of 'no strings' and 'no exclusives'? I thought you promised not to ever get possessive, and above all, never get involved."

"I did and I'm not!" he said, feeling flustered and hiding it well, he hoped. He *was* jealous. "But I know your weaknesses as well as anybody."

"Maybe so. But he didn't camp on my doorstep in any way, shape, or form." Her face clouded. "It was awful."

She told him about the mob outside Bulmer's house Monday evening, forcing its way in, how he had been bruised and battered and his clothes half torn from his body.

Charles shuddered at the thought of being in that position. All those people reaching, touching.

And then she told him about how they had received word that his house had burned down.

"We went there Tuesday," she said softly. "There was nothing left, Charles! It had rained like crazy the night before, yet the ashes were still smoldering. You should have seen him—stumbling around the foundation like a drunken man. I don't think he truly believed the place had burned until he got there and saw it. Before that it had only been a story from a voice on the phone the night before. But when he pulled up in front of his yard, oh, you should have seen his face."

A tear slid down Sylvie's cheek, and the sight of it, knowing it

was for another man, was like a drop of nitric acid slipping down
the outer wall of his heart.

"You should have seen his face!" she repeated, volume rising
with her anger. "How could they do that to him?"

"Well," Charles said as cautiously as he could, "when you play
with fire—"

"You're so damn sure he's a phony, aren't you?"

"I'm absolutely positive." Charles could not remember being more
sure of anything else in his life. "Diseases don't disappear at the
touch of someone's hand, even if that someone is the wonderful
Dr. Bulmer. He's had a lot of free publicity, a lot of new patients,
and now it's backfired on him."

"You *bastard!*"

"My-my!" he said, giving her a dose of her own medicine. "Is
this the woman who swore she would never get emotionally tangled
up with anyone ever again?"

"He's a good man and he didn't need any new patients! He had
all he could handle already!"

"Then he's daft!"

Charles had expected a quick retort, but instead he faced silent
uncertainty. Which meant he had struck a nerve. Sylvie herself had
questions about Bulmer's mental status. Yet she had taken him into
her home. Charles realized with a pang he did not wish to acknowledge that her feelings for Bulmer must run deep. Quite a bit deeper
than her feelings for him. He could not help but resent that.

"Do you love him? Or is he just another stray you've taken in?"

"No," she said with a sudden ethereal smile that bothered him
more than anything else since she had sat down. "He's not just a
stray."

Charles found the whole conversation unpleasant and wanted off
the subject.

"Why don't we go up to my—"

He stopped in midsentence because he had suddenly noticed that
the cafeteria had gone silent. He glanced around and saw that everyone in the room was staring at a point somewhere behind him. He
turned to look.

Senator McCready had entered the cafeteria and was heading in their direction. His progress was slow, what with the way he had to lean against his cane, but there was no doubt that Charles' table was his destination.

When he reached the table, Charles stood up and shook his hand— a formal gesture for the sake of the rest of the people in the room. They spoke a few banal words of greeting, then McCready turned to Sylvie, his political twinkle in his eye.

"And who might this be?"

Charles introduced them and then the senator asked if he might join them for a few minutes. After he sat down, the normal buzz of the cafeteria returned, but at a higher volume than usual.

Charles was nearly struck dumb by McCready's appearance. Since the Foundation had bought this building, he had never—*never!*— shown his face in the staff cafeteria. And to show up in public in the afternoon when his strength was fading was unheard of! Charles knew the physical toll this was taking on him. What the bloody hell was he up to?

"Where are you from, Ms. Nash?" he asked, acting as if this were just another one of his routine daily visits to the caf.

"I'm one of your constituents, Senator," Sylvie said with her half smile that Charles knew to mean that she was amused but not impressed by McCready's presence. "I live in Monroe. Ever hear of it?"

"Of course! As a matter of fact, I remember reading a piece in Tuesday's paper about a house fire in Monroe. Said the place belonged to a Dr. Alan Bulmer. I wonder if that's the same Dr. Bulmer I know."

Sylvie's smile and insouciant manner evaporated. "You know Alan?"

"Well, I'm not sure. There was a Dr. Bulmer who testified before one of my committees a few months ago."

"That's him! He's the one!"

McCready shook his head and *tsk*ed. "A shame. Lightning is such a capricious thing."

"Oh, it wasn't lightning," Sylvie said, and launched into her story about the mob. When McCready professed to know nothing about Bulmer's publicity as a healer, she filled him in on what the press had been saying.

Charles folded his arms across his chest, trying to keep a self-satisfied smile off his face. It was all clear now. McCready was here to pump Sylvie about Bulmer. Charles had to admire the way the senator had broached the subject so gracefully without wasting as much as a second. The man was smooth.

"That really is too bad," McCready was saying with a slow, sympathetic shake of his head. "We were on opposite sides of the political fence at the committee hearings, but I deeply respected his integrity and obvious sincerity."

The lopsided smile was suddenly back on Sylvie's face. "Oh, I'm *sure* you did."

The senator rapped the tabletop with his knuckles as if he had just thought of something.

"I'll tell you what," he said. "If Dr. Bulmer is agreeable, I will put the resources of the Foundation at his disposal to investigate this power he is supposed to have."

Charles watched Sylvie blink in surprise. "You will?"

Charles wasn't the least bit surprised, however. This surely had been the senator's aim all along: Get this Bulmer chap here and see if he's for real. And now that Charles knew where the play was going, he leaned back and enjoyed the performance.

"Of course! The *raison d'être* of the Foundation is research. What if Dr. Bulmer truly has some power of healing that is as yet unknown to medical science? We would be negligent of the very purpose of this institution if we did not at least attempt to subject his supposed power to the scientific method. If he has something—*truly* has something—then I will place my reputation and the full weight of the Foundation's prestige behind vindicating him to the world."

"Senator," Sylvie said, eyes bright, "that would be wonderful!"

She's really got it bad for Bulmer, Charles thought. *Otherwise she'd never swallow this load of tripe.*

"But be warned," the senator said, his voice turning stern and stentorian. "If we determine that he's a fake, we will publicly expose him as such and advise anyone who is sick, even if they suffer from but a runny nose, to have nothing to do with him. Ever!"

Sylvie was quiet for a moment, then she nodded. "Fair enough. I'll convey it to him in just those terms. And we'll let you know."

Charles felt his jaw clamping. *We'll let you know.* Already they were a team.

I've lost her, he thought. The realization brought a sharp stab of pain, surprising him with its intensity. He didn't want to let her go. Their relationship had atrophied, but it wasn't dead. He could still revive it.

"And I will assign Dr. Axford to oversee the investigation." He glanced pointedly at Charles. "Providing he agrees, of course."

Nothing could have made Charles refuse. He would take the greatest pleasure in exposing Alan Bulmer as a fraud. *Then* what would Sylvie think of him?

"Of course," he said without missing a beat. "I'd be delighted."

"Splendid! Let's see . . . today's Thursday. Most of the week is shot. But if he can come in tonight, we can start the work-up right away. Right, Charles?"

"Whatever you say, Senator."

"There's one more thing," Sylvie said slowly, as if measuring her words. "This power of Alan's is *doing* something to him."

Power corrupts, my dear, Charles wanted to say. *Just look at the senator.*

"If he agrees to come in, will you check out his memory?"

"Memory?" Charles' interest was suddenly piqued. "How so?"

"Well, he can recall things from his childhood clear as day. But by lunch he's forgotten what he had for breakfast."

"Interesting," he said, thinking how it could mean nothing, or could be something very serious. Very serious indeed.

___ 34. ___
The Senator

"Front security just called, sir," said his secretary's voice through the intercom speaker. "He just arrived."

"Very good."

Finally!

McCready had been on edge for hours, wondering if Bulmer would really show. Now he could allow himself to relax.

Or could he?

He settled deeper into the thickly padded chair behind his desk and allowed his nearly useless muscles to rest. But his mind could not rest; not with the possibility of a cure so near at hand. To regain the strength of a normal man, to walk across the Capitol parking lot, to climb a single flight of stairs, to pursue a woman, to take part once again in the innumerable daily activities the average person took for granted. The prospect set his adrenaline flowing and his heart pumping.

And then there were the ambitions that went beyond the average man's—to once again look upon the possibility of capturing the party's nomination and running for the White House as something more than an empty pipe dream.

So many doors waiting to open for him if Bulmer's power proved to be real.

And Bulmer was here at last.

But at what cost? said a small voice from some dim, boarded-up corner of his mind. Were all the maneuverings and machinations to get him under your roof really necessary? Couldn't you simply have arranged to meet with him and asked him straight out if those incredible stories were true?

McCready squeezed his eyes shut and pushed the voice back to wherever it had been hiding.

It sounded so easy in those simplistic terms. But how could he go to that man as a meek and humble believer and put himself at his mercy? His whole being recoiled at the idea of assuming the role of supplicant before any man. Especially before a doctor. Most especially before Dr. Alan Bulmer.

How could he ask that man for a favor?

And what would Bulmer demand in return?

And worst of all: What if Bulmer turned him away?

He almost retched at the thought.

No. This way was better. This way he could call the shots. The Foundation was *his* territory, not Bulmer's. When all the data were in, he would know for sure one way or the other. If Bulmer was a fraud, it would be another in a long list of dead ends.

But if the data supported the stories, Bulmer would owe him.

Then McCready could go to Bulmer with his head high. And collect.

35.
Alan

"I can't do it now," Alan said, looking up at Charles Axford, who concealed his annoyance so poorly.

"Well, when *can* you do it?" Axford said.

Alan consulted his notes. Thank God for the notes. He couldn't remember a damn thing without them. The Hour of Power had come between 4:00 and 5:00 on Monday, and this was Thursday, so that meant it would probably come between 7:00 and 8:00 this evening. He glanced at his watch.

"Should be ready in about an hour."

"Super." He pronounced it *seeYOO-pah*. "Make yourself at home until then." He rose. "I've got a few things to check on in the meantime."

So Alan found himself alone in Charles Axford's office. He didn't want to be here, hadn't wanted to come to the McCready Foundation at all. But Sylvia had insisted. She had come home from the Foundation with Jeffy and McCready's proposal and had worked on him relentlessly all afternoon, saying that he would never know peace, never be able to practice any sort of reputable medicine again, that he owed it to himself, to his regular patients, to the special ones only he might be able to help, and on and on and on until he had capitulated out of sheer exhaustion.

Very persistent, that woman.

But he loved her. No doubt about that. She made him feel good about himself, good about her, good about the whole damn world. He hated leaving her, even for the few days it would take to go through this clinical investigation here at the Foundation. He had come here as much for her as for himself. That *had* to be love.

Because he hated being here.

It was a nice-enough place. Rather impressive, actually, with its steel and granite exterior and that huge art-deco lobby. But beyond the lobby, all twenty stories had been refurbished and furnished with state-of-the-art medical equipment.

The decor didn't make him feel the least bit comfortable, however. He hated being probed and studied and looked at and treated like an experimental lab rat. None of that had happened as yet, but it was coming. He could feel it coming. He had signed a waiver of liability and had agreed to sleep here and stay within the confines of the Foundation building for the duration of his testing in order to minimize the variables that might otherwise be introduced.

He sighed. What choice did he have? Either go on as he had been and lose his license and his reputation as a reliable, conscientious physician, condemned to practice miracle medicine on the fringes as some sort of quack or tent-show healer; or let someone like Axford do a hard-nosed, nitty-gritty scientific work-up under controlled conditions, get hard data, replicate the results, and document first the existence and then the whys and wherefores of the Touch.

Alan wanted to know—for Sylvia, for the world, but mostly for himself. Because the Touch was doing something to him. He didn't know exactly what, but he knew he wasn't quite the same person as when he started with this back in the spring. Axford's conclusions might not be good news, but at least he would know, and maybe the knowledge would help him reassert some modicum of control over his life. He sure as hell hadn't had much control over it lately.

* * *

The digital LED display on the desk clock said 7:12 when Axford returned.

"Are you quite ready now?" he said with his haughty air.

"Won't know for sure until I try."

"Then let's try, shall we? I've kept my secretary and a few others after hours on your account. I trust you won't disappoint us."

Axford led him down an elevator and into the opposite wing of the building, talking all the while.

"A man you shall know only as Mr. K has agreed to allow you to 'examine' him. He knows nothing about you—has never heard of you, never seen your picture in the paper, knows nothing about you other than the fact that you are another physician who is going to examine him and possibly contribute something to his therapy."

"Pretty much the truth, hmmm?"

Axford nodded. "I don't lie to people who come here for treatment."

"But you're also trying to avoid any hint of placebo effect."

"Bloody right. And we'll have the room miked and you'll be on videotape to make sure you don't try to sell him on a miracle."

Alan couldn't help but smile. "Glad to see you're taking no chances. What's the diagnosis?"

"Adeno-CA of the lung, metastatic to the brain."

Alan winced. "What's been tried so far?"

"That's a rather involved story—and here we are." He put his hand on a doorknob. "I'll introduce you and leave you alone with him. From then on you're on your own. But remember—I'll be watching and listening on the monitor."

Alan bowed. "Yes, Big Brother."

* * *

Mr. K was tall, very thin, and his color was awful. But his eyes were bright. He sat shirtless and stoop-shouldered on the examining table, and showed more empty spaces than teeth when he smiled. There was a two- or three-month-old scar, one inch long, at the base of his throat above the sternal notch—mediastinoscopy, no doubt. Alan also noticed knobby lumps above his right clavicle—lymph nodes swollen with metastasized cancer. Mr. K wheezed at times when he spoke, and he coughed intermittently.

"What kind of doctor are you?"

"A therapist of sorts. How do you feel?"

"Not bad for a dead man."

The reply startled Alan. So casual, and so accurate. "Pardon?"

"Didn't they tell you? I got cancer of the lung and it went to my head."

"But there's radiation therapy, chemotherapy—"

"Horseshit! No death rays, no poisons! I'll go out like a man, not some puking wimp."

"Then what are you doing here at the Foundation?"

"Made a deal with them." He pulled out a pack of Camels. "Mind if I smoke?"

"After I examine you, if you don't mind."

"I don't mind." He put them away. "Anyway, I made a deal: Keep me comfortable and out of pain." He lowered his voice. "And grease the chute on the way out when the time comes, if you know what I mean. Do that and I'll let you study me and the effects of all this cancer. So they're gonna keep giving me tests to see what happens to my mental function, my moods, my—what they call it? Oh, yeah—motor skills. All that shit. Never did much with my life these last fifty-two years. Figure I can do something on the way out. Man's gotta be good for something sometime in his life, ain't he?"

Alan stared at Mr. K. He was either one of the bravest men he had ever met or a complete idiot.

"But you know all this already," Mr. K said. "Don't you?"

"I like to find things out on my own. But tell me. If for some reason your tumors just disappeared and you walked out of here a healthy man, what would be the first thing you'd do?"

Mr. K winked at him. "Quit smoking!"

Alan laughed. "Good enough. Let's take a look at you."

He placed a hand on each side of Mr. K's head. There was no waiting. The shocklike ecstasy surged through him. He saw Mr. K's eyes widen, then they rolled upward as he went into a brief grand mal seizure.

Axford rushed into the room.

"What in bloody hell did you do to him?"

"Healed him," Alan said. "Isn't that what you wanted?" It was time to wipe that smug, superior look off Axford's face.

"You son of a bitch!"

"He's all right."

"I'm fine," Mr. K said from the floor. "What happened?"

"You had a seizure," Axford said.

"If you say so." He brushed off Axford's attempt to make him lie still, and got to his feet. "Didn't feel a thing."

"Check him out tomorrow," Alan said, feeling more confident of the Touch than ever before. "He's cured."

"Tomorrow, hell!" Axford said, leading Mr. K to the door. "I'm hauling in the on-call techs right now! We'll see what a chest X ray, EEG, and CT scan have to say tonight!"

36.
Charles

It's a mistake! It's got to be!

Charles sat before the light boxes, staring at the chest X ray. The PA view on his left was two months old; it showed an irregular white blotch in the right hilar area, a mass of cancerous tissue. The view in the middle had been shot a week ago; the mass was larger, with tendrils reaching out into the uninvolved lung tissue, the hilum swollen with enlarged lymph nodes. The third film, to the right, was still warm from the developer.

It was normal. Completely clean. Even the emphysema and fibrosis were gone.

They're having me on! Charles told himself. *They're pissed at being called in at night so they've stuck in a ringer to give me a scare!*

He checked the name and date on the third film: Jake Knopf—known to Bulmer as Mr. K—and today's date were printed in the upper right corner. Then he checked the film again and noticed an irregularity of the left clavicle in the third film—an old fracture that had healed at a sharper than normal angle. A glance at the other two studies almost froze his blood—the same clavicle abnormality was in all three!

"Wait a minute now," he said to himself in a gentle tone. "Just wait a minute. No use getting your knickers in a twist just yet. There's got to be an explanation."

"Did you say something, Doctor?" a voice said from behind him.

Charles swiveled his chair around. Two men, one blond, one dark haired, both in white lab coats that were tight across their shoulders, stood inside the door.

"Who are you?"

"We're your new assistants."

Assistants, my ass! These two were goons. He recognized one of them from the senator's personal security team.

"The hell you are. I don't need any assistants and didn't ask for any."

The blond fellow shrugged. "This is where we've been assigned. This is where we'll stay. Personally, I'd rather be out on the town, but the orders came straight from the senator's office."

"We'll see about that." He jabbed at the intercom. Here he was, faced with the most astounding puzzle of his medical career, and he had to put up with interference from McCready. "Marnie—get me the senator. Now." He was glad he had had her stay tonight; it would save him the trouble of tracking McCready down.

"Uh, Dr. Axford?" she said, uncertainly. "He's already on the line. He called about a minute ago and said you'd be calling him very shortly and he'd hold until you did."

Despite his anger, Charles had to laugh. That sly bastard!

"He's on 06, Doctor," Marnie said.

"Right." He picked up the handset.

"I was expecting your call," McCready said without preamble. "Here's why I must insist on Henly and Rossi staying with you: You are aware no doubt of Dr. Bulmer's penchant for publicity; I want to make sure that none of his test results leak out until you are completely finished. I will not have him use the Foundation and some inconclusive data as a springboard to greater heights of notoriety. And I won't have any of the staff tempted into leaking some of these results to the outside.

"Therefore, Henly and Rossi will be on hand to see that all— and I do mean *all*—records of Dr. Bulmer's stay remain locked in your office files until you and the Foundation are ready to issue a statement."

"You really think all this is necessary?"

"I do. And I ask you to cooperate with me."

Charles thought a moment. It would be a pain in the ass to have these two characters traipsing around after him, but if all the data were to be confined to his office, where he could have access to it at any time, then how could he object?

"All right. As long as they don't get in my way."

"Thank you, Charles. I knew I could count on you. Any results yet?"

"Of course not! I've only just begun!"

"Very well. Keep me informed."

Charles grunted and hung up. He edited Henly and Rossi from his mind and studied the X rays again. There had to be a mistake there. Somewhere along the line somebody had either screwed up or was trying to make a fool out of him.

He'd find out which, and heads would roll.

*   *   *

Charles just missed Mr. Knopf at the EEG lab.

"He's on his way to radiology," the tech told him.

Charles picked up the thick, fan-folded EEG record and spread part of it out on a desk. He felt his mouth go dry as he pulled more and more of it across the desk.

It was normal. None of the typical irregularities signifying an underlying mass, no hint of a recent grand mal seizure.

He had the tech pull out a previous tracing. Yes, all the usual signs of brain tumor had been there. All gone now.

He rushed down to radiology, idly noting Henly and Rossi entering the EEG lab after him and gathering up all the tracings he had been reading.

Knopf was already in the CT scanner. Charles paced the floor in front of the developer. He was sweating, whether from the extra heat thrown off by the machine or from tension, he didn't know. The radiologist wouldn't be in until morning, but that didn't matter.

Charles could read the scans himself. As the films rolled out of the developer, each with four radiographic cuts of Knopf's brain, he grabbed them one by one and slapped them up on the view box.

Normal! One after the other: *Normal!*

He was almost frantic now. This was a nightmare! Things like this just didn't happen in the real world! Everything had an explanation, a cause and an effect! Primary tumors and their metastases simply didn't disappear because some balmy faith healer put his hands on a head!

He saw that the red light over the door was out so he rushed into the scanner room. Jake Knopf was sitting on the edge of the roller table.

"What's up, Doc?" he said. "You look like you need a transfusion."

I do! Charles thought. *Straight vodka!*

"Just want to check your neck, Jake."

"Sure. Check away."

Charles pressed his fingers above Knopf's right clavicle where the lymph nodes had been swollen and knotty. They were gone now. The area was clean.

Nausea rose up like a wave. He felt as if his world were coming apart. He lurched away and hurried toward Bulmer's quarters.

It was true! Knopf was cured! And Bulmer had done it! But how? Jesus H. bloody fucking Christ—!

He cut himself off with a bitter laugh. If Bulmer's power was possible, then anything was possible. Even Jesus Christ was possible. Better watch his tongue. He might really be up there. Or out there. Or somewhere. Listening.

*   *   *

"Nope," Bulmer said with a slow, deliberate shake of his head from where he sat by his room window. "Can't do it."

"Why the bloody hell not?"

"Too late. It only lasts for an hour and then it's gone."

"How convenient."

"I've got no control over it."

"So when will it be back?"

He glanced at his watch. "Sometime tomorrow morning, probably, but definitely somewhere around eight tomorrow evening."

Axford sat down on the bed. He suddenly felt exhausted.

"You're so sure?"

"Been keeping track of it for months." He indicated a manila envelope.

"Records?" Charles said, feeling his lethargy lift slightly. "You've kept records?"

"Sporadically at first, but pretty consistently lately. You want to use them, you can have them. I mean *borrow* them. I want them back."

"Of course." Axford sifted through the contents—there were index cards, scratch pad sheets emblazoned with the logos of various pharmaceutical companies, even prescription blanks with notes jotted on the back. There were a few audio microcassettes, too. "What is all this?"

"Names, dates, times. Who, what, where, when—when the Hour of Power started and when it ended."

The Hour of Power—sounded like one of those Sunday-morning gospel shows. Charles could feel his excitement growing. Here was something he could deal with—dates, times, *data!* He could work with these. He could understand and toy with and analyze these. But Jake Knopf . . .

How could he deal with what had happened to Jake Knopf today?

"You never asked about Mr. K," he said to Bulmer.

"Who?" Bulmer looked genuinely puzzled.

"The chap with the brain metastases. You saw him a few hours ago."

"Oh, yes. Of course." Bulmer smiled. "He's fine, I'm sure. A remarkable 'spontaneous remission,' no?"

"You read minds, too?" Charles blurted in surprise. That had been exactly what he had been thinking.

Bulmer's smile was laconic. "I've heard that one a few times before."

"Right. I'll bet you have."

He looked Bulmer in the eye and hesitated before asking the question. *The* question. Because he was afraid of the answer.

"Is all this for real?"

Bulmer held his gaze. "Yes, Charles. It's for real."

"But *how,* dammit?"

Bulmer went on to tell him about a former Vietnam medic who eventually wound up in the Monroe Community Hospital, where he touched him and died.

A fantastic story, but certainly no more fantastic than Jake Knopf's remission. He studied Bulmer. The man's bearing, his laid-back manner, the pile of notes in the envelope, all indicated a sincere man.

But it can't be!

Charles stood and hefted the envelope.

"I'm going to sift this stuff through the computer and see if any correlations fall out."

"There's a definite rhythm to the Touch, but I haven't been able to figure it out."

"If it's there, we'll find it."

"Good. That's why I'm here. You're going to do a work-up on me, aren't you?"

"Starts first thing in the morning."

"Do a good one. The works."

"I intend to." He noticed Bulmer's grim expression. "Why do you say it like that?"

"Because there's something wrong with me. I don't know if it's stress, or if it's something else, but I can't seem to remember things the way I used to. I can't even remember half the people I cured. But I cured them. That I know."

"Short-term or long-term memory?"

"Mostly short-term, I think. It's pretty spotty, but there's definitely something wrong."

Charles didn't like the sound of that, but he reserved judgment until he had some data to work with. "Rest up tonight, because tomorrow and the next day you're going to be tested like you've never been tested before."

As Charles turned to go, Bulmer said, "You do believe me just a little now, don't you?"

Charles saw something in his eyes at that moment, a terrible loneliness that touched him despite his desire to prove Alan Bulmer a cheap fraud.

"I don't believe in believing. I either know or I don't know. Right now I don't know."

"Fair enough, I guess."

Charles hurried out.

* * *

It was late, but Charles made the calls anyway.

He had looked through Bulmer's notes and couldn't believe that the man would put all this down in black and white. He had listed dates and times. He named names! He even listed other physicians caring for the patient! If he was a phony, he was either a very naive or a very stupid one. It would be so easy to trace these people and check out their medical records.

But, of course, if Bulmer was completely caught up in a delusional system, he could be expected to record his imagined data rigorously.

Charles couldn't say exactly why he had looked through Bulmer's manila envelope before sending it down to data processing, but now that he had, he was compelled to call at least one of the other doctors mentioned within the mess to check out a "cure" Bulmer described.

He picked one at random: Ruth Sanders. Acute lymphocytic leukemia. He called information, found the number of the hematologist Bulmer had listed, and called him. After blustering his way past the answering service, he got Dr. Nicholls on the line.

The hematologist was instantly suspicious and very guarded. And rightly so. He did not want to give out privileged information over the phone to a voice he didn't know. Charles decided to lay his cards on the table.

"Look. I'm at the McCready Foundation. I've got someone here who says he cured Ruth Sanders' leukemia three weeks ago. I'm looking for proof that he's bonkers. I'll hang up. You call me back here at the Foundation—that way you'll know I'm really calling from here—and ask for Dr. Charles Axford. Then give me a few straight answers. I promise you they'll go no further."

Charles hung up and waited. The phone rang three minutes later. It was Dr. Nicholls.

"Ruth Sanders' leukemia is in complete remission at this time," he said immediately.

"What protocol were you using?"

"None. She had refused further treatment due to side effects."

"And her peripheral smear is suddenly normal?"

"It happens."

"What about her bone marrow?"

Dr. Nicholls hesitated. "Normal."

Charles felt his throat go dry.

"How do you explain that?"

"Spontaneous remission."

"Of course. Thank you."

He hung up and pawed through the envelope for more "cures" that listed consultants. He found one that Bulmer apparently wasn't sure about: a teenage girl with alopecia universalis—bald as a billiard ball when she came and left the office. He called her dermatologist. After going through a similar rigamarole with the consultant, he finally got the man to admit reluctantly:

"Yeah. Her hair's growing back. Evenly. All over her scalp."

"Did she tell you about a Dr. Bulmer?"

"She sure did. According to Laurie and her mother, that quack will be raising the dead next."

"You think he's a rip-off artist, then?"

"Of course he is! These guys make their reputations on placebo effect and spontaneous remissions. The only thing about this Bulmer character that doesn't fit in with the usual pattern is his fee."

"Oh, really?" Charles hadn't thought about how Bulmer must be cleaning up on these "cures" of his. "What did he take them for?"

"Twenty-five bucks. I couldn't believe it, but the mother swore that was all he charged. I think you've got a real kook on your hands. I think he may really believe he can effect these cures."

"Could be," Charles said, feeling very tired. "Thanks."

With steadily growing alarm, he made five more calls, which yielded three more contacts. The story was always the same: complete spontaneous remission.

Finally he could not bring himself to dial another number. Each doctor he had spoken to had had only one encounter with a "Bulmerized" patient and had easily written off the incident as a fluke. But Charles had a sheaf of names and addresses, and so far Bulmer was batting a thousand.

Charles fought off a sudden desire to throw the envelope into his wastepaper basket and follow it with a match. If what Bulmer had said about his failing memory was true, he wouldn't be able to recall much of the data. It would be gone for good. And then Charles would feel safe.

He smirked at the thought of Charles Axford, the relentless researcher and pursuer of scientific truth, destroying data to save himself from facing the collapse of all his preconceptions, the repudiation of his precious *weltanschauung*.

It was a perfectly heinous idea, yet oh, so attractive.

For the events of the day—first Knopf and now these phone calls with the unbroken trail of "spontaneous remissions" they revealed—were making Charles physically ill. He was nauseous from the mental vertigo it caused him.

If he could destroy the data, he was sure he could make himself forget they had ever existed. And then he could once again return his mind to an even intellectual and philosophical keel.

Or maybe he couldn't. Maybe he would never recover from what he had learned today.

In that case the only thing to do was follow it through.

He looked once more—longingly—at the wastebasket, then stuffed Bulmer's papers back in the envelope. He was locking them in his office safe when his secretary popped her head in the door.

"Can I go now?"

"Sure, Marnie." She looked as tired as he felt.

"Need anything before I leave?"

"Do you have any Mylanta?"

"Your stomach bothering you?" she said, her brows knitting together in concern. "You look kind of pale."

"I'm fine. Something I ate. Crow never did agree with me."

"Pardon?"

"Nothing, Marnie. Go home. Thanks for staying."

How could he tell her or anyone else how he felt? It was as if he were the first astronaut in space, and he had looked down from orbit and seen that the earth was flat.

37.
Sylvia

"What's the matter, Jeffy?"

She had heard him whimpering in his sleep. As she looked in, she saw him raking at his pajamas and neck. She went over to investigate. He had never shown tendencies toward self-destruction or self-mutilation, but she had read of autistic children who developed them. With the way he was regressing, she feared every change was for the worse.

She pulled his hands away and saw the rising welts on the skin of his neck. Lifting his pajama top, she saw more on his back.

Hives.

There had been nothing new in his diet, and she hadn't changed her detergent or fabric softener. She could think of only one thing that had been recently added to his intake—his new medicine from the Foundation.

Sylvia slumped down on the bed next to Jeffy. She wanted to cry. Wasn't anything going to help this child? Jeffy was slowly fading away and there seemed to be nothing she could do other than sit and watch him vanish. She felt so damned *helpless!* So impotent! It was like being paralyzed. She wanted to *do* something, anything but cry.

She took a deep breath and settled herself. Crying never solved anything—she had learned that after Greg's death.

She phoned Charles at home. His housekeeper said he hadn't returned from the Foundation yet. She called him there.

"You'll have to stop the medication," he told her. "Were you seeing any results?"

"No. Too soon to see any change, wouldn't you think?"

"I suppose. But it's a moot point now. He could have a more severe reaction with the next dose, so pour the rest down the toilet. And have you got some Benadryl around?"

She ran a mental inventory of the medicine cabinet. "I think so. The liquid."

"Good. Give him two teaspoons. It'll stop the itching."

"Thank you, Charles. Will do." She paused, then: "How's Alan?"

His voice sharpened. "Your precious Dr. Bulmer is doing fine. Better than I, for that matter."

Something odd about his voice . . . strained . . . Charles almost never showed emotion. It made her uneasy.

"Something wrong?"

"No." A tired sigh. "Everything's fine. We start testing him in the a.m."

"You won't hurt him, will you?"

"Jesus, Sylvie, he'll be fine. Just don't ask bloody stupid questions, okay?"

"Okay. Pardon me for asking."

"Sorry, Love. I'm a bit rushed here. I'll ring you up later to see how the Boy's doing."

He made some excuse about checking reports and said good-bye, leaving Sylvia standing there, holding the phone. Charles was upset about something and that wasn't good. But Charles also sounded indecisive . . . almost unsure of himself. That was unsettling.

She hung up and went to get the Benadryl. The house seemed so empty as she walked down the hall to the medicine cabinet. Alan had been here only three days and nights, but he had filled Toad Hall for her in a way that she had not known since buying the old place. It seemed all the emptier now for his leaving.

After all these years it was so strange to miss somebody.

She had just spooned the antihistamine into Jeffy when the phone rang. Her heart tripped a few beats when she recognized the voice.

"A lonely froggy calling Mrs. Toad."

"Alan!"

He told her about Mr. K and how he had cured the man, and how Charles had reacted.

"No wonder Charles was acting so strangely!"

"You don't sound quite yourself tonight, either."

She didn't want to burden him with her own problems, but she had to tell him.

"It's Jeffy. He's allergic to that new drug."

"Oh, I'm sorry to hear that. But look," he said, and she could hear his voice brighten, "when I get out of here we'll know all about the Touch. *Then* will you let me try it on Jeffy?"

She felt every muscle in her body suddenly tighten of its own accord. Was it possible?

"Alan—will it work?"

"I don't know. Seems to work on everything else. Why not autism?"

God, if I could believe for just a minute, for just a second.

"Sylvia? You still there?"

She took a breath. "Yes, Alan. Still here. Hurry home, will you? Please?"

"I'm on my way!"

She laughed, and that relaxed her a bit. "Wait till they're finished with you."

"Good night, Mrs. Toad."

"Good night, Alan."

She hung up the phone and went over to Jeffy. She gathered him up in her arms and hugged him close, ignoring his struggles to get free, struggles that were as impersonal as someone in a deep sleep trying to untangle himself from his sheets.

"Oh, Jeffy. Everything's going to be all right. I can feel it coming."

And she could. The bitter discouragement of a few moments ago was gone. She wouldn't let herself get carried away, but she felt that somewhere up around the bend she might catch sight of the light that was supposed to wait at the end of every tunnel.

38.
Alan

So this is what it's like to be a patient.

Alan was into his second full day of testing and he didn't like it.

Starting at 6:00 a.m. yesterday, they had stuck leads to his scalp and attached a box to his belt for a twenty-four-hour EEG by telemetry. They had punctured him and poked at him for the rest of the day. And all without a word of explanation. This morning had started off with hour after hour of written psychological tests.

At least he knew what was going on. But how must a patient feel when everything around him was strange and mysterious and vaguely threatening?

And he was lonely. He missed Sylvia desperately. Just a few days with her and he felt like a new man. To be away from her now was an almost physical pain. But he was doing this as much for her as for himself. If their relationship was to have any sort of future, he had to know what he was getting her into.

And so he would be a patient for a while. And like any patient he was afraid of what these tests would show. It might be just another routine work-up to Axford, but there was nothing routine about the ordeal to Alan. He was seriously concerned about his erratic memory, the gaps that had seemingly been cut out of his life, especially his recent life. That suggested a diagnosis too awful to consider.

Better to have a brain tumor than Alzheimer's disease. He knew he was out of the usual age range, but the signs were there.

He was now lying on a hard-surfaced table in the Foundation's radiology department, waiting to be rolled into the maw of a machine that looked like a CT scanner. A young technician wearing a good four pounds of eye makeup approached with a syringe.

"This place even runs full blast on Saturdays?" he said as she swabbed his arm with alcohol.

"Every day," she said around a big wad of chewing gum.

"By the way, I had a CAT scan a few weeks ago." He remembered the rush of warmth when the contrast material had been infused into his veins.

"This is similar but different," the girl said nonchalantly. "This here's a PET scan."

"Ah, yes," he said, putting on a pedantic tone. "Positron Emission Tomography." He was pleased that he had remembered the meaning of the acronym. Maybe his memory wasn't so bad after all.

The technician cocked her head as she looked at him. "Hey. Pretty good. How'd you know that?"

"Read about it in *Newsweek*. What's that you're going to inject into me?"

"Just sugar."

More than just sugar, Alan knew. FDG—*radioactive* sugar that would show the most active and least active areas of his brain. He remembered a few articles he'd read in the journals had said that PET scans had demonstrated abnormalities in the brain metabolism of schizophrenics. Is that what Axford was after—proof that he was a grade-four tweety bird?

"Dr. Axford wants you to walk around for a while before you're scanned," she said as she withdrew the needle from his vein.

Evidently Axford wanted to see the overall activity of his brain.

And what if he found a schizophrenic pattern on the PET? What if everything Alan had seen and done lately had never happened? What if it were all part of an elaborate delusional system?

No, he wasn't going to fall into that trap. *I'm NOT crazy,* he thought, and then realized that they all say that, don't they?

*   *   *

The tests were finally finished and he was sitting in his bare little room on the seventh floor when there came a knock on the door.

It was Mr. K. Alan didn't recognize him at first—his color was so much better. A suitcase rested on the floor beside him.

"Just came to say good-bye," he said, thrusting out his hand.

Alan shook it. "Leaving?"

"Yep. Goin' out for a Saturday afternoon walk and I ain't coming back. Said they can't use me anymore 'cause I'm not sick anymore."

"Did they tell you how your cancer cleared up?" He was curious how Axford & Co. would explain that.

"Said it cleared up by itself. Nocturnal emission or something like that," he said with a grin and a wink. "But I know what it was and so do you."

"What?"

He poked a finger at Alan's chest. "It was you. You did it. I don't know how, but you did it. Only explanation I can think of is you're an angel or something sent down by God to give me another chance. Well, I'm taking it! I screwed up the first time around, but I ain't screwin' up again!"

There were suddenly tears in Mr. K's eyes. Obviously embarrassed, he pulled something from his pocket and thrust it into Alan's hand. It crinkled.

"Here. Take these. I won't be needing them."

Thinking it was money, Alan began to protest. Then he saw that it was a half-empty pack of Camels.

"Good-bye," said Mr. K, averting his face as he picked up his suitcase and hurried off.

Alan went to throw the cigarettes into the wastebasket, but stopped in midstride and stared at the crumpled pack. He decided to keep it. Every time he had his doubts about the reality of what he was experiencing, he'd take it out and use it as a reminder of Mr. K's "nocturnal emission."

__ 39. __
Charles

"This everything?"

Henly nodded as he placed the last print-out on Charles' desk. "Every last bit."

"You're sure?"

"We're paid to be thorough."

Charles had to admit that McCready's two goons were extremely thorough. They had dogged Bulmer's progress from department to department for the past two days, gathering up each scrap of data as it was produced and tucking it away for Charles' eyes only.

For two days now he had suppressed the gnawing desire to scan each test result as it came in, afraid that he would prejudice himself by forming a hasty diagnosis. He wanted to see the whole picture at once.

"You waiting for something?" he asked Henly and Rossi as they stood across the desk from him.

"Yeah," Rossi said. "We're waiting for you to put that stuff in the safe."

"I want to look at it."

"Everything's on the computer, Doc. Filed under your access code. We're not supposed to leave until all that stuff's locked away."

"Forget it," Charles said, his annoyance rising. "I like to see the originals."

"Give us a break, Doc," Henly said, agitatedly running a hand through his blond hair. "It's Saturday night and the women are waitin'. Lock up the safe and we're gone. What you do after that ain't our problem."

Charles sighed. "Anything to speed you on your way." He went to the wall safe, tapped in the code, and shoved all the papers inside. After slamming it shut and pressing the *clear* button, he turned to the two security men. "Happy?"

" 'Night, Doc," they said in unison, and they were gone.

Charles seated himself before his computer terminal and found a three-by-five index card taped to the screen. It read:

All data from Bulmer notes and cassettes entered into memory as "Hour of Power," your access only.

He stared at the dull, lifeless surface of the CRT, almost afraid to turn it on, afraid that he would find no explanation for the incredible phenomena Bulmer had left in his wake for the past few months.

But he had to start sometime, somewhere, and Bulmer's notes seemed as good a place as any. He flipped on the power and soon the square little cursor, blinking bright green in the blank darkness of the screen, made its appearance. He entered his access code, then had the computer list sequentially the data Alan had given him.

It was a mess. He scrolled through, noting that times would be recorded for three consecutive days, then a gap of two days with no data, then four days with times, then three without. He could see no pattern. It looked completely random, chaotic. He entered:

CORRELATE WITH ALL KNOWN HUMAN BIORHYTHMS

He watched the cursor stop blinking for a few seconds, then the answer flashed on the screen with a beep:

NO CORRELATION

Charles typed:

CORRELATE TO MEMORY

That would initiate a search through the computer's entire memory bank, one of the most complete bioscience data bases in the world. It was a longer wait, but finally came the beep:

NO CORRELATION

This was looking like a dead end, but for the hell of it, Charles decided to let the computer search the memory banks of other computers all over the world:

CORRELATE RHYTHM WITH ALL OTHER ACCESSIBLE DATA BASES

PROCESSING flashed on the screen.

This search would take considerable time, so while that was going on, he cleared the screen and prepared to find out what there was to know about Dr. Alan Bulmer. He decided to start with the basics, so he cued up Bulmer's blood profile.

TEST	ABNORMAL	NORMAL	UNITS	REF. RANGE
CALCIUM		9.6	MG/DL	8.5 - 10.5
FREE CALCIUM		4.2	MG/DL	3.5 - 5.8
INORGANIC PHOSPHORUS		3.4	MG/DL	2.5 - 4.5
TOTAL BILIRUBIN		0.6	MG/DL	0.2 - 1.2
DIRECT BILIRUBIN		0.2	MG/DL	0.0 - 0.3
INDIRECT BILIRUBIN		0.4	MG/DL	0.3 - 0.9
TOTAL PROTEIN		7.2	GM/DL	6.0 - 8.0
ALBUMIN		4.6	GM/DL	3.0 - 5.5

GLOBULIN	2.6	GM/DL	1.5 - 3.6
ALB./GLOB. RATIO	1.8		1.1 - 2.2
ALKALINE PHOSPHATASE	60	IU/L	30 - 115
SGOT	27	IU/L	0 - 50
SGPT	29	IU/L	0 - 45
LDH	193	IU/L	100 - 225
BUN	19	MG/DL	10 - 20
CREATININE	1.1	MG/DL	0.7 - 1.5
BUN/CREATININE RATIO	20.0		7.0 - 29.0
GLUCOSE	94	MG/DL	60 - 115
URIC ACID	1.9	MG/DL	2.0 - 9.0
SODIUM	142	MEQ/L	135 - 145
POTASSIUM	4.1	MEQ/L	3.5 - 5.5
CHLORIDE	106	MEQ/L	96 - 106
CARBON DIOXIDE	26	MEQ/L	24 - 30
CHOLESTEROL	187	MG/DL	135 - 300
TRIGLYCERIDES	92	MG/DL	10 - 150
T4 RIA	8.2	MCG/DL	5.0 - 13.0

HEMOGRAM

WBC	5.3	K	4.5 - 11.0
RBC	5.12	M	3.5 - 5.9
HEMOGLOBIN	15.2	GM%	10.0 - 18.0
HEMATOCRIT	44.6	%	36 - 54
MCV	87		80 - 100
MCH	30		22 - 35
MCHC	34		27 - 37

WBC DIFFERENTIAL

NEUTROPHILS	56	%	46 - 79
LYMPHOCYTES	36	%	15 - 44
MONOCYTES	4	%	0 - 9

| EOSINOPHILS | 3 | % | 0 - 5 |
| BASOPHILS | 1 | % | 0 - 2 |

For the hell of it, he had ordered a drug screen.

TEST	ABNORMAL	NORMAL	UNITS	
ALCOHOL, ETHYL		0	MG/DL	
		10 - 50	MG/	
			DL:	NO INFLUENCE
		50 - 100	MG/	
			DL:	SLIGHT INFLUENCE
		100 - 150	MG/	
			DL:	MODERATE INFLUENCE
		150 - 200	MG/	
			DL:	MODERATE POISONING
		200 - 250	MG/	
			DL:	SEVERE POISONING
		350 - 400	MG/	
			DL:	DEEP COMA
AMPHETAMINE				NONE DETECTED
METHAMPHETAMINE				NONE DETECTED
PHENOBARB				NONE DETECTED
SECOBARB				NONE DETECTED
DORIDEN				NONE DETECTED
QUININE				NONE DETECTED
MORPHINE				NONE DETECTED
METHADONE				NONE DETECTED
PHENOTHIAZINE				NONE DETECTED
CODEINE				NONE DETECTED
COCAINE				NONE DETECTED
DILAUDID				NONE DETECTED
AMOBARB				NONE DETECTED
DARVON				NONE DETECTED
DILANTIN				NONE DETECTED

As expected, no abusable substances were floating around in his blood or urine.

So far so good. His cardiogram and chest X ray were normal, too. Next he cued up Bulmer's CT scan from Downstate and reviewed the series of radiographic slices of the brain at various levels with and without contrast: no infarcts or masses evident anywhere. The MRI studies done here were negative as well.

So Bulmer didn't have a brain tumor and hadn't had any previous strokes. No surprise. He moved on to see what his brainwaves looked like.

An edited version of Bulmer's twenty-four-hour EEG from yesterday scrolled horizontally across the screen. The computer presented a good sample of the six parallel zigzag lines that formed the basic electrical pattern of his brain, then edited that particular pattern out of the rest of the record, leaving only irregularities and significant variations for review.

Charles noticed immediately that the basic pattern was diffusely abnormal. Nothing terribly specific, but the background activity was disorganized, showing generalized slowing.

That puzzled Charles. This was not the type of EEG he would associate with an active professional pushing forty. It was a senile old man's EEG.

He scrolled on. The first variation showed around 7:15 a.m., when an undulating pattern began to appear, barely noticeable at first, but growing more pronounced with every passing minute. It wasn't confined to any one section of the brain, but affected all the leads, causing the lines to glide up and down. The undulation was most pronounced at 7:45, after which the magnitude of each wave began to slacken off, finally disappearing at 8:16.

Charles leaned back and chewed his lip. Odd. He couldn't remember ever seeing anything like that before. He shrugged it off. Probably some transient electrical disturbance in the telemetry. He scrolled on, finding nothing until 7:37 p.m. last night, when the same pattern repeated itself, peaking shortly after 8:00 and disappearing by 8:35.

Doubly odd. Two apparent artifacts, both identical, approximately twelve and half hours apart, each lasting an hour.

The Hour of Power!

A tingle ran up Charles' back.

He shook himself. This was ridiculous. It was just an artifact—a unique one, he'd grant that, but a mere artifact nonetheless.

He cleared the screen, cued up Bulmer's PET scan, and gasped. The EEG had been unsettling, but this was outright shocking. He ran through a number of slices on the PET, then flashed back to the CT scan and MRI. Those were definitely normal, with normal ventricles and sulci and no sign of impaired circulation in any area of the brain. Back to the PET scan—grossly abnormal. The FDG injected into Bulmer had not been taken up by his brain cells in the usual way. The CT scan showed that nothing was stopping the glucose from getting there, but in the PET, the yellow and orange areas of active brain were markedly reduced, while other areas of the scan were dark, showing no uptake at all of the glucose. The neurons there weren't working.

Which meant that areas of Bulmer's brain were not functioning.

Charles' mind whirled in confusion. He had seen PET scans with similar abnormalities before, but not in a brain that was perfectly normal in anatomy and vasculature.

The computer beeped and flashed in the lower left corner of the screen:

SEARCH COMPLETED—0.95 CORRELATION FOUND

Charles quickly cleared the screen and typed:

LIST CORRELATION

The computer beeped and wrote:

SOURCE: NATIONAL WEATHER SERVICE
DATA BASE. CORRELATION: TIME
COORDINATES OF ALL DATA ENTERED
APPROXIMATE TIME OF HIGH TIDE IN LONG
ISLAND SOUND OFF GLEN COVE, NY.
COMMENCING APPROXIMATELY 30 MINUTES

BEFORE HIGH TIDE AND CEASING
APPROXIMATELY 30 MINUTES AFTER.

Charles slumped back in his chair. Well, he had wanted to identify the rhythm of Bulmer's so-called Hour of Power, and here it was. The oldest rhythm in the world.

The tide.

It gave him the creeps.

He stood up and walked around his desk and back again to relieve the tension that had begun to grip his muscles. He remembered the two sine-wave artifacts that had risen and fallen about twelve hours apart. Didn't the tide rise and fall twice a day, about twelve hours apart? He rechecked the tracings on the screen and jotted down the time each artifact appeared and disappeared—7:15 a.m. to 8:16 a.m. and 7:37 p.m. to 8:35 p.m. If the artifact represented Bulmer's Hour of Power, and it was linked to the rise and fall of the tide, then high tide should occur right in the bloody middle of those two periods. He figured the midpoints, then sat down at the terminal again.

> CORRELATE WITH HIGH TIDE IN LONG
> ISLAND SOUND OFF GLEN COVE JULY 11:
> 7:45 A.M. AND 8:06 P.M. REFER TO
> N.W.S. DATA BASE

The computer beeped almost immediately.

NO SIGNIFICANT CORRELATION

Damn! If that had correlated, he'd have had something concrete to go on.

Wait! Bulmer hadn't been near Long Island Sound when the tracing was made. He'd been here, on Park Avenue in Manhattan. The East River was the nearest body of water.

Charles leaped to the keyboard.

CORRELATE WITH HIGH TIDE IN THE
EAST RIVER JULY 11: 7:45 A.M. AND
8:06 P.M. REFER TO N.W.S. DATA BASE

An instant beep:

0.97 CORRELATION

Got it!
But exactly *what* did he have?

___ 40. ___
Alan

Alan felt his heart throw a few premature beats when he answered the knock on his door and saw Axford standing there.

This is it, he thought.

Axford had a bottle in one hand and a sheaf of papers under his other arm. He looked like he had already sampled the bottle a couple of times before his arrival.

"Is this a party?" Alan said, stepping back to let him in. "Or a wake?"

"Get some glasses," Charles said gruffly. "This is good stuff, even if you don't like bourbon."

He poured an inch or so into each of the two plastic cups Alan got from the bathroom and they tossed it off together.

"Smooth. What's the brand?"

"Maker's Mark," Axford said. "Have some more." He quickly poured another shot, but Alan didn't drink.

"Well?" Alan said, forcing himself to ask the question that had made the last two days a living nightmare. He had envisioned himself slowly deteriorating over the next few years until he became a drooling vegetable sitting in a pool of his own excrement. "Do I have Alzheimer's disease or don't I?"

Axford emptied his glass and walked over to the window.

"You know something, Bulmer? Sometimes I have to wonder about myself. I'd have found it so much easier to tell you you've got Alzheimer's than what I really have to say. Some kind of bloody bastard, what?"

"I'll tell *you* something, Axford," Alan said, allowing his rancor to rise to the surface. "You've got the bedside manner of Attila the Hun! *What did you find?*"

"I don't know."

"You don't *know?*" He knew he was shouting, but he couldn't help it. "All those tests—"

"—reveal something I can't explain."

Alan sat down on the bed and sipped at his glass. "So there *is* something after all."

"Your memory changes are similar to the Alzheimer pattern, but as you know, the way things stand now, the only way to make a definitive diagnosis is at autopsy."

Alan couldn't help but smile. "I signed a lot of consents, but I don't remember agreeing to that."

Axford's face was completely deadpan as he looked at Alan. "You did. You just don't remember. It's scheduled for nine a.m. tomorrow."

"Not funny."

"But seriously, though, we can make a pretty good presumptive diagnosis of Alzheimer's clinically and radiographically without cutting into your brain and finding some neurofibrillary tangles."

Alan realized that Axford was speaking to him as he might to a layman, probably not sure of how much Alan had retained about the disease. Alan himself didn't know what he knew or had forgotten, so he let Axford go on.

"Clinically you might be suspected of having a case, but your CT scan shows none of the usual stigmata—no cerebral atrophy or ventricular dilation, no widening of the sulci."

"That's a relief."

"Your PET scan, on the other hand, is markedly abnormal. Areas of the cortex and hippocampus have shut down, showing no metabolism—a classic picture of the advanced Alzheimer brain."

Alan's insides knotted. "Well, is it or isn't it?"

"I can't say. If you have Alzheimer's, you don't have any form I've ever seen."

Alan held out his cup for more bourbon. He didn't know whether to laugh or cry.

"Do you think it's the Touch that's doing it to me?"

Axford shrugged. "I don't know."

"Don't know much, do you?" Alan snapped.

"We know what rhythm your 'Hour of Power' follows."

Alan felt his spine stiffen. "I'm listening."

"It comes and goes with high tide."

It was like a punch in the gut. "High tide?"

Axford nodded.

Feeling shaky, Alan got up and took his turn at the window, looking down at Park Avenue below, barely hearing Axford talk about a periodic disturbance in his EEG.

High tide! God! Why hadn't he seen it? The clues were all there—the way the power traveled around the clock, coming an hour or so later every day. It was so obvious once it was pointed out. If he'd only known! It would have been so easy to work with it. All he needed was a tide chart. If he'd had one in his pocket at the Board of Trustees hearing, he wouldn't be in this mess.

But *the tide* controlling the waxing and waning of the Touch. It had such an elemental feel to it, hinting at something incredibly ancient at work.

He turned to Axford as a thought occurred to him.

"You realize, don't you, that you've just so much as admitted that the Touch exists."

Axford had dispensed with his cup and was now taking pulls straight from the bottle.

His voice was slurred. "I don't admit a bloody damned thing. Not yet. But I do want to do a repeat PET scan on you tomorrow. Confirm those dead areas."

Alan wanted to confirm those areas, too. "Fine. I'll be here." He watched as Axford walked unsteadily for the door. "You're not driving, are you?"

"Hell, no. Only a bloody idiot would keep a bloody car in this bloody city!"

He slammed the door behind him, leaving Alan alone with the prospect of trying to find sleep while thinking about dead areas in his brain.

__ 41. __
Charles

"I'll be damned!" he said aloud as he looked at the computer analysis of the repeat PET scan.

It was still grossly abnormal, but the computer said that the glucose uptake had increased over the past twenty-four hours as compared to Saturday's scan. The improvement wasn't visible to the naked eye, but the computer saw it, and that was good enough for Charles.

And good news for Bulmer, although it didn't bring Charles any closer to a diagnosis.

He now spread out the new two-hour EEG on his desk top. Despite the cotton mouth and pounding headache from too much bourbon last night, he'd managed to remember to pick up a tide chart for the East River on his way to the Foundation this morning. When he had seen that high tide was due at 9:17 a.m., he had ordered a stat EEG on Bulmer at 8:30.

And here before him on paper was the same sine-wave configuration that had appeared on the twenty-four-hour EEG two days ago, rising approximately thirty minutes before high tide at 8:46 and ending at 9:46.

He took a certain perverse satisfaction in his newfound ability to predict the occurrence of something he had been absolutely sure did not exist.

His private line buzzed. He picked it up, wondering who would be calling him here on a Sunday morning.

He recognized the senator's hoarse voice immediately.

"Why haven't I seen a report yet?"

"And a very good morning to you, too, Senator. I'll be finishing up testing today."

"You've done enough tests! The Knopf case is proof enough for me."

"Maybe so, but it explains nothing."

"I don't care about explanations. Can you deny that he has a healing power? Can you?"

"No." It killed him to admit that.

"Then that does it! I want you to—"

"Senator," Charles said sharply. He had to put McCready off for a little while longer. He couldn't let Bulmer go just yet. "This power, or whatever it is that he has, works sporadically. By tonight I'll have the exact pattern of its occurrence confirmed. With that nailed down we can predict to the minute when it's operating. Until we do that, we'll just be fumbling around in the dark. One more day. That's all. I promise."

"Very well," McCready said with obvious reluctance. "But I've waited a long time."

"I know. Tomorrow morning for sure."

Charles hung up and stared at Bulmer's EEG without seeing it. The report McCready was looking for had already been dictated, and tomorrow Marnie would type it into the main computer's word processor. But Charles hadn't mentioned that, because he knew the senator was not really after a report.

He was after a cure.

McCready wanted Alan Bulmer to touch him and make his myasthenia gravis go away. So he was becoming more anxious, more impatient, and more demanding than usual. And why shouldn't he? If he was going to restore Bulmer's reputation and credibility as a physician, he had a right to a touch.

But in order to give Bulmer back his credibility, he needed Charles Axford's signature on the report stating that Dr. Alan Bulmer could indeed, at the right time of day, cure the incurable with a simple touch of his hand. Charles, however, needed one last bit of proof, one final shred of irrefutable evidence before he would sign.

He intended to acquire that proof tonight, sometime after 9:00. But first he wanted a tête-à-tête with Bulmer.

*   *   *

"So that's the Hour of Power, ay?" Bulmer said, looking down at the sine waves flowing through the EEG laid out on his bed.

"If you want to call it that."

Bulmer looked at him. "You never give in, do you?"

"Not often."

"And you say my PET scan is better?"

"Minimally, yes."

"Then I might as well get out of here."

"No!" Charles said, a bit more quickly and loudly than he would have liked. "Not yet. I just want to hook you up to the EEG tonight and have you use your so-called power on a patient while we're recording."

Bulmer frowned, obviously not happy with the idea. "This place is getting on my nerves. I'm bored out of my mind."

"You've come this far. What difference is another twenty-four hours going to make?"

Alan laughed. "Do you know how many times I've said those exact words to inpatients with hospitalitis? Thousands!" He shook his head. "Okay. One more day and then I'm out of here."

"Right." Charles turned at the door. He didn't want to ask this question, but he needed the answer. "By the way, how do you make this bloody power work?"

"What power?" Bulmer said with a smile. "The one that doesn't exist?"

"Yes. That one."

He scratched his head. "I don't really know. When the hour's on, I just put my hand on the person and sort of . . . *will* it."

"Just touching them in passing's not enough?"

"No. Many times I've done a physical on someone—ENT, heart, lungs, blood pressure, and so on—and nothing's happened. Then I've found something, wished it gone and"—he shrugged—"it went."

Charles saw the light in Bulmer's eyes and realized for the first time that the man was a true healer, power or no power. Charles knew plenty of physicians who loved the practice of medicine—ferreting out the cause of a problem and then eliminating it. Bulmer was that sort, too, but Charles had come to see that he had another, almost mystical dimension. He wanted to *heal*. Not merely to stamp out the disease, but to make a person *whole* again, and he was bloody damned elated when he could. You could be taught to do the first; you had to be born to do the second.

And damned if he wasn't starting to like the man.

"Do you have to know the diagnosis?"

"I don't know. I usually know because I talk to them and examine them." He cocked an eyebrow toward Charles. "Just like a *real* doctor."

"Do you feel anything when it happens?"

"Yeah." His eyes got a faraway look. "I've never shot dope or snorted cocaine, but it must be something like that."

"That good?"

"Great."

"And the patients? Do they all have seizures?"

"No. Mr. K probably had his because all of a sudden his brain metastases were gone and that triggered something off. A lot of them seem to feel a brief pain in the target organ, but he's the only one ever to seizure on me. Why the interest all of a sudden?"

Charles started for the door again and did not look back. "Just curious."

*   *   *

Since it was Sunday night and there were no technicians around, he had brought the EEG telemetry set to Bulmer's room and hooked him up himself. Just as well. He didn't want an audience tonight. The leads were now fastened to his scalp and the telemetry pack hooked to his belt. Charles flicked the switch and started transmission.

He checked his watch: 9:05. High tide was scheduled for 9:32. The Hour of Power had begun and it was time for Charles to perform the most difficult task of his life.

"I want you to meet someone," he told Bulmer. He went to the door and motioned Julie in from where she had been waiting.

"Dr. Bulmer," he said as she stepped into the room, "I'd like you to meet my daughter, Julie."

A look of confusion passed over Bulmer's face, then he stepped up to Julie, smiled, and shook her hand.

"Hello, Ms. Axford!" he said with a bow. "Do come in."

Julie threw Charles an uncertain look but he smiled and motioned her forward. He had warned her that the man would have wires on his head, but had said nothing else beyond the fact that they were going to meet a man he knew. He couldn't bring himself to say anything more than that, couldn't risk allowing the slightest glimmer of hope to glow in her when he didn't dare hope himself.

Bulmer made a big fuss over Julie, seating her in his chair, finding her a Pepsi in his little refrigerator.

"I can only have two ounces," she told him.

He paused and then nodded. "Then that's all you shall have."

He turned on the telly for her, and as she turned her attention to a situation comedy, Alan turned to Charles.

"When's her next dialysis?"

Charles was speechless for a few seconds. "Did Sylvie tell you?"

He shook his head. "Didn't even know you were a father. I saw how pale she was, the puffiness around her eyes, and then I spotted the fistula when her cuff slipped up. Care to tell me about it?"

Charles made the long story short—chronic atrophic pyelonephritis due to congenital ureteral atresia, a contracted bladder, donor rejection, high cytotoxic antibody titers.

"Poor kid," Bulmer said, and there was genuine feeling in his eyes. But not all of it seemed to be for Julie.

"Why are you looking at me like that?" Charles asked.

Bulmer tapped his forehead. "I can imagine what it cost you up here to bring her to me."

He went over and talked to Julie, gradually drawing her away from the telly. She responded to him, and soon she was babbling on and on about her dialysis treatments and how she measured her daily fluids and took her dozens of pills. Charles found himself responding to Bulmer, almost wishing, despite his abhorrence of the very thought of being in private practice, that he had his knack with people.

Suddenly Bulmer grasped both of Julie's shoulders and closed his eyes for a second. He shuddered and Julie gave a little cry of pain.

Charles leaped toward her. "What's wrong?"

"My back!"

He could feel his teeth baring as he turned toward Bulmer. "What did you do to her?"

"I think she'll be all right now."

"I'm okay, Daddy," Julie said. "He didn't touch my back. It just started to hurt."

Not knowing what to think, Charles hugged Julie to him.

"You're pretty lucky with your timing, you know," Bulmer said.

"What do you mean?"

"Bringing her here during the Hour of Power."

"It wasn't luck. I used the tide chart."

Bulmer looked at him as if he were crazy. "Tide chart? What's that got to do with it?"

"It's high tide now. That's what brings on your so-called Hour of Power."

"It does? When did you find that out? Why didn't you tell me?"

Charles felt a cool lump of dread settle on the back of his neck. "You don't remember me telling you?"

"Of course not! You never did!"

Charles had no intention of arguing with him. He called radiology and ordered a repeat PET scan in the morning, top priority. He had a dreadful suspicion as to the cause of Bulmer's cognitive deficits and abnormal scans.

But right now he wanted to get Julie home. It was time for her dialysis.

They said good-bye to the slightly confused Alan Bulmer and headed for the elevator. He let Julie press all the buttons, and she seemed as happy as a clam until they were about halfway to the ground floor. Suddenly she leaned forward and bent her knees, jamming her thighs together.

"Oh, Daddy, it hurts!"

Alarmed, he crouched beside her. "Where?"

"Down there!" she cried, pointing toward her pubic region. Then she was sobbing. "And it's all *wet!*"

He looked and he saw the wet stain spreading down her thighs, turning her jeans a darker shade of blue. The air within the elevator car filled with the unmistakable ammonia odor of the urine that was pouring out of a child who hadn't produced more than an ounce a week for years, pouring into a bladder that had forgotten how to hold it.

Charles hugged his daughter against him as his chest threatened to explode. He closed his eyes in a futile attempt to muffle the sobs that racked his body from head to toe, and to hold back the tears that streamed down his cheeks.

42.
Alan

"When can we expect you?" Sylvia's voice said from the phone.

It was a sunny Monday morning and Alan longed to be with her. Now that his stay at the Foundation was nearly over, every extra minute here seemed like an eternity. He wished she were stretched out beside him on the bed right now.

"In a few hours," he said.

"In time for dinner?"

"I sure hope so. The food here isn't bad, but institutional food is institutional food. After dinner I'll see what I can do for Jeffy."

There was a pause on the other end, then: "Are you sure he'll be all right?"

"Can he be any worse?"

"Not much." Her voice suddenly brightened. "Anyway, it'll be nice to have a doctor around the house again."

"Not for long. I'll move into a motel and start getting the insurance straightened out on the house and get construction going on a new place."

"Alan Bulmer! You are staying here with me, and that's final!"

Her words warmed him. This was what he had wanted her to say, but he still felt compelled to put up a show of resistance.

"What will the neighbors say?"

"Who cares? What can either of us do to make our reputations any worse?"

"Good point, Mrs. Toad. I'll see you later." *If I can remember how to get back to Monroe.*

As Alan sat up on the bed and hung up, Axford walked into the room without knocking. He took three paces in from the doorway and stood there, staring at Alan. His face was pale and lined and haggard. He looked physically and emotionally exhausted.

"Her BUN is down to twenty-six," he said in a flat voice. "Her creatinine is down to two-point-seven. Both are still dropping. We spent most of the night running back and forth to the loo until about four a.m., when her sphincters started toning up and her bladder started stretching." His voice quavered and Alan could see the muscles of his throat working. "Her renal sonogram shows both kidneys have enlarged since her previous study, and a renal-flow scan shows normal function."

Alan was completely baffled. "Charles, is something wrong?"

He closed his eyes and took a deep, tremulous breath. He pulled a handkerchief from his pocket and wiped his eyes. Then he looked at Alan again.

"Whatever you want that I have or can get for you is yours. Just say the word. My right hand? I'll cut it off. My balls? Say the word."

Alan laughed. "Just get me out of here! And tell me what the hell you're talking about!"

Axford's eyes widened. "You really don't know?"

"Know what?"

"Oh, Christ! I—" He glanced over at the chair. "Can I sit down?"

Once he was seated, he faced Alan squarely and leaned forward. He seemed more in control of himself now and started to speak in low, measured tones.

Charles told Alan how he had cured Julie, Charles' daughter, of her chronic renal failure last night. And with each word Alan felt a terrible sick feeling grow within him, because he did not remember seeing Charles since yesterday afternoon, and didn't remember ever knowing that he had a daughter.

"All this leads to what I'm about to say, which is going to be tough for you to hear. But you've got to know and you've got to do something about it."

Charles paused, then said:

"You've got to stop using the Touch."

"What?"

"It could kill you."

Alan's mind whirled. How could something that healed kill him?

"I don't understand."

"That repeat PET scan you had this morning—it shows a significant increase in the nonfunctional areas of your brain."

"And you think there's a connection?"

"I'm sure of it. Look: You say your memory has deteriorated during the past few months. The Touch started a few months ago. Your baseline PET scan was abnormal and consistent with Alzheimer's. After a couple of days of not using the power, your PET scan improved and so did your mental function. Then you used the Touch last night and suddenly forgot that the Hour of Power coincides with high tide."

"It does?" It was news to Alan.

Charles ran a hand over his eyes. "This is worse than I thought. We discussed it Saturday, and again last night. I even showed you an EEG of yours that demonstrated it."

"Jeez." He felt sick.

"Right. Bloody damn Jeez. So with your short-term memory all shot to bloody hell, and your PET scan this morning significantly worse than yesterday morning's, there's only one conclusion I can come to. How about you?"

Alan sat in numb silence for a moment, then: "My brain's shutting down."

"Not by itself it isn't, mate. Bit by bit, a little piece of who you are and what you are gets eaten up by this power every time you use it."

"But you just said my second scan was better."

"Right. By not using the power, your brain function improved an infinitesimal degree. By using the power *once*—and remember it or not, you cured the most precious person in the world to me last night—you knocked out a grossly appreciable area of your brain."

Alan jumped to his feet and paced, his heart pounding, his stomach in a knot. He didn't want to believe what he had heard. "You're sure of this?"

"It's all there on the scans. It comes down to the ratio of a centimeter forward over a period of two days to a meter backward in an instant."

"But if I'm really careful, I can rest up, so to speak, and use the Touch judiciously." He was grasping at straws, he knew, but he was desperate. He kept thinking of the people who needed that power to live. He thought of Jeffy. He couldn't possibly say no after he had promised Sylvia.

"You ever play Russian roulette?"

"Of course not!"

"Well, it's the same thing. You've already damaged lots of nonvital parts of your brain. But what happens if you knock out the basal ganglia or the motor cortex, or the limbic system, or the respiratory center? Where does that leave you?"

Alan didn't reply. They both knew the answer: Parkinsonism, paralysis, psychosis, or death. Some choice.

"One more thing I should warn you about," Axford said. "Senator McCready will be expecting to have a meeting with you tonight."

"Tonight? Why tonight? I expect to be gone by then."

"He has myasthenia gravis, if you get my drift."

Alan got the drift. "Oh."

"Right. It's a decision you'll have to make when the time comes. But I wanted to be sure you knew all the risks."

"Thanks. I appreciate that." He smiled at a grim thought. "Maybe I should write all this down. I might not remember it an hour from now. But no matter what the risk, there's one person who's *got* to get a dose of the Touch."

"Who?"

"Jeffy."

Charles nodded. "That would be wonderful, wouldn't it?"

He stood up and thrust out his hand. "I'll send you a copy of my report. But in case I don't see you before you go, remember: You have a friend for life, Alan Bulmer."

When he was gone, Alan lay back on the bed and reviewed all Charles had told him. It still seemed clear to him. His retention seemed good at the moment. But knowing that there were pieces of his memory missing—maybe permanently—terrified him. For what was anyone but a sum of their memories? Where he had been, the things he had done, why he had done them: They all made him Alan Bulmer. Without them he was a cipher, a *tabula rasa*, a new-born.

Alan shuddered. He had made his share of mistakes, but he liked who he was. He didn't want to be erased. He wanted to remain Alan Bulmer.

But what of the senator? If McCready could save his reputation and tell the world that Dr. Alan Bulmer was not a charlatan or a nut, then Alan would owe him. And he would pay that debt.

But Jeffy came first. Nothing would stop him from putting the Touch to work on Jeffy. And if the senator wanted to give it a try after that, fine. But Jeffy came first.

After all that was settled up, maybe it would be time for him to go away with Sylvia and Jeffy for a while to recharge the batteries. When he returned, he'd get his life in order, get everything in perspective, and try to get back into a regular practice. And maybe save the *Dat-tay-vao* for rare cases of dire need.

One thing was certain: He would not allow himself to fall into the rut that had put such distance between Ginny and him.

No, sir. Alan Bulmer was going to learn to say *no* once in a while.

__ 43. __
Charles

"Dr. Axford!" Marnie said, running up to him as he entered the corridor. "I've been looking all over for you!"

She looked positively frazzled. "What's up, Love?"

"Those two new assistants of yours came down to your office and just about emptied your safe!"

"What? Did you call security?"

"They were wearing security uniforms!"

Baffled and alarmed, Charles hurried to his office. He found the safe closed and locked.

"They had the combination," Marnie said in response to his look. "And they were neat. Seemed to know exactly what they wanted."

"I didn't have any money in there," Charles said to himself as he tapped in the combination. "What on earth did they—"

His question was answered as soon as he opened the door. All the Bulmer data were missing. This didn't make sense.

"Call the senator for me."

"I was about to suggest that, since he's the one who sent them down."

A shock ran through Charles. "The senator?"

"Sure. He called first thing this morning. When I told him you weren't in yet, he said that was just as well and that he was sending Henly and Rossi down to pick up some papers from your office. I had no idea he meant from your safe. I'm sorry about this . . . I didn't know how to stop them."

"It's okay, Marnie."

"Oh, and one more thing," she said as she tapped at the phone buttons. "The senator said to compliment you on your report. But I just typed it in this morning."

Charles felt his intestines knot. He quickly depressed the cradle arm on Marnie's phone.

"Cue it up for me," he said, and directed her to her CRT. "How did you file it?"

"I named it Bulmerrep."

Try as she might, she could find no trace of the report.

"It's been erased," she said. "I swear I typed it in."

"Don't worry, Love," Charles said, laying a comforting hand on her shoulder and hiding the turmoil within him. "Nothing's perfect. Not even a computer. By the way, did you see which way Henly and Rossi went?"

"As a matter of fact, yes. I followed them all the way to the elevators trying to find out what was going on and I noticed that they went *down*. I was a little puzzled 'cause I figured they'd head for the senator's office."

"Did you happen to notice where they stopped?"

"Yes. One stop down—the ninth floor."

"Right. You sit tight here and I'll go have a talk with the senator."

Charles hurried toward the fire stairs. But he headed down, not up. The events of the morning had suddenly taken on a sinister tinge, but he was sure it was just his own mind creating melodrama out of a series of incidents that no doubt had a simple, rational explanation. He couldn't imagine what that explanation might be, but he did know that he wanted his data back. The ninth floor was the central records section. If Henly and Rossi were storing the data there, he would see what he could do to unstore it, and then pay a little visit to McCready and find out what in bloody hell was going on!

He was storming along the main corridor on the ninth floor when he spied a familiar profile through a magazine-sized window in a door. He stepped back and looked inside.

Henly and Rossi were calmly running a stack of papers—much of it EEG tracings that he recognized as Alan Bulmer's—through a shredder. Charles' first impulse was to burst in, but he backed away and forced himself to walk down the hall the way he had come. There was little to be gained by confronting the two security men— most of the data was already confetti, anyway—but he might well learn a lot by pretending he knew nothing more than what Marnie had told him.

He was sure now that it wasn't his imagination. Something nasty was going on.

He could understand the senator's anxiety to read the report and saw nothing wrong with his dipping into the word-processing files for a sneak preview. But he wasn't just gathering up data—he was destroying it.

Why?

At least all the data was still available to Charles in the main computer.

Or was it?

He fairly ran back to his office and keyed in his access code to retrieve the Bulmer data.

FILE NOT IN MEMORY

A chill rippled over him. It was almost as if someone were trying to eradicate every trace of Alan Bulmer from the Foundation's records.

Again—why?

Only one man could answer that question.

Charles headed for the elevator.

*   *   *

"Charles!" the senator rasped from behind the desk as Charles entered his office. "I was expecting you."

"I'm sure you were."

"Sit down."

"I'd rather stand." Charles found he could best hide his uneasiness over the last hour's events by acting properly angry.

"Now, now," the senator said with a friendly chuckle. "I know you're upset, and with good reason. But I had to get those records to a safer place. You'll forgive me a little paranoia, won't you?"

Charles went cold at the lie. "They're in a safer place than my safe?"

"Oh, yes! I have them in my own ultra-secure hidey-hole where I keep very sensitive documents. The Bulmer data are there."

"I see."

Charles could almost admire the smoothness of the senator's line. Beautifully done, even down to that cute, folksy, hidey-hole bit.

But the bloody damn *why* of it all still plagued him. He suppressed the urge to call the senator out on his lies and wring the truth out of him. That would be futile. Besides, he had just thought of another avenue of approach.

"So," McCready said in a conciliatory tone, "are we still friends?"

"We were never friends, Senator. And let me warn you: I'm changing the combination to my safe, and if it's ever even *touched* by one of your stooges, you'll be looking for a new director."

With that, he strode from the senator's office and hurried for his own.

*   *   *

Charles sat in his locked office and punched Senator McCready's access code into his computer terminal.

He had seen the senator use it on occasion when they had to call up his personal medical file. For some reason—perhaps because the senator knew everyone's code and no one knew his—Charles had memorized it.

He now ran through all the files keyed exclusively to the senator's code.

He found the missing Bulmer data; everything regarding Bulmer that had been keyed to Charles' access had been transferred to the senator's exclusive access. Most of the rest was pure rubbish—

McCready's most recent medical test results, notes, memos. Charles came across a public opinion projection done by the computer and was about to move on when he spotted the word "healed" in the center of a paragraph. He read it through.

The projection exhaustively covered the effect of illness and its cure upon public reaction to a presidential candidate.

It found that a seriously ill candidate had little chance of nomination and virtually no chance of winning.

Franklin Delano Roosevelt to the contrary, a candidate who had been seriously ill but somehow miraculously cured was haunted by a specter of doubt as to if and/or when the illness might recur, and was severely handicapped against a healthy opponent.

But even worse off was a candidate who had hidden a serious illness from the public and had then been cured. A question uppermost in many voters' minds concerned what else he might be hiding from them.

Everything was suddenly perfectly clear to Charles. Except for one thing: The "somehow miraculously cured" in the second scenario obviously referred to Bulmer, but the date on the report was June 1—almost six weeks ago.

He didn't have time to figure that out now—he had to get to Bulmer immediately.

44.
Alan

"So that's his plan," Charles said in a fierce, whispered voice. "He's going to dump you in the street!"

Alan struggled to disbelieve all that he had just been told.

"Charles, I never thought much of the man, but this . . . *this!*" He felt cold.

"It's true. I owe you too much to play games with you. But you don't know what I know. He's going to have you work your magic on his myasthenia gravis and then he's going to say he never heard of you. And I'll tell you straight, mate: If I had to prove we'd ever done so much as a urinalysis on you here, I couldn't."

"But you said that computer projection was dated almost a month and a half ago. That would mean he's been planning since May. That's crazy! Nobody in the world could have predicted back in May that I'd wind up here. Everything looked fine back then."

Alan knew he had a point, and so, apparently, did Charles. His voice lost some of its intensity.

"There was no hint that things were going to get dodgy for you?"

"Not the slightest. There was a little flak when the article in *The*

Light came out, but hardly anybody takes them seriously." He closed his eyes and rubbed his forehead, trying to remember. "No. Near as I can say, things started falling apart when the local paper got on my case. That led to the hospital hearing and everything just escalated from there."

Charles' head snapped up. "Local paper? Jesus bloody Christ! What's it called?"

"The Monroe *Express*. Why?"

"I'll know in a second."

He picked up the phone and began jabbing at the numbers. Alan turned to the window and fought the sense of betrayal that threat-ened to overwhelm him.

He turned as he heard Charles hang up the phone and saw the reluctant excitement in his eyes. Apparently Charles had confirmed his deduction, but he didn't look happy about it.

"Everybody thinks of either politics or medical research when the McCready name is mentioned. We all forget where his money came from: a chain of newspapers! And your hometown paper is part of the McCready chain!"

Alan slumped into a chair. "The *Express*! I never dreamed!" His mind marveled and recoiled at the subtlety and pervasiveness of the conspiracy McCready had engineered. Those seemingly public-spirited editorials calling for Alan's removal, and the immediate trumpeting of the news that he had been suspended from the hospital staff. They had accomplished their purpose: He had been left with no place to turn and had fairly leaped at McCready's offer of help.

"That bastard!" he shouted, feeling the rage surge up in him. His marriage, his practice, his reputation—they all might still be intact if not for McCready. "That son of a bitch! I still can't believe it."

"Let's try one more thing, then, shall we?" Charles said as he picked up the phone and laid it in Alan's lap. "I haven't checked this out, but try it yourself. Dial the operator and ask her to connect you with Alan Bulmer's room."

Alan lifted the receiver, pressed "O," and asked for himself.

"I'm sorry," said the voice. "We have no one by that name listed as a Foundation patient."

Despite the sensation of a lead weight settling in his stomach,

Alan told himself that this didn't necessarily confirm Charles' theory. Today was his last day here; perhaps they had simply removed his name from the inpatient list a little ahead of time.

"When was he discharged?" Alan asked.

"I'm sorry, sir, but our records don't list that name as having ever been a patient here within the past year."

Fighting the sick feeling that slithered up inside him, Alan slammed the receiver down.

"Let's get out of here," he said.

"I was going to suggest that."

"But first," Alan said, feeling the muscles of his jaw knot as he spoke through clenched teeth, "I want to pay a little visit to the senator and tell him just what I think of him and his rotten little scheme."

"That might cause more problems than we can handle," Charles told him.

He had a strange feeling that Charles was afraid. "Like what?"

"Like you may find yourself detained here longer than you wish."

"Come on, Charles!" Alan said with a laugh. "You're letting this make you paranoid. I came in here of my own free will and I can leave whenever I want."

"Don't count on it, mate. And don't call *me* paranoid. You're the bloke whose psychological profile shows delusional activity."

"What are you talking about?" Alan said, feeling the first twinges of alarm now.

"The MMPI and all those other multiple choice tests you took on your second day here—they portray you as a chap who sees himself as possessing a God-like power. Just hold on now!" he said quickly as Alan opened his mouth to protest. "I'm a believer. Those tests were designed to ferret out the schizoid types. They're invalidated by a chap who can *really* do the things you can. So you and I both know you haven't broken with reality. But let me tell you, friend: Little red flags went up all over the place when your tests were scored."

"So you're saying they might be able to justify detaining me if they want?"

"Right. I don't know how much you remember about New York

State commitment laws, but believe me, you could be out of circulation for a bloody long time."

It cost him a lot of effort, but Alan managed to smile. "Maybe I'll just leave now and send the senator a telegram. Tomorrow."

"Good. And just to be on the safe side, I'll get you a lab coat to wear on the way out. Everybody on staff here wears them. It'll be the next best thing to being invisible. I've got an extra in my office. Lay low until I get back."

Alan quickly gathered up the few incidental belongings he could stuff in his pockets. He was traveling light, anyway. He had lost all his clothes except for what he had been wearing when the house burned down. He checked and made sure he had his wallet and car keys, then sat down to wait.

Through the closed door he could hear almost constant movement out in the hall—footsteps back and forth, carts being wheeled by. He did not recall that much activity during the past few days, but then, he hadn't been waiting anxiously for someone to arrive and lead him out of here.

He had been on edge to begin with. After half an hour, he was one tight knot of tension. Where the hell was Charles?

He had intended to stay out of sight until Charles returned, but he could not sit still any longer. For want of doing something, he decided to take a look and see if Charles was anywhere in sight.

The hall was eerily silent. He noticed immediately that the door leading to the elevator atrium was closed. That struck him as odd. It had always been kept open during the day and was closed only after 10:00 p.m. He hurried down to it and pulled on the handle.

It wouldn't budge.

Beyond the small pane of wired glass, the elevator area was empty. As Alan rattled the handle and pounded on the door, a face appeared at the glass. He was dark, wore a security guard's cap, and looked vaguely familiar.

"The door's jammed!" Alan said.

"No, sir," said the guard. His voice was slightly muffled through the door. "It's locked."

"Well, unlock it, then!"

The guard shook his head apologetically. "It's for your own protection, sir. A violent patient escaped from the security ward. We're pretty sure we've trapped him between the fourth and sixth floors, but until we catch him we're sealing off all the wards and administrative areas."

Alan rattled the handle. "I'll take my chances. Open it."

"Sorry, sir. Can't do that. Orders. But as soon as this loony's caught, I'll be right here to open up."

He moved away from the door and, despite Alan's repeated pounding and calling, did not reappear.

Anger and fear intermingled. He was tempted to run into the nearest room, grab a chair, and use it to smash out the little glass window in the door. Not that it would get him out of here, but it sure as hell would make him feel a lot better. Of course, the act could later be used as proof that he was not only deranged, but violent. Why play into their hands? Why make it easy for them?

He gave the door a final frustrated kick and then headed for the nursing station to see if the guard's story was on the level. As he moved along the hall, he noticed that all the rooms were empty. The wing hadn't been filled to anywhere near capacity, but now there was no one in any of the rooms.

He increased his pace. By the time he reached the nursing station, he was not surprised in the least to find it deserted.

Alan didn't have to search any further. He knew from the dead silence of the wing that he was the only one here.

He hurried back to his room and picked up his phone. Dead. He had half expected that.

Alan took a deep breath and sat down. He wasn't afraid; he was angry. But as he sat there, he felt his anger cool from the wall-pounding, lamp-throwing type to a sharp, icy rage that put his teeth on edge and set his fingers to drumming.

He knew what was up. He would be kept here for the rest of the afternoon and most of the early evening under the ruse of protecting him from a deranged patient. And then at, oh, say, about 9:45 or so—approximately half an hour before high tide—the security ward escapee would be captured and the door to Alan's wing unlocked.

Alan would be free to go, but first the good senator would like to have a friendly word or two with him to explain what wonderful things the Foundation planned to do for him now that his healing ability had been proven.

And by the way, while you're here, and since it happens to be high tide at the moment, would you mind clearing up this little ol' neuromuscular disease I've got?

Obviously Senator McCready didn't know that Alan was on to him. Else why put on this elaborate charade?

So Alan waited patiently, grinding his teeth and drumming his fingers on his thigh as he stared out his window at the Manhattan skyline. He had had it with being pushed around. He had lost control of his own life somewhere along the way. He had become a pawn, moved here and there at various times by circumstance, by the hospital Board of Trustees, by the *Dat-tay-vao,* and now by Senator James McCready.

Well, it stopped here and now. Alan Bulmer was climbing back into the driver's seat. He was reclaiming his life and making his own decisions from here on in.

And he actually was looking forward to seeing the senator.

He had a surprise for him.

___ 45. ___
Sylvia

"Charles!"

Sylvia was shocked to see him at her front door. She glanced behind him. "Isn't Alan with you?"

He shook his head and walked past her. He was still in his white lab coat and obviously upset. His normally high coloring was higher than usual. "He was supposed to be, but they're keeping him there."

"Keeping him?" Her heart tripped over a beat, paused to catch itself, then went on in rhythm. "How long?"

"Till after high tide, I imagine. *If* he cooperates."

"Charles, what are you talking about? Why isn't he with you?"

"They kicked me out! Just like that!" Charles snapped his fingers and talked on at breakneck speed. " 'Here's your severance pay and please leave the premises now, thank-you-very-much.' Must have found out I was snooping into his personal-access-only files."

"*Charles!*" Sylvia was frightened and baffled and Charles wasn't making any sense.

"Okay! Okay! I'll tell you in a minute!" he said, heading for the library. "Just let me get a bleeding whiskey!"

Eventually he told her. She sat on the arm of the leather sofa while he paced back and forth the length of the library, swirling and sipping from the glass of Glenlivet clutched in his hand as he told her incredible things—about a man with metastatic cancer to the brain who suddenly didn't have a tumor cell in his body, about abnormal scans and EEG sine-wave artifacts coinciding with high tide and Alan's Hour of Power, and an Alzheimer's-like syndrome that Alan's use of the *Dat-tay-vao* seemed to be causing.

"You mean it's damaging his brain?" She wanted to be sick. Alan . . . senile at forty. It was too awful to imagine.

"I'm afraid so."

"But that fits in with the poem Ba showed me. Something about 'keeping the balance.' If only I could think of it."

She stepped over to the intercom and called Ba in from the garage, asking him to bring the *Dat-tay-vao* poem. Then she wandered the room, rubbing her tense palms together.

It was all frightening and bewildering to Sylvia, yet she still hadn't had her question answered.

"Why is he still there?"

"Because our great and wonderful friend, Senator James Mc-Cready, who has used all of us so very neatly, wants to use Alan as well and then throw him to the wolves!"

Another explanation followed, this one even more fantastic than the first, concerning McCready's manipulation of events to get Alan into the Foundation and the subsequent destruction of all the data.

"Then it's true?" Sylvia said, finding her voice at last. "He really can . . . cure? With a touch? I'm hearing this from you of all people?"

She watched Charles nod, saw his lips tremble.

"Yes." His voice was barely a whisper. "I believe."

"What happened?"

"Julie—" His voice broke. He turned and faced the wall.

Sylvia's heart leaped. She came up behind him and put both her hands on his shoulders.

"Julie's cured?"

He nodded but remained faced away.

"Oh, Charles!" she cried, throwing her arms around him. The

burst of joy inside her brought tears to her eyes. "That's wonderful! That's absolutely wonderful!"

Sylvia had only met Julie a few times, but had been deeply touched by the child's quiet courage. There was, however, another more personal reason for her joy: If Julie could be cured, then there was real hope for Jeffy.

Charles seemed to read her mind. He turned around and gathered her in his arms.

"He says Jeffy's his next patient."

"But didn't you say the *Dat-tay-vao* was damaging his mind?" The realization was like a dark cloud drifting past the sun. Would Alan have to trade a part of his mind to break through Jeffy's autism? She didn't know if she could allow that.

She didn't know if she could refuse.

She pushed it all to the rear of her mind, to be dealt with when the time arose. Right now she had to concentrate on getting Alan back to Toad Hall.

But there was something different about Charles. She noticed a change in him. He had mellowed in the past few days. His hard, glossy façade had peeled away in spots, leaving soft, vulnerable areas exposed.

"He touched you, too, didn't he?" she said after watching him for a long moment.

"Rubbish! I didn't have anything that needed curing."

"No. I mean the other way—with his own personal touch—the one he's had all along. His empathy, his caring."

"He really does care, doesn't he?" Charles said. "I thought it was an act, part of the dedicated, hardworking family doctor role he was playing. You know: foot soldier on the front lines in the never-ending battle against death and disease, and all that sort of rot. But he's the real thing. And I always thought someone like him would be a wimp who'd carry his devotion to his practice like a cross. But he's a *man*." Charles bit his lower lip. "Jesus! The things I thought about him! *Said* about him!"

Sylvia gave him a hug. "Now maybe you can understand why he's been staying here."

Charles looked at her. She saw pain in his eyes, but it was distant, and fading. "I daresay I do. And I hope you're both very happy together."

"You called for me, Missus?" Ba said from the doorway.

"Oh, yes, Ba. Did you bring that poem—the one about the *Dat-tay-vao*?"

He handed it to her and she read it to Charles:

> *"It seeks but will not be sought.*
> *It finds but will not be found.*
> *It holds the one who would touch,*
> *Who would cut away pain and ill.*
> *But its blade cuts two ways*
> *And will not be turned.*
> *If you value your well-being,*
> *Impede not its way.*
> *Treat the Toucher doubly well,*
> *For he bears the weight*
> *Of the balance that must be struck."*

Sylvia turned to Charles. "See? 'He bears the weight of the balance that must be struck.' That sounds like what's happening to Alan: Every time he uses the Touch, it takes something from him. For every something given, something is taken away."

"Sounds like a variation on the old 'No Such Thing as a Free Lunch' thing: Somewhere along the line somebody gets stuck with the bill. But that's not what concerns me most right now. We should waste no time setting the wheels in motion to get Alan out of the Foundation."

"Won't he be getting out tonight? He'll use the *Dat-tay-vao* on the senator and then he'll be on his way."

"I don't think so," Charles said with a slow shake of his head. "Alan was mad—I mean really angry when I told him how McCready had set him up."

"You don't think he'll refuse to heal him, do you?" Sylvia said, her alarm slipping back on her. "That's not like Alan."

"You didn't see his eyes. And if McCready doesn't get what he wants, he won't let Alan go."

"But he can't hold him!"

"He can for a while. I thought he had destroyed all of Alan's original test results, but now that I think of it, I'll bet he kept the originals of his psychological profiles."

"Why?"

"Because Alan scores out as a bloody paranoid schiz. They could hold him on the grounds that he's dangerous to himself or others."

"I'll call Tony," Sylvia said, angry as well as frightened now. "He'll turn that place upside down."

"Don't count on it, Sylvie. Those profiles, along with the Foundation's reputation and the senator's personal influence . . . well, it could be a long time before we spring Alan."

"Pardon me," said Ba, who hadn't moved from the doorway. "But does the Missus want the Doctor returned from the Foundation?"

"Yes, Ba," she said, noting the hint of eagerness in his voice. She knew how highly he regarded Alan. "Any ideas?"

"I shall go there and bring him back."

He said it so matter-of-factly, yet Sylvia saw the determination in his eyes.

"Forget it!" Charles said with a laugh. "The Foundation's security is airtight."

"I have been there many times with the Missus. I shall go there tonight and bring the Doctor back."

Charles laughed again. But Sylvia watched Ba's face, remembering what Greg had told her about the simple fisherman who had attached himself to the Ranger group and trained with them, and whom Greg had said he wanted most at his side in any combat situation. Ba wanted to do this. And Sylvia realized with a sudden tingle of excitement that she wanted him to do it.

"Very well, Ba. But be careful."

The smile dropped from Charles' face as if he had been shot. "What? Just like that? Go get Alan? Are you crazy?"

Sylvia returned Ba's grateful little bow, but stopped him as he turned to make his exit. "Wait, Ba." She turned to Charles. "Would you draw a few floor plans and tell him where you think Alan may be? It would greatly help matters."

"But this is *insane!* Security will be all over him as soon as he sets foot inside!"

"Let's hope Ba doesn't have to hurt too many of them." She was enjoying the befuddled expressions playing over Charles' face.

He finally settled down and she watched as he sketched out the floor plans of the upper levels. Ba leaned over them in silence.

"Where's Alan now?" Sylvia asked. She didn't know why, but it was important to her to know the location of his room.

"Most likely he's still in the seventh-floor patient wing—room 719—but he could be anywhere in the complex." He pointed to a section of the top floor. "Your safest bet is here: Alan will be in McCready's private quarters between 9:45 and 10:45 tonight."

"How can you be sure?"

"Because I remember my chart saying that high tide is 10:18 tonight. That would probably be the best place and time to find him."

Ba shook his head. "The best time is when he is between. It would be very hard to enter the senator's private place."

Charles was looking at him with new respect. "That makes good sense, old boy. I daresay you might bring this off after all. Although I sincerely doubt it." He took off his lab coat. "Here. Take this. I can't imagine any place or circumstance in the Foundation where you wouldn't stand out like a sore thumb, but this might make you less conspicuous."

"Want to go along, Charles?"

He smiled sardonically. "Sounds like I'd have a wonderful time— I'm especially entranced by the possiblility of being arrested for breaking and entering and spending a few nights in a New York City jail. No, Love. I'll pass on this. Doubt if I'd be much use anyway. They know me there, and all security shifts have surely been informed that I'm persona non grata. And besides, I've got to get home to Julie. A functioning renal system is still a very new thing for her. I want to be there if she needs me."

That reminded Sylvia that she would have to catch Gladys and ask her to stay with Jeffy for a few hours while she was out. She waited until Ba showed Charles out, then caught him as he headed back toward the garage.

"I'm coming along tonight, Ba," she told him, and watched the usually placid features reflect his bewilderment and concern.

"Missus, there might be trouble! You cannot come!"

"Oh, but I must, Ba. And if you won't have me along, I'll drive there on my own. So let's not waste time arguing."

"But why, Missus?"

Sylvia thought about that. Why, indeed? Why get personally involved in something like this when Ba could probably do just as well on his own? Maybe it was because she felt so helpless in the face of Jeffy's regression. Would this make her feel useful? She wasn't sure, and it really didn't matter. She only knew she loved Alan and wanted to be there for him. And that was enough.

"Because, Ba," she told him. "Just because."

— 46. —
At the Foundation

Ba had a bad feeling about tonight as he pulled into the curb before the Foundation building. His initial plan had been simple: one man moving stealthily through the halls. Now it had been complicated by the Missus.

He was still recovering from the shock of the Missus' insisting on coming along tonight. He had planned to take his AMC Pacer, but now he was driving the Graham, and the Missus was in her usual place in the rear seat.

During the drive, Ba had argued strenuously to limit her to the most marginal involvement, such as waiting at the wheel of the car while he went inside, but she had flatly refused. She wanted to *be there*.

So he had reluctantly given the Missus a safe assignment: Go to the front entrance and make a scene—create a diversion.

"That's my specialty," she had said. "Making scenes."

As he put on the emergency brake, Ba heard the top twist off a bottle. He turned and saw her pouring liquor into a short glass. She took some in her mouth, rinsed it around like mouthwash, then swallowed with a grimace.

"Ugh! How do people drink scotch?" She breathed into her palm. "At least I'll smell the part. Let's go. It's showtime." Her eyes were bright with excitement.

Ba got out and stepped around to let her out, then watched as she walked up to the brightly lit front entrance, glass in hand, staggering just enough to look like someone who had had more than enough to drink.

He took a small duffle bag from the front seat and left the car under the lights at the curb. It would be safe there for a while, and he had decided that the best way to bring Dr. Bulmer out was straight through the front door.

He hurried off toward the side of the building.

*   *   *

It was 9:20 and he could wait no longer.

Senator McCready had rested all day. Sleep in other than short dozes had been almost impossible due to the excitement and anticipation of tonight. But he had resolutely stored up his strength, all but screaming at the clock for the unbearably slow caress of the hands across its face.

Now the time was almost here. He was going to Bulmer. At first he had intended to have him brought up here to the top-floor residence, but had dropped that idea in favor of one with more psychological appeal. He would go to Bulmer, thus appearing to be a humble supplicant rather than someone expecting a command performance.

Yes, this was the better approach. And after he was cured, Bulmer would have to be discredited. Try as he might, McCready could think of no alternative solution. That small, almost forgotten part of him let out a faint cry of protest. He turned a deaf ear to it. He couldn't relent now. He couldn't ignore the polls or the computer projection. A vindicated Dr. Alan Bulmer would be too much of a liability. McCready had to ruin him. There was simply no other way out.

The doors slid open and Rossi wheeled him into the elevator. They headed for the seventh floor.

*   *   *

The guard spotted her from his marble-enclosed guard station and was moving toward her before she was halfway through the revolving door.

"Sorry, miss," he said, holding out his hands in a "Stop" gesture. "We're closed to all visitors now."

Sylvia took a deep breath and launched herself into character.

"Wanna shee my doctor."

"None of the staff doctors are here now. Only a few resident physicians. Who's your doctor? We'll leave a message for him."

She had decided to be a belligerent drunk. She had seen enough of them at her parties—she hoped she could be convincing.

"I'm not talkin' 'bout one of your goddamn staff doctors! I'm talkin' 'bout Dr. Alan Bulmer. He's a *patient* here!"

"Visiting hours ended at seven. They start again at one tomorrow."

"I don't give a shit about your visiting hours! I'm here now . . . and I wanna shee Bulmer *now!*" She started toward the elevators. "What floor is he on?"

He grabbed her gently but firmly by the arm and guided her back toward the door. "Tomorrow, lady. Tomorrow."

Sylvia snatched her arm away. "Do you know who I am, you . . . you *lackey?*"

"No. And I don't care. Git!"

Sylvia had to hand it to the guard—he was keeping his cool. But it was showing signs of wear.

"Call the senator!" she cried as he grabbed her shoulders from behind and firmly propelled her toward the door. "He'll tell you who I am!"

It was time to play her ace card. She lurched away from him and leaned over the front of the guard station. There was a large panel of green and red lights there. Only the green were lit; they glowed steadily. She let her knees buckle.

"I'm gonna be sick!"

"Not there you ain't!" He pulled her away and eased her onto a bench a few feet away. "Sit here. I'll get you some water." He reached for her glass of scotch. "And you've had too much of that already."

"Doncha *touch* that! Just get me some water."

As he stepped over to the water fountain and filled a paper cup for her, Sylvia took a breather. So far, so good. She glanced at her watch.

Almost time.

She stood up again and staggered over to the guard station.

"Hey! Get away from there!" the guard cried as he returned with her water.

"You're right," Sylvia said, holding up her glass of scotch. "I don't need any more of thish." She placed the glass carefully on the marble rim directly above the control panel, then she made sure to hit it with her elbow as she swung around to return to the bench.

The guard's cry of "Oh, shit, no!" mixed with the tinkle of breaking glass, followed by a chorus of electrical pops and hisses accompanied by acrid white smoke rising from the control board as twelve-year-old scotch leaked down into the printed circuits.

As buzzers and bells began to sound, Sylvia moaned. "Oooh, I'm gonna be *so* sick!"

*   *   *

The small aluminum grappling hook had caught the ledge of a darkened second-floor window on the third try. Ba hauled himself up the length of the attached quarter-inch nylon cord until he could grab the ledge and pull himself up and balance there. He repeated the process with the window directly above.

This was as far as he would go on the outside. Dr. Axford had said that the administrative offices were on the third floor. As Ba had hoped, they were deserted at this time of night, and there was no sign that the windows were hooked up to the alarm system. A brief flick of his flashlight revealed that the floor inside was carpeted. Good. He pulled the duffle bag up to the ledge, withdrew Dr. Axford's white lab coat, and wrapped it around his right hand. Turning his face away, he struck the window a hard backhand blow.

A splintering crash was followed by a softer clatter of the shards falling against each other as they hit the carpet, then silence.

Ba hooked his grapple inside the frame and waited, ready to slide down to street level at the first sign of anyone coming to investigate. No one showed, so he climbed in. He donned the lab coat, which was far too short in the arms, and waited until it came: a cacophony of bells and beeps. It sounded as if every alarm in the building was going off at once.

Ba checked his watch: 9:32. He bowed his respect to the Missus. His old friend Sergeant Nash had chosen well for a wife. She was as resourceful as she was compassionate. He stepped into the deserted hall and from there made his way to the fire stairs near the elevator alcove. He was on the third floor; the senator's domain was on the twentieth.

He began to climb.

He was breathing hard when he reached the top level, so he stopped and rested a moment, peering through the small rectangle of wired glass. There was only one elevator door at this level, and one doubtlessly needed a key to travel this far. He checked the latch on the door. It was unlocked. A warning sounded in his brain. It would be senseless to lock a door to a fire stair, but if the senator was as security conscious as Dr. Axford had said, this door would be wired with an alarm. The security system, however, was in chaos now, so it might be safe to open it and check around for any other possible entry to the top floor besides the single elevator.

He moved out into the alcove and followed a short hallway to a set of double doors that was tightly closed. It was the only doorway on the entire floor. He briefly put his ear against it but could hear no sound from within. The entire level had a deserted feeling to it. He checked his watch: 9:40. He was on schedule, and it was apparent that Dr. Bulmer hadn't arrived yet.

Ba hurried back to the stairwell to wait. He had decided that the simplest and safest course was to intercept Dr. Bulmer as he stepped from the elevator and bring him back down to street level—leaving behind whoever had been escorting him to the twentieth floor, of course.

*   *   *

When he heard the knock on the door, Alan glanced at the clock. Nine twenty-six. Right on time.

He opened the door and found himself face to face with the swarthy security guard who had refused to let him leave the wing hours ago. With him was another guard. They looked familiar, and then he recognized them as Axford's assistants. Their name tags said "Henly" and "Rossi."

He swallowed the anger that had been simmering for hours and said: "What happened to the white coats?"

"Traded them in," Henly, the blond guard, said.

"Catch that maniac?" Alan asked Rossi.

He nodded. "Yep. And we brought you a visitor."

Leaning heavily on his cane, Senator McCready shuffled into the room. An empty wheelchair sat behind him in the hall.

"Good evening, Dr. Bulmer!" he said, genially enough. "I hope the unavoidable extension of your stay here hasn't inconvenienced you too much."

Alan hid his shock at seeing the senator come to him. He had expected the opposite. Much of his rage evaporated at seeing the infirmity and debility of the man close up. The slowness of his movements, the exertion they cost him—he was in sad shape.

"What an unexpected pleasure!" he managed to say. "And don't give my incarceration a second thought. How often does a man get a chance to be alone with his thoughts for nearly half a day? A little introspection is good for the soul." He grabbed McCready's hand and shook it. "I can't thank you enough for what you've done for me!"

That last sentence, at least, was true. By coming to the Foundation, Alan had learned that he could prove the existence of the *Dat-tay-vao* and could predict the hour of its occurrence with a simple tide chart. He had also learned that it was destroying his mind. He had gained something despite McCready's treachery.

McCready smiled. "As the barker said, 'You ain't seen nothin' yet!' " He fairly dropped into the chair. "We've gathered enough evidence to polish up your reputation and safeguard your medical license."

But you've destroyed it! Alan thought, his anger rising.

"We'll be sending out a general press release first thing tomorrow morning."

You lying bastard! It would never be composed, much less released.

Alan forced a smile. "I can barely wait to see it."

Suddenly the air was full of whooping sirens and clanging bells.

McCready snapped a glance at the two guards. "What's that all about?" His voice was barely audible above the din.

"Beats me," Henly said, his expression concerned and puzzled as he unclipped his walkie-talkie from his belt. "Sounds like fire and break-in and everything else. I'll check with Dave."

He turned and stuck his head into a relatively quiet corner while Alan and the others waited in silence. Finally Henly turned back to them.

"It's all right. Dave says some lady came in stewed to the gills demanding to see a patient and spilled a drink on the control console. Says it's a mess down there."

"Go help him out," McCready said. He turned to Rossi. "And you wait outside. I have a personal matter to discuss with Dr. Bulmer."

The guard stepped out and closed the door, muffling somewhat the continued clamor of the alarms.

"Personal matter?" Alan said.

"Yes." The senator rested both hands atop his cane and leaned forward. "As I'm sure you can see, I'm not a well man. By this time of night I'm usually fast asleep from exhaustion. It is only from sheer force of will that I made it here tonight."

"What's the problem?"

McCready removed his dark glasses. "You tell me, Doctor."

Alan saw the pathognomonic drooping, half-closed eyelids.

"Myasthenia gravis."

"Correct. A relentlessly progressive case. I . . . this is so difficult to ask . . . I was wondering if you might—"

"Heal you?"

"Yes. If you would."

Over my dead body! was what Alan wanted to say, but he kept his expression bland.

"Do you happen to know when high tide is, Senator?"

"It's at ten-eighteen." McCready checked his watch. "Just a little over thirty minutes away."

"Good. Then the *Dat-tay-vao* should be working soon."

"The what?"

"The Touch, Senator. The Touch that heals. Let's give it a try, shall we?"

Alan waited a few moments until his watch ticked around to 9:50. He had had a long time to think today, and had decided that his life had been manipulated too often for too long. He was reclaiming control, and here was where it began. McCready could wreck his career, ruin his reputation, send his teetering marriage over the edge, and convince the world that he was insane. But Alan Bulmer could still decide if and when to use the *Dat-tay-vao*. It was all he had left.

And it was all that McCready wanted.

Not quite knowing what would happen next, Alan stood up and placed his hands upon the senator's head.

Out in the hall, the alarms stopped.

*   *   *

Ba's watch said it was almost ten o'clock. All was quiet—too quiet. No one had come or gone on the top floor here. This troubled him. If they were going to bring the Doctor up to the senator's quarters, they surely would have done so by now.

Which left two possibilities: Either Dr. Bulmer wasn't coming up here tonight or the senator had gone to him. Dr. Axford had seemed quite sure that the senator would stay where he was and have Dr. Bulmer brought up. But Dr. Axford had been wrong before.

Seven-nineteen. That was the number of Dr. Bulmer's room.

Ba started down the steps.

*   *   *

"Had a few too many, lady?"

The blond guy was leering down at her as she slumped on the

bench. He had arrived like the cavalry to help the downstairs guard stop the racket and reset all the alarms. He strutted before her as if he knew without question that his uniform made him irresistible to women. Sylvia hated uniforms. Especially paramilitary models.

"Buzzsh-off, bozo," she said. "I ain't feelin' too good."

"Oh, but you're looking *fine!*"

"Yeah. Right."

He took her gently but firmly by the arm. "Let's you and me take a walk back to the overnight quarters where we can talk about this privately."

Sylvia snatched her arm away. She wanted to lash out at lover-boy, here, but held back.

"Talk about what?"

"About how much trouble you're in, honey. But maybe we can work something out."

Sylvia had a pretty good idea of how he wanted to work out. "Ain't in no trouble. Senator's a friend of mine."

"Yeah? What's your name?"

"Toad. Mrs. S. Toad."

The guard waved her off with disgust. "Get her out of here, Dave. I've got to get back upstairs to the senator."

Sylvia's heart leaped. Alan would be wherever the senator was. She took a fresh and sudden interest in the guard.

"You're gonna see the senator?" she cried, rising and following him toward the elevator. "Take me with you! I gotta see him!"

"Get lo—!" he began, then stopped. A calculating gleam lit his eyes. "Well . . . okay. What say I take you up to the senator's personal quarters and see if he's there? And if he ain't there"—he winked at Dave—"we can wait for him."

"S'go," Sylvia said, taking his arm. She wanted in the worst way to get upstairs to where Alan was, and this seemed as good a route as any. "Senator's an ol' buddy of mine."

The guard patted her hand as he led her toward the elevator. "Mine, too."

As the elevator doors closed and the car started up, he leaned against her and ran a hand up her flank.

"Ooh," she said, swaying against the side wall of the car. "This elevator's making me sick."

He backed away. "Hold on, hon. It's a short ride."

*   *   *

"Nothing's happening," McCready said after Bulmer's hands had rested on him almost a full minute. He fought the uneasiness creeping into him like a chill. "Does it usually take this long?"

"No," Bulmer said. "It usually happens instantly."

"Why isn't it working?" McCready fought off a rising panic. Bulmer seemed so unconcerned. "It's supposed to work half an hour before and after high tide! What's wrong? All the conditions are right! *Why isn't it working?*"

"Something's missing," Bulmer said.

"What is it? What? Just tell me and I'll have Rossi get it! What?"

Bulmer glared into his eyes.

"Me."

"I don't understand."

"I've got to *want* to cure you."

And then it was all clear. "So. Axford got to you."

"He sure did, you son of a bitch."

McCready repressed a desire to scream in rage at Axford's treachery. He kept cool on the outside.

"That makes things difficult, which is unfortunate, but it doesn't change anything."

"Meaning?"

"You'll remain our guest until you do something about my condition."

"I do have friends, you know."

McCready allowed himself a bitter laugh. "Not many. Hardly any, in fact. I had my people take a careful look into your life, hoping to find some sort of lever against you. But there was none. No mistress, no vices. You're pretty much a work-obsessed loner, Alan Bulmer. Much like me. The only friend who might present a problem is that lawyer, DeMarco. But I can deal with him. So you can consider yourself out in the cold."

Bulmer shrugged carelessly, almost as if he had been expecting this. Wasn't he frightened? His uncaring attitude worried Mc-Cready.

"Don't you understand what I'm saying to you? I can tie up your life indefinitely! I have personality profiles, answered in your own hand, that any psychiatrist in the country will interpret as the product of a severely psychotic and probably dangerous mind! I can keep you here or have you committed to state institutions for the rest of your life!"

Bulmer leaned back and folded his arms. "You exaggerate. But that's okay. You still won't get what you want."

"Oh. You want to deal, is that it?"

"No deal. Either I stay or I go free, but in neither case do you get the *Dat-tay-vao.*"

McCready stared at him, his mind whirling in confusion. What was the matter with this man? The determination in his eyes was unnerving.

"So that's how it's to be?" McCready said finally, leaning heavily on his cane as he struggled to his feet. "Suit yourself."

"All you had to do was ask."

McCready felt his legs go weak—the weakness now was due to more than just the myasthenia gravis—and sat down again. *All you had to do was ask.* Such a naive statement . . . yet it cut him to the core to think that he could have avoided all the intrigue and plotting simply by walking into Bulmer's office two months ago when he first got wind of those stories. Oh, God, if that were true, if he could have been well all that time, if he could have—

No! This was a crazy way to think. Bulmer was lying!

McCready stood firm against the wave of uncertainty. He had proceeded the only way he could.

"That was impossible. I couldn't give you a gun like that to let you hold to my head. You showed what you think of my politics at the committee hearing in April. I couldn't take the risk that you'd exploit what you knew and what you'd done as soon as I decided to run for President."

"I'm a doctor. Anything that went on between us would be privileged."

McCready snorted. "Do you really expect me to believe that?"

"I guess not," Bulmer said, and for an instant McCready thought he saw pity break through the anger in the other man's eyes. "You assume I'm like you."

He could no longer fight the overwhelming fear that he would never be free of this disease.

"I'm *sick!*" he cried through a sob that tore itself from his heart. "And I'm sick of being sick! I'm desperate, can't you see that?"

"Yes, I can."

"Then why don't you help me? You're a doctor!"

"Oh, no!" Bulmer said, rising and stepping toward him. "Don't try to run that game on me, you cold-blooded bastard! You were going to have me committed for the rest of my life a minute ago. That didn't work, so now you do the poor-broken-down-old-man number. Forget it!"

*   *   *

Alan hoped his words were convincing, because inside, much to his frustration and dismay, he was actually beginning to sympathize with McCready.

"I want to live again! Make love again! Shout again!"

"Stop it!" Alan said, trying to block out the words, made all the more compelling by the steadily fading power of McCready's voice.

"No! I won't stop! You're the only hope I have left!" With a sudden burst of strength he grabbed Alan's hands and pulled them down against his shoulders. "Heal me, damn you! Heal me!"

"*No!*" Alan said through clenched teeth.

And then it happened. Lancing pain, like fire, like ice, like electricity, ranged up his arms and throughout his body. Alan fell back and McCready screamed, a howl from the depths of his lungs.

Rossi lunged into the room.

"What the fuck's goin' on here?"

He looked at McCready, who was gray in the face and rapidly shading toward blue as he tried to pull air into his lungs.

"What'd you do to him?"

"Nothing!" Alan said, hugging his burning arms against his chest. "Nothing!"

"Then what's the matter with him?"

"Myasthenic crisis, I think. Get a house doctor or somebody up here with oxygen! Quick!"

"You're a doctor!" Rossi said, looking from Alan to the senator and back again. "Help him out!"

Alan hugged his arms more closely against himself. Something awful had just happened at his touch, and he was afraid to lay a hand on McCready again, afraid he'd make it worse.

"I can't. Get somebody else."

As Rossi leaped to the phone, Alan glanced at the open door that led to the hall. He started for it. He wanted out of here.

He made it all the way out to the elevator area, where he pressed the *Up* and *Down* buttons. He was waiting for the doors to open and take him away from there—he didn't care in which direction—when Rossi rushed up and grabbed his arm.

"Wait a minute, pal. You ain't goin' *no*where!"

It was fear and it was anger and it was sheer frustration at being told what he could and could not do once too often that made Alan lash out at the guard. He rammed his elbow into Rossi's solar plexus; as he doubled over, Alan got both hands against the back of the guard's head and pushed him toward the floor. Rossi landed with a grunt as the air wooshed out of him.

But then he was rolling over onto his back and pulling his revolver from its holster.

Suddenly a foot and a long leg, both in black, appeared and pinned Rossi's gun arm to the floor.

Alan jerked his head up and nearly cried out in fright and pleasure. Ba! The lanky Vietnamese stood there like a pallid vision from a nightmare. The door to the fire stairs was swinging closed behind him.

"Excellent, Dr. Bulmer."

He bent and casually plucked the weapon from the guard's hand. Rossi looked up at him in wonder and terror.

Just then the elevator doors opened. The blond guard stood within, a woman slouched next to him.

"Sylvia!" Alan cried in shock. How could she be—?

"What the hell are you doing out here?" Henly said, stepping forward as Sylvia straightened up behind him and beamed at Alan.

Ba stepped up beside Alan, the pistol dangling in his hand.

"Good evening, Missus," he said, then turned to Henly. "We shall need this car."

Henly said, "What the fuck—?" and reached for his own pistol. Ba stepped into the car and slammed him against the back wall.

"Take us down, please, sir," he said.

Alan stepped in and took Sylvia in his arms. She clung warm and soft against him.

Henly was nodding and fumbling with his key ring. "Yeah. Sure." He keyed an override and the car started down.

"Thank God you're all right!" Sylvia said, hugging Alan close.

"I'm fine," Alan said, "but I don't know about the senator." He suddenly realized that he was touching Sylvia and nothing was happening. Whatever had caused the sudden progression of the senator's disease seemed to have passed.

"What's wrong with him?"

"I don't know. The *Dat-tay-vao*—some sort of reverse effect."

His eyes were drawn to Ba, who was holding his hand out to Henly. The awestruck guard meekly handed his revolver over to the gaunt figure that towered over him. Ba emptied the cartridges from both pistols, put them in his pocket, then handed the empty weapons back to Henly. "Please not to do anything foolish."

The doors slid open and they were on the ground floor. Alan hurried Sylvia toward the doors while Ba brought up the rear.

"Dave!" Henly yelled from behind them as they passed the front desk. "Stop 'em!"

Dave looked at Alan and Sylvia, then looked at Ba and shook his head.

"*You* stop 'em!"

47.
Ba

Ba felt refreshed in the warm, humid air of the outdoors. He had never been able to adjust to air conditioning. He stepped ahead of the Doctor and the Missus and opened the rear door to the Graham for them. It was a proud moment for him to be able to lead these two safely from the Foundation. He would have freed anyone had the Missus asked, but it was especially pleasing to aid the Doctor. It lessened the weight of his debt to the Doctor for Nhung Thi; it helped to balance the scale between them.

Once they were inside, he got in the driver's seat and made a U-turn into Park Avenue's downtown flow at the next cross street.

"I don't think it would be wise to take the Dr. Bulmer back to Toad Hall just yet, Ba," the Missus said from the back seat.

Ba nodded. The same thought had occurred to him. "I know a place, Missus."

"Then take us there."

"Now hold on, everybody!" the Doctor said. "Just hold on a minute! I'm a free man and I want to go home!"

"Alan," the Missus said softly, "you haven't got a home anymore. It's gone. They burned it."

"I know that! I mean Monroe. That's where I live. I'm not going to hide from anybody!"

"Alan, please. I know you've been pushed around a lot lately, but Ba and I have just gone to a lot of trouble to get you out of the Foundation. A little legal finagling could put you back there in no time—or worse. If something has happened to McCready, they could blame it on you and you could wind up in Bellevue!"

There was silence in the rear. Ba thought he knew what might be going through the Doctor's mind. It seemed not only cowardly, but an apparent admission of guilt to run and hide. But the Missus was right—better to seek shelter until the storm passed.

Still, he could not help but sympathize with the Doctor, who must be feeling that his life was no longer his own. And truly it wasn't. Ba had now been privileged to meet two men with the *Dat-tay-vao*, and neither had been fully in control of his life. For the Touch has a will of its own, and knows no master.

The Monday night traffic was thin. He reached Canal Street quickly and followed it east between Little Italy and Chinatown, then turned downtown on Bowery until he came to a tiny sidestreet where refugees from his country had collected during the seventies. They all shared the kinship of strangers far from home, but none so close as those who had risked the open sea together in his boat. Most of his fellow villagers had settled in Biloxi, Mississippi, still living as fishermen, only now in the Gulf of Mexico instead of the South China Sea. But one or two had straggled to the Northeast. He stopped now before the ramshackle tenement that housed one of the elders of his former village.

The trip had taken less than fifteen minutes. Ba set the emergency brake and turned in his seat.

"You will be safe here," he told the Doctor.

Dr. Bulmer looked up and down the dark, ill-lit street, then up at the rickety building. "I'll have to take your word on that, Ba."

"Come," he said, stepping out and opening the door.

"Go, Alan," said the Missus. "If Ba says it's all right, then you can take it to the bank."

Ba glowed with pride at her words as he watched them embrace and kiss.

"All right," the Doctor said. "But just for tonight. Twenty-four hours and that's it. Then I'm coming home."

As the Doctor stepped out of the car, Ba closed and locked the door behind him. He didn't like leaving the Missus alone here on the street, but the motor was running and he would only be a few minutes.

He guided Dr. Bulmer into the building and up the flaking stairway to the fourth floor.

"Chac is an old friend," he said as they climbed. "If my fishing village still existed, he would have been an elder there."

"What's he do now?"

"He sells newspapers."

"What a shame."

"Better than what was in store for him at home. The communists wanted us to work for them in exchange for a ration of rice. We call that slavery. We have always worked for ourselves."

"You work for Mrs. Nash."

Ba did not pause or look back at the Doctor. He knew the question and knew the answer. "When I work for the Missus, I work for myself."

"I hear you," the Doctor said. And by the tone of his voice, Ba knew that he understood and there was nothing more to be said.

They reached the fourth-floor landing. Ba knocked softly but persistently on the door that read 402. His watch said 11:16. Chac might be asleep—he rose daily at four and was on the street in less than an hour. He hated to disturb the older man's sleep, but the time of his arrival was not of his choosing and Chac would understand.

A voice spoke from the other side of the door. "Who's there?"

Ba announced himself in the Phuoc Tinh dialect. There came the clicks of locks and the rattle of chains, and then the door was pulled open and Ba felt himself embraced by the shorter, older man.

"I cannot stay," Ba said, fending off offers of food and drink. He heard a child cough in the back room. He glanced questioningly at Chac.

"My grandson, Lam Thuy. He's almost three now. He stays here while Mai Chi and Thuy Le work at the restaurant. Here. Sit and let me make you tea."

"The Sergeant's wife awaits me below. But I have a favor to ask."

"Anything for Ba Thuy Nguyen! You know that!"

Ba smiled, warmed by the elder's approbation. "A friend needs shelter for a few days—shelter from the weather and from all eyes except those of this household."

Chac nodded. "I understand perfectly. It shall be done. This is he?"

Ba brought the Doctor forward and spoke in English for the first time. "This is Dr. Bulmer. He did all that could be done to make Nhung Thi's last days peaceful."

"Then he shall be as one of us," Chac replied, also in English.

He shook the Doctor's hand and brought him forward, welcoming him into his home.

"I must go," Ba said, feeling the urgency to get back down to the street where the Missus waited unprotected. But first there was something he had to tell the Doctor.

He drew him aside as Chac bustled toward the kitchen to make tea.

"Doctor," he said in a low voice, leaning very close. "Please not to mention the *Dat-tay-vao* to anyone."

The Doctor's eyebrows lifted. "I hadn't planned to. But why not?"

"Not time to explain now. All will be made clear later. Please do not mention the *Dat-tay-vao* here. Please?"

The Doctor shrugged. "Okay. Fine with me. But, listen"—he touched Ba's arm—"thanks for tonight. And take good care of that lady."

Ba gave him a slight bow.

As he left the apartment, he heard the child coughing again. Louder.

— 48. —
Alan

"You were Nhung Thi's doctor?" Chac said in thickly accented English after Ba had gone and the kettle had yet to boil.

"Yes. Not much I could do for her, I'm afraid." He worked to shut out the memory of her death agonies. A horrible way to go. He'd prefer almost any form of death to being eaten alive by lung cancer.

Alan distracted himself by studying Chac's grotesquely arthritic hands, noting the thickened and gnarled joints, the ulnar deviation of the wrists and fingers. How did this man manage to hand out his papers? How on earth did he make change?

He let his gaze wander around the tiny front room. The cracking plaster had been freshly painted; the furniture was old and rickety but waxed and dust free. A chubby plaster Buddha sat cross-legged on a corner table; a crucifix hung on the wall above it.

The child coughed again from the rear of the apartment. It carried a higher-pitched sound this time.

"Your son?" Alan asked. It seemed unlikely, but you never knew.

"Grandson!" Chac said, puffing himself up.

The coughing persisted, its bark becoming distinctly seal-like. But that wasn't what alarmed Alan. It was the whistling intake of breath, the increasingly labored stridor between coughing spasms that lifted him to his feet and drew him toward the sound.

That child was in trouble!

Chac, too, recognized the distress in the cough. He darted ahead of Alan and led the way. Halfway there, a thin woman of about Chac's age in a long, dark blue robe came out into the hall and joined the procession to the bedroom at the far end of the apartment.

Just before they reached the door, the cough shut off abruptly, as if a noose had been tightened around the throat. Chac turned on the light as they rushed into the room. Alan took one look at the black-haired boy with the mottled face and wide, panicky, black eyes, and knew there wasn't a second to spare.

Croup—with epiglottitis!

"Get a knife, small and sharp!" he said to Chac, shoving him back toward the kitchen.

He was going to have to try an emergency tracheotomy. He'd seen it done twice during his clinical training a dozen or so years ago, but had never yet been called upon to do one himself. He'd always prayed the situation would never arise. Cutting open someone's throat and then crunching through the cricothyroid membrane to form an airway without severing an artery or lacerating the thyroid was a difficult enough proposition on a still patient. On a squirming, bucking, fear-crazed child, it seemed madness to try. But this boy was going to die if he didn't get air soon.

Chac rushed back in and handed him a small knife with a sharp, two-inch blade. Alan would have preferred a narrower blade— would have loved the 14-gauge needle he'd kept in his black bag for a decade now just for an occurrence such as this. But his bag was in the trunk of his car.

The child was rolling and thrashing on the bed, arching his back and neck in a hopeless effort to pull air into his lungs.

"Hold him down," Alan told Chac and his wife.

The woman, whom Chac called Hai, looked at the blade with horror, but Chac shouted something to her in Vietnamese and she steadied her hands on either side of the child's face, now a dark blue. When Chac had situated himself across the boy's body, pinning his arms under him, Alan moved forward. With his heart pounding and the knife slipping around in his sweaty palm, he stretched the skin over the trachea.

Ecstatic voltage shot up his arm.

With a vortical wheeze, air rushed into the child's starved lungs, then out, then in again. Slowly his color returned to normal as he sobbed and clung to his grandmother.

Alan stared at his hand in wonder. How had that happened? He glanced at his watch: 10:45. Was the Hour of Power still on? What time had McCready said for high tide? He couldn't remember! Damn!

But did it matter? The important thing was that the little boy was alive and well and breathing normally.

Chac and his wife were staring at him in awe.

"Dat-tay-vao?" Chac said. "You *Dat-tay-vao?"*

Alan hesitated. For some strange reason he had a feeling he should say no. Had he been told to deny it? But why? These people knew about the Touch.

He nodded.

"Here?" Chac said, leaning closer and looking in his eyes. *"Dat-tay-vao* here in America?"

"So I'm told."

The Vietnamese couple laughed and wept and hugged their sobbing grandson, all the while babbling in Vietnamese. Then Chac came forward, holding out his deformed, arthritic hands, smiling timidly.

"Help me? Please?"

Another warning bell sounded in a distant corner of his mind. Hadn't Axford told him that the Touch was damaging his mind? But how could he say such a thing? Alan felt fine!

"Sure," he said. It was the least he could do for the man who was giving him shelter. Alan enclosed the gnarled fingers in his own and waited but nothing happened.

"The hour has passed," he told Chac.

The Vietnamese smiled and bowed. "It will come again. Oh, yes. It will come again. I can wait."

*   *   *

"I'm getting cabin fever," Alan told Sylvia.

He had spent a restless night and had been delighted to hear from her this morning. But talking on the phone was a far cry from being next to her and did little to ease his growing claustrophobia. The little apartment occupied the southeast corner of the building. Nice and warm in the winter, no doubt, but the sun had been blazing through the windows since 6:00 a.m. and the temperature of the soggy air here in the front room had to be pushing into triple figures already.

Hai, dressed in the classic loose white blouse and baggy black pajama pants of her people, bustled around the kitchen while her grandson munched on a cracker, both unmindful of the heat. It all came down to what you were used to.

"I've been cooped up for days—first in that glorified hospital room at the Foundation, now in an apartment so small you rub shoulders with somebody every time you move!"

"You promised to stay one day."

"And I will," he said, looking at the clock. It was 9:00. "In just a little over twelve hours I'm walking out of here. I don't care who's looking for me—McCready or the Mafia—I'm gone."

"I don't think the senator will be doing much looking. He's in a coma in Columbia Presbyterian."

"You're kidding!"

"Of course not! You sound surprised."

"Shouldn't I be?"

"Well, didn't you tell me last night that he went into some sort of convulsion when he tried to make you heal him? What'd you call it—a myasthenic crisis?"

Alan groped for the memory. The story sounded familiar. It came back slowly, like a slide projection very gradually being brought into focus.

"Oh, yeah. Sure. They say anything else about him?"

"No. Just that he's critical."

Did I do that? Alan asked himself after he had said good-bye to Sylvia.

Had he wanted to harm the senator? Had that somehow influenced the Touch to worsen his illness rather than cure it? Or had McCready simply worked himself into such a state that he brought the crisis upon himself?

Why try to kid himself? He had felt an odd sensation in his arms before McCready collapsed. Not the usual electric pleasure. Something different. Had he brought that on or had the power itself initiated it?

He didn't know. And not knowing worried him.

He shifted in the chair, felt something crinkle in his pocket, and pulled out Mr. K's empty Camel pack. Smiling, he set it on the table. Mr. K . . . Alan wondered if he had really stopped smoking.

There came a click of a key in the lock of the apartment door and Chac came in, dressed in a blue work shirt and denim coveralls. He bowed to Alan, then embraced his wife. Hai brought tea for both of them. Alan accepted it with what he hoped was a gracious smile. He was swimming in tea.

He watched with amazement as Chac deftly lit an unfiltered cigarette with his deformed hands. As Alan tried to hold up his end of a halting conversation about the weather, he detected a growing murmur of voices in the hall outside the door. He was about to ask Chac about it when the Vietnamese slapped his hands on his thighs and said, "It is time!"

"Time for what?"

"*Dat-tay-vao.*" He held out his hands to Alan. "Please?"

Was the Hour of Power on? And if so, how did Chac know? Alan shrugged. Only one way to find out.

He grasped the twisted fingers—

—and there it was again. That indescribable pleasure. Alan found something very comfortable in the Touch today. Maybe it was because Chac took its existence and effects for granted; there was no doubt to overcome, no preconceptions to butt against, no need to cover it up, just simple acceptance. And maybe it was because the *Dat-tay-vao* itself was back among the people who knew it best and revered it most. In a sense, the Touch had come home.

Chac raised his new hands and wrists before his eyes and flexed his slim, straight fingers. Tears began to roll down his cheeks. Speechless, he nodded his thanks to Alan, who placed an understanding hand on the older man's shoulder.

Chac stood and showed Hai, who embraced him, then went to the door and opened it.

The hall was filled with people. It looked like half of the city's Southeast Asian population was on the landing. They gasped in unison at the sight of Chac's normal, upraised hands, then broke into a babble of singsong voices, none of them speaking English.

Chac turned to him and dried his eyes. "I thank you. And I wonder if you would be so kind as to let the *Dat-tay-vao* heal others."

Alan didn't answer.

Why me? he wondered for the thousandth time. Why should he wind up with responsibility for the *Dat-tay-vao*? To decide whether to use it or not? He vaguely remembered being told that it was hurting him, that he paid a personal price every time he used it.

Do I want this?

He looked across the table at the happy little boy sitting with his grandmother, alive and well this morning instead of dead or on a respirator. He saw Chac flexing and extending his new fingers again and again. And he saw Mr. K's empty cigarette pack.

This was what it was all about: second chances. A chance to go back to when and where the illness had struck and start fresh again. Maybe that was the answer to *Why me?* He wanted to provide that second chance—give them *all* a second chance.

"Doctor?" Chac said, waiting.

"Bring them in," he told Chac. "Bring them *all* in."

Alan waited in anticipation as Chac went back to the door. This was going to be good. He could be up front about the Touch here. No worry about newspapers and hospital boards and conniving politicians. Just Alan, the patient, and the *Dat-tay-vao*.

He motioned to Chac to hurry. There would be no holding back today, no pussyfooting around. The Touch would recede in an hour and he wanted to treat as many as he could.

Chac brought the first forward: a middle-aged man with both arms locked at right angles in front of him.

"The Cong broke his elbows so that he would go through life unable to take food or drink by himself."

Alan wasted no time. He grabbed both elbows and felt the familiar shock. The man cried out as his arms straightened at the elbows for the first time in years, and then he began to swing them up and down. He fell to his knees, but Alan gently pushed him aside and motioned a limping boy forward.

On they came, in a steady stream. And as the *Dat-tay-vao* worked its magic on each one, Alan felt himself enveloped in an ever-deepening cloud of euphoria. The details of the room faded away. All that was left was a tunnel view of his hands and the person before him. A part of him was frightened, calling for a halt. Alan ignored it. He was at peace with himself, with his life. This was as it should be. This was what his life was about, this was what he had been born for.

He pressed on, literally pulling the people toward him and pushing them aside as soon as the pleasure flashed through him.

The haze grew thicker. And still the people came.

*   *   *

The flashes of ecstasy stopped coming but the haze remained. It seemed to permeate all levels of his consciousness.

Where am I?

He tried to remember but the answer wouldn't come.

Who *am I?*

He couldn't even think of his name. But there was another name surfacing through the haze. He reached for it, found it, and said it aloud.

"Jeffy."

He clung to the name, repeating it.

"Jeffy."

The name ignited a small flame within him. He turned his face northeast. He had to find Jeffy. Jeffy would tell him who he was.

He stood and almost fell. His left leg was weak. He called for help, and shadowy figures babbling gibberish propped him up until he was steady. As he began to walk toward the door, gentle hands tried to hold him back. He said one word: "No." The hands fell away and the figures parted to let him pass. He came to a set of stairs and paused, unsure of where his feet were. He tried to reach out for the banister with his left hand but could not raise it high enough. It was so heavy.

"Help," he said. "Jeffy."

Hands and arms lifted him and carried him down and around a number of times and finally brought him into the bright, hot sun where they set him on his feet again.

He began to walk. He knew the direction. Jeffy was like a beacon. He moved toward it.

"Jeffy."

___ 49. ___
Sylvia

Sylvia sat on the library couch where she and Alan had made love last week and patiently listened to the noon news, waiting for further word on McCready. There was nothing new. She rose and reached to switch off the weatherman when the camera abruptly cut away from him to the anchorman.

"This just in: Senator James McCready is dead. We have just received word that the senator has died from complications of a long-standing illness. We will break into our regular programming as more details become available."

Her heart pounding, Sylvia strode forward and spun the dial. She searched across the band, hunting more details, but heard only the same information in almost exactly the same wording. All the stations must have received identical releases.

She flicked off the set.

Complications of a long-standing illness.

That was a relief. She had worried that the senator or his staff might try to lay the blame for what had happened on Alan. Normally such a fear would never have crossed her mind, but after what had happened lately. . . .

The realization struck her: Alan could come home!

She checked the slip of paper that Ba had given her and called Chac Tien Dong's number. It went four rings before it was answered by a Vietnamese woman. Sylvia could barely hear her over the wild babble of voices in the background at the other end of the line.

"May I speak to Dr. Bulmer, please?" There came a confusion of noise over the wire. "How about Chac?" Sylvia said. "Can I speak to Chac?"

More confusion, then a male voice.

"Yes? This is Chac."

"This is Mrs. Nash, Chac. May I speak to Dr. Bulmer?"

There was a long pause, then Chac said, "He not here."

Oh, my God! "Where is he? Where did he go? Did someone come and take him away?"

"No. He leave all by self."

That, at least, was a relief. It meant that none of the Foundation people were involved.

"But why didn't you stop him?"

"Oh, no," Chac said. "Never stop *Dat-tay-vao*! Very bad!"

Alarm spread through her like a cold wind. Ba said he had warned Alan against mentioning the Touch. How did Chac know?

"Did he use the *Dat-tay-vao*?"

"Oh, yes! Many times!"

Sylvia slammed the receiver down and shouted, *"Ba!"*

— 50. —
Ba

Ba pushed his way through the thinning crowd in the tiny apartment to where Chac was standing and waving his reborn fingers in the air. His anger must have shown in his face, for the older man looked up at him and paled.

"I couldn't help it, Ba!" he said, retreating a step.

"You promised!" Ba said in a low voice, feeling hurt and angry. "You said you would keep him from all eyes except your family's, and here I find a party!"

"The *Dat-tay-vao*! He has the *Dat-tay-vao*!"

"I know that. It was why I asked you to hide him."

"I didn't know that! Perhaps if you had told me, it would have made a difference!"

"Perhaps?"

"Little Lam Thuy would have died if he hadn't been here! Don't you understand? He was sent here! He was meant to be here at that very moment! The *Dat-tay-vao* knew it would be needed and so it brought him here!"

"*I* brought him here! And I'm glad with all my heart that he saved

Lam Thuy, but that does not justify inviting the entire community to come here!"

Chac shrugged sheepishly. "I boasted. I was so honored to have the *Dat-tay-vao* in my home that I had to tell someone. The news spread. Like fish to the spawning ground, they descended on me. What could I do?"

"You could have turned them away."

Chac gazed at him reproachfully. "If you had heard that someone with the *Dat-tay-vao* was down the street when Nhung Thi was dying of the cancer, would you have been turned away?"

Ba had no answer. None, at least, that he wished to voice. He knew that he would have fought like a thousand devils for a chance to let the *Dat-tay-vao* work its magic on his withering wife. He sighed and placed a gentle hand on Chac's shoulder.

"Tell me, old friend. Which way did he go?"

"He was looking northeast. I would have kept him here, but he was seeking someone. And as you know, one never impedes the *Dat-tay-vao.*"

"Yes, I know," Ba said, "but I've never understood that."

" 'If you value your well-being/Impede not its way.' What more is there to understand?"

"What happens if you do impede its way?"

"I do not know. Let others learn; the warning is enough for me."

"I must find him for the Missus. Can you help me?"

Chac shook his head. "We did not follow him. He was under the spell of the *Dat-tay-vao*—he was not walking right and his thoughts were clouded. But he kept saying the same word over and over again: 'Jeffy.' Again and again: 'Jeffy.' "

Spurred by a sudden and unexplainable sense of danger, Ba stepped to the phone and dialed the Missus. He now knew where the Doctor was going. But if he was walking and if his mind was not right, he might never reach his destination. Ba would do his best to find him, but first he had to call the Missus.

Glancing out the window, he saw the first thunderheads piling up in the western sky.

___ 51. ___
During the Storm

Sylvia had watched the gathering darkness with a growing sense of foreboding. Her longtime general fear of all storms paled before the dread that rose in her minute by minute as she watched the billowing clouds, all pink and white on top but so dark and menacing below, swallow the westering sun. Alan was out there somewhere. And he was coming here. That should have thrilled her; instead it filled her with an even greater unease. Ba had hinted that Alan wasn't quite in his right mind. Alan and the storm—both were approaching from the west.

The phone rang. Sylvia rushed to it.

It was Charles. He seemed to have regained his composure since yesterday. Quickly, Sylvia relayed what Ba had told her.

"The bloody fool!" he said. "Did Ba say how many people he worked his magic on before he wandered off?"

"He wasn't sure, but from what he could gather from Chac, maybe fifty."

"Good lord!" Charles said in a voice that was suddenly hoarse.

Sylvia pressed on, hoping that if she kept feeding information to

Charles he might be able to give her an idea of what had happened to Alan.

"Chac also told Ba that Alan was walking funny—as if his left leg wasn't working right."

"Oh, no!"

"What's wrong?"

"That poor stupid bastard! He's gone and knocked out part of his motor cortex! God knows what will go next."

Sylvia felt as if her heart were suspended between beats. "What do you mean?"

"I mean that this Touch or whatever you call this bloody power of his has apparently used up most of the nonvital areas of his brain, and now it's moving into more critical areas. No telling what will go next if he goes on using it. If it hits a vital motor area, he could wind up crippled; if it knocks out a part of the visual cortex, he'll be partially or completely blind. And if he should happen to damage something like the respiratory center in the brainstem, he'll die!"

Sylvia could barely breathe.

"God, Charles, what'll we do?"

"Isolate him, keep him safe and happy, and don't let him go around touching people when the tide is in. Given time, and, assuming he hasn't caused too much damage, I think his brain will recover. At least partially. But I can't guarantee it. Of course, the first thing you've got to do is find him."

"He's coming here," Sylvia said with a sinking feeling.

"Well, good. No problem then."

"He's coming for Jeffy."

"Oh, yes, he mentioned Jeffy at the Foundation." There was a lengthy pause, then: "That does present a problem now, doesn't it? A moral dilemma, one might say."

Thunder rumbled.

Sylvia couldn't answer.

"Let me know if there's anything I can do," Charles said. "*Any*thing. I owe that man."

Sylvia hung up and corralled Jeffy from the now dark sunroom. She pulled the drapes closed across the tall library windows, then sat on the couch and snuggled with the ever more placid Jeffy as she listened to the growing din of the storm.

On the Five O'Clock News, Ted Kennedy and Tip O'Neill were extolling the courage and integrity of the late Senator James A. McCready. Sylvia tuned them out.

What am I going to do?

She knew the choice that faced her and she didn't want to choose. According to the chart, it would be high tide off Monroe at 10:43 tonight. If Alan arrived then, she would have to make a decision: a meaningful life for Jeffy against brain damage, maybe even death, for Alan.

She hugged Jeffy against her and rocked back and forth like a child with a teddy bear.

I can't choose!

Maybe she wouldn't have to. Maybe Ba could intercept him and bring him to Charles or someplace where he could rest and become himself again. That would rescue her from the dilemma of either letting him go ahead with what he thought he had to do, or standing in his way and delaying him until the hour of the *Dat-tay-vao* passed.

And later, after Alan had had days and weeks to rest up, and if he recovered the parts of his mind he had lost over the past few weeks, and knew what he was doing and was fully aware of the risks involved, *then* maybe she could let him try the *Dat-tay-vao* on Jeffy.

But what if the *Dat-tay-vao* was gone by then?

Sylvia squeezed Jeffy tighter.

What do I do?

She looked at the old Regulator school clock on the wall—5:15. Five and a half hours to go.

*   *   *

Alan realized he was wet. The water poured out of the sky in torrents, soaking through his clothes and running down his arms and legs. His feet squished in his shoes as he walked.

He had been walking as fast as his weak left leg would allow him for a long time. He wasn't sure where he was, but he knew he was closer to Jeffy. He had crossed a bridge over a river and was now walking down a narrow alley between two run-down apartment houses. He came to a spot where an overhang gave shelter from the downpour. He stopped and leaned against the wall for a rest.

Two other men were already there.

"Beat it, asshole," one of them said. Alan strained his vision in the dim light to see the one who had spoken. He saw a filthy man who wore his equally filthy long brown hair tied back in a ponytail, dressed in torn jeans and a T-shirt that might have been yellow once. "This spot's taken."

Alan didn't know why the man was so belligerent, but he took it as good advice. He had to keep on moving. Had to get to Jeffy. Couldn't let a little rain stop him. He started for the end of the alley toward which he had been heading, but tripped and almost fell.

"Hey!" said the other man. He too was wearing dirty jeans, and his greasy, gray sweatshirt cut off at the shoulders exposed crude tattoos over each deltoid. His hair was short and black. "You kicked me!"

In a single motion, he levered himself off the wall and gave Alan a vicious shove. Off balance and stumbling backward, Alan's windmilling arms caught the wall, but his left leg wouldn't hold him. He went down on one knee.

"Bad leg, ay?" Ponytail said with a smile as he stepped forward. Alan felt a stab of pain in his good leg as the man kicked him. He went down on the other knee.

Hurt and afraid now, Alan struggled back to his feet and turned away.

"Hey, gimp! Where y'goin'?" one of them said from behind.

"Jeffy," Alan said. How could they not know that?

"What he say?" said the other voice.

"Dunno. Didn't even sound like English."

"Hey! A foreign dude. Let's check him out!"

A hand clamped on his shoulder and spun him around. "What's the rush, pal?" Ponytail said, grabbing his arms and pinning them to his sides. Sweatshirt came up beside him and rammed his fingers into Alan's left rear pocket.

"Fucker's got a wallet!"

A vaguely female voice shouted from far above. "Hey! What's goin' on down there?"

"Eat me, sweetheart!" Sweatshirt yelled, almost in Alan's ear, as he struggled with the button on Alan's rear pocket.

"Jeffy!" Alan said.

Ponytail stuck his face almost against Alan's. His breath was foul. "I'll Jeffee your head, asshole, if you don't shut up!"

Alan freed his right arm and pushed against him.

"Jeffy!"

And suddenly Ponytail began to gurgle and writhe in his grasp. His eyes rolled upward and a swollen tongue protruded from his mouth.

"What the fuck?" Sweatshirt shouted. "Hey, Sammy! Hey!"

He pulled on the front of Alan's shirt and Alan fended him off, grabbing his wrist with his newly freed left hand.

Sweatshirt began to shudder uncontrollably in Alan's grasp, as if suddenly struck with a malarial chill. His short black hair began to fall out and rain down on Alan's arm.

Alan glanced back at Ponytail, now swaying drunkenly. Lumps had appeared all over his skin; as Alan watched, they swelled, pointed, and burst, oozing trails of purulent, blood-tinged slime down his quaking body.

Reeling in confusion and shock, Alan tried to loosen his grip but found his fingers locked. Sweatshirt's knees crumbled under him. As Alan watched, the man's stomach began to swell, becoming enormously distended until it ruptured, spewing loops of his intestines out of the cavity to drape over his thighs like strings of boiled sausage.

A woman's voice screamed from high above. Ponytail, now an unrecognizable mass of festering sores, sank to the ground. As the buzz of the gathering flies mixed with the shrill sound of the woman's continued screaming, Alan turned and started walking once more. The images of the scene behind him were already fading into unreality as he picked up the beacon that lay to the northeast.

"Jeffy," he said.

*   *   *

Ba wheeled his Pacer up and down the rain-soaked streets. Chac had told him that the Doctor had headed northeast, and so Ba had driven that way, weaving a path from street to street through the teeming housing projects until he came to the East River. From there he took the Williamsburg Bridge and crossed into Brooklyn. He was unfamiliar with this area of the city. That, coupled with the maniacal fury of the storm and the almost nightlike darkness, slowed his search to a frustrating crawl.

Wherever this was, it was a nasty neighborhood. He did not like to think of the Doctor walking through here alone. Anything could happen to him. The storm, at least, was in his favor. It seemed to be keeping most people indoors.

He turned a corner onto a wider street and saw flashing red lights a few blocks down—two squad cars and an ambulance. Saying a silent prayer to his ancestors that the lights were not flashing for the Doctor, he accelerated toward them.

Ba double-parked and pressed through the buzzing crowd of rain-soaked onlookers to see what had drawn them out into the storm. Over their heads Ba could see a number of attendants in the alley fitting the second of two body bags around the gangrenous and shriveled remains of what had once been a human being. Despite the rain, he caught a whiff of putrescence on a gust of wind from the alley. And even in the red glow of the flashers, Ba detected a grim pallor to the attendants' faces. Both body bags were loaded into the ambulance. The sight of them brought back unwanted memories of the war back home.

"A murder?" Ba said to the man next to him.

He shrugged. "Two rotted bodies. Somebody must have dumped them there." As he glanced up at Ba, his eyes widened. He turned and hurried away.

A man who appeared to be a police detective cupped his hands around his mouth and called to the crowd. The man next to him held an umbrella over the two of them.

"I'll ask you all one last time: Did anyone see what happened here?"

"I told you!" said a wizened old woman from the stoop of the building behind the scene. "I saw the whole thing!"

"And we have your statement, ma'am," the policeman said in a tired voice without turning around. He rolled his eyes at his companion.

No one came forward. The crowd began to thin. Ba hesitated, unsure of what to do. Two rotted corpses . . . at least he was now sure that the Doctor had not been in one of those body bags. He should leave and continue the search, he knew, but something held him here.

That old woman on the stoop. He wanted to speak to her.

*   *   *

Alan walked up a ramp toward a highway. Cars rushed by him; the sheetlike cascades of dirty water from their tires added to the downpour, leaving not a dry spot on his body. He barely noticed. He did not know the name of the highway but sensed that it traveled in the right direction.

He reached the main span of the road and continued walking. Lightning blanched the dark sky and thunder drowned out the rumble of the cars and trucks speeding by. Wind lashed the rain into his eyes. He walked on, faster now, a sense of urgency lighting inside him. He was late, behind schedule. If he didn't hurry, he'd arrive too late for Jeffy.

Without thinking, he turned and began walking backwards. Of its own accord, almost as if by reflex, his arm thrust out toward the traffic, his thumb pointing toward his destination.

It was at a point in the road where the water was particularly deep and the cars had to slow to a crawl to pass through, that a car pulled to a stop beside him and the passenger door flew open.

"Boy, do you look like *you* could use a lift!" said a voice from within.

Alan got into the car and pulled the door closed after him.

"Where y'going?" said the plump man in the driver's seat.

Alan said, "Jeffy."

*   *   *

Finally, the crowd, the ambulance, and the police cars were all gone. Only Ba and the old woman on the stoop remained, he in the rainy darkness, she in the pool of light under the overhang on her front stoop.

Ba walked over and stood at the bottom of the steps.

"What did you see?"

She gasped as she looked down at him. "Who the hell are you?"

"Someone who has seen strange things in his lifetime. What did you see?"

"I told the police."

"Tell me."

She sighed, looked over to the opening of the alley beside the building, and began to speak.

"I was watching the storm. Sitting at my window, watching the storm. I always sit at my window, rain or shine. Not much going on outside most of the time, but it's sure a helluva lot more than's going on inside. So I was sitting there, watching the lightning, when I seen this guy come walking down the alley, walking kind of funny, like he'd hurt his leg or something. And he's walking in the rain like he don't know it's raining. I figure he's on drugs, which means he's right at home around here."

"Excuse me," Ba said, his interest aroused now. "But what did this man look like?"

"Maybe forty. Brown hair, blue pants, and a light blue shirt. Why? You know him?"

Ba nodded. That described the Doctor perfectly. "I'm looking for him."

"Well, you better hope you don't find him! You should have seen what happened to those two bums, God rest their souls"—she crossed herself—"when they tried to rob him! He grabbed them and they went into fits and died and rotted, all in a few minutes! You've never seen anything like it! And neither have I until today!"

Ba said nothing, only stared at her, stunned.

"You think I'm crazy, too, dontcha? You and those cops. Well, go ahead. Think what you want. I saw what I saw."

"Did you see which way he went?" Ba said, as he found his voice again.

"No, I—" was all he heard, for she flinched as a particularly bright bolt of lightning cut through the rain and gloom, and whatever else she might have said was lost in the thunderclap that followed on its heels. She turned and opened the door to the building.

"I didn't hear you!" Ba called.

"I said I didn't *want* to see."

Ba hurried back to his car. As he sped along the streets, looking for a phone, his mind raced in time with the engine.

What was happening? First the senator, now these two men. Was the *Dat-tay-vao* turning evil? Or were these examples of what was meant by that line from the song: "If you value your well-being/ Impede not its way"?

Perhaps Chac had been wise after all not to prevent the Doctor from leaving. He might have ended as a rotted corpse.

Ba was no longer searching for the Doctor. That could wait. Before he did anything else, he had to find a phone. The Missus had to be warned. If the Doctor made it to Toad Hall, the Missus might try to keep him from Jeffy, thinking it was for the Doctor's own good.

His mind turned away from what might happen.

He came to a light at a main thoroughfare, but couldn't find a sign to tell him its name. He saw a Shell station half a block to his left and headed for it. Fortunately, the pay phone there hadn't been vandalized and he called Toad Hall.

A recorded voice came on the line: *"We are sorry, but your call did not go through. Please hang up and dial again."*

Ba did, and received the same message. A third try with the same result left one conclusion: The lines were down again in Monroe.

Ba asked the station attendant the quickest route to the Long Island Expressway and then sped off, his mind consumed with a vision of the Missus withering and rotting under the Doctor's hand as she tried to stop him.

A glance at the dashboard clock showed 8:15. Plenty of time. Still he hurried, weaving through the traffic, dodging the potholes. A sign pointed straight ahead for the L.I.E./495. The red light ahead turned green so he accelerated.

And then he saw the delivery truck careen into the intersection as it ran its red light. Ba all but stood on the brakes. As the Pacer went into a spin on the wet pavement, he saw the driver's wide eyes and shocked, open mouth, saw the name IMBESI BROS. in big yellow letters on its side, and then the world disappeared.

*　　*　　*

"Sure this is where you want to get out?"

Alan nodded. He had remembered his own name—at least his first name—and recognized some of his surroundings. The sign had said, EXIT 39—GLEN COVE RD. The car was stopped under the overpass, out of the rain. He knew that Jeffy was directly off to his left, due north of here. The driver was heading farther east.

"Yes."

The driver glanced around at the narrow shoulder of the road. "This is where this Jeffy is gonna meet you?"

"Not far," Alan said as he opened the door and stepped out into the rain.

"It's eight-forty-five now. What time they comin'?"

"Soon."

"You're gonna catch *pneumonia* soon."

Alan said, "Jeffy."

"Just remember me the next time you're driving along and see someone soaked and walking in the rain."

"Yes," Alan said and closed the door.

After the car had sped off, Alan struggled up the embankment to the road above and turned north.

It wasn't far now. He was tired, but he knew that once he reached Jeffy he would be able to take a long, long rest.

*　　*　　*

Where was Ba?

Sylvia paced the library, dark but for the glow of a few candles placed here and there around the room. The power was out, the phones were out, and the tide was coming in. Quarter to ten now. An hour to high tide.

An involuntary yelp of fright escaped Sylvia as a jab of white-hot lightning lit the room and thunder rattled Toad Hall on its foundations.

Would this storm *never* stop?

Futile as it was to rail at nature, Sylvia took comfort in the gesture. It vented her tension. And it was better than thinking about the decision facing her.

If Ba had found Alan and was keeping him away until the hour of the *Dat-tay-vao* had passed, then she was home free. But if Alan was still on his way here. . . .

If only she knew! If only Ba would call!

I'm copping out.

She had to make a decision. If she was ever going to respect herself after this nightmare was over, she would have to get off the fence and stop hoping for someone to decide for her.

She started to sigh but it came out as a sob. She bit her lip to hold back the tears. There was only one choice.

She had to stop Alan.

God, how she ached to give Jeffy a chance at being a normal little boy. But the price . . . the price.

How could she allow Alan, in his brain-damaged state, to risk further damage, perhaps death, on the chance that he might cure Jeffy's autism? So far the *Dat-tay-vao* had been used only on physical ills. Who even knew if it could help Jeffy at all?

And if it could, wasn't that the most frightening prospect of all?

In that moment, she faced the gut-wrenching realization that she wasn't afraid for Alan as much as she was afraid for Jeffy and herself. What if Jeffy's autism *was* suddenly cured and he became a normal, responsive child? What kind of child would he be? What if he loathed her? Or even worse—what if she loathed *him?* She couldn't bear that. Almost better to have him stay the way he was and still love him than to face the unknown.

Still, her mind was made up: If Alan arrived, she'd stop him, even if it meant physically blocking his way.

She should have felt relieved now that she had finally reached a decision. Why did she feel so defeated?

She took the flashlight and ran upstairs to check on Jeffy. She found him sleeping peacefully despite the storm. She sat on the edge of the bed and smoothed his curly, sun-bleached hair.

A tear rolled down her cheek, and she felt her resolve weaken, but she took a deep breath and held it until she hurt. Then she let it out, slowly.

"Your day will come, little man," she whispered, and kissed his freckled forehead.

Then she went back downstairs to wait for Alan.

*   *   *

The jostling brought Ba back to consciousness. Flashing red lights glowed dimly through the blur that coated his eyes like thick jelly. As he blinked and his vision cleared, he saw a concrete overhang a few yards above with a sign that read EMERGENCY ENTRANCE. From below him he heard a clank and felt one firm, final jostle. He realized with a start that he was on a stretcher that had been slid out of an ambulance and had its wheels lowered. He tried to sit up but found straps buckled across his chest. The effort caused a blaze of pain to rip up the back of his neck and explode in his head.

"Let me up," he said in a voice that did not quite sound like his own.

A brusque but gentle hand patted his shoulder. "Take it easy, mac. You'll be okay. We already thought you was dead but you ain't. We'll be unstrapping you in a minute."

He was wheeled up next to a gurney, unstrapped, and moved laterally. Only then did he realize that he was on a wooden back-board. Ba waited until the backboard had been removed, then made his move before any more straps could be fastened around him.

The room swam and a wave of nausea washed over him as he sat up. He clenched his teeth and bit back the bile that welled up in his throat.

"Just a minute there, pal," one of the attendants said. "You better lie down until they get a doctor in here."

"What time is it?" Ba said. The room had righted itself and was holding steady. He realized there was a bandage around his head. There were other people on other gurneys spaced evenly along the walls of the emergency ward, some enclosed in curtains, some open. Activity swirled and eddied around him.

"Ten-seventeen," said the other attendant.

Two hours! Ba slid off the gurney onto his feet. *I've lost two hours!* He had to get to Toad Hall, to the Missus!

As he began to walk toward the door to the outer hallway, ignoring the protests from the ambulance attendants, a middle-aged nurse, clipboard in hand, marched up to him.

"And just where do you think you're going?"

Ba looked at her once, then brushed by her. "Please do not stop me. I must leave."

She stood aside and let him pass without saying another word.

He went through the automatic doors and stood there on the curb, his fists clenching and unclenching against his thighs.

He had no car!

A door slammed to his right and he saw an ambulance driver walking away from his rig. The diesel engine was still running.

Before actually making a conscious decision, Ba found himself walking toward the vehicle as the driver passed him and went through the emergency doors. The door was unlocked. Without looking back, Ba seated himself behind the wheel, put it in gear, and pulled out onto the street. Because a right turn would take him out of sight more quickly, Ba turned that way and came upon an arrow pointing straight ahead to 495.

He found the switches for the flashers and the siren and turned them on. With no little sense of satisfaction, he floored the accelerator and watched cars slew out of his way to let him pass. He began to think that he might have a chance to make it to Toad Hall in time after all.

*   *   *

The streets here looked vaguely familiar, yet try as he might, Alan could not remember the name of the town. A number of times he wanted to turn from his path and investigate a side road or follow a tantalizing thread of familiarity to see where it led.

But he found he could not. Whatever was guiding him—*driving* him—would not allow him to veer from the path toward Jeffy. There was a monumental singularity of purpose within him that had all but taken control.

He turned off the road and walked between two brick gateposts onto an asphalt driveway, then off the driveway and into a stand of willows where he stopped and stood among the drooping leafy branches that swayed like soft bead curtains in the wind. He was glad to stop; he was exhausted. If it were entirely up to him, he'd drop onto the sodden ground and go to sleep.

But it was not up to him. So he stood and waited, facing the huge, dark house across the lawn. Beyond the house he could hear water lapping high and hungry against the docks. The tide was almost in. He didn't know how he knew that, but there was no doubt in his mind. And that was what he seemed to be waiting for—the crest of the tide.

He felt a new sensation, a tension coiling within him, pulsating eagerly, readying to spring. His hands felt warm.

And then he began to walk toward the house.

It was time.

"Jeffy," he said to the darkness.

*   *   *

Finally, the storm was dying. The lightning was now dim flashes and the thunder only low-pitched rumbles, like an overfed stomach with indigestion.

Thank God! Sylvia thought. *Now, if only the lights will come back on. . . .*

Phemus began to bark.

Sylvia went to the window that looked out on the driveway, but saw no car. She glanced at her watch and saw that it was 10:40. Three minutes to high tide. A chill ran over her. Someone was out there in the darkness, moving this way across the lawn toward the house. She wished she could turn on the outside spotlights. At least then she could see him. Not that it really mattered. She could sense his presence.

Alan was coming.

But how could that be? How could he get all the way here from lower Manhattan? It just didn't seem possible. Yet he was out there. She was sure of it.

Flashlight in hand, she took Phemus by the collar and led him back to the utility room where she closed him in with the washer and dryer. As she was moving toward the library, she heard the front door swing open. She stopped for a minute, listening to her heart thudding in her chest. She thought she had locked that door! What if it wasn't Alan? What if it was a burglar—or worse?

Turning her flashlight off, Sylvia steeled herself and crept softly along the hall until she got to the front foyer. A distant flash of lightning flickered though the still-open door, reflecting off wet footprints on the floor and backlighting a dark figure starting up the stairs.

"Alan?"

The figure didn't reply, but continued to climb. It seemed to be limping as it took the steps one at a time. Ba had said that Alan was limping when he left Chac's. It had to be him.

She flicked on the flashlight and angled the beam until she caught his face.

Yes, it was Alan, and yet it was not Alan. His face was slack, his eyes vacant. He was different.

"Alan—don't go up there."

Alan glanced her way, squinting in the beam of light.

"Jeffy," he said in a voice she barely recognized.

Cajole him, she told herself. *Talk him down. He's not all there.*

She held the light under her own face. "It's me—Sylvia. Don't go to Jeffy now. He's asleep. You'll only disturb him. Maybe you'll frighten him."

"Jeffy," was all that Alan said.

And then the lights came on.

Sylvia gasped at the sight of Alan in his entirety. He looked terrible. Wet, dirty, his hair matted and twisted by wind and rain, and his eyes—they were Alan's and yet not Alan's.

He continued up the stairs one at a time at his painfully slow pace, moving like an automaton.

With fear and pity mixing inside her, Sylvia started toward him. "Don't go up there, Alan. I don't want you to. At least not now."

He was halfway up the staircase now and didn't look around. He simply said, "Jeffy."

"*No,* Alan!" She ran up the stairs until she was beside him. "I don't want you to go near him! Not like this. Not the way you are."

The lights wavered, flicked off for a second, then came back on. "Jeffy!"

Fear had taken over now. There was no longer any question in her mind that Alan was completely deranged. In the distance she heard a siren. If it was the police, she wished they were coming here, but it was too late to call them now. She couldn't let Alan near Jeffy. She'd have to stop him herself.

She grabbed his arm. "Alan, I'm telling you now—"

With a spasmodic jerk of his left arm, he elbowed her away, slamming her back against the banister. Sylvia winced at the pain in her ribs, but what hurt more was that Alan did not even look around to see what he had done.

The siren was louder now, almost as if it were passing directly in front of the house. Sylvia scurried up to the top of the stairs ahead of Alan and faced him, blocking his way.

"Stop, Alan! Stop right there!"

But he kept on coming, trying to squeeze by to her left. She tightened her grip on the banister and wouldn't let him pass. She was so close to him now, and she could see the determination in his eyes. He pressed against her with desperate strength as the lights flickered again and the siren's wail became deafeningly loud.

"Jeffy!"

"*No!*"

He grabbed her arms to push her aside and then everything happened at once. Pain—it started at her core and began to boil within her, tearing at her, making her feel as if she were being turned inside out. Her vision dimmed. She heard a pounding sound—footsteps on the stairs or the blood in her ears? Then Ba's voice shouted,

"*Missus, no!*"

She felt an impact that knocked the wind out of her, felt strong arms around her, lifting her, carrying her, falling to the floor with her.

Sylvia's vision cleared as the pain faded away. She was lying on the second-floor landing. Ba was beside her, breathing hard, a bloody bandage around his head.

"Missus! Missus!" he was saying, shaking her. "You all right, Missus?"

"Yes, I think so." She saw Alan limp by. He looked down at her, and for a moment seemed to start toward her, a confused and concerned look on his face. Then he turned away, as if drawn by an invisible cord, continuing on his path toward Jeffy's room. "Alan, come back!"

"He must go, Missus," Ba said soothingly as he restrained her. "You must not try to stop him."

"But why?"

"Perhaps because he has always wanted to help the Boy, and perhaps his time with the *Dat-tay-vao* is near its end and he must complete this final task. But you must not try to stop him."

"But he could die!"

"As you would have died if you had barred his way any longer."

There was a note of such finality in Ba's voice, and such unfailing certainty in his eyes, that Sylvia did not dare ask how he knew.

The lights went out again.

Sylvia looked down the hall and saw Alan's shadowy form turn into Jeffy's room. She wanted to scream for him to stop, to run down the hall and grab him by the ankles. But Ba held her back.

Alan disappeared through Jeffy's doorway. A pale glow suddenly filled the room and spilled out into the hall.

"No!" she cried and broke away from Ba. Something awful was going to happen. She just knew it.

She rolled to her feet and ran down the hall, but was brought to a halt for a frozen second as a child's cry of pain and fear split the silent darkness.

And then the cry took form.

"Mommy! Mommy-Mommy!"

Sylvia's knees buckled. That voice! God, that voice! It was Jeffy! The lights flickered again as she forced herself forward, through the door, and into the room.

By the glow of his Donald Duck night-light she could see Jeffy crouched against the wall in the corner of his bed.

"Mommy!" he said, rising to his knees and holding his arms out to her. "Mommy!"

Sylvia staggered forward, heart pounding, mouth dry. This couldn't be true! This kind of thing only happens in fairy tales!

Yet there he was, this beautiful little boy, looking at her, *seeing* her, calling for her. Half-blinded by tears, she ran forward and gathered him up against her. His arms went around her neck and squeezed.

It was true! He was really cured!

"Oh, Jeffy! Jeffy! Jeffy!"

"Mommy," he said in a clear, high voice. "That man hurt me!"

"Man? What—?" *Oh, God! Alan!* She frantically looked around the room.

And then she saw him, crumpled on the floor like a pile of wet rags in the shadows by the foot of the bed.

And he wasn't moving. God in heaven, he wasn't even breathing!

AUGUST

___ 52. ___
Jeffy

Jeffy felt a warm inner glow at the sight of Dr. Bulmer. It was always the same whenever he saw him. He didn't know exactly why; he just knew that he loved the man, almost as much as Mommy.

Jeffy stood beside his mother now as Mr. Ba pushed Dr. Bulmer's wheelchair through the front door and into the house. It had been a month since the doctor had been carried out of Jeffy's room and rushed to the hospital. He still didn't look too good, but he looked better than he had that night.

Jeffy would never forget that night. It was as if his life had begun then. He could remember very little before it. But that night . . . the world had become a glorious new place that night, opening up like one of the morning flowers in the garden when the sun shone on it.

Life before then had been like a dream; half-remembered, disjointed scenes from that time flashed sporadically in his new wakeful state. Everything now seemed new and not-new, as if he had been here before, seen and done so many things before, and forgotten them. Seeing them again was like a gentle jog to his memory, causing a burst of recognition in which pieces out of nowhere seemed to fall into place.

Mommy said that everything good that had happened to him since that night was because of Dr. Bulmer. Maybe that was why he got such a good feeling whenever he saw the doctor.

Mommy took over the job of pushing the wheelchair and started talking to Dr. Bulmer. She always talked to him. Jeffy had noticed that on the times when he had visited the doctor in the hospital. Mommy talked and talked, even though the doctor hardly ever answered her back. She pushed him into the room that the men had been working on for the past few weeks.

"Remember this place, Alan?" she said. "We spent some time here, you and I."

"I . . . I think so," he said in his flat voice.

"Used to be the library. Now it's your room. You're going to stay here until your legs are strong enough to get you up and down the stairs. We're going to have doctors and physical therapists and speech therapists coming and going in and out of here like there's no tomorrow. You're getting better every day. Two weeks ago you couldn't even speak; now you're talking. And you're going to keep on getting better. And Jeffy and I are going to help you. You're going to be the same person you used to be." Mommy's voice got sort of choked-sounding for a second. "I swear it. No matter how long it takes, I *swear* it!"

"How was I?" he said.

"You were the greatest. Still are, in my book."

She grabbed his hand and squeezed it. For a moment Jeffy was afraid she was going to cry again. She didn't cry as much now as she used to, but she still did it a lot. Jeffy didn't like to see her cry.

"Jeffy," she said, turning to him. He saw that she wasn't going to cry. Not now, anyway. "Why don't you take Mess and Phemus out in the yard for a while. They've been cooped up in the house all morning. But stay away from the dock. The tide's in and I don't want you getting wet."

"Goody!" He felt like running around himself. He scooped Mess up from her sunny spot on the window seat, then slapped his hand against his thigh. Phemus came running from the back room. And then they were out into the yard and the warm August air.

As Mess stalked off into the bushes, Jeffy found a stick and began to toss it for Phemus to chase. On the third throw, it caught in the branches of one of the peach trees—the one Mommy called The New Tree, the one with the really big peaches. With Phemus barking and running in circles around him, Jeffy tried to climb up to retrieve it. He succeeded only in scraping his legs and shaking loose a few of the riper peaches.

They looked good. As he bent to pick one up, Mess strolled out of the bushes and approached him. She was carrying something in her mouth . . . something that moved. Mess deposited the gift in front of Jeffy and walked off.

It was a bird. Jeffy looked down with horrid fascination at its bloody, mangled wing as it struggled in vain to right itself.

His heart went out to the poor creature. As he reached out, it cheeped weakly and flapped its good wing to get away.

"I won't hurt you," he said. Maybe he could keep it and feed it and fix its wing. Then the bird would be his very own pet. As he gathered the wounded creature into his hands, he felt a sudden thrill run up his arms.

It felt so good!

And then the bird was squawking and fluttering its suddenly perfect wings. It wriggled free of his grasp and took to the air. It soared, circling once over his head, then it flew off into the trees.

Jeffy didn't understand what had happened, but he felt good.

Somehow the bird's wing had been made all better. Had he done that? He didn't know. He'd have to try it again sometime. Maybe he could even make Dr. Bulmer all better. That would make Mommy happy. Sure. Maybe he'd try that someday. Right now he was more interested in the peach that lay before him on the grass. He picked it up and took a big bite.

Delicious!

7986